## PRAISE FOR MAYA BANKS

"A must-read author . . . her [stories] are always full of emotional situations, lovable characters, and kick-butt story lines."  —*Romance Junkies*

"Heated . . . romantic suspense . . . Intense, transfixing."
—*Midwest Book Review*

"Grabbed me from page one and refused to let go until I read the last word."  —*Joyfully Reviewed*

"Searingly sexy and highly believable."  —*Romantic Times*

## PRAISE FOR KARIN TABKE

"Tabke masterfully creates sexual tension."  —*Romantic Times*

"Exhilarating . . . Ms. Tabke heats up the era."  —*Midwest Book Review*

"[A] guilty pleasure."  —*The Romance Reader*

"Karin Tabke has left me craving for more!"  —*Romance Novel TV*

## PRAISE FOR SYLVIA DAY

"Her books are a luxury every woman deserves."  —Teresa Medeiros

"An incredible author."  —*The Romance Studio*

"Sylvia Day's storytelling dazzles."  —Lara Adrian

# Men Out of Uniform

## MAYA BANKS
## KARIN TABKE
## SYLVIA DAY

HEAT | NEW YORK

**THE BERKLEY PUBLISHING GROUP**
**Published by the Penguin Group**
**Penguin Group (USA) Inc.**
**375 Hudson Street, New York, New York 10014, USA**
Penguin Group (Canada), 90 Eglinton Avenue East, Suite 700, Toronto, Ontario M4P 2Y3, Canada
(a division of Pearson Penguin Canada Inc.)
Penguin Books Ltd., 80 Strand, London WC2R 0RL, England
Penguin Group Ireland, 25 St. Stephen's Green, Dublin 2, Ireland (a division of Penguin Books Ltd.)
Penguin Group (Australia), 250 Camberwell Road, Camberwell, Victoria 3124, Australia
(a division of Pearson Australia Group Pty. Ltd.)
Penguin Books India Pvt. Ltd., 11 Community Centre, Panchsheel Park, New Delhi—110 017, India
Penguin Group (NZ), 67 Apollo Drive, Rosedale, Auckland 0632, New Zealand
(a division of Pearson New Zealand Ltd.)
Penguin Books (South Africa) (Pty.) Ltd., 24 Sturdee Avenue, Rosebank, Johannesburg 2196,
South Africa

Penguin Books Ltd., Registered Offices: 80 Strand, London WC2R 0RL, England

This book is an original publication of The Berkley Publishing Group.

This is a work of fiction. Names, characters, places, and incidents either are the product of the authors' imaginations or are used fictitiously, and any resemblance to actual persons, living or dead, business establishments, events, or locales is entirely coincidental. The publisher does not have any control over and does not assume any responsibility for author or third-party websites or their content.

PRINTING HISTORY
Heat trade paperback edition / October 2011

Library of Congress Cataloging-in-Publication Data

Banks, Maya.
   Men out of uniform : three novellas of erotic surrender / Maya Banks, Karin Tabke, Sylvia Day.—
Heat trade pbk. ed.
      p.   cm.
   ISBN 978-0-425-24316-9
   1. Erotic stories, American.   2. Criminal justice personnel—Fiction.   I. Tabke, Karin.
II. Day, Sylvia.   III. Title.
   PS648.E7B37 2011
   813'.60803538—dc23

                                                                    2011019140

PRINTED IN THE UNITED STATES OF AMERICA

10   9   8   7   6   5   4   3   2   1

# Contents

# Soul Possession

MAYA BANKS

*To my twisted but awesome agent, Kim Whalen, who wanted
so badly to be a serial killer in one of my books.
To Kirsten, a fabulous reader who plays a terrific part in this story.
To Vicki Lane and Laurie Kap, two wonderful friends that
I count myself so fortunate to know.
Thank you for just being you and real.*

# Chapter 1

This case is pissing me off," Rick said to his partner as he picked up his beer bottle and drained half the contents.

Truitt grimaced and sipped at his beer, his gaze tracking across the room. Rick knew who he was watching. It was a ritual he and Tru had fallen into for weeks now.

Jessie Callahan. A gorgeous brown-eyed doll with the sweetest smile he'd ever seen on a woman. Honey blond curls so thick he itched to plunge his fingers into the thick mass.

They'd flirted with her and propositioned her every time they came in, and she always flirted right back and then turned them down flat.

She didn't seem overly shocked that the proposition included both men. In fact, her face turned the prettiest shade of pink every time they promised her a night she wouldn't forget. The thing was, she looked downright interested, which is why they persisted. She was going to cave. Rick and Truitt knew it. And it was fun as hell in the meantime to up the ante every time they came in.

"This bastard has to make a mistake sooner or later," Truitt said, turning his gaze from Jessie to eye his partner. "What kind of a sick fuck gets off on torturing women and then turning them loose in the woods to hunt them? I want this son of a bitch. I want him bad."

Rick nodded. The images of the victims still burned brightly in his mind. Cuts, bruises, blood. Lots of blood. Caked-on mud and dirt, scratches from head to toe. They'd all run blindly through the dense woods until the bastard tracking them ended his sick hunt with a bullet from a high-power rifle.

They didn't stand a chance, and yet he gave them hope by turning them loose after terrorizing and torturing them for God knew how long. Stripped of clothing and bleeding, they ran for their lives.

The police hadn't been able to determine a link between the women. No common factors. It was all frighteningly random, which frustrated Rick and Truitt and their department to no end.

The media had labeled the asshole the Big Thicket Killer. Not terribly original, but fitting all the same. No leads had turned up. Forensics had been a bust so far. The bastard was either meticulous or damn lucky.

The only way the police even knew to look for a body was because after every kill, the arrogant son of a bitch called it in. Complete with GPS coordinates.

Who knew how many women this psychopath had murdered before he decided to go public? How many test subjects had he experimented on before taking the game to the next level and all but daring the police to come after him?

Rick drained the last of his beer and set the bottle back on the table with a thud. This was their first night off in days. They had a backlog of cases and they were still spinning their wheels on the serial killer. He hated sitting around waiting for the bastard to make his next move. How many more innocent women were going to lose their lives before they took him down?

"Let it go, man," Truitt said, interrupting his thoughts. "At least for tonight."

Rick lifted his gaze, searching out Jessie in the crowd. Sometimes the assholes who liked to hang out in the pub enjoyed giving her a hard time, and he liked to look out for her when he and Truitt came in. He wished they could be here more often, but lately nights off were few and far between.

She was one gorgeous woman, but more than being beautiful, she had a sunny personality that just warmed you through. And when she smiled . . . man, her smile did funny things to his chest and other parts of his body.

He didn't immediately find her. Maybe she'd gone in the back to get something.

"We're going to take her home tonight," Rick announced.

Truitt raised his brows. "Getting impatient? What if she isn't ready?"

"She's ready. She's been giving it back to us for weeks. She's adorably shy but she's interested. She watches us every bit as much as we watch her. I think we just need to push it a little more. I'm tired of sitting around and waiting. We aren't the only ones who come in here to drool over her, and if we don't make a move, she's going to be going home with someone else."

"Well, when you put it that way," Truitt drawled. "I don't want to scare her, but I damn sure don't want her in someone else's bed."

Rick frowned as he finally located her. "She looks upset about something. Motion her over here like we want another beer. I want to make sure everything's okay and then we'll find out what time she gets off."

Truitt followed Rick's gaze and his eyes narrowed. He lifted his hand when he caught her eye and crooked a finger at her.

━━━━━━

Jessie stalked out of Merriam's office, her lips tight and fury ripping through her. She'd have liked to have ripped Merriam's hair out by the roots. The bitch had the nerve to accuse of her of skimming money from the register and then fire her.

She very generously told Jessie she could finish out the night, and if Jessie didn't need the money so desperately, she would have told Merriam to shove it.

Jessie didn't even go near the register. How the hell was she supposed to be stealing from it? Denise, the bartender, guarded the register like a jealous lover and looked accusingly at anyone who got within ten feet of it.

And yet Jessie was going to take the fall for a few hundred dollars that Merriam said had mysteriously disappeared?

She was so pissed she wanted to throw a chair across the room. She wasn't normally a vindictive type of person but right now she wished Karma would bite Merriam on the ass, and she'd told her as much.

Merriam was a hard-ass, uptight bitch who was an absolute monster to work for. But Merriam paid good wages and Jessie made good tips at the popular pub. Her regulars always took good care of her. The money had made the crap that Jessie had to put up with worth it.

Her shoulders sagged and her hands still shook from her confrontation with Merriam. They were already shorthanded and Jessie really, really wanted to say to hell with all of them and walk out, because then Merriam would have to come out and help tend bar and she hated to be dragged out of her office for any reason.

It only made Jessie feel marginally better that she'd told Merriam exactly what she thought of her. She'd left by telling Merriam that she hoped she was run over by a bus. Okay, so maybe that wasn't the classiest exit, but really, how was being Miss Manners going to help? It wasn't like by being polite she'd suddenly get her job back.

"Problem, Jessie?" Denise barked from behind the counter. "You've got customers waiting. Get your ass in gear."

"Fuck off," Jessie snapped. Oh God, did that feel good. She almost laughed at Denise's look of shock.

She turned to see Truitt Cavanaugh motion for another round of beers. Her mouth drooped as she realized that this would be the last night she'd get to serve her two sexy detectives. She'd miss flirting with them, and those smoldering stares they sent her way when they thought she wasn't looking. Or, hell, maybe they did know.

They'd been angling to get her into bed for weeks and she'd always put them off. The idea of having a threesome was shocking but titillating in an exciting oh-my-God kind of way, but she'd never mustered the nerve to go for it.

She wasn't a virgin, but she was woefully behind in the sex education department, and somehow she knew they were so far out of her league that she hadn't a prayer of satisfying either.

They were bad boys and she was a wholesome, sweet good girl, and if that wasn't enough to disgust her, she didn't know what was.

Still, she wouldn't mind signing up for Sex Ed if they were teaching.

Rick was all dark and brooding. Quieter than Truitt. His hair hung to his shoulders, sleek and black, just made for a woman's fingers. She was fascinated by a man who'd have the words *Courage, Honor,* and *Heart* tattooed around his wrist like a bracelet. It made her wonder all manner of things about his hidden depths and how much she'd like to plumb them.

Truitt was no less of a badass, and in some ways he was fiercer-looking than Rick. He was big and broad-shouldered, a few inches taller than Rick with a body builder's physique. He wore an earring in one ear but she'd been close enough to know that both ears were pierced.

Spiraling bands with sharp points and flowing edges circled both arms and disappeared into his sleeves. She always wondered how far up his body his tats went, and what other secrets hid behind the T-shirts and jeans he wore.

Between the two of them, they'd fueled some serious bad-girl fantasies. She could be bad. She could *totally* be bad given the right provocation, and damn if they didn't provoke some serious desire to be really, really naughty.

She sighed. One day. Maybe. But then why not tonight?

She grabbed a few bottles and made her way through the crowd, trying to smile despite wanting to cry. She hated looking for a job. She hated walking into a place and asking for an application. She hated being conspicuous in these situations, and she always felt like everyone in the world was watching her and judging.

And now she'd have to start that process all over again and she didn't have any days to spare to be off work. Money was tight and she couldn't miss her classes. Not when the semester was almost up.

Halfway across the floor, someone backed into her and all her weight came down on her bad knee. It buckled and she hit the floor, but she managed to keep the beer bottles held high, a fact she was absurdly happy about.

Pain shot through her leg and she bit her lip to keep from crying out. The guy who knocked her down quickly bent over, his expression one of genuine regret. But before he could offer to help her up, Truitt and Rick were both bending down, concern bright in their eyes.

"Jessie, you okay?" Truitt demanded.

Embarrassed to be the center of attention in the crowded pub, she nodded, her cheeks hot.

"Let me help you up, sweetheart," Rick said as he gently guided her to her feet.

Her knee gave way immediately and Truitt hauled her to his side until she was steady. She offered a shaky smile and then held out the beers.

"At least I didn't spill your beer," she joked.

"I don't give a damn about the beer," Truitt growled. "Come sit down. You're hurt."

They helped her to their table and eased her down into one of the chairs. Rick bent down on one knee and slid his hands up her bare leg. He frowned when he got to one of the scars around her knee.

"What happened here?"

She tried to pull her leg away, but he kept a firm hold. His fingers were gentle, but he didn't allow her to escape.

"Car accident," she mumbled. "My knee still gives me trouble sometimes."

"What the hell are you doing working a job that requires you to be on your feet all the time if you've got a bum knee?" Truitt demanded.

This time Rick relinquished his grip when she tried to pull away. She tucked both legs under the table and glanced quickly around, relieved to note that everyone had gone on about their business and quickly forgotten about her.

"Are you hurting, sweetheart?" Rick asked in a voice that made her melt. He had a flirty way with words that hit her in the right spot every time. Only this time he was less flirty and more concerned, and she loved that even more.

"I'll be fine," she said, managing a reassuring smile. "Just put too much weight on it too quickly."

"Not to worry. Rick and I are planning to take you home with us after you get off work. We'll pamper you until you've forgotten all about that knee," Truitt said in a low, husky voice.

Her legs trembled and she thrust her hands into her lap under the table so they wouldn't see how nervous she was. Which was ridiculous because they flirted, she flirted, and nothing ever came of it. But tonight . . . well tonight was just a different night all the way around. She kept looking at him, expecting him to tease or wink, but he seemed dead serious, and that sent another flutter of awareness winging through her body.

The truth was she could use some pampering and whatever else they chose to do after the night she'd had. She couldn't think of a single, solitary reason to turn them down.

Provided they were serious. And there was only one way to find out. If she made a fool of herself, it wasn't as if she'd ever see them again.

"As it happens, I can leave anytime," she said. "Does all that pampering you're promising come with a foot rub?"

Rick's eyes suddenly gleamed dark, making her all shivery inside. Truitt went quiet and the tats on his arms rippled as his muscles jumped and flexed.

"It comes with a hell of a lot more," Truitt said. "Did you just say yes? Don't tease, Jessie. We've been waiting a hell of a long time for you to put us out of our misery."

Her heart was about to thump out of her chest. She was positively light-headed. They really weren't flirting or teasing. They were dead serious, and right now they were both staring her down with eyes that were so hot she was about to melt. Waiting. For her to put them out of their misery.

Well damn, but that made her giddy.

"Just let me clock out and get my keys," she managed to get out. "I'll meet you in the parking lot."

# Chapter 2

Rick and Truitt were waiting by her car when she walked into the parking lot.

"You shouldn't be driving with your knee hurting," Truitt said as he wrested the keys from her grip. "I'll take your car. You ride with Rick."

She winced and glanced between Truitt and her tiny beat-up old car. The idea of him fitting his large frame into her ten-year-old Toyota Corolla was laughable.

"I can drive," she said. "You'll never fit."

He pulled her against him until she fit flush against his chest. Lord, but the man smelled as sexy as he looked and she loved the feel of his hard body.

He lowered his head and kissed the tip of her nose. Then he pushed her toward Rick and patted her on the ass. She sighed, rolled her eyes, but let Rick guide her to his truck while Truitt crammed himself into her car.

Rick closed the passenger door after Jessie was inside and then walked around the front to get in on the driver's side.

"All set?" he asked as he keyed the ignition.

She nodded, suddenly nervous as realization sank in. She was really doing this. She was really going home with two sinfully gorgeous men who were going to do sinfully decadent things to her body.

She couldn't freaking wait.

He pulled onto the highway and Jessie glanced in the side-view mirror to see Truitt pull in behind them. She started when Rick reached over and slid his fingers through hers. He picked up her hand and pulled it toward him, resting it on top of his thigh.

It was such a small thing, but it felt intimate.

"Everything okay?" he asked.

Startled, she looked up at him in question.

"You looked upset in the bar. Right before you fell. Need me to kick anyone's ass?"

Laughter escaped and some of the stress of the evening lifted away. There was nothing she could do about it now, and she wasn't about to let Merriam ruin what could possibly be the best night of her life.

"No, but thanks for the offer. It's kind of nice to have someone willing to kick ass on demand."

"Anytime," Rick said with a grin. "Just say the word. Tru and I will be more than happy to take care of it."

"You two are a trip."

He glanced sideways. "What's that supposed to mean?"

She ducked her head, a little embarrassed and suddenly a lot shy.

"Jessie?" he prompted in a coaxing voice.

"You've been flirting with me for weeks. I didn't really think you were serious. Well, until tonight when I decided to chance making a fool out of myself."

He groaned. "Are you telling me you would have taken us up earlier if you had realized we were absolutely serious?"

"Weeelll. Maybe?"

He sighed. "Clearly we need to work on our presentation."

She smiled. "I needed the time to work up my nerve anyway. You and Truitt are . . . intimidating."

"Darlin', the last thing we want is to intimidate you."

He squeezed her hand and then picked it up and raised it to his mouth. His lips were a warm shock to her palm. And then if that wasn't enough, he licked over the tips of her fingers and gently sucked each one into his mouth.

Holy hell, but the man had reduced her to a gaping, speechless blob in thirty seconds flat.

"If you had any idea how much I've fantasized about you, you'd know that you effectively have me by the balls and I'm yours to command," he said in amusement.

She had nothing to say to that.

Ten minutes later, they pulled into the driveway of a smallish brick house that looked like a lot of other small brick houses in the neighborhood.

It was a cookie-cutter subdivision. It made her positively wistful. While others might dream of huge houses on huge lots with individuality in spades, her dream house was in a quaint neighborhood with nice people, where kids played in the streets and the houses were all neat and uniform.

But then anything at all would be a step up from her efficiency apartment in a not-so-great neighborhood across town from this middle-class subdivision.

Still, it gave her a happy sigh to dream. One day she'd be beyond her current circumstances. She held on to that hope and knew that she had the power to make it reality. Hard work and a never-quit attitude had gotten her through a devastating car accident. It would get her through her current jobless state.

And at least for tonight she planned to cut loose, have some fun and temporarily forget about her less than ideal circumstances.

Before she had time to open her door, Truitt appeared at her

window and opened the door for her. He reached inside and helped
her down, holding her to his side until he was sure her knee would
support her.

Her chest caved in a little at the thoughtfulness of the gesture.

Rick went ahead of them and opened the door. She and Truitt followed and she looked curiously around when he flipped the light on.

If she expected a slovenly bachelor pad, she was wrong. The living room was neat and uncluttered. A masculine dark brown leather
couch lined the wall in front of a flat-screen television mounted to
the opposing wall. There were two recliners on either side of the
couch and a solid oak coffee table in front of the sofa.

It had a cozy, homey look that she was instantly drawn to.

"So which one of you lives here? Or do you both?"

"He's living here temporarily," Truitt said, gesturing toward
Rick. "His lease ended on his apartment so he's crashing with me
until he decides what he wants to buy and where."

Why she was surprised that this was Truitt's house, she wasn't
sure. He had a wild edge to him that contradicted the clean, earthy
look to the house. It was very *traditional*. That was the word she was
searching for and Truitt looked anything but traditional.

Truitt curled an arm around her and pulled her into his body. He
kissed her brow first but then lowered his mouth to capture her lips
in a hot, toe-curling kiss.

Lust hit her like a hammer. She purposely put all her weight on
her good leg because if she didn't she knew she'd go down like a
rock.

Truitt must have felt her shift because he pulled away and then
steered her toward the couch. She sat and he knelt in front of her, his
big hands closing around her aching knee.

As soon as he touched her she let out a soft moan. Warm and
gentle, his palms brushed over her skin. He removed her slides and
tossed them a few feet away while Rick settled on her other side.

"I'm probably supposed to be patient and sensitive right now given that you've been on your feet all night and your knee hurts, but what I really want is to get you naked. Then I want to lavish all sorts of loving on you," Rick said as he dropped a kiss on her shoulder.

"He's the impatient one," Truitt said with an eye roll. "He has about as much finesse as a bull in rut."

"And you don't want to get her naked?" Rick asked mildly.

"Hell yeah, I want her naked. But these things should be savored. I've fantasized about this moment for so long, the last thing I want is for it to all be over in two seconds. I want to take her clothes off one piece at a time and enjoy every damn minute."

This wasn't happening. It simply wasn't happening. The only explanation was that she was at home and her own fantasies were manifesting themselves in a surprisingly realistic dream. A really fantastic, never-want-it-to-end dream at that.

She cleared her throat delicately. "How does this work exactly?" Then she wanted to die of embarrassment. She sounded like a moron.

Rick grinned. "Darlin', you have the most gorgeous feminine blush. I just love it when your cheeks get all pink. Makes me want to do all sorts of outrageous things just to get you to do it again."

"I know I sound like an idiot," she mumbled. "It's just that I've never had sex with two guys. At the same time, I mean. I'm not at all sure what I'm supposed to do."

Truitt ran his hand up her leg to rest at her waist. "You don't have to do a single thing but lie back and let me and Rick make you feel good. We're going to touch you . . ." He rose up on his knees and leaned in to slide his mouth over hers. "And kiss you . . ." He moved down her jaw and then angled her neck so that he nibbled at the sensitive point below her ear. "And then we're going to fuck you."

She reacted strongly to the picture he painted in her mind. The comparison between the slow and sensual kissing and touching, culminated by hot, sweaty fucking nearly had her panting.

"But in order to do that, your clothes have to come off," Truitt murmured just below her ear.

Rick's hands slid up her body, tugging gently at her T-shirt. It came free of her denim shorts and he pulled it over her head, leaving her in her bra.

"Pretty," Truitt said as he leaned back in to nibble at the strap over her shoulder.

He dragged at the strap, pulling it down her arm while Rick tugged at the button of her shorts.

"Stand up for just a minute, sweetheart," Rick said. "Hold on to me so you don't put weight on that knee. I'll have you undressed in just a minute and we can take this to the bedroom."

Truitt pulled her upward and she braced herself on Rick's shoulder while Truitt held her other arm. Rick unzipped her shorts and then parted the waistband, baring the thin silk of her panties.

Her shorts slid down her legs. Her bra was half on, half off. Rick and Truitt both hooked a finger in the waistband of her panties and eased them downward.

"Damn. Golden, just like the rest of you," Truitt breathed as he stroked his fingers through the curls between her legs. "Pretty and sweet. I can't wait to taste you."

Her legs trembled uncontrollably. Her fingers curled into Rick's shoulder as she leaned her weight to her right leg. Rick quickly reached up to unclasp her bra and then he pulled it away, tossing it back onto the couch.

Before she could think to be self-conscious about her sudden nudity, Truitt rose and gathered her into his arms. He followed Rick down the hall to a bedroom at the end and when he walked inside, he laid her gently on the bed.

Both men stood over her, greedily devouring her with their gazes. And then they began to undress.

She lay there, riveted to the sight of them peeling away their clothing. Her breath caught when Truitt tossed his shirt aside and revealed the intricate pattern of tattoos that snaked their way up his arms and over his shoulders. Over the firm expanse of his belly, and around his navel, was a matching swirl of Bengal markings.

Rick's body was devoid of tattoos save the one around his right wrist, and she still wondered about its meaning. If you took the time to have words permanently inked onto your skin, they meant something.

When they both reached for their pants, she forgot to breathe. Truitt was first to shed his jeans and underwear. His cock jutted upward, thick and long. His muscled thighs and lean, rigid abdomen just made him look even bigger and more fearsome.

Rick was a little slower to work his way out of his jeans, but he was no less impressive when he finally stood naked by the bed. Surrounded by dark, silky hair, his cock extended high toward his navel, impressive in both length and girth.

Hell, she had no idea what she was going to do with all this cock but she was sure as hell going to have a good time figuring it out.

Truitt stared down at the golden goddess lying in his bed and it was all he could do to remember his name or how to breathe. From the moment he'd laid eyes on Jessie when she'd started working at the bar he and Rick liked to hang out in, he'd been completely and utterly fascinated.

She wasn't the most gorgeous woman on earth. But there was a sweetness to her that was compelling. He and Rick weren't the only ones to notice either. She had every man who went into that damn bar completely and utterly gobsmacked. And she was completely oblivious to it all.

No, she might not be the most gorgeous woman on earth, but she was the most beautiful woman in *Truitt's* world, and he was exposed to women every day.

He and Rick dated separate women. It wasn't like they went around all the time looking for a threesome. But they'd both looked at Jessie and neither of them was going to bow out. So the only recourse they had was to seduce her together. Which, well, was weird, but hell, he wasn't going to step aside so Rick could put the moves on her.

"You are so damn beautiful," he murmured.

Jessie's face lit up in a smile so sweet that it made his teeth ache. Her cheeks were delightfully pink and she was looking at them both with those big, shy brown eyes.

Rick groaned and then crawled up on the bed on her right side. He lowered his lips to hers and took her. There was no other way to describe the savagery with which he possessed her mouth.

Taking advantage of their distraction, Truitt slid his hand over her bum knee, caressing it a moment before nudging her legs apart.

The soft golden curls parted and her pink feminine flesh came into view, swollen and glistening with her moisture. Above him, Rick moved down to her breasts and began sucking and nipping at her nipples until they were dark pink and rigid.

Hell, he didn't know what he wanted to taste first, her pussy or her breasts. But since Rick had already claimed her plump, delectable breasts, Truitt settled between her thighs and carefully slid a finger down her damp seam.

She moaned softly and arched her slim hips upward. He smiled and nuzzled through her folds until his mouth touched her slick heat.

He swept his tongue out, savoring the first burst of her flavor as it filled his mouth. Then he licked her from her tiny entrance to the top of the delicate hood that surrounded her clit.

He traced a path around the taut nub and then sucked it gently into his mouth, being careful not to hurt her. She writhed restlessly beneath him and he could hear Rick sucking at her breasts.

The sound was hot. Erotic. The only better noise was the sound of hips slapping against ass and the light sucking sound of a pussy around a cock.

Man, he couldn't wait to get inside her.

He tongued her entrance. She quivered harder. He slid his tongue inside, tasting her, sipping at her essence. Like drinking sunshine and honey.

"God damn, Truitt. You're going to have to move before I die up here," Rick ground out.

Truitt raised his head to see Rick suck strongly at one nipple before turning his gaze down to Truitt. He had that crazed look like he was about to come.

Truitt grinned. "You get her mouth. This pussy is all mine."

"Hell, we can't make her get on her hands and knees," Rick said. "She'll hurt herself."

"Put her head over the edge of the bed."

Jessie pushed upward, her eyes glazed, her lips and breasts swollen and red from Rick's attentions.

"Where do you want me?" she asked in a husky, passion-laced voice that had Truitt doing his own desperate gritting of his teeth to keep from shooting his wad everywhere.

"Just turn around, darlin'," Rick said. "Rotate so that your head is off the bed on my side."

The two men helped her get into position and no sooner had she levered her head downward then Rick had straddled her and slid his cock into her mouth.

For a moment Truitt stared at the erotic sight of Rick fucking her mouth. Holy hell, but the sight of her throat bulging to accommodate his deep thrusts had Truitt's nuts about to burst.

He yanked open the nightstand drawer and with shaking fingers dumped a box of condoms out, snagging one. He ripped it open, rolled it over his aching cock, and then he climbed onto the bed and positioned himself between her thighs.

"Ease off a minute, Rick," Truitt said.

Rick withdrew his cock, now shiny with her saliva. The head was so swollen and purple that it looked damn painful. Rick reached down and lifted Jessie up so that she could look at Truitt.

She looked drunk. High on pleasure. Delectably mussed, her hair in disarray and that fuckable swollen mouth that just begged to be kissed and then fucked some more.

"I'm about to get inside you, Jessie," Truitt said. "I don't want to hurt you, sweetheart. If I do, if anything either of us does makes you uncomfortable or hurts you, you get Rick's attention, okay? We're both impatient bastards right now because seeing you spread out and naked in front of us has us crazy, but we want this to be good for you and we plan to spend all night making you scream our names."

Wordlessly she nodded, her eyes wide and unfocused. Then Rick lowered her head and pushed his cock back between her lips.

Ah hell, Truitt couldn't hold back another minute. He slid his cock up and down her dampness to lubricate the condom and then he positioned himself at her tiny opening and pushed inside.

He stopped after an inch because holy shit she was tight. It was like forcing his dick into a closed fist. He was never going to make it like this.

Holding a thumb to her clit and then rubbing over it in feather-like strokes, he tensed and then thrust hard.

She opened around him but her body fought the sudden invasion. She spasmed and gripped him so tight that he nearly lost consciousness. He'd never felt anything so good in his life.

Rick was riding her mouth hard and Truitt knew he couldn't make slow, sweet love to her this time. He withdrew and thrust hard and deep, his thumb stroking her flesh.

Her hands flew up to grip Rick's hands that were holding the sides of her head as he fucked her mouth. For a moment Truitt thought she wanted them to stop and so he went still, though it damn near killed him. Rick did the same, pulling out in a hurry.

"No," she gasped. "Oh God, no, please don't stop."

Even as the plea slipped out, her body was arching and undulating, on the verge of her orgasm.

Both men thrust back into her body at the same time and they began riding in relentless rhythm. Truitt closed his eyes as his balls drew up and his release pushed painfully up his cock.

Mindlessly he pumped against her, no longer taking care. He wasn't thinking of whether he hurt her. He was only thinking that if he didn't move, he'd die.

He heard Rick's cry, felt Jessie clutch him in her velvet sheathe and then go wet around him, bathing him in her heat.

He began coming, pumping harder, coming even harder. On and on in endless spurts. Even when he finally came down over her, he could feel his cock still pulsing inside her, could feel the warm, slick semen rising up the condom around his dick.

Shit.

With a groan he rolled to the side, pulling out so the condom wouldn't leak. Hell, he'd pumped it so full it was a wonder it hadn't burst.

He quickly disposed of it and then returned to Jessie. Rick was tenderly wiping the semen from her mouth and then he lifted her and rolled so that she was fully on the bed.

Truitt pulled her into his arms and she snuggled up tighter than a bedbug. Rick spooned up close behind her and they lay there panting, their hearts racing.

"Holy hell," Rick said hoarsely. "My fantasies didn't even come close to the reality."

# Chapter 3

Jessie lay between Rick and Truitt, her mind scrambling to get a grip on what had just happened. They hadn't lied. They'd fucked her. Hard. And it had been glorious.

There was nothing nice and sweet about their possession. They'd taken her, they'd owned her. And they'd given her the single most mind-blowing orgasm of her life.

She shivered at the memory, and her clit still pulsed, sensitive to even the slightest movement.

Rick kissed her shoulder and then slid his hand down the length of her body, until it rested possessively on her hip.

"You okay?" he murmured.

She snuggled a little deeper into Truitt's neck. "Mmm hmm."

Truitt chuckled. "You're quite a snuggle bug and if you burrow any closer to me you're going to find yourself on your back again with me inside you."

"I believe that pleasure is mine this time," Rick growled.

She laughed. She was lying between two men who were fighting over her like she was queen of the universe. They certainly knew how to stroke a girl's ego.

"What are you laughing at?" Rick demanded.

"You two arguing over who gets to fuck me where," she said, her voice muffled by Truitt's neck. "I like it."

"Before the night's over, we're going to fuck you in every conceivable way," Truitt vowed. "So there's no argument. Maybe just impatience."

Then he pulled her head back so he could kiss her and his voice gentled. "Did we hurt you? Were we too rough?"

She smiled. "No. It was perfect. Really, really perfect."

"If you thought that was perfect, you're awfully easy to please," Rick grumbled. "It was too fast and we didn't spend enough time making it good for you."

"Well, as you said, we have all night," she said mischievously. "Though, I have to say, I have no complaints so far. If you guys make it any better I may not survive."

Truitt caressed the curve of her behind and massaged one plump cheek. "Have you ever had anal sex?"

She was sure her cheeks went pink again. Both sets of cheeks. She shook her head, too mortified to squeak out a no.

"Would you want to try it?"

Rick nibbled at her shoulder and his hand went to her ass too, squeezing and massaging as if to tell her his opinion of the whole idea.

"Maybe. I've heard it's . . . painful."

"Well, if you get with an uncaring dickhead who just wants to shove it in, yeah, it'll hurt. But we'll take it nice and slow. We'll make it good for you, baby. We'll make it damn good. You can take one of us in your ass and the other in your pussy."

"I thought the only people who did that were porn stars," she mumbled.

"How would you know this?" Rick asked in mock surprise.

"A girl can watch porn too," she defended. "We like sex, same as guys do."

"I can't speak for porn stars, but it's pretty damn hot," Truitt said. "There's nothing like the sensation of taking a woman at the same time, having her between you, small and delicate, while you fuck her from both ends."

She shivered at the crudeness and the vividness with which he described the act. It was suddenly something she wanted to experience very much. And if this was going to be her sole night of debauchery, then the more debauched she was, the better. When the hell else was she ever going to get an opportunity like this? It wasn't like she had guys lining up to ask her to have threesomes with them.

"The idea is to get you so horny, so unbelievably aroused, that you'll agree to anything," Rick teased.

"Already there," she muttered.

"There's no hurry," Truitt said in an easy voice. "We don't have to do it all tonight. There's always tomorrow night. Or the next. But if you want to give it a try tonight, we'll certainly accommodate you."

She didn't know quite what to say to that. It sounded like they wanted more than a fling, more than some one-night stand, but how did that work with more than two people involved. Were they wanting a regular fuck buddy?

While she wasn't opposed to sex for the sake of sex, it had never been something she indulged in. Not that she was a prude, she simply hadn't had the opportunity. Neither had she had sex with a guy she wanted to commit to doing the act with often.

"Tell me about your knee," Rick said against her shoulder. "You said you had a car accident. It must not have been very long ago if it still bothers you."

"It was two years ago," she said in a quiet voice.

Truitt frowned. "Two years? And your knee still hurts you?"

"It was . . . a bad accident. It took me a long time to recover. I've

had six surgeries on my leg and knee. They had to completely reconstruct parts of the bone."

"Why in the hell are you working as a waitress? That can't be
good for your leg," Rick said.

"I was in school when the accident happened. I had to quit. I started
back but it's hard to find a job that works around my class schedule. I
have bills to pay so I can't be too picky about the work, you know?"

Neither man looked happy with her response but they let it go.
The last thing she wanted was to get into the fact that she no longer
had a job.

There had to be a way of convincing Merriam that she hadn't
stolen money. Suddenly the idea of not seeing Rick and Truitt on a
regular basis depressed the hell out of her. They always managed to
brighten her day no matter how shitty it had been to that point.

She wasn't a quitter. If she was, she'd have given up a long time
ago when the odds were against her walking again. It might not be
the best job in the world, but it was hers and she was damn good at
it, and she wasn't about to let her asshole boss pin the blame on her
for missing money.

"Hey, what's the fierce expression for?" Truitt asked.

She relaxed and smiled. "Oh, nothing. Just wondering when act
two begins. I may be new to the whole being in bed with two gorgeous male specimens thing, but I've decided that Waste Not, Want
Not is a very good motto."

Rick chuckled and nipped at her neck, sending shivers racing down
her spine. Truitt lowered his head and pulled at one nipple with his
mouth and then sucked strongly until she moaned low in her throat.

"You are absolutely delicious," Truitt said as he pushed her over
so that both breasts were available to him.

Rick scooted back on the bed to give Jessie more room and she
reached for him, wanting to touch him. She hadn't been able to
touch either man yet. Things had happened so quickly.

She slid her fingers through Rick's hair as Truitt teased and tormented her nipples.

"I love your hair," she said.

Rick seemed uncomfortable with the praise but his eyes glowed as he turned to look at her. He caught her hand as she trailed her fingers through the silky ends and kissed her palm.

"And I love yours," Truitt said even as he delved a hand into her thick curls. "I've been dying to run my hands through it ever since I first saw you."

Rick laughed. "Face it, man, you've been dying to touch her since we saw her."

Truitt shrugged. "Yeah, that too."

"I don't get it," she said, marveling at their words.

"What don't you get?" Rick asked.

"Why me? I mean you both act like I'm something special. I feel like a goddess the way you two look at me and talk about me."

"That's how you're supposed to feel," Truitt said as he drew away, his eyes gleaming. "As for why you? Honey, you're just it with a capital *I*. No other way to explain it. I saw you and it was kind of like taking a bullet."

She frowned. "I'm not sure that's the way I want to be immortalized. Have you ever been shot?"

"He hasn't. I have," Rick said dryly. "If he had, he wouldn't be throwing around that colorful little descriptor."

Truitt grinned. "I have a good imagination."

Jessie pushed herself upward and got to her knees so she could stare down at the two men in bed with her. It was a feast of male flesh and she couldn't control her itchy fingers. She placed her palms on their chests and let them wander over the muscled dips and ridges and downward to their taut bellies.

She absently traced the outline of Truitt's tattoo while her hand stilled on Rick's pelvis just above the dark patch of hair surrounding his cock.

"I love your tats," she murmured. "I used to stare at you and wonder how far up your body they went." She turned and took her hand from Rick's abdomen and picked up his hand. "Why do you have *Courage, Honor,* and *Heart* tattooed on your wrist? Does it have a special meaning?"

A dark shadow passed over Rick's face as he stared down at the words encircling his wrist. "They're for my brother. He was a cop too. He was killed in the line of duty. They were his creed. Words he lived his entire life by. Values our father taught us to uphold every day of our lives."

"They both sound like awesome people," she said softly.

"They were," Rick said. "World isn't quite the same without them."

"What happened to your father?" she asked.

"He retired from the force and then a year later he died of a heart attack. The same year my brother was killed."

Her heart aching for him, she bent and pulled him into her arms, hugging him fiercely. "I'm sorry. What a terrible time for you."

When she pulled away, Rick seemed a little dazed. Then he reached up, touched her cheek and smiled. "Thanks. Nobody's hugged me since my dad died. It felt . . . nice."

She smiled back. "Glad I could be the first then."

She put her hand back down, low on his abdomen, and then shyly went lower until her fingers brushed across his erection.

It pulsed hot and hard against her palm as she wrapped her hand around the satiny smooth flesh.

Truitt bent and nuzzled her ear. "Why don't you hop on top. I have an idea. If you'll let Rick take care of you for a while, I'll get some lubricant and work you up to taking us both."

She sucked in her breath as her mind flashed with the images of her on top of Rick and Truitt behind her. It was so darkly erotic, like nothing she'd even ever imagined. But now that the idea had been planted, she was riveted, intrigued, and wildly turned on.

Rick reached blindly for a condom even as Jessie gingerly climbed over his legs and settled her knees on either side of him.

But when he tossed the opened condom to the mattress beside Jessie, he reached for her and started to pull her up his body.

"I haven't got to taste that sweet pussy of yours yet," he murmured. "And no way I want you to try to take me when you're unprepared. Move up and straddle my face."

Her face burned. She could feel the flush spread over her entire body. Her hands shook as he began to help her scale up his muscular body. Oh God, she wasn't a sex goddess. How was she going to pull this off?

But by the time she levered herself over his face, she forgot all her inhibitions. All she wanted was to feel the magic of his tongue.

He gripped her hips and guided her down.

"Open yourself for me, sweetheart."

Swallowing back her nervousness, she reached tentatively down, sliding her fingers through damp, swollen flesh. She spread her folds just as his tongue swept over her opening and up to her clit.

"Perfect," he breathed. "Fucking perfect. Stay just like that, doll."

Soon though, remaining still was impossible. She moved back and forth, guiding his mouth to the places she most wanted his tongue. He nuzzled, nibbled, and licked and she had to reach with her other hand to grip the headboard so she didn't collapse on him.

"You two are killing me," Truitt groaned.

Jessie tensed as the beginnings of her orgasm built rapidly, burning like an intense fire. Rick eased her backward until she sat on his chest and they stared at each other, both trying to catch their breath.

"I didn't want you to come yet," he said. "I want to be inside you when that happens."

He reached for the condom and she moved back down his body. With shaking hands, he rolled the latex over his rigid cock and then held out his hand to her.

She slid her fingers into his and then arched over him, reaching with her other hand to position him. They both held their breath when the head lodged against her entrance.

She slid slowly down, closing her eyes at the exquisite fullness. He stretched and strained her limits. She pulled tight around him, clutching him deeper, and she wondered if she'd even be able to take all of him in this position.

"Be easy, sweetheart. Don't hurt yourself," he gasped out.

But she was determined to bring them both ultimate pleasure.

She inched downward, sucking in her breath. She was light-headed with the sheer decadent thrill of his possession. Or was it her possession?

As her ass came to rest on the tops of his thighs, she paused, absorbing the sensation of having such a large cock wedged tightly inside her pussy. She felt impossibly full and stretched tight.

Warm hands slid sensuously down her back and she arched into Truitt's touch like a cat. He pushed her forward the tiniest bit and then stroked over her behind, allowing his fingers to brush over the seam.

He parted her cheeks and touched the tip of his finger to her opening, eliciting a gasp of surprise. He pushed inward just a bit and she was surprised at the ease with which he penetrated her tight ring. It was then she realized that he'd used lubricant.

"Just relax and enjoy it," Rick said as he smoothed his hands over her waist and then over to cup her breasts. "We want to make you feel good. We want you to want this as much as we do."

He brushed his thumbs across her taut nipples and ripples of pleasure rolled through her body. Then Truitt pushed in a bit more even as he pressed a tender kiss to the middle of her back.

With one hand he caressed and kneaded the flesh of her behind as his other finger worked carefully in and out of her ass. Rick stroked and toyed with her nipples and every once in a while he'd flex his cock, sending mini spasms through her pussy.

She was already impatient, even though she knew she'd never be able to take Truitt so soon. She sighed and lifted her ass when Truitt eased another finger through her opening and stroked in an out, spreading the cool gel. Then he slid one finger all the way in and she gasped in surprise—and pleasure.

"God, you're tight," Truitt gritted out. "It's killing me to think of fucking this sweet ass."

"Ditto," she muttered, moving back, impatient for more.

When he added a third finger, stretching her to accommodate the added width, she felt the first pinch of pain. Instead of shying away, she moaned softly and embraced the stretching burn.

"That's it, sweetheart," Truitt whispered. "You're so fucking beautiful, Jessie."

His fingers moved faster and with more force. Occasionally he stopped to add more lubricant, always making sure his entry was slick and easy.

She closed her eyes and began to anticipate just how it would feel when he thrust his big cock into that tiny opening, stretching her, forcing his way in, making her accommodate him.

Sweat beaded her forehead and her breaths came in short, erratic puffs.

"Jesus, Tru, you need to hurry or she's going to come and I'm not even moving," Rick groaned.

"She's not ready," Truitt said. "I'm not going to hurt her."

"Please, just try," she begged. "I'll stop you if it's too painful. What you're doing feels so good. I want you inside me. I want you both inside me."

Truitt muttered a curse and then his fingers left her. A moment later she felt his hands on her ass again, parting her cheeks. This time the blunt crown of his penis replaced his fingers at her opening. She could feel the cool slide of the lubricant over the condom as he pushed forward.

Inch by agonizing inch, he applied pressure but never too much. Every time she thought she wanted him to stop, he seemed to sense her discomfort and he'd pause. Then he and Rick would caress her, kiss her, offer words of encouragement and praise.

Rick pulled lightly at her nipples, working them between his thumb and finger. Just as he pinched a little harder, Truitt pushed into her, shoving past her resistance so he was all the way inside her ass.

Her back bowed and she threw back her head. She twitched and jittered as she reacted to the pulsing heat of two cocks buried deep inside her body.

Her hands curled against Rick's chest, her fingers digging into his flesh as she shuddered atop him, trying desperately to control her out-of-control nerve endings.

"Shhh, it's okay, baby. We're there now," Truitt whispered against her back. "Just relax. Adjust to our size. We've got all the time in the world. You tell me when it's okay to move. I won't do anything until you're ready."

She leaned forward, panting, her mouth dry, her eyes squeezed tightly shut as she fought off her orgasm. She didn't want to come yet. Not when it was just beginning. She wanted to know exactly what it felt like to be fucked long and hard, her body accommodating not one but two huge cocks.

"It's okay," she said in a low, strained voice. "I want this. Want you both. It's overwhelming. Not painful. It doesn't hurt. Different kind of oh-my-God."

Rick chuckled and reached up to frame her face before rising up and pulling her down at the same time to meet his kiss. "You have a way with words, darlin'."

Truitt withdrew, his cock dragging through the distended, tight opening until she moaned helplessly, digging her fingers back into Rick's chest. Then he surged forward again and she gasped at the instant fullness.

Finally Rick gripped her thighs. Truitt put his hands higher at her waist. They both held her tightly and both began to move in slow, sensual strokes.

Her brain promptly melted.

Her orgasm rose sharp and unrelenting. She could no longer control the momentum. It barreled over her with the force of a tidal wave.

Her cry was sharp and biting. Her entire body tightened to the point of pain. The pressure was unbearable and beautiful all at the same time.

The two men surged into her, over and over, taking, possessing, commanding her without mercy. She begged them to stop then demanded they didn't.

Then Truitt's hand tangled in her hair and he pulled sharply, bending her neck back so he could kiss the side of her neck. He nipped once and then sank his teeth into her pulse point.

She melted. She literally went to pieces, each one going in a different direction. Her vision blurred, her mind went blank, and she was adrift in a haze of absolute euphoria.

She didn't even realize that she'd collapsed onto Rick's chest until she slowly became aware of her cheek resting over his heart as she panted for breath. Truitt was pressed tightly to her back and his chest heaved against her as he too fought for air.

Rick kissed her head and ran his fingers through her hair.

They were both still wedged inside her ass and pussy. She was so sensitive she dreaded any movement whatsoever. If they so much as touched her, she'd shriek.

"Hold still, baby, while I pull out," Truitt said.

She held her breath but he was exquisitely tender, sliding carefully from her body with only a slight twinge. She sighed and relaxed against Rick, all energy sapped by her intense orgasm.

"Don't wanna move," she mumbled against Rick's chest.

His hands stroked over her back, caressing and petting.

"No one says you have to, darlin'. Just lay here awhile and let me hold you."

# Chapter 4

Jessie was draped over Rick, warm and completely limp, her soft, even breathing signaling her sleep. Rick smiled and idly ran his fingers through the thick curls, twining the ends around his hands.

"She out?" Truitt asked as he pulled on a pair of sweats and a T-shirt. He eased onto the bed and lay on his side, watching Jessie with hungry eyes.

No matter that they'd just had her, Rick felt that same hunger. He had no idea what Truitt was presently thinking. Truitt was . . . well, he was unpredictable. You never could quite tell where he was coming from.

He'd know soon enough just how deep his friend's feelings ran for the petite angel in Rick's arms.

"I'm not letting her walk out of here," Rick said.

He glanced over to gauge Truitt's reaction to his statement.

Truitt frowned but remained silent for a long while. His lips pursed and twitched like he wanted to say something but wasn't quite sure of what it was he wanted to get out yet.

Then he cursed. "Hell, Rick, is this going to be an issue? Because you know damn well I'm not letting her walk away either."

Rick shrugged. "It doesn't have to be. Or it could be. That entirely depends on what you want and what you expect."

"And what she wants and is willing to accept," Truitt said grimly.

Rick nodded. "Yeah. That's kind of the key right there."

Truitt blew out his breath. "Jesus. I really didn't want complicated right now."

A chuckle escaped Rick and he promptly went quiet so he wouldn't wake Jessie with the noise or the movement of his chest.

Truitt flopped over onto his back to stare up at the ceiling. Rick could tell he wore a disgruntled look on his face and he was probably muttering under his breath.

"It doesn't have to be complicated," Rick said mildly. "We've already overcome the most difficult hurdle. She's had sex with us both. She didn't freak out. And she's obviously attracted to both of us. Who says it has to be this complicated matter? Can't we take it easy, see where it takes us?"

Truitt rolled back over. "No, we damn well can't. I don't want her sleeping with anyone else. Hell, I don't even want her *looking* at anyone else. Now that means complicated. No matter how you look at it, because if I don't want her with another man, that means we're committing to something deeper here. Not that I want to look at another woman, not after her, but shit. This has complicated written all over it. I don't like the way I'm feeling right now. Gut-shot with my balls flapping in the wind."

Silent laughter shook Rick. So like Truitt. Uptight. Always overthinking things. Rick shook his head. "You're a mess, man. Seriously. We've had sex with her twice. How do you know that's not all she wants? Maybe she won't want to hang around. We have to sell her on the idea of even sticking around us, both of us, before we can worry about whether another man is looking at her."

"I'm a fucking pansy," Truitt said in disgust. "I swear to you the moment I saw her I knew I was fucking done. Over. Stick a knife in me. Done. And the hell of it is, I don't even mind."

"Quit your bitching. You're getting way ahead of yourself."

"Oh, like you aren't thinking the same damn thing," Truitt muttered. "You're over there plotting ways to convince her to stay with us. You don't want her going back to work. You want to keep her home so you can fuss over her and that bum knee."

"Am I that obvious?"

"No, I just know you. You like to take over. You're a black-and-white kind of guy. You see what you want. You hatch a plan. Then you carry it out to the letter."

"I think I hear an insult in there somewhere."

"Nah, it's what makes you a good cop. You're focused."

"Okay so maybe I do want her to stay. I may want that, but I also know that when she wakes up, if we start spouting that kind of shit after only being with her a few hours, she's going to think we're freaks and she'll probably break her neck getting the fuck out of here. And, hell, I wouldn't blame her. The cop in me would warn any woman away from a man who's thinking the things I'm thinking."

Truitt frowned again. "This is crazy. *We're* crazy."

"That might be true, but no matter how crazy we are, we damn sure don't want her leaving with the idea that this is a one-time fling and that we're adding her to the notches on our bedpost."

"Speak for yourself. I've been celibate. Mostly."

Jessie stirred, turned her head so that her other cheek rested on Rick's chest. She did one of those sweet snuggle moves and sighed as if she was perfectly content. Rick stroked a hand over her hair.

"I don't know what it is about her," Rick said in a low voice. "But you're right. She's it. When I see her I can't look away. There's something that's just irresistible about her. And the thing is, she's just as sweet as she looks. She hugged me for God's sake."

"Awww, are you sad because I haven't hugged you?" Truitt drawled.

Rick scowled and held up his middle finger. "Fuck you, man."

Truitt chuckled. Then he stretched and put his arm above his head. "I'm beat. It's been a long-ass week. If we aren't planning to let her go, I vote we get some sleep, let her rest, and spend the day fucking her brains out tomorrow."

"Smooth," Rick said. "Real fucking smooth." He shook his head again. Truitt was . . . well, he was Truitt. After being partners for five years, Rick knew it was hopeless to comment on Truitt's lack of tact.

Truitt could fight his own battles anyway. If Jessie was going to be with them for any length of time, she'd learn to deal with Truitt's uncouthness. Or not.

Carefully he rolled, easing Jessie down onto the bed between him and Truitt. Truitt was quick to tuck an arm around Jessie and pull her into his chest.

"Get some damn clothes on," Truitt grumbled. "Jessie's not awake and I don't want to see your naked ass."

Rick swung his legs over the bed and then went to get a pair of shorts from his room. By the time he returned, Truitt was sound asleep, his cheek resting against Jessie's ear.

Yeah, his partner had it bad all right. But Rick couldn't say a damn word because he had it every bit as bad.

# Chapter 5

Jessie woke, the room dark around her. She was aware of a hard body behind her but she could feel the heat of another in front of her.

Her cheeks went warm and she rolled her eyes at the idea that she was lying here blushing in the dark because she'd had a wild night of sex with two hot-as-hell guys.

She raised her head, staring around for a clock, but didn't see anything that was visible. Well, she had to pee anyway.

Carefully she eased down the bed, not crawling over either of them. She had no idea if they had to work today or not and she figured they needed the rest after being up so late.

She stumbled around for her clothing and dug into the pocket of her shorts for her phone to check the time. It was early. Or late, depending on your schedule. Often Jessie wasn't getting into bed until now after a long night at the bar and cleanup.

Merriam would still be in her office as she always was until 6:00 A.M. every morning. She holed up doing God knows what, muttering over expenses. The waitresses heard her bitching regularly about cutting costs.

Once in the bathroom, Jessie sat on the closed toilet seat for a long moment weighing her options. Last night she'd been pissed and ready to say fuck it and find a new job. But she couldn't afford to miss even a few days and there was no guaranteeing she'd find a job that quickly.

Which meant she really needed to swallow her pride and go back to try to convince Merriam that she hadn't stolen money and to beg for her job back.

She grimaced because, man, it was hard to swallow her pride. She'd never been good at it. She rubbed absently at her knee and then stared down at the scars that lined either side of her leg.

Bill collectors weren't particularly understanding, and she did have to eat and pay tuition. If she had any hope of getting back on her feet both literally and figuratively, she had to suck it up and go back to the bar.

If she went now, she could be back in time to cook breakfast for the guys. They wouldn't even know she'd been gone if things went well with Merriam. And if worse came to worst, she'd collect her tips and her paycheck and resign herself to having to go job hunting instead of taking a long lazy day.

Saturdays were the only day she gave herself off. The rest of her time was spent studying or working.

She hurriedly dressed, splashed water on her face, and pulled the unruly mass of her hair back and twisted it into a knot. Then she tiptoed back through the bedroom, stopping in the kitchen to leave a quick note. Just in case they got up before she did.

On second thought, she'd better check to see if they had the fixings for breakfast, because if not she'd need to stop off at the twenty-four-hour grocery down the street. Eggs were cheap, as were cheese and mushrooms. She could make a mean omelet and she could make biscuits from scratch.

She shook her head after searching the fridge. Judging by the takeout cartons and the pizza boxes, they ate out often and weren't much on cooking.

Satisfied with her plan, she quietly let herself out of the house and headed for her car.

Twenty minutes later, she pulled into the parking lot of Powell's Pub. As expected Merriam's jeep was parked on the side, but the rest of the lot had long since been deserted.

Digging into her purse for the key she hadn't yet returned, she got out and hurried to the door. After letting herself in, she headed toward Merriam's office in the back, and sure enough, light shone from underneath the door.

Jessie paused, sucked in her breath, squared her shoulders, and knocked.

"Who the hell is it?" Merriam demanded. "I've got a gun, just so you know."

Jessie was well acquainted with the gun Merriam kept behind her desk. Merriam liked to flash it around and generally let it be known she armed herself. She said it discouraged dumbasses from trying to score easy cash.

"It's Jessie, Merriam. I need to talk to you."

There was a long pause. "Come in."

Jessie opened the door and peered in to see Merriam sitting behind her desk, a scowl on her face.

"You've got a lot of nerve coming back here after walking out last night."

Jessie's mouth dropped open. "You fired me! What the hell else was I supposed to do?"

"You seemed interested enough in working the night out until those two cops started sniffing around you."

Jessie was convinced the woman had never smiled in her life. She was wrinkled, looked about seventy, even though Jessie knew she was in her fifties, and she had the deep rasp of a lifelong smoker.

"Look, Merriam, I didn't steal anything from you. You have no proof and I want my job back."

Jessie was absurdly proud of how confident and forceful she sounded.

Merriam's lips thinned. "I know you didn't steal the money. But I'm not happy about you skipping out of here last night so I haven't decided if you get your job back yet."

Again Jessie's mouth flopped open. "You know I didn't steal the money? And you fired me anyway? Are you crazy?"

"You aren't making a case for me rehiring you," Merriam said dryly. "I didn't find out you didn't steal the money until after closing. That's all I'll say about that. Now I'm short one more employee so if you'll get your ass into work tonight to cover, you can have your job back."

For a moment Jessie stood there at a loss for words. She'd expected to have to fight. She'd been prepared to fight. Then her eyes narrowed because, really, it had been far too easy and Merriam was anything but easy.

Merriam scowled. "Quit gawking. I made a mistake. You won't hear me saying so again. You either want your job back or you don't, but make up your mind so I can figure out if I need to hire *two* new employees."

Jessie smiled then. "Yes, ma'am. I'll be in tonight."

Merriam waved her hand in dismissal. "Get on out of here then. I've got work to finish up so I can go home and go to bed."

Feeling giddy and triumphant, Jessie turned and hurried out of the office.

"Don't forget to lock the door back on your way out!" Merriam hollered behind her.

Jessie shook her head and walked out, locking the door before she headed for her car. Halfway there, she stopped and did a fist pump. The day was definitely looking up.

And she had time to run by the store and be back before the guys were even out of bed.

———

Truitt stirred and automatically reached his hand out only to grasp air. He patted the place where Jessie had been and frowned when he felt the coolness of the spot. He raised his head, blinking bleary eyes to see Rick sprawled on the other side of the bed.

He sniffed as the aroma of cooking food wafted through his nostrils. Whatever it was, it smelled damn good. His stomach growled and he rolled over, rubbing his abdomen. Actual home-cooked food was a novelty. He and Rick either ate out, got delivery, or cooked out of a can. They'd given up on microwaving shit because, well, it tasted like shit.

He debated whether to shower first or go see what Jessie was up to. He finally decided to go check her out just in case she had plans to leave anytime soon.

He ambled into the kitchen to find Jessie bending over to peer into the oven. Her cute little ass strained at the not-much-to-them denim shorts and his morning hard-on just got harder.

Lord, but he had to learn to control himself around her.

Then she shut the oven and turned, her eyes lighting up when she saw him. That look warmed him to his toes.

"Oh good, you're up! Breakfast will be ready in about ten minutes."

"Have I got time for a shower?" He looked self-consciously down at his rumpled appearance. He was lucky she hadn't run screaming in the other direction. He rubbed his jaw and decided he'd have to be extra fast in the shower because he needed to shave too.

"If you hurry," she said, her eyes sparkling. "The biscuits aren't good when they're cold."

"Biscuits?" He almost whimpered. "Like homemade biscuits or biscuits out of a can?"

"My grandmother would roll over in her grave at the idea of biscuits out of a can," Jessie said with a laugh. "Now go or you'll have to eat them cold."

"I'm going, I'm going," he said as he turned and all but fled to the bathroom.

By the time he emerged exactly eight minutes later with only one razor cut to show for his hastiness, Rick was already seated at the breakfast table while Jessie put out plates. She smiled again when she saw Truitt and he felt that funny tightening in his chest all over again.

"Have a seat. I'm dishing up the omelets now. The biscuits are ready to come out of the oven and the gravy's done."

"Ah hell. Gravy," Truitt breathed.

Rick chuckled. "It's been so long since we had anything resembling real home cooking. We might fall all over ourselves kissing your feet."

Jessie arched an eyebrow and her lips twitched. "I might like that."

She motioned for Truitt to sit and then she hurried around the counter. She was back in just a second with the omelets and then she went back. Two more trips and biscuits so light and fluffy were set on the table, along with a bowl of steaming brown gravy.

The smell was divine.

Truitt dug into his food and when it hit his tongue he about orgasmed all over again.

"Good?" Jessie asked.

Rick had his mouth full and eyes closed in delight.

"You're a dream," Truitt said when his mouth was free of food. "You're gorgeous, sweet, *and* you cook? Do you have any faults?"

She blushed that pretty pink again, but pleasure shone in her eyes.

For the next half hour, he and Rick ate like they hadn't been fed in a week. His stomach was probably going to scream What the Fuck? since he wasn't currently poisoning it with shit out of a can.

When his plate was clean and he'd downed the last biscuit, Truitt leaned back in his seat and sighed. Jessie got up to clear the table, but Rick wrapped his fingers around her wrist and pulled her back down to sit.

"You don't need to be up on that knee after hurting it last night. Why don't you just stay here. Truitt and I will take care of the dishes later."

"Okay. I should probably be going now anyway. I have to work tonight. We're going to be shorthanded."

Truitt sat forward just as Rick stroked his fingers over Jessie's wrist. Rick was just about to open his mouth when his cell phone rang.

Rick swore and Truitt groaned. "Not now. Anytime but now."

Jessie shot them a puzzled look.

"Chief has his own ringtone," Rick said dryly. "Sorry darlin', I have to take this."

He pulled out his cell phone and issued a short greeting. Truitt watched keenly as Rick frowned, then glanced quickly in Jessie's direction before focusing his gaze on Truitt.

Whatever it was, it couldn't be good if Chief was calling on their day off. He hoped to hell their serial killer hadn't struck again.

"We'll be there," Rick said grimly.

He hung up and cast an uneasy look in Truitt's direction again. Then he tugged Jessie's hand into his and rubbed his fingers over her knuckles.

"Truitt and I have to go and I don't know how long we'll be. But I want you to stay here. Get some rest. Do whatever you need to do. I'll call you. Give me your cell number."

Jessie frowned but recited her number as Rick put it into his phone. Then Rick rose and gestured for Truitt.

"Let's go. I'll tell you about it on the way."

# Chapter 6

Rick stood over the body of Merriam Powell and blew out his breath. This was going to be sticky in more ways than one. He glanced at Truitt, who had the same look of resignation. But at least Jessie wouldn't be going to work tonight.

To the side, Rick heard one of the other detectives who'd been called to the scene mention Jessie's name. He quickly tuned in and then walked over to interrupt the conversation.

"What about Jessie Callahan?" Rick asked.

Trevor "Bull" Phillips narrowed his eyes, clearly irritated by the interruption. "You know her?"

"Yeah, I know her. Truitt and I both come in here a lot. Jessie's a waitress. She worked here last night."

"Well your waitress is our prime suspect in the case. From what's been gathered so far, I'd say this is going to be a slam dunk."

"What the fuck?" Truitt demanded as he shoved in.

"She's not at her apartment. I've already sent Jones to bring her in. You happen to know where to find her?" Bull asked.

Rick exchanged looks with Truitt. This was a clusterfuck. No way they could pull this case now. Not if Jessie was mixed up in it. But at least they could clear her.

"Where's the chief?" Rick asked. "He's going to need to hear this."

"On his way. Merriam Powell was an old friend of his. He's pretty hot to trot to nail her killer to the wall."

On cue Chief Markham strode into the office just as Jud Hennessee was pulling a sheet over Merriam's head. Chief stopped Hennessee and carefully pulled the sheet back just enough to see Merriam's blood-spattered face.

"Jesus," the chief muttered. Then he got up and walked over to where Rick and Truitt stood with Bull.

"You got leads?" the chief demanded.

Bull nodded.

"I want the son of a bitch who did this," the chief snarled.

"Look, Chief, we need to tell you something. It involves the primary suspect in this case. I don't have all the facts. Bull was just about to fill me in. But Jessie Callahan couldn't have murdered Merriam Powell because she was . . . she was home with me all night," Rick finished tightly. "She was with Truitt and I. We just left her a few minutes ago."

The chief snapped his gaze to Bull. "And this is your prime suspect?"

Bull stared hard at Rick and Truitt, in a way that pissed Rick off. Like he didn't believe Rick or maybe he thought he'd even lie to protect Jessie.

"We have witnesses that place her here at the bar around five A.M., which is the estimated time of death," Bull said.

"Bullshit," Truitt said. "She was in bed with me."

The chief raised one eyebrow. "I thought she was in bed with Rick. Make up your mind here."

"She was in bed with both of us, okay?" Rick bit out. "It isn't important who she was having sex with. What's important is that she has an alibi."

Bull crossed his arms over his chest. "What time did you leave the bar with her last night?"

"Are we being questioned?" Truitt challenged.

The chief held up his hands. "Outside, all of you."

The four men walked outside the bar and over to the chief's car. The chief leaned against his car and stared at Rick and Truitt and then at Bull.

"Let's get this over with as quickly as possible. Answer Bull's question. If she was with you then this will be resolved shortly but if you two are involved, we need to make this clean and by the book."

"We left around eleven," Rick said.

"And is that her usual time to get off?" Bull asked.

Truitt shook his head. "No, she usually closes. She hurt her knee though and said she could leave."

"Well here's what I know," Bull said quietly. "She was fired from her job last night. I have two witnesses plus an entry in Merriam's business journal stating that Jessie was suspected of stealing money and Merriam let her go. That was at approximately 10:45. Witnesses also heard Jessie threaten her. Now you say she left with you at eleven. Did she say anything about losing her job?"

A sick ball formed in Rick's stomach. He glanced at Truitt who looked a little shell-shocked himself.

"No," Truitt muttered. "She said she had to be in tonight because they were going to be shorthanded. She told us that just a little while ago."

"Okay now. How sure are you of her whereabouts at five this morning?" Bull continued.

Rick swallowed. "I didn't wake up until close to seven. She was in the kitchen cooking."

Truitt nodded. "Yeah, I was up just a few minutes earlier. We were asleep by three."

"What exactly is your relationship with Miss Callahan?" the chief interjected. "How long have you known her?"

Rick didn't like the direction this was heading and that ball was getting bigger in his gut.

"A few weeks. We'd come in, have a few drinks. Flirt. Proposition her."

"And did she ever take you up on your offer?" Bull asked.

Truitt shook his head. "Not until last night."

"Did she know you were cops?" the chief interjected.

Rick nodded. "Yeah. She knew. It wasn't a secret."

Bull and the chief fell silent a long moment. Truitt looked a little green. Then he muttered, "No way. I don't care how it looks. She didn't do this. She's so damn . . . sweet."

Rick dragged a hand through his hair and looked away. He was feeling like a fool and he didn't like that feeling at all. Had they been taken in by a pair of big brown eyes?

"Did it occur to you that she seized an opportunity to give herself an alibi?" the chief asked quietly. "She gets fired, gets pissed at her boss, sees a way to get revenge, and have an airtight alibi? I mean who's going to doubt the word of two detectives when they say she was home all night with them in their bed?"

Truitt rubbed his hand over his belly, a tight grimace working its way across his face. He was steadily shaking his head in denial.

As much as it grieved Rick to say it, he knew it had to be done.

"How much do we really know about her, Tru?" Then he turned to Bull. "How credible are your witnesses?"

"Two employees reported overhearing the argument between Miss Callahan and Miss Powell last night. This morning her car was spotted parked outside the bar by an off-duty security guard and a jogger who runs a path by the bar every morning."

"Shit," Rick swore.

Truitt was absolutely and completely silent. His brows had drawn together in a dark cloud and his jaw was tight.

"Okay, well you two are off the case. Bull will take lead. I want you to stay away from Jessie Callahan in the meantime. You two will have to be formally questioned at the station if she claims you as her alibi and denies being present at the bar this morning."

Bull's phone rang and he held up a finger as he turned away to answer it. Rick didn't pay attention to what was being said. His mind was numb with disbelief. He felt like a complete idiot.

The coincidence of her deciding to come home with him and Truitt on the same night she'd been fired and made threats against her boss was too staggering to ignore.

Bull ended his call and turned back around, a grim expression on his face. "You said you left Jessie at your place when you were called out?"

"Yeah," Rick said.

"Jones just picked her up outside her apartment. He's bringing her in now."

———

Jessie sat in the interview room of the police station, her stomach tight and her nerves shot. No one had told her crap about why she was here, only that she was being questioned. For what? And why?

She supposed she shouldn't have agreed to come. They weren't arresting her so she had a right to refuse, right? The truth was, she'd been so intimidated by the hulking police officer who'd not so politely "asked" her to come into the station with him, that she'd mechanically gotten into his car—into the backseat of his car like some damn prisoner.

She was mortified by the idea of anyone seeing her, and by the stares that had been cast her way when the officer had escorted her into the station.

He'd seated her inside a small room that had only a table and chairs. It was cold and sterile and it heightened her unease.

Could something have happened to Truitt and Rick? But surely no one would know to say anything to her. Unless maybe they'd mentioned her in some way?

She shook her head. It did no good to speculate. All she had to do was wait and then she'd be able to go home.

She sat for what seemed like forever. It was silent and empty. She could walk out, surely. They couldn't hold her here. The door was wide open. Was it a test?

She shook her head for a second time. She was losing her mind and she was paranoid.

Finally two men entered the room. One was an older man with graying hair, dark bushy eyebrows, and wrinkles around his piercing eyes. He carried himself with authority, but it wasn't him who took a seat in front of her. He stood off to the side, arms crossed as he stared her down.

Discomfited by his regard, she turned her attention to the man in front of her. Then she swallowed because he looked like he could squash her like a bug.

"Miss Callahan. I'm Detective Phillips. I'd like to ask you a few questions."

"Okay," she breathed out. "What about? Is something wrong? Did something happen to Truitt and Rick?"

Detective Phillips's eyes narrowed. "I'll ask the questions here. Earlier this morning, Merriam Powell was found murdered in her office at Powell's Pub."

Jessie's mouth dropped open. She slapped her palms on the table and shot to her feet. "That's not possible! She was alive. I saw her. I talked to her. And I locked up after I left."

The detective's eye flickered and he glanced over at the older man who still stood to the side.

"So you admit to being at the pub this morning."

Jessie frowned and eased back down into her chair. "Of course I do. I went to see her about my job. We talked maybe ten minutes and then I left."

"And what time was this?"

She put a hand to her head and rubbed. "Five I think? It was close to five. I woke early and knew she'd leave by six and I needed to catch her."

"Were you angry? Did you argue?"

"No. Not at all. I fully intended to argue my case. You see, the night before she accused me of stealing money from the register but it was complete crap because I never touch the register. She fired me and at first I was going to let it go, but I can't afford to lose any days. So I went to her office to tell her that it was bullshit and that I needed my job. But when I got there she told me she knew I hadn't taken the money and that she knew by closing time the night before but she was peeved because I left early, even though she fired me!"

She broke off long enough to take a breath.

"Continue," the detective prompted.

"So she said that we were going to be shorthanded. I assume she fired whoever it was she decided was stealing from her. I don't know, but she said if I wanted my job back, I had to go in tonight to work."

"I see."

Again he glanced to the older man and Jessie looked rapidly between them both as realization dawned. Okay so she was slow but it was suddenly crystal clear why she'd been brought in for "questioning."

"You think I did it," she whispered.

The detective leaned forward. "Well, let me tell you how it's been explained to us by eyewitnesses. Ms. Powell calls you into her office. Fires you for stealing money. You get into an argument. You threaten her. A few minutes later, you leave with two police officers. Go home with them. Have a little fun. Then you sneak out when they're asleep, go back to the pub, get into another argument with Ms. Powell and when she won't give you back your job, you kill her. Then you go back to Truitt Cavanaugh's house, slip in while they're still sleeping, cook some breakfast, pretend nothing's wrong, tell them you have to be in to work and then you bolt as soon as they leave. Am I getting it right so far?"

The blood drained from Jessie's face. She was so numb and freaked out that she honest to God couldn't even open her mouth. Was this what they thought? Was it what Truitt and Rick thought? They had to have already told this detective everything or else how would he know?

"Are you suggesting I used them so I could murder someone?" she croaked out.

The idea sounded so outlandish that all she could do was sit there and stare dumbly as the detective coldly judged her.

"What I think is that it's pretty damn convenient that you suddenly take Rick and Truitt up on their proposition when you put them off for weeks. And on a night when you were fired from your job and threatened your former employer. She turns up dead the very next morning and you were present at the crime scene. In fact, it would appear that you were the last person to see her alive. Now you tell me. How does that look?"

She bolted to her feet again. "I don't give a damn how it looks. I didn't do it. She gave me back my job! She obviously fired someone else. Why don't you question the other employees?"

"Oh, we'll question them. We've already questioned several. It's not looking good for you, Miss Callahan. Why don't you make things easier for all of us and tell us what really happened. Maybe you did go to try and talk her around. Maybe you got upset when she refused. The DA might consider the lesser charge of manslaughter if you tell us exactly what happened."

Tears of rage swam in her eyes and it pissed her off that these jackasses would see her cry. Her fingers curled into tight balls and it was all she could do not to punch the condescending jerk right in the face.

"I didn't do anything," she bit out. "And unless you're arresting me, I'm out of here. Don't come near me again without a warrant."

"You'll make this a lot easier on yourself if you cooperate now."

For the first time the older man spoke and Jessie turned her ire on him.

"Fuck off. I'm out of here."

She stomped toward the door and nearly ran smack into Truitt and Rick, who were standing just outside in the hall. She took a hasty step back as relief made her wilt.

"Thank God you're here," she whispered. "Tell them I didn't do this. Make them understand."

"I can't do that, Jessie," Rick said in a formal sounding voice.

Her brow wrinkled in confusion as she looked between the two men. Rick looked . . . stoic. Truitt looked raw, angry, and confused. Yeah, well, join the club.

Realization hit her with the force of a cement block. They thought she'd done it too. They were staring at her like she'd somehow betrayed them. Like she'd used them.

Disappointment was so keen that it nearly buckled her knees. Then she steeled herself because she wouldn't let them know how much it hurt for them to look through her the way they were doing.

"I didn't do it," she said quietly. "Please believe me."

Something flickered in Rick's eyes. He hesitated and looked . . . torn. Did he want to believe her? She couldn't tell. He was so hard to read. She wanted to see doubt in his eyes, and maybe it was there, but how could she know it wasn't just wishful thinking?

"Why were you gone so long, Jessie?" Truitt asked. "You said you were at the pub no longer than ten minutes. The timeline doesn't add up. Give us something to work with here. Tell us what happened so we can help you."

She stared at them, growing more numb by the minute. "I was at the store buying stuff to make you breakfast."

No longer able to stand their scrutiny, or the idea that they entertained that she could do this, even for a moment, she turned sideways to brush between them and walked down the hall, slowly at first but with growing speed. She heard one of them call her name, but she refused to turn around. They'd see how utterly devastated she was.

She burst out of the doors and took off down the street, no clear direction in mind, only that she wasn't spending another minute in such a hostile environment. God, they all thought she'd *killed* another person in cold blood. They were crazy but the frightening part was just how serious they were and it scared her to death.

Whatever happened to how sweet they thought she was? And how nice and cute and beautiful. Blah, blah, blah. It made her head hurt to know just how stupid she felt right now.

Three blocks from the police station, she dug out her cell phone and sank onto the sidewalk, drawing her knees to her chest as she clumsily punched in the phone number.

"Please, please be there," she whispered.

"Hello?"

"Kirsten, thank God. It's Jessie."

"Jessie? Hon, are you okay? You sound like you're crying. What's going on?"

Jessie wiped angrily at the tear trickling down her cheek and tried to work the knot out of her throat.

"I need you to come get me," she said in a shaky voice.

# Chapter 7

"Want me to go kick them all in the balls?" Kirsten asked with a scowl.

Jessie closed her eyes, cupped her hands around the warm mug of coffee, and inhaled the aroma. No matter how hard she tried, she couldn't stop the shaking. Her arms shook, her hands shook, even her teeth kept clanking together to make the most annoying sound.

She opened her eyes when Kirsten gently took the coffee from her and set it on the table in front of the couch.

"You're going to spill that all over you, hon. You're still shaking like a leaf."

"Thanks for coming," Jessie said because she didn't know what else to say. She was so grateful that Kirsten had come immediately and had brought her back to her apartment. The idea of going back to her place alone knotted her stomach.

"Stop thanking me. What are friends for?"

Jessie's eyes went watery again. "You're the best friend I could ask for. You've had my back since sixth grade."

"Damn straight. And you've had mine."

Kirsten was a beautiful woman and she had a warm smile that just drew people to her. She was only slightly taller than Jessie but thinner by far. She was lanky, had a jean size that made Jessie green with envy, and she moved with a grace that made people stop and watch her go by.

She had long, straight auburn hair that in the sunlight reflected about six different shades. And she had the bluest eyes, light and clear. Mesmerizing to look at.

"You didn't answer my question. Should I go down there and kick their asses?"

Jessie smiled. Or tried to. "No. I'm the dumbass in this. I never should have gone home with Rick and Truitt. I was upset over Merriam firing me. I wasn't thinking straight. I hurt my knee and they were offering . . . comfort."

Kirsten snorted. "That wasn't all they were offering."

"True," Jessie acknowledged. "But of all nights to have given in. They not only think I murdered a woman but they think I'm some tramp who lured two detectives into her bed so I could sneak out to do my evil deed."

"Sounds like something out of a B movie."

"Yeah, tell me about it," Jessie muttered. She covered her face with her hands. "God, I don't know what I'm going to do. They totally think I did it. They supposedly have witnesses. What am I going to do, Kirsten? I can't afford a lawyer. I can't afford to be without a job, but who's going to hire me now with this hanging over my head?"

Kirsten reached over and squeezed her hand. "You didn't do it. Of course you didn't do it. You couldn't hurt a fly, Jessie. Try not to freak out yet. They haven't arrested you. They still have to build their case. They'll find who really killed Merriam. If worse comes to worst, I can call my dad. You know he loves you like a daughter and he'd be more than glad to help."

Jessie lost the battle to hold her tears back and she threw her arms around her friend. "I love you," she said fiercely. "I'll never forget that you were there with me when I was in the hospital, and when I was struggling so hard just to walk again."

Kirsten hugged her back and kissed her cheek. "And you were there for me when I absolutely needed you most, when I thought my entire world was going to end. You made me want to keep living."

Kirsten leaned back and stroked her hand over Jessie's bedraggled hair. "You need some rest, hon. I know it's hard to sleep when you're so scared and upset. Let me give you one of my sleeping pills. It won't hurt you to take something to help you sleep."

Jessie nodded, her eyes closed wearily. She was exhausted. Right now she'd do just about anything for a few hours of oblivion.

———

When the phone at his desk rang, Rick picked it up and barked a greeting. For a moment there was silence before the eerie, familiar electronic synthesizer crackle sounded.

He went tense and turned violently, motioning frantically for Truitt and anyone else he could get to notice.

"Good afternoon, Detective Broughman. I have to tell you, I'm disappointed. This latest one just wasn't a challenge. Hardly worthy of my skills. Clearly I'll have to do better next time. I'd give you coordinates but she won't be hard for you to find."

Rick's stomach revolted and before he could respond, the phone went dead. He sank into his chair, still gripping the receiver just as the chief and several other police officers ran up.

"It was him. Christ, there's another. He said this one wasn't a challenge."

Curses rang out. The chief pinched the bridge of his nose and closed his eyes. "Damn it," he said. "Nothing else?"

"Just that he would have to do better next time. Said she wasn't worthy of his skills. He didn't give a location this time. Said she wouldn't be hard to find."

"He's escalating," Truitt said. "It's just been two weeks since the last. Half the time between the last two victims."

"Sounds like he'll be out hunting again soon," Bull said with a scowl. "We have to nail this son of a bitch."

"Call it out," the chief said. "We need to start looking. Do it as quietly as possible. We don't want to alert the media before we even have a body. People will run all over those woods and mess up our crime scene."

The officers slowly dispersed. Rick ran a hand through his hair. His head ached like a son of a bitch. This sucked. The timing sucked. As much as he wanted nothing to do with the investigation involving Jessie, a part of him refused to believe she could be responsible. Last he'd heard it was just a matter of formalities and that the case would be turned over to the DA soon. And even though he wasn't supposed to go near this case—or Jessie—he had no intention of just leaving it alone. He needed to know himself just what Jessie's role in this was. Only now, every minute of his time would have to be spent on the recovery of the newest victim.

With a weary sigh, he picked up the phone to call in his group of volunteers. The very last thing he wanted was the body of another young woman to haunt his dreams. But she at least deserved to be found and buried with dignity, not left to rot with no marker to celebrate her life.

━━━━━━━

Jessie and Kirsten sat cross-legged on Kirsten's couch, a pint of Blue Bell ice cream in their hands. Jessie's poison was Cookies 'n Cream. Really. There wasn't a better ice cream. Anywhere. Kirsten liked the more froufrou stuff and so she'd gotten some weird mix of flavors and nuts. Jessie shuddered at the mere thought of all that stuff in her ice cream.

Kirsten flipped through the channels, a practice that made Jessie crazy, but she didn't say anything and instead focused on her ice cream. Every delicious calorie. Hey, when your life sucked, eat ice cream.

"Holy shit, Jessie, that's you!"

Jessie's head jerked up, her eyes narrowed in confusion. "Wha?"

She quickly focused on the screen as Kirsten turned up the television. She froze when she saw a snapshot of herself plastered across the news. The anchor was babbling on about the murder of a local pub owner but the only thing Jessie heard was her name and that she was a person of interest in the case. The story then went on to give information about Jessie, including that she had been a waitress at the pub until she'd been let go under suspicion of theft.

"What the fuck?" Kirsten bit out. "I don't believe this. Holy shit. They can't do this! You haven't been arrested. They can't just smear your reputation like that."

"Though no charges have been filed, the police are expected to make an arrest soon."

Jessie's stomach dropped and her mouth went dry. She sat staring at the TV long after Kirsten turned it off and hurled the remote across the room.

"That does it! I'm calling my dad. This is outrageous. They can't do this to you. A 'source inside the police department'? What the everloving hell? We need to find out who sold you out and sue their asses," Kirsten snarled. "They can't go around leaking crap to the media when you haven't been charged with a crime. Whatever happened to innocent until proven guilty? They've already started your trial, goddamn it."

Jessie couldn't speak. Her throat was too closed off. This was a nightmare. Yeah, she'd been freaked out by being brought into the police station for questioning, and yeah, it had pissed her off that they'd come right out and said they thought she killed Merriam. But not even then had she really thought that it would come to this. Maybe she was in denial, but innocent people didn't really get convicted did they? Only in the movies or mystery novels. God, she felt like a naïve moron.

"What am I going to do?" she whispered to Kirsten.

Kirsten sat down next to Jessie and gripped her shoulders. "What we're going to do is hire a lawyer. A damn good one. Daddy will know someone. I'm going to call him right now. And listen to me, Jessie. If they come for you, don't you say a word. Not a single word. You just look through them and refuse to speak until your lawyer is there to advise you. Okay? Do you understand? Not even a peep. They'll try to get you to confess. Hell, they'll try to get you to say all sorts of things that they can twist around on you in court. So if you don't say anything, they can't do that."

Jessie nodded dumbly. Then she hugged Kirsten to her and hung on for dear life. "I'm scared. These things aren't supposed to happen in real life."

Kirsten squeezed her and then pulled away. "Tomorrow, I want you to go to your apartment and get all your stuff. You're moving in with me until this is all over with."

"But I can't do that. I don't even have a job," Jessie protested.

"Exactly. You can't pay rent if you don't have a job and if you don't stay with me, you'll be out on the streets. That is so *not* going to happen. You can take me to work then take my car to get your stuff and pick me up after my shift."

"I love you," Jessie said fiercely.

Kirsten smiled. "I love you too. We're going to kick some cop ass. Now let me go call Daddy. He's going to be pissed. We'll get you through this, Jess. I promise."

# Chapter 8

Even after seeing countless dead bodies in his years on the force, Truitt still had to turn away from the sight of the young woman sprawled on the ground, half covered in leaves, dirt and mud caking her body, mixing with blood from numerous cuts. The killer had been right. The victim hadn't been hard to find at all because the arrogant asshole had left her for the police to find in the area they always staged in when they searched the woods.

The utter callousness, the fact that the killing was sport for some son of a bitch who got a thrill from hunting down a defenseless woman, filled him with rage.

The girl's final moments had been filled with pain, terror, and the helpless realization that she was going to die. This time the shot wasn't from a distance. No, judging by the marks on her knees and the position of the entry wound, the bastard had caught up to his captive, made her kneel, and then shot her execution style.

Or maybe he'd never turned her out for the hunt. Maybe he was changing his game up. But then he'd complained in his phone call to Rick that the woman hadn't been a challenge. Maybe she'd refused to run. Maybe she'd realized the futility. Or maybe she'd simply given up.

The crime lab had marked off a wide perimeter, and beyond it, other police officers searched meticulously for something, anything, the killer could have left behind. Sooner or later he had to fuck up.

But the bastard even picked up his shell casings, and the bitch of it was, he either had the lightest feet known to man or he covered his tracks extremely well, because they could find absolutely no disturbance in the soil or the forest floor. Only blood and footprints and disturbance from the victim.

She was a pretty girl. Looked like a college student. A good twenty years younger than the last victim. Her blue eyes were glassy and fixed in death, her hair smeared with blood. Truitt shook his head and heaved out a frustrated sigh. Sometimes his job sucked.

Soon she was packed in a body bag and carried to where the coroner's van waited. The scene was wrapped up, and as dusk settled over the woods, Rick and Truitt dragged themselves along with the other volunteers toward their vehicles.

They were dirty, tired, and disheartened.

Truitt's mood only got blacker when he saw the news vans parked around their vehicles. The chief was already fielding questions and it looked well on its way to becoming a circus.

"Let's get the fuck out of here," Rick muttered. "Pick up a six pack or five and get wasted."

Truitt didn't argue.

As they climbed into Rick's truck, Truitt's cell phone rang. When he glanced down he recognized the number and his gut tightened.

"It's Bull," he muttered to Rick. Hell, he had probably arrested Jessie. Just what they needed to cap an already stellar day.

"Cavanaugh," Truitt barked into the phone.

"Truitt, it's Bull. Look man, I think you should come by the

station. I know you've had a long day but I think you'll be interested
in knowing this."

Truitt sighed. "All right. We'll be there ASAP."

He shoved the phone back into his pocket.

"He wants us to come to the station."

Rick's lips thinned. "Great. Just when I thought this day couldn't
get any worse."

They rode back into town in silence, passing through the smaller
communities, many of which had been homes to the women victim-
ized by the Big Thicket Killer.

When they finally pulled up outside the station, it was well past
dark. Truitt was starving and he had a date with a case of beer.

They got out of Rick's truck and Truitt stared up the steps to the
entrance.

"Shit," he muttered.

"Come on. Let's get it over with," Rick said sharply. "It's been a
hell of a day."

They walked through the door and Rick waved when the dis-
patcher cheerfully greeted them.

"Hey guys, Bull's in his office. He's been waiting for you."

"Bull seems a bit eager to shove Jessie down our throats," Truitt
said in a terse voice.

Rick's lips tightened but he didn't say anything as they walked
down the long hallway to Bull's office on the end. Bull was behind his
desk up to his nose in paperwork. When he heard Rick and Truitt he
looked up and then put down his pen.

"Have you made an arrest?" Rick bit out.

"Yeah, I have."

Truitt's lips curled up into a snarl. "Okay, so why did we need to
be here? You couldn't have said this over the phone?"

Bull leveled a stare at him. "Jessie didn't do it. She was telling the
truth."

Rick went still. Truitt's heart started to pound harder.

"Okay, wait," Rick began. "You made an arrest. Just yesterday she was all but convicted in your eyes. What changed?"

"Have a seat. You'll need to see this."

Bull swung around and aimed a remote at the television monitor a few feet away as Rick and Truitt lowered themselves into chairs.

As they watched the news story that all but painted Jessie as a convicted killer, Truitt's fingers curled into tight fists.

"What the hell was that?" Rick demanded. "Where the fuck did they get their information? Who's the goddamn leak?"

"I don't know," Bull said. "Chief's pissed. Hell, we're all pissed. Nobody here likes to see the goddamn news blabbing shit before we're ready."

"Son of a bitch," Truitt swore. "So she didn't do it and now that doesn't matter because everyone will *think* she did."

Bull held up his hand. "We're doing damage control. We have a confession. The chief is going to handle the press conference himself to say that an arrest has been made, charges will be filed, and that Miss Callahan was instrumental in the department's discovery of the true killer."

"Too little too late," Truitt said bitterly. "Who the hell did it?"

"Jessie's alibi about being at the grocery store checked out. She told the truth about being at the pub no more than ten minutes. Not to say she couldn't have killed Ms. Powell in that time, but there was a lot of blood at the scene and there's no way she could have cleaned up and gone to the grocery store so quickly. When we started to question other employees, one of the stories waffled. When we pressed the bartender, she folded in about thirty seconds. She was a sobbing mess inside of five minutes and couldn't confess fast enough."

"Then why the hell was that information leaked?" Truitt demanded. "Son of a bitch. Nothing had been decided for sure. We aren't a bunch of fucking amateurs. You don't go to the press ever, but you damn sure don't go around telling people who you *think* killed someone."

"I want to know just as badly as you do," Bull said with a scowl. "It compromises my investigation."

"Has anyone informed Jessie that she's no longer a suspect?" Rick cut in.

Bull paused before turning his gaze to Rick. "I thought maybe you two would want to do the honors. Up to you though. I wanted to tell you first. I got a confession just an hour ago and I called you as soon as I was done."

Truitt thrust his fingers into his short hair. Jessie probably wouldn't ever give them the time of day again, but she deserved to know she was off the hook.

"Thanks, Bull. Appreciate it," Truitt said as he rose.

Rick also stood and they nodded their good-byes and then headed back out to Rick's truck. For a long moment, Rick sat behind the wheel staring moodily out the windshield.

"Goddamn it," he finally said and he pounded the steering wheel with his fist. "She was telling the truth all along. She went home with us because she wanted to."

Truitt nodded tightly. "Yeah. We fucked up. Christ. What a load of crap. The coincidence of all that going down like that? Has to be astronomical."

"Or maybe it wasn't coincidence," Rick said grimly. "We don't have the details, but it's entirely possible someone saw their opportunity and used Jessie as the scapegoat."

"We need to get over to her place. Do you have her address?"

Rick swore and then picked up the phone to call Bull.

Twenty minutes later they pulled up outside Jessie's apartment to see her car parked out front. Truitt breathed a sigh of relief. At least she was home. They would make her listen. They had no other choice.

Both men got out and just as they got to the door, it opened and

Jessie nearly ran into them, lugging a suitcase behind her. She stopped hard and would have fallen but Rick caught her arm and steadied her. Truitt could still see the wince when her leg took too much weight.

As soon as she locked onto them, she hastily backed away. The suitcase fell to the porch with a clunk.

"Are you here to arrest me?" she asked in a shaky voice.

She looked small and fragile and Truitt swore at the fear in both her voice and her eyes. He reached out to touch her, to somehow offer reassurance but she jerked back, making herself a smaller target.

"No honey, we're not," Rick said gently. "We're here to tell you that an arrest has been made. You're no longer a suspect."

She stared blankly at them for a long time, her mouth open. Her gaze darted back and forth and then she shook her head as if she hadn't fully understood what Rick had said.

"Just like that?" she asked hoarsely. "I'm not being arrested?"

Truitt shook his head. "No. You're under no suspicion."

Tears filled her eyes and then she looked away as she wiped at her eyes with her palms. "Everyone will think so though. It was all over the news today. I'll never get another job."

"We're going to fix that," Truitt vowed. "The department owes you. The chief is going to take care of it. No one will think you're remotely guilty."

She swallowed hard and then color suffused her cheeks. "You can't fix it for me. You can't control what other people think. What they think they know. What they know is that my face was all over the news. Some may not even remember why, but they'll know there was something about me that they should be cautious about. So, no, you can't fix this for me."

Truitt couldn't stand it any longer. "Sweetheart, let's go inside. Were you going somewhere?"

"Yeah, I was going to my friend's apartment to stay with her. She called her dad about a lawyer since we were convinced I'd be arrested any moment. I'm not going inside with you. I'm not going anywhere with you."

"Jessie, please," Rick said softly.

Her eyes flashed. "Do you know I said the same thing? I said please believe me. But I get that it was your job, okay? I'm not mad, because it looked like I killed someone and you had to do your job. I get why you had to stay away from me. Do you want to know what I don't get and why I'm angry?"

Truitt swallowed and let his hand fall.

"I don't get why you looked through me like I was nothing to you. Like I had betrayed you. I get that you may have *thought* so, but you condemned me without ever asking. You never once *asked* me if I did it."

Shit. There was nothing he could say because they hadn't asked. They'd been too wrapped up in their anger over thinking they'd been used.

"I know you had a job to do, but would it have killed you to have said I know it looks bad, Jessie, but tell me what happened? Would it have killed you to ask me if I did it? You *never* asked. No one did! You assumed you had all the facts and you looked right through me and basically agreed with the assumption that I was some whore who used sex with you to cover up a crime."

The misery and humiliation on her face gutted Truitt. Rick didn't look any better.

"I need to go," she muttered. She reached down for her suitcase and started down the steps toward her car.

When she got to the bottom, her knee buckled and she went down, clutching at the suitcase for leverage.

"Damn it, Jessie," Rick said as he hurried down to help her. "At least let me get your suitcase. You need to stay off that knee."

"Just let me go," Jessie said quietly, her voice laced with pain. "I honestly can't do this with you right now. I'm tired. I haven't slept in days."

Truitt walked up behind her and slid a hand over her shoulder. He squeezed and kneaded, lightly stroking in a comforting manner. She tensed but didn't pull away.

"I'm sorry, Jessie. I misjudged you. You're right. I should have asked you. I should have done a lot of things. I don't want this to be it for us."

Jessie turned those soulful brown eyes on him, eyes that dripped with fatigue. "Who's us, Truitt? Me? You? Rick?" She shook her head. "It was a nice night. A lot of fun. The sex was great. I'm not sure what more you're wanting here."

"A hell of a lot more," Rick growled.

Startled, she turned to look at Rick as he wrested the suitcase from her grasp.

"We want you, Jessie," Truitt said. "We both want you. Not just for one night. Definitely not for just one night. We fucked up. We know that. But I'm hoping like hell you'll give us another chance here."

Jessie brought her hand up to her forehead and it was then he could see the very real pain she was in. Something came loose in his chest as he watched her grapple with her anger and also the sadness that tinged her every word.

"I can't do this now," she said again in a soft whisper. "I need to go."

She started for her car, but she took it slow this time. Rick followed with her suitcase and silently stowed it in her trunk.

"Don't carry that in wherever you're going," Rick said gruffly. "Get someone to help you."

She nodded and started to get back into her car.

"When will you be back?" Truitt rushed to say, because hell if he was just going to let her walk away.

She shrugged. "I don't know. Things have changed. I need a few days to figure out what I'm going to do now."

"Don't take too long, Jessie," Rick added quietly. "We'll be waiting."

# Chapter 9

So you told them what?" Kirsten asked as she licked the ice cream off her spoon.

In what was fast becoming a nightly—and fattening—ritual, the two women were seated on the couch devouring a pint of Blue Bell ice cream.

"You realize it would be cheaper if we just bought a gallon," Jessie pointed out.

"It's all about intentions," Kirsten said. "If I buy a gallon, my intention is to eat the whole gallon. Whereas I buy a pint, I'm only committing to a pint."

Jessie laughed. "Your logic is flawed! We eat a pint every night. The same amount of ice cream is being consumed."

Kirsten wrinkled her nose. "I don't feel as guilty buying a pint."

Jessie sucked another creamy spoonful into her mouth and sighed. Some of the panic had abated but her anxiety level was still through the roof. She had to pay rent in three days and she still didn't have a job. So she had a decision to make. She couldn't make the rent and pay her utilities. Kirsten had offered to let her stay until she could get another job and get another place to live. Which meant if she did that, she had three days to be out of her apartment.

And then she laughed because really, apart from dishes and clothes and a few items like the TV she rarely watched, there wasn't anything to move.

"So?" Kirsten prompted. "What exactly did you say to your cops? You avoided my question a while ago."

Jessie sighed. "They aren't my cops. And I didn't tell them much. I was upset. A little shell-shocked. They didn't want me to go, but what else was I going to do?"

"Were they properly contrite?"

"Define properly."

"Did they beg?" Kirsten asked with a mischievous grin.

Jessie frowned. "Well, no. I wouldn't have wanted that. They just looked and sounded . . . sorry. I don't know. Honestly at the moment I wasn't too worried about how messed up they were. Not to be rude but I was dealing with my own issues and it wasn't about them. They hadn't been accused of murder. They hadn't had their picture all over the news while it being broadly hinted that they were going to be arrested and charged with a crime."

"Preach it sister. So what are you going to do?"

Jessie blew out her breath. "Hell if I know. I don't even understand what they want from this. I mean it was supposed to be a fling. Now they're acting like they want more. Both of them. How the hell is that supposed to work?"

"Well you didn't seem terribly concerned about how it worked when you were having sex with them both," Kirsten pointed out with an amused smile. "I'd say it works just like it did the first time. You sleep with both of them."

"You're such a cheeky bitch," Jessie grumbled. "I get how the sex works, okay? It's everything else I'm clueless about."

Kirsten shrugged. "Okay, so what? Figure it out as you go."

Jessie drew back in mock surprise. "Are you lobbying for the two men you called dickheads just a few nights ago? The same men you thought castration was too good for?"

"All right. So I have a slightly vicious streak. But they seem genuinely sorry and they worry about you and your knee. I have a hard time finding fault with them if they want you to take better care of yourself."

Jessie rolled her eyes. "Look, I just need a few days to sort out my mess of a life. The last thing I need is to begin any sort of relationship whether casual or serious in the middle of this clusterfuck I call my life."

"Okay yeah, I can agree with that. But after you've moved in with me and after you've gotten another job I vote you call them up and at least give them the chance to grovel. I love a man who grovels well."

"You need to stop before you make me all weepy again."

Kirsten looked at her strangely. "What did I do now?"

"You make me laugh and I really need that right now. I'm so glad I have you."

Kirsten chuckled. "You'll forget about me soon enough when you have those two hot cops back in your bed. When you told me about the night you had with them, I wanted to stab you. I was so jealous. They sound absolutely hot and gorgeous even if they're a little thickheaded. They are male after all. If we wanted perfection, we'd put penises on women and cut off their boobs."

"Stop," Jessie said with a shudder. "I think you just ruined them for me."

The two burst into laughter again and Jessie went limp with relief. Just a short time ago she'd been convinced that her life as she knew it was over. She'd been scared out of her mind and contemplating the very real possibility of going to jail.

No matter how hard she might think her life had been since her accident, she had so much to be grateful for and she'd prefer every hard knock to a life behind bars.

"I think we need to celebrate," she said impulsively.

Kirsten's face lit up. "I agree. We're being pathetic sitting here stuffing our faces with ice cream when we need to be celebrating the fact that you did not kill your evil employer."

Jessie sighed. "She wasn't evil. She was just . . ."

"Evil. She was evil and moody. She was a crusty old bat and she probably hadn't gotten laid since fire was discovered."

Jessie tried to hold back her laughter because . . . well, it was just wrong to speak ill of the dead.

"I'll concede that she was moody. I won't, however, speculate on her sex life because that's just . . . gross."

Kirsten snickered and then threw her legs over the end of the couch. "Okay, so what are we going to do? Powell's is obviously out and we'd never set foot in that place again even if it reopens. I vote we go somewhere, get absolutely shitfaced, and then take a cab home. I have bra twenties for both of us."

Jessie laughed. "Okay, I'm in. No one will recognize me if we're in some dark bar anyway, right?"

―――――――――

After spending hours making calls, interviewing the victim's family members and friends, Rick had a headache from hell, and he was frustrated because nothing made sense.

He and Truitt as well as the entire team assigned to the Big Thicket Killer had tried to connect the dots between the most recent victim and the ones before. With no success. They couldn't find anything that linked the women.

It was seemingly random, which made it all the more frightening. What was the killer's selection criteria? Did he just drive around, see a woman, and decide she was the one?

The women weren't from the same area or town. They had no common interests. They didn't shop in the same places, go to church at the same churches. Their jobs were varied, some being students, and some not working at all.

The only common denominator was that they were women. And that left a hell of a lot of potential victims in the running.

"Let's pack it in," Truitt said. "It's been a long day and we're not getting anywhere. We all need some sleep. We can start back in the morning."

There were murmurs of agreement but after everyone had filtered out of the conference room, Rick still sat, staring broodingly at the crime-scene photos.

"Come on, man. Let's get out of here. Go have a beer."

Rick sighed. "Yeah, you're right."

He was getting out of his chair when his cell phone rang. Frowning when he saw the incoming call listed as private, he punched the button and brought the phone to his ear.

"Detective Broughman."

Chills raced down his spine when he heard the telltale metallic silence and then, "Detective, I just wanted you to know that I've already selected my next victim and I'm sure she'll be more of a challenge than my last."

"You son of a bitch!" Rick roared into the phone. "Stop playing your sick game. These are innocent women you're killing."

There was a distinct pause. "No, Detective. They aren't innocent. Not at all."

The phone went silent and Rick swore.

The chief stuck his head in the door. "Something wrong, Broughman?"

"He just got another call from our killer," Truitt said quietly.

"And?" the chief demanded.

"He said he's already selected his next victim. Jesus Christ, Chief. What the hell do we do? I've never felt so helpless in my life," Rick said. "How are we supposed to keep these women safe when we have no idea how he's choosing them? We're just sitting around waiting for him to fuck up."

The chief looked ten years older than he was. His hair seemed grayer and the lines in his face were more pronounced. "I think we need to go public. We should at least warn the women in this area that this bastard has already chosen his next victim. We need to go stronger on our public warnings. We've issued several statements to the females in the area, but we need to bring home the seriousness of them having their personal safety foremost in their minds."

Truitt let out a strangled sound. "We'll incite panic."

"Yeah, well what else are we supposed to do?" Rick challenged. "We can't just do nothing. We have no idea how these women are being taken. There's no sign of struggle in their house. No strangers lurking around their homes. No unusual activity. It's like this guy just walks them right out of their house and they willingly go with him."

"Maybe they do," Truitt said slowly. "What if this guy is someone they would trust?"

"But there's no connection between these women. What are the odds that they'd all know this guy and trust him?" the chief asked.

"We could call around and see if anyone from the cable company, electric company, gas, city whatever has been seen at the victim's residence," Rick suggested.

Truitt shook his head. "We've already covered that angle. No utility trucks or men in uniform or otherwise were spotted in these neighborhoods. It was one of the first things I thought of."

Rick blew out his breath. His headache was only getting bigger.

"You guys go home," the chief said. "You aren't any good to me in your present condition. I'm going to get with the mayor and call a joint press conference immediately. I don't care what kind of panic I incite. The women of our city are going to have to be careful."

Rick nodded, resigned to the fact that there was another woman out there that he likely couldn't save, who might already be in the hands of a maniac.

"Let's go get a drink," he said to Truitt.

It wasn't like he'd ever sleep, because when he closed his eyes, he was haunted by the image of a beautiful young woman covered in dirt and blood.

# Chapter 10

With makeup and her hair fixed, Jessie didn't resemble the photo that had aired on the news. She wasn't sure how the hell they'd managed to drag up the picture they had. Jessie had looked hung over, and since she rarely imbibed to excess, it wasn't like she'd had many opportunities to be photographed drunk off her ass.

Tonight, though, she was going to make an exception and blow off some serious steam and anxiety.

"Holy crap, it's loud in here!" Jessie exclaimed when they entered the corner bar.

"What?"

Jessie leaned in closer. "I said it's loud in here!"

Kirsten nodded and grinned. Then she motioned toward the bar and the two women threaded their way through the crowd. As they reached the counter, the music stopped, though Jessie's ears kept thumping right along.

"Thank God," Kirsten said. "Now we won't have to holler to order a drink."

The bartender was cute in a preppy sort of way but Jessie found her mind wandering to the two rough-edged cops who'd rocked her world in bed and shattered it out of bed.

The women accepted their drinks and Kirsten turned around, drink in hand, to survey the assortment of people in the dimly lit interior.

"Looks like pickings are slim tonight," Kirsten muttered. "Not too many cute ones."

"That's your problem," Jessie said. "You like them cute when you should be looking for a harder edge. Something that screams badass and I'll rock your world in bed."

"Uh-huh, well we're not all queen of the threesome," Kirsten said dryly.

"Oh God, that sounds so dirty when you say it," Jessie groaned.

Kirsten chuckled. "You're cute when you blush. Besides, don't listen to me. I'm a jealous bitch right now because I'd die a happy woman to get it on with two gorgeous guys."

She threw back her drink and chugged it down then she held out the hand with the glass in it and bumped Jessie's arm. "Bottoms up, girlfriend. The night is young and we're wasting good booze."

Jessie complied, tipping up her glass and swallowing down the tart drink.

Kirsten turned around, ordered refills, and then asked for six shots of Patrón.

"Oh, hell no," Jessie said. "You aren't getting me to shoot tequila."

"Don't be a whiny bitch and drink up. I'm buying tonight."

Jessie grimaced then gingerly picked up one of the shot glasses. "We're crazy."

"But we're cute crazy," Kirsten said with a grin.

She held up her shot glass, clinked it against Jessie's, and then both of them put the rim to their mouths and tipped back their heads at the same time.

It was like swallowing fire.

Jessie came back wheezing, her eyes watering. Around them applause broke out and it was then she realized that she and Kirsten had an audience.

"Shit," she muttered.

Kirsten shrugged. "Let's give them a show."

Chants of "Drink, drink, drink" filled the air and Jessie reached for the second shot. A moment later it felt like the lining was stripped from her esophagus but the alcohol was down and swimming around her stomach.

"One more and then let's dance," Kirsten said. She thumbed in the direction of the band that was returning from break.

By now Jessie couldn't remember what her original complaint had been but she was game for some dancing. It had been a while and she could shake her ass with the best of them.

They toasted again, slogged down the shot, and then Kirsten hollered to the bartender. "Get us another set up. We'll be back after this song!"

She grabbed Jessie's arm and dragged her to the dance floor just as the first chords blared over their eardrums.

Within moments they had a crowd around them, a mixture of guys and girls. Jessie let the music and rhythm roll through her body, already loosened by the alcohol. She closed her eyes and let the rush of exhilaration flood her chest.

Relief. Bone-melting relief. Freedom from the fear that had permeated the very air around her for the last few days.

She and Kirsten whooped it up, together and separately. It was probably well established that they were lesbians with the way they bumped and ground all over each other. The shouted "I love you"s also might have done the trick, but none of the guys seemed to mind. The more exuberant she and Kirsten got, the more guys flocked to the dance floor.

When the long set was over, Kirsten dragged her toward the bar where their drinks waited.

"Okay, let's do this again," Kirsten shouted over the music. "Then we dance."

"If I don't puke first!"

By now a few others had joined in the shotfest and the bartender lined up an entire row of Patrón. Eager hands grabbed the glasses, and after a raucous count of three, they began downing them one after another.

"Do you see what I see?" Rick muttered as he and Truitt stood in the doorway of the pub.

Truitt's eyes narrowed as he zeroed in on the bar where Jessie stood with a crowd around her. She was rapidly downing shots along with another woman about her age.

"Yeah, I see."

"What the ever-loving hell is she doing?"

"Looks like she's getting drunk," Truitt said dryly.

Before they could move in the direction of the bar, the woman with Jessie slammed down her glass and then took Jessie's hand and dragged her onto the dance floor.

What followed left Truitt's tongue hanging down and his pants uncomfortably tight. The woman moved like a dream, all curves and softness, undulating in rhythm to the music.

Her breasts were plumped up—had to be one of those Wonderbra contraptions—and nearly spilling out of the top she wore. Or didn't wear. Hell, it was hard to tell from here whether she was more into the shirt or more out of it.

But what really set his teeth on edge was the number of men surrounding Jessie, all trying to touch her and get up in her space.

"She's wasted," Rick growled.

"Oh, you think?"

"Well, we can't barge in and flash our badges. After her experiences with the police this week, she'd never speak to us again. Which means we're just going to have to pretend we're her pissed-off boyfriends and wade in to drag her off."

"Uhm, there might be a problem with that," Truitt pointed out. "It would appear she's here with her friend. I didn't see Jessie's car in the parking lot. Which means we're going to have to take both of them."

"Whose boyfriend are you going to be?" Rick drawled.

Truitt scowled. "I'll take Jessie. You take the other one."

"She's not bad," Rick said. "She's not Jessie, but she's a looker. If I hadn't seen Jessie first, I'd absolutely do her."

Truitt rolled his eyes. "Come on. I can't stand this a minute longer. There's no telling how long they've been at it."

They waded through the crowd, Truitt scowling at people who seemed all too willing to give him and Rick a wide berth. When they reached the women, they were sort of squatting, Jessie's back and ass nestled against her friend's chest and groin, and they bobbled up and down looking for all the world like they were putting on an erotic peep show.

At least Truitt understood why they'd drawn such a crowd now.

Truitt stood there, waiting for Jessie to see him and Rick. He planted his feet and crossed his arms over his chest. Some of the crowd had moved back to widen the perimeter so that it now encompassed him and Rick. And they all looked on with avid interest like they were sure the fireworks were about to start.

When Jessie and her friend did finally turn, their reactions were nothing short of amusing. Jessie halted abruptly, her eyes wide. Beside her, the friend also stopped and she stared boldly, raking her gaze up and down his body until he felt a might embarrassed.

"Are these your cops, Jessie?"

Now the problem with that question is that it just happened to pop out just when the last note died and a window of silence crept in before the room erupted in applause and whistles.

Jessie seemed to recover from her surprise and scowled. It was a cute scowl too. Her nose scrunched up and she had such a look of belligerence that Truitt was reminded of a bulldog.

"No, they aren't my cops," she shouted.

Rick took a step forward until he was so close to Jessie she was forced to tilt her neck to look up at him.

"Yes, we *are* her cops."

Jessie shook her head, all the while Rick nodded.

"I don't suppose you'll take just one and leave the other to me?" her friend asked mournfully.

Rick grinned and Truitt's mouth twitched.

"You can have them both. With my blessing," Jessie said crossly. "They're jerks."

"Well yeah, but they're gorgeous jerks. Do y'all know how to grovel?"

Truitt blinked in confusion at the abrupt change in direction of the conversation. "Grovel?"

"Yeah, I'm thinking you'll need to do some serious groveling to get Jessie to forgive you. She's been through hell the last few days. We're out to blow off some steam. You might have just ruined her night."

"What's your name, doll?" Rick asked.

"Kirsten, and I'm her friend. Her *best* friend. So if she doesn't want to go with you then she stays with me," she said fiercely.

"You're both coming with us," Truitt said. "You're both wasted and we're going to make sure you get home safely. Now you can come quietly or we can haul you out over our shoulders. Either way, you're coming."

Kirsten blinked and Jessie's eyes widened again. Neither seemed to know quite what to make of that.

Then Jessie's brows scrunched together and she thrust up her chin. "You wouldn't dare."

It was the wrong thing to say. Particularly to Rick because telling him he wouldn't dare was like waving a pork chop at a starving pit-bull.

Rick simply plucked her up, tossed her over his shoulder, and rested his hand possessively on her ass.

"I'm going, I'm going!" Kirsten exclaimed as she put her hands in the air. "Just point me in the direction."

"Hey, put me down!" Jessie exclaimed.

Truitt was already pulling out his badge as he herded Kirsten toward the door. Rick followed close behind and Truitt held up his badge when the security guard got a look at Jessie and frowned.

The guard relaxed when he saw the badge and motioned for Rick to pass on out the door.

When they hit the parking lot, Rick strode toward his truck with Jessie's pert little ass thrust skyward. He opened the back, eased her onto the seat, and then scowled at her as he stood inside the door.

"I don't know what the hell you were thinking. You shouldn't have been out on the dance floor drunk off your ass when you've got a bum knee. You're going to regret it tomorrow."

Truitt guided Kirsten around so she could sit beside Jessie in the backseat and then he climbed into the front. He turned just as Rick shut the door and he slid his gaze over Jessie.

"You okay? Your knee hurt?"

"No," Jessie mumbled.

"She's not feeling anything right now," Kirsten said smugly.

"I guess not," Rick said as he climbed in. "Just how much have you girls had to drink?"

Kirsten shrugged. "Six . . . seven . . . maybe ten shots."

"Jesus," Truitt muttered. "Ten? That's enough alcohol to put an elephant to sleep, for God's sake. What were you shooting?"

"Patrón."

"Oh my God," Rick groaned. "Are you two insane?"

"She wanted to celebrate," Kirsten defended. "Isn't that right, Jessie?"

She turned as she said the last and then leaned over Jessie who'd gone quiet.

"Jessie?"

Jessie had her head on the window, mouth half open, and she was passed out cold.

# Chapter 11

Why don't you just take me home and then you can take Jessie home with you," Kirsten said as they pulled out of the parking lot. "I'm sober. Really. And then you could do your groveling in private. That is, when she regains consciousness . . ."

Rick glanced back at Kirsten. "I'd feel better if you weren't alone."

Kirsten made a face. "I'm a big girl. Besides, I can hold my liquor. Mutant genes or something. I can pack a lot of alcohol into a small body. No one ever knows how I do it without passing out in my own puke."

Truitt grimaced at that visual and Rick chuckled.

"Okay, doll. We'll take you home and put you to bed. And then we're taking Jessie home with us so we can do our . . . groveling."

Kirsten smirked. "I knew you two couldn't be all bad."

After getting directions to Kirsten's apartment, which suited Rick just fine because now they knew where to find Jessie, he dropped Kirsten off and saw her inside, testing her sobriety himself. The woman hadn't lied. She could drink an astonishing amount of liquor and still be completely coherent.

Jessie on the other hand . . .

He glanced back to where Jessie still lay against the glass and then drove toward Truitt's place. When he pulled into the drive, Truitt got out and carefully opened the door so Jessie wouldn't flop sideways.

Truitt unbuckled her and lifted her out. He held her close as he walked toward the house, and Rick felt keen disappointment that she wasn't snuggled in his arms. He wanted to touch her so badly he ached.

The last days had been torture for him and Truitt both. First the thought that she'd used them and then the fear that no matter what she'd done that she'd be arrested and jailed. And finally the realization of just how wrong they'd been about her and the dread of losing her when they'd only just managed to finally get with her.

"Should I put her straight to bed or attempt to sober her up?" Truitt asked when they were inside.

"Put her on the bed. I'll make some coffee and we'll see if we can wake her up."

Truitt shouldered his way down the hall carrying Jessie, and Rick went to put on a pot of coffee.

Ten minutes later, he carried a steaming mug to the bedroom and found Jessie curled up against Truitt. Truitt met Rick's gaze as Rick set the cup down on the nightstand and then leaned down close to Jessie's ear.

"Jessie, Jessie, baby, wake up, okay?"

Truitt trailed a finger over her cheek and suddenly Rick couldn't stand it another moment. He crawled on the bed and levered himself down so he was close to her. He didn't want her to wake up and be freaked out. He wanted her . . . comfortable. Secure.

"Jessie," he murmured, adding his voice to Truitt's. "Wake up, honey. Open those gorgeous brown eyes and look at me. I've got some coffee you need to drink."

At that her eyelids fluttered and her unfocused stare met Rick's. Then her nose wrinkled.

"Don't want coffee," she muttered.

Rick chuckled and his heart softened. Hell, he wanted to pull her onto his body and let her sleep there like a warm blanket.

"What are you doing here?" she asked.

Just then Truitt nibbled at her shoulder and she jerked her head back, her eyes flaring in surprise as her gaze settled on him.

"We live here," Truitt said.

"Then what am *I* doing here?" she grumbled. "You were jerks. I don't want to talk to you right now. I was celebrating and having fun. Now I'm not having fun."

"If you weren't such a cute drunk kitten we'd show you how much fun you could be having," Rick said.

She gave him a disgruntled look but she didn't argue further.

"The room is spinning and I don't feel so good," she said.

Sure enough she'd gone awfully pale and sweat beaded her forehead.

"You need to puke?"

"Dunno. Maybe I should just go take a shower."

Truitt raised a brow from behind her shoulder. Yeah, Rick wasn't stupid. He wasn't about to let her go take a nosedive in the shower and crack her skull.

"You get a shower only if one of us goes in with you," Rick said.

She frowned again but then swallowed and licked her lips. "I don't care. I just need to get up. My stomach's queasy."

Rick scrambled up and reached down to pluck her off the bed. When he got to the bathroom he parked her by the toilet and after making sure she wasn't going to fall face-first into the bowl, he reached over to turn the shower on.

When he turned back, she was asleep again, her cheek pressed against the toilet seat. His chest shook with laughter and he reached down to hoist her up so he could get her clothes off.

Quickly deciding this was a two man job, he called for Truitt who popped in a second later. Truitt lifted a brow and amusement twinkled in his eyes.

"Having trouble?" Truitt asked with a grin.

"You could say that. Help me get her clothes off."

Between the two of them, they managed to hold Jessie upright and get her clothes off.

"I'll take her while you get undressed and in the shower. Then I'll hand her in to you," Truitt said.

Truitt lifted her to sit on the towel that covered a portion of the counter by the sink and he leaned her forward so her head rested against his neck and the rest of her body was pressed against his.

Rick stripped down, reached a hand in to test the water temp, and grimaced at the lukewarm feel. Bracing himself, he ducked in and then motioned for Truitt to bring Jessie over.

As soon as the water hit Jessie's back, she let out a yelp and her eyes flew open.

Rick pulled her into his arms and pressed his lips to her forehead as she trembled against him. After a moment she relaxed and went limp. At first he thought she'd passed out again but when he pulled her away he saw that she was very much awake.

"I'm thinking maybe I should have choked down the coffee," she said, her mouth quivering. "It was warm at least."

"We'll warm you up in just a minute," Rick promised.

She leaned in against him again, resting her forehead just underneath his chin as the water poured down over them both.

"I haven't forgiven you yet," she said.

He smiled. "But you will."

He could positively feel her frowning over the arrogance in that statement but she didn't refute it.

"Want a full body scrub while we're in here?" Rick asked.

She shook her head. "If it's all the same to you, I'd like to get out before I become an ice cube."

He reached behind her to shut off the water and her sigh of relief was audible in the sudden quiet. He pushed open the shower door to find Truitt waiting with a large towel that could probably be wrapped around Jessie twice.

Jessie stepped out shivering from head to toe, her teeth clinking together like ice tinkling against glass. Truitt enfolded her in the towel and began to rub briskly in an effort to warm her.

Rick grabbed another towel and stepped around them to head back into the bedroom. A moment later, Jessie walked out wrapped in the towel with Truitt on her heels.

Rick quickly pulled on a pair of shorts and a T-shirt and then held out his arms to Jessie. To his satisfaction she walked right into them and snuggled against his chest.

"Crawl into bed," he said as he kissed the top of her damp hair.

"I don't have anything to wear," she said. "Just what I had on before."

Truitt reached into one of his dresser drawers and then tossed a shirt across the bed to Rick.

"Here, put this on. It's good to sleep in."

Her cheeks blooming with color, she tugged the towel downward and then hastily pulled the huge T-shirt on over her head. The hem fell to just above her knees and Rick decided that he'd like to keep her like this all the time. In just an oversized T-shirt, where he could have access to her in a matter of seconds.

His dick stood up and paid attention to that particular fantasy and Rick shifted to alleviate the discomfort in his groin.

Jessie turned and crawled onto the bed and then burrowed under the covers, pulling them to her nose. Rick and Truitt crawled in after her, pressing close from both sides. After a moment she sighed in contentment and some of the shaking ceased.

"Are you sober enough to hear us grovel?" Rick asked seriously.

Her eyes narrowed. "You've been talking to Kirsten. I swear the girl's obsessed with groveling. A simple apology works fine for me."

"Does it?" Truitt asked softly. "Because we're not just asking you to forgive us, Jessie. We're asking you for more. A hell of a lot more."

She swallowed visibly and stared up at Truitt and then over to Rick. "How much more?"

Rick put a finger to her cheek and trailed it softly down to her jaw and then traced the line to her chin. "Everything. We want you to be ours. We want to take care of you, make sure you stay off your knee when it hurts, make love to you as often as we can, come home to you after a rough day at work, eat your wonderful cooking. That sound like anything you'd be interested in?"

Jessie blinked rapidly and wondered if this was just a direct result of too much alcohol. Alcohol induced hallucinations, didn't it?

She suddenly wasn't so cold anymore. She was warm all the way to her toes and then some. Both men stared at her like . . . Damn. Like they meant every single word.

"I'm still drunk, aren't I?"

Truitt chuckled close to her ear. "No, sweetheart. Not that drunk anyway."

"What do you want, Jessie?" Rick asked, his eyes intense as they scorched over her body. "Don't think about anything else. Just tell me what you want. What your gut tells you."

"I'm crazy but I want that too," she said before she could chicken out. "I don't even know how to wrap my mind around how such a thing works—"

Rick put his finger over her mouth. "Stop right there. All we need to know, all that is important is what you want. We know what we want. We'll make it work."

He sounded pretty darn convincing.

Her mouth trembled and she glanced up at Rick and then back over her shoulder to where Truitt was positioned. "You hurt me." It had to be said. She had to get it out. She had to be sure that they wouldn't ever think she could be capable of such a thing again.

Rick looked gutted. Guilt crowded into Truitt's eyes.

Before they could respond, she took a breath and went on. "I know I probably don't understand how things work, and you probably weren't allowed to so much as speak to me. But the way you looked at me, and the fact that you said nothing while those people said horrible things to me in that room—it hurt. I know we didn't really know each other, but I felt a connection to you both. I mean, you'd both been coming into the pub regularly. And when we finally had sex, it was like . . . I don't know. It was like we'd been leading up to it forever and had already been on a dozen dates. I know you didn't know me. Logic tells me that you had every reason to be suspicious. But my heart was hurt because that night was special to me and I wouldn't have gone home with you if I didn't trust you on some basic, instinctual level. I guess I wanted that same level of trust back from you both."

"No, you're right," Truitt said in a quiet voice. "We owed you that much. We did have doubts about you committing murder even in the face of some pretty damning evidence at the time. But we didn't express those doubts to you. We didn't give you any sign that we were anything but sure you'd fucked us over, and for that I'm sorry."

Rick nodded. "And you were right about us not being able to talk to you or see you. But that was no excuse. We could have said we believed in you. We could have done a lot of things. But we didn't and it hurt you. We won't hurt you again, Jessie. At least not intentionally. I know we're asking for a chance we didn't give you. But give us one. We won't make you regret trusting us this time."

"Okay," she whispered.

Truitt's mouth slid warmly over her shoulder again and Rick lowered his head until his lips brushed hers.

She could feel the relief pulsating from their big bodies. Some of the tension that knotted their muscles went away, leaving them more relaxed against her.

"I was supposed to move in with Kirsten," she said when Rick pulled away. "I can't afford rent on my place without a new job and I haven't been able to look yet. I'm supposed to go get my stuff tomorrow. I thought you guys should know since . . . well, you know, we'll be sort of involved now."

Truitt scowled. "Sort of involved?"

"You'll just move in with us instead," Rick said, cutting off Truitt before he could finish. "How much stuff do you have? I don't want you moving anything heavy."

She blinked in surprise. "Not much. The apartment came furnished. All I have are my clothes, a few dishes, and my TV. Shoes and stuff, maybe a few boxes worth."

"Rick and I have duty tomorrow afternoon. We're working a tough case. We might be late but you can go over and move what you can and Rick and I will get the rest when we get off."

Jessie licked her lips. This was so . . . fast. And yet excitement sparkled through her veins, that new, giddy rush you got when you just knew that something was right.

"Are you guys sure this is what you want? You can't be used to having a woman underfoot in your house."

"It's not under out feet where we want you," Rick said with a grin. "But, yeah, we're sure. We want you here. We don't want you anywhere else."

"I—I want to be here too," she said honestly.

She could sense the relief in both men. She cuddled into Rick's chest even as Truitt moved in closer behind her to spoon.

Their hands were warm and soothing on her skin.

"I was so scared," she whispered.

Truitt tensed and then his lips nuzzled past her hair and to the spot just behind her ear.

"You don't have to be scared anymore, Jessie. I'm sorry for what happened. We didn't trust you, but that's going to change. From now on we'll ask before we make up our minds."

She nodded, accepting the earnestness in his voice. Rick tipped her chin up and then maneuvered so she could look him in the eye.

"I'm sorry too, Jessie. Give us another chance. We won't let you down again."

She smiled and then yawned. Rick caressed her jaw and then eased her back until she was snuggled against him once more.

"Sleep, sweetheart. We'll get you moved tomorrow and then we'll go from there."

# Chapter 12

Jessie woke to a warm mouth nuzzling the soft skin just below her ear. Her pulse sped up, and she sighed as teeth followed the wetness of a tongue and grazed up to her earlobe.

"Mornin'," Rick said huskily against her skin.

She stirred, then stretched lazily and turned more fully onto her back so she could stare up at him. On her other side, Truitt also woke and snuggled up close to her, his palm caressing a line up her waist to her breasts.

"Morning," she returned.

"How are you feeling? Headache?"

She considered his question for a moment and then shook her head. "I'm good actually. What time is it?"

"Nearly ten. Truitt and I are going in after lunch. I couldn't resist waking you to see if you were up for . . ."

He leaned down to kiss her, his mouth moving hotly over hers.

"For what?" she whispered as he pulled his mouth away.

His grin was slow and wicked and sent chills cascading over her body. "For us to make love to you for a couple of hours."

"Oh."

"Is that a good 'oh' or a bad 'oh'?" Truitt growled.

She turned, feeling deliciously naughty and a little more confident of herself than she had the first time they'd had sex. Leaning up, she nibbled at his firm jaw, enjoying the rasp of stubble on her tongue.

When she got to his mouth, she licked over his bottom lip and then kissed him.

"Definitely a good 'oh,'" she murmured.

He cupped her chin in one hand, returned her kiss, and then pulled away to stare into her eyes. Intense warmth and desire radiated from his gaze. Buzzed over her like a tangible burst of fire.

"Take off your shirt," he ordered softly.

Not hesitating, she slipped the T-shirt over her head. Rick took it from her and tossed it away. She knelt between them as they leaned against the headboard to stare at her.

She felt beautiful. The way they looked at her made it impossible for her to feel any other way. There was clear adoration in their gazes but there was also intense need and desire.

"Play with your breasts," Rick said, giving his own command. "Fondle them and touch your nipples."

She blushed and her breasts immediately began to ache. She hesitantly slid her hands up her belly to cup the tender mounds and brushed her thumbs over the taut points.

A shudder worked through her body, tightening every muscle in its wake. She pinched her nipples between her fingers and gently plucked until they were dark and rigid.

"Tell us what you want, Jessie," Truitt said in a soft voice. "Tell us how to please you. Today we're yours. We have a hell of a lot to make up for."

Oh hell. She had a buzz going on that had nothing to do with alcohol and everything to do with an overdose of sexy, seductive males.

She ducked her head for a moment, but Rick put a finger underneath her chin and gently nudged upward. His smile was warm and delighted as he took in her shyness.

"Come here," he said huskily.

Rick pulled Jessie into his arms until she straddled his lap. Arms full of naked, sweet woman . . . Was there anything better? Her pink-stained cheeks were adorable and the way she peeked at him and Truitt made his heart squeeze.

"Now tell us what you want."

She smiled shyly again and glanced over at Truitt, who was every bit as captivated as Rick was.

"I want you both. Like last time. Can we do that again?"

"You mean both at the same time, one in your pussy and one in your ass?" Truitt asked.

Rick winced at just how bluntly it came across but Jessie's breathing sped up. She seemed to like the crudeness of his explanation.

She nodded, her bottom lip caught firmly between her teeth. He was intrigued by the mix of sensual tigress and shy kitten. At first she'd seemed determined and comfortable to take the initiative and be aggressive with her wants and needs. Then she'd backed off and had become shy and self-conscious.

He wondered if she even knew how beautiful he and Truitt found her. Or how desirable. Or how he couldn't look at her without his gut twisting into a knot.

He reached up to push her hair over her ear, stroking his fingers through the thick tresses. He let his hand wander down her body, over the generous curves of her breasts, to her waist and then to her hips.

"You're beautiful, Jessie," he said hoarsely. "So beautiful that my hands shake around you."

She stared back at him, eyes wide and surprised. Happiness exploded deep in their warm brown depths and she sparkled. It was the only word to describe the way she lit up.

He leaned forward, wrapped his arms around her, and pulled her flush against his body. Her breasts pressed against his chest, soft and silky. He nibbled delicately at her neck, inhaling her scent as he kissed his way up to her mouth.

"What I want to do is lay you out between me and Tru and shower you with so much love that you damn near pass out."

She moaned softly and went limp against him, her curves melded to his harder body. Carefully he leaned forward, holding her as he lowered her to the bed.

She landed with the softest of bounces, her hair splaying out around her head. She stared up at him and Truitt with lazy, passion-drugged eyes that practically begged for them to touch her.

As if she ever needed to beg them for anything.

Truitt stood and rapidly pulled his clothing off in impatient jerks. Then he crawled back onto the bed and stretched out next to Jessie.

Rick backed off the bed as well but he was slower to undress, his gaze never leaving Jessie as she focused on Truitt and the gentle caresses he bestowed on her.

Truitt rose over her, part of his body shielding her from Rick's view. He lowered his mouth to kiss her, his hand going to her body to pull her even closer. It was a possessive move that Rick understood. Even though they were both in a position of having to share a woman they cared deeply for, there was still a part of them that screamed she was theirs and they wanted to somehow brand her.

He wasn't threatened by Truitt's desire to possess Jessie. He understood it all too well. And in time, when they weren't both so consumed in the newness of this relationship, they would both have time with Jessie.

Maybe he should be more concerned with the dynamics of the

relationship and worried about the potential pitfalls, but what he knew was that he couldn't give Jessie up. Neither would Truitt. And if she was willing to take on both of them, she would have the more difficult role. Rick would do whatever it took to ensure she was happy and secure with them both.

He made a quick grab for condoms in the nightstand, tossed the packets onto the bed and then slid back onto the mattress so he could view firsthand the luscious, sweet woman he'd lost his heart to.

Truitt's fingers were between her legs, petting and coaxing their way through the soft folds of her pussy even as his tongue tangled hotly with hers. Rick bent down to suck her nipple into his mouth, and she arched immediately, her soft cry explosive in the quiet room.

Truitt moved slightly to the side to allow Rick more room, and Rick slid his own hand down her belly through the curls to stroke her clitoris while Truitt teased her entrance.

"You have to stop," she groaned.

"Stop? You don't like it?" Truitt asked.

Her eyes were half lidded and she looked drugged. High on desire and arousal. Her lips were swollen and looked so damn delectable that Rick wanted nothing more than to slide his cock into that tight mouth.

"I love it," she gasped out. "I'm about to come and I don't want it to end so soon."

Truitt smirked but removed his hand from between her legs.

Rick nuzzled her cheek and then found her mouth, kissing her as he licked over her lips. "I have the perfect position in mind," he murmured. "I don't want any pressure on your knee. I want you to be able to lie back and enjoy everything we give you, not worry over whether you'll hurt yourself."

"Mmm, and what's this position?" she asked in her sweet, husky voice.

Remembering how she reacted to Truitt's raw language, he

decided to paint her a very colorful picture of exactly what he had in mind.

"You're going to sit on my cock and take me deep into your ass. Tru got that pleasure last time. This time it's mine. Then you're going to lie back while I hold you, and Tru is going to slide into your pussy. I'm going to continue holding you while he fucks you, and I'm simply going to enjoy being deep inside your ass until he finishes. Then I'm going to fuck your pretty little ass until you beg me for mercy."

Chill bumps rose on her skin and danced across her flesh, scattering delicately. Her nipples hardened and puckered until they strained upward, begging for attention. She stirred restlessly and let out a tiny whimper of need.

"Goddamn," Truitt swore. "Get her up and ready before I come right here all over her."

Rick chuckled. His words had been intended to get Jessie all hot and bothered, but they'd excited Truitt every bit as much.

"Help her," he directed Truitt. "And get me the damn lube."

Rick stood and walked around to the front of the bed before settling down on the edge. He waited until Truitt tossed him the lube and then leaned back so that his legs dangled over the edge and his cock jutted upward.

He smoothed lubricant over his erection until it was slick and then tossed the tube back to Truitt so he could prepare Jessie.

A moment later, Truitt lifted her and carried her around before carefully easing her down between Rick's thighs. Rick raised himself up and clasped his hands around her hips, guiding her back until the cleft in her legs cradled his dick.

"I'm going to lift you up to straddle his thighs," Truitt said to Jessie. "Dangle your legs over his and then let him guide you where you need to go."

Jessie glanced over her shoulder and sent Rick a look that would set fire to an iceberg. Her gaze positively smoldered, and a surge of pure, unadulterated lust hit him so hard that he nearly hauled her back onto his erection right then and there.

"Hurry," he gritted out in Truitt's direction.

Truitt easily lifted her up and settled her so she was astride him, facing away. Her legs dangled down and he bore all her weight. Mindful of this, he was careful as he fit his cock to her tiny opening. He lifted her slightly and then tilted his hips upward, pressing to gain entrance.

He pulled her down as he thrust upward, and he groaned in agony as she slid snugly over the head of his dick, caught momentarily before, with another tug, he had himself more fully embedded.

She gripped his knees and her nails dug into his skin.

"Am I hurting you?" he demanded.

She shook her head vehemently and then tried to push herself down farther, taking more of him inside her.

Finally he was balls deep inside her ass and he couldn't breathe. Every time he tried to suck air into his lungs, it felt like he was trying to thread a needle with a piece of rope.

He clutched at her hips and then slid his hands up and down her body, touching, caressing, reaching around to cup her full breasts. He was about to come all sorts of unglued and he tried like hell to get a grip before it was all over with.

He wrapped his arms around her and pulled her into his chest. She sighed and snuggled into his embrace, purring like a contented kitten. He loved the feel of all that soft, feminine flesh pressed against him. So trusting. And her scent. He inhaled deeply and then buried his nose in her hair, wanting more, wanting to draw her to the very heart of him.

Truitt stared at the erotic sight of Rick buried deep in Jessie's ass, her astride him, thighs splayed wide, her pussy completely bared to his view and impending possession.

Her head was thrown back, nestled in the curve of Rick's neck, her eyes closed, her expression one of complete abandon. She looked like an angel.

Rick cupped her breasts, holding them up, and Truitt couldn't resist such an invitation. He went to his knees between their tangled legs and sucked strongly at the breast being presented like a gift.

Jessie cried out and arched forward, her hand flying to tangle in Truitt's hair. She held him there, her grip strong as he suckled first one nipple and then the other.

"Take me please, Truitt," she pleaded. "I won't last much longer and I want this so much. I want you both inside me."

Hell if she'd ever have to beg for anything. He quickly rose, stepped closer so that he crowded in on her. He grabbed a condom, rolled it on, and then fit his dick to her opening.

She was going to be delectably tight with her ass full of Rick's dick. It made her pussy even smaller, and she was already so tight that being inside her was like a slice of heaven.

He inched forward.

Sweet Jesus, she gripped his head like a fist squeezing for all it was worth.

Rick curled his fingers over her legs and pulled them even farther apart, which made her groan as she stretched around Rick's cock.

Knowing if he didn't get in soon, he'd come being just an inch inside her, he pushed relentlessly forward until he was halfway in.

Jessie was uncontrollable. She twitched and writhed between him and Rick and it took their combined strength to keep her still enough that she didn't unseat them both.

Truitt withdrew just enough to open her a little more and then thrust forward as he fused his mouth to hers.

He took her mouth and he took her pussy and he wasn't gentle with either one. He'd reached his limit and he'd never had any finesse anyway.

Her breasts pressed hotly to his chest, her nipples little hard points, digging into his skin. She was sandwiched tightly between him and Rick, and Truitt had never seen a hotter sight in his life.

Delicate pale flesh caught between much darker, rougher skin.

He slid his hands down her body, gripped her waist, and then began thrusting in and out of her, loving the sounds that each thrust forced from her lips.

"How close are you, baby?" Truitt groaned.

"No," Rick said harshly. "Not yet. I don't want her to come yet. You finish but I need her still worked up or I'll end up hurting her."

Truitt tenderly cupped her cheek, a direct contradiction to the force with which he was pounding into her pussy. Then he closed his eyes and clenched his jaw so tight that he worried he'd break his teeth.

He came in a hot rush, his entire body trembling with the force of his orgasm. His legs went weak, his knees shook, and hot flashes rolled through his body until he panted for breath.

One last stroke to her very heart and he held himself there as he shuddered with the last of his release. For a long moment he simply stood there, buried inside her body. She was his. There was no more intimate possession than this. Bodies joined. Souls inexorably entwined.

His pulse raced, and as he pulled gently out, he nearly stumbled. As soon as he stepped back, Rick rose, still holding on to Jessie, lifting her but keeping himself buried deep inside her ass.

He turned then and lowered her, belly down, onto the bed. He slipped from her ass, eliciting a moan from Jessie.

"I want you flat, honey. Don't put any pressure on that knee. I want you relaxed."

She went limp on the bed, her cheek pressed to the mattress, and she closed her eyes as he mounted over her. He barely even spread her legs. He simply parted her ass cheeks, fit his cock to the seam, and then pressed forward.

As soon as he was inside, her stretched over her body, covering her as he thrust in and out.

He blanketed her completely, his hips cupped over her ass, the smack of flesh meeting flesh erotic and electric in the air. Faster. Harder. He rose and fell over her until finally he pushed himself up so he was supported by his palms flat on the mattress on either side of her shoulders, and he fucked her every bit as ruthlessly as he'd promised.

Truitt was already hard again, unbelievably turned on by the sight before him.

Just when Truitt was sure Rick would come, he tore himself away and impatiently turned Jessie over.

"Hold her injured knee so I don't hurt it," he said to Truitt even as he took her other leg and pushed it outward, baring her pussy and ass to him once more.

Truitt hurried forward, cradled her leg and gently held it while Rick lifted just enough so he could thrust into her ass once more.

On her back, his entry made her far more vulnerable. She was pushed upward as he drove into her ass. He reached between then and brushed his thumb over her clit as he powered inside again.

Her entire body tightened and she arched upward. Then he slid his thumb inside her opening and stroked her clit with his fingers.

"Come, Jessie baby. Come for me," Rick panted.

They both looked near to pain. Jessie's face was drawn into tight lines. She slammed her eyes shut as Rick grew more forceful with his fingers. Then she cried out. Screamed both their names as Rick slammed home one last time.

Rick slumped down over her, and Truitt carefully lowered her leg until he was sure she was comfortable. Rick rolled away long enough to take care of both himself and Jessie, and then he motioned for Truitt to better position her.

Truitt was more than happy to pull her into his arms and let her snuggle against his chest. Rick climbed in behind her and pressed a row of tiny kisses over her bare shoulder.

"Are you all right?" Rick asked in a low voice.

Jessie smiled and turned just enough that she could meet his gaze. "That was amazing. You and Truitt are so . . . perfect."

Truitt didn't entirely agree with that, but damn if it didn't make him puff up like a blowfish to hear her say it. He kissed her brow even as her eyes were closing.

"How long before you leave?" Jessie murmured.

Rick sighed. "I wish we didn't have to. We have maybe an hour."

"I'll have Kirsten come pick me up and take me over to my apartment. That way you guys don't have to leave even earlier to drop me off."

Rick smoothed her hair back and nuzzled her ear. "That sounds like a plan. We can use the remaining hour for much, much better pursuits."

"I like that plan," Truitt said as he fit his mouth to hers.

# Chapter 13

So it wasn't her best day but it was far from her worst. Her worst were hopefully behind her and her best were definitely ahead.

Feeling particularly philosophical, Jessie climbed into her car and waved at Kirsten as she pulled out of Kirsten's drive.

Kirsten had come by Truitt's house to pick her up and take her back to Kirsten's apartment so Jessie could have her car. Kirsten had offered to go help Jessie pack up her apartment, but really, there just wasn't much to do and Kirsten had to work.

Already she'd had a text from each of the guys, which she thought was incredibly sweet. She half wondered if she was crazy for jumping in so quickly, but wasn't everyone entitled to one rash decision in their life?

She hoped like hell she wouldn't ever regret it, but oh well, if she did, she'd have fun in the meantime.

She pulled up to her apartment and sighed. She wouldn't miss this place. It had been a place to live. Not home. A place in which she'd been biding her time until she paid off her debt, finished school, and got a better job.

Accounting was boring, no doubt, but who didn't need an accountant? Companies always needed number crunchers and accountants were usually the last to be laid off. It seemed like a stable job, and above all, Jessie wanted some stability in her life.

Maybe in time she could open her own business. Do taxes and small-business accounting. The idea of having her own office space with her name outside gave her a ridiculous thrill.

The sooner she packed up and gave her notice, the quicker she could move on with her life. Things could only look up from here.

She let herself in and stared around the tiny efficiency, where she'd lived since her accident. No, she wouldn't miss it.

Cheered by the thought of embarking on something new and exciting, she went into the bedroom and began packing her clothes. She went into the bathroom and tossed all her toiletries into a duffle bag and then lugged her suitcases to the front and left them by the door.

She was about to start into the kitchen when movement out her front window caught her eye. Frowning, she went over to peek out. Her frown got deeper when she saw a patrol car pulled right up to her front door on the narrow concrete driveway. Hell, she didn't even park there and it galled her that some dumbass cop was blocking her now.

And then she thought that maybe Rick and Truitt were the dumbass cops in question and her cheeks warmed. Even if she hadn't voiced the insult out loud she still felt guilty. Knee-jerk reaction after her experience with the police over the last few days.

She went to the door and stepped out onto her walkway, glancing toward the patrol car. To her surprise a tall, slender policewoman got out of the driver's side and flashed a smile in Jessie's direction.

Jessie frowned back at the woman.

The woman continued forward. "Are you Jessie Callahan?"

"What's it to you?" Jessie asked belligerently.

"I wondered if you could come to the station with me. We need to ask you a few questions about one of your coworkers. We're still investigating Merriam Powell's murder."

Oh, now they wanted her help? She didn't care if this woman worked with Rick and Truitt. She could kiss Jessie's ass. She may have forgiven Rick and Truitt but she wasn't so forgiving to the rest of their department.

"I'm busy," Jessie said shortly.

The woman's eyebrows arched. "It won't take long."

"If it won't take long then ask me here while I finish packing."

Jessie started to turn away but to her surprise the woman quickly closed the distance and gripped Jessie's arm.

"You going somewhere?" the woman asked softly. She let go and abruptly took one step back.

"That's none of your b—"

The words broke off in midsentence as fire surged through Jessie's body. Her entire body stiffened and she jittered from head to toe. She couldn't move, she couldn't speak, she couldn't cry out. Her lips were numb and her tongue instantly dry in her mouth.

Her bad knee buckled and she would have hit the ground but the woman pushed forward and held her up, smiling the whole while. Casually she half-carried, half-dragged Jessie the three feet to the passenger side of her patrol car.

She opened the back and eased Jessie in as if she worried they were being watched. Then she leaned in as Jessie started to sag sideways.

All Jessie saw was the butt of a pistol flying toward her head and then her entire world went black.

"I wonder why Jessie won't answer her cell. She answered my text hours ago but then nothing else afterward."

Truitt yawned and rubbed a hand through his hair. It had been a long-ass day spent interviewing the victim's family, friends, and coworkers.

All he really wanted was to go home, feel Jessie in his arms, and then sleep for about twenty-four hours straight.

He glanced up at Rick and saw that his partner was worried. Not just a little bit either. He frowned. "She was moving stuff today. She's probably busy. She might be with her friend."

"That doesn't explain why she won't answer her cell. It isn't turned off or it would go straight to voice mail."

Truitt frowned but before he could respond, the phone at his desk rang.

"Cavanaugh," he said in greeting.

"Is this Truitt Cavanaugh?"

"Yes it is. Is this Kirsten? Jessie's friend?" He recognized the voice.

"Yeah, it is. Look, have you heard from Jessie since I picked her up from your house?"

Dread began to form in Truitt's stomach and he glanced over at Rick, who was still frowning at his phone.

"No, Rick was just saying she hadn't answered her phone or his texts. You haven't seen her either?"

Rick came to immediate attention and hovered over Truitt, his brows drawn together as he listened to the conversation.

"No," Kirsten said. "And the thing is, I went over to her apartment. Her car is still there but the front door is locked. It doesn't look like she's there but where else would she be unless she was with you?"

"Okay, thanks for letting me know, sweetheart. Rick and I will find her. I promise."

"Let me know that she's okay. I worry about her."

"Will do."

Truitt hung up and then stood abruptly, grabbing for his keys. Rick was leaned over Truitt's desk, his palms planted on the surface and his face a mask of worry.

"What's going on?" Rick demanded.

"Kirsten's worried. She hasn't heard from Jessie all day and she said she drove by Jessie's apartment and her car is still there but the door is locked and it looks like she isn't home."

"Shit," Rick said. "It's after eight and it's been hours since we last heard from her. I knew I should have gone by to check on her. What if she's inside the house hurt?"

"Let's go," Truitt said as he hurried out of his office.

Several minutes later they roared up to Jessie's apartment and parked behind her car. Rick was out of the truck before Truitt had come to a full stop. Cursing, Truitt got out and ran to the front door behind Rick.

They tried the door but found it locked. They both put a shoulder to the wood and then rammed forward. On the second attempt, the door burst open and they rushed in.

"Jessie!" Truitt yelled. "Jessie, are you in here?"

Rick nearly tripped on her suitcases. They ran to the bedroom, the only other room besides the bathroom, but the apartment was empty.

"Where the hell is she?" Rick demanded.

"She's mostly packed. Everything is out of the bedroom and bathroom. Looks like she only had the kitchen. Her suitcases are by the door and her car is out front. Where the hell could she have gone?"

"I've got a bad feeling about this," Rick said. "This is going to sound crazy, Tru, but I can't get the idea out of my head."

"What? Spit it out, man."

"The killer called *before* this time. He's never done that. But this time he made it a point to call us and say that he'd already chosen his next victim. I know it sounds insane but it's screaming in my head right now. What if the son of a bitch tagged her from the news story?"

"That's a hell of a coincidence. What are the odds? Unless this guy is watching us. Then he'd know that we were involved with Jessie, but that's just crazy."

"Why does he call me every time?" Rick asked quietly. "Why not someone else. Why not the chief? It's not about attention. He's obviously focused on me. And if he's focused on me, then he'd damn well know about Jessie. Or it could be a raging coincidence. Either way I have a sick feeling that the bastard has his hands on Jessie and if we don't do something, we're going to lose her."

# Chapter 14

Jessie woke to throbbing pain in her head. Her entire body hurt. Her muscles were still jittery and she couldn't make sense of where she was or what had happened.

The first thing she became aware of was rain. The sound of rain, a gentle patter that soothed some of the vicious ache. She started to raise her head, because for some reason, the rest of her body wasn't cooperating, but as soon as she moved, agonizing pain ripped through her knee.

She screamed and tried to flinch away, but she couldn't move. She was tied to a wooden table, completely naked.

A face appeared above her. A face she remembered. And it all came back. The cop at her apartment. The bitch had Tased her.

The woman rammed the butt of her pistol into Jessie's knee again.

The pain was so horrific that Jessie gagged and turned her face to the side, breathing fiercely through her nose so she wouldn't vomit.

"Glad you're awake. The hunt is about to begin."

The words were said with such coolness and calm that they sent a shiver down Jessie's spine. She lay there panting, frantic to make sense of her situation. What the hell was happening? This woman was a police officer for God's sake.

"This is the way it's going to happen," the woman said.

Her hair was pulled back into a sharp ponytail, so tight that the skin stretched across angular cheekbones. She'd be pretty with makeup. Jessie almost laughed hysterically at the idea that she was contemplating how a maniac would look spiffed up.

She was tall. Even taller than Jessie had first realized. She had an athletic build that Jessie envied and was toned, with not an ounce of fat anywhere on her body.

She had on camo pants and a black tank, but what Jessie's gaze was drawn to was the wicked-looking hunting knife in her hand. It gleamed in the low light, and as Jessie dragged her gaze from that knife, she realized that she was in what looked to be a hunting camp and God only knew where they were.

The woman leaned in closer until the knife was so close Jessie could see her own reflection in the blade.

"I'm going to let you go and you're going to run. Then I'm going to hunt you and make the kill. It's fair. You get a fighting chance. Everyone before you has been too stupid to know what to do with it, but that's not my fault. I gave it to them."

"If you wanted to make it fair, you wouldn't have bashed my knee," Jessie said through gritted teeth. "You have to know I can't run."

The woman shrugged. "I imagine you can do lots of things you don't think you can when you're life is on the line."

She yanked the knife down Jessie's side and Jessie felt her flesh split open. She screamed in shock and horror as pain assaulted her all over again. The smell of blood rushed through her nostrils and she gagged again.

"What the hell are you doing?" Jessie yelled hoarsely. Oh God, it hurt. It felt like she was on fire. This bitch was crazy. Batshit crazy. And you couldn't reason with crazy.

"Tracking a kill is all about a good blood trail. I can hardly follow a blood trail if there's no blood," the woman replied calmly.

She dragged the knife down Jessie's uninjured leg, making a shallow cut from her hip to her knee. Jessie arched off the table, straining against her bonds as she screamed once again. Tears trailed down her cheeks and she closed her eyes, praying for a way out. Praying for the strength to run when the time came.

"Why aren't you begging?"

The obvious puzzlement in the woman's voice made Jessie open her eyes and focus.

"Just let me go and let's get on with it," Jessie gritted out.

The woman chuckled. "So impatient to die. I like you. I knew from the moment I watched your interview with the chief and Bull that you'd prove more of a challenge than my past hunting trips. The last one was a huge disappointment. She wouldn't even run. What's the fun in that?"

"You are one fucked up bitch," Jessie snarled. "Let me up so we can get on with this. I want to stand over you when your ass is arrested and kick you in the teeth a few times."

The woman adopted a bored look. "Think your detectives will save you?"

The pain was starting to get past the anger-induced adrenaline burst and if she wasn't set free soon, there was no way she'd make it even a few steps into the woods.

"I don't think they're going to save me," Jessie said tightly. She sucked in steadying breaths as she fought the horrific pain eating away at her. "I'm going to save myself."

This time the woman laughed but she started to cut the ropes tying Jessie to the table that was slick with Jessie's blood.

"Consider this an adult version of hide-and-seek," the woman said. "I'm going to go into the next room and give you a five minute head start. After that I'm coming after you."

She slung a rifle strap over her arm and strode through the doorway into the back of the house. Jessie didn't waste a single second. She pulled herself upright and slid off the table, testing the strength of her knee.

Pain tore through her leg and the knee buckled, leaving Jessie grasping the table so she didn't fall. She staggered toward the door but her mind screamed at her to stop and not to panic.

She was bare-ass naked and had nothing to stop the blood that streamed down her body and left small puddles wherever she stepped. Shit, this was going to make it easy for the homicidal maniac to find her.

She didn't see anything in the cabin that would help her stop the blood but then she remembered the sound of rain. Excitement coursed through her body and gave her a renewed adrenaline burst.

She limped out of the doorway and bolted off the rickety porch, swallowing the cry of pain when too much weight landed on her knee. She stood long enough to wash the blood off her body and then she ran toward the densest section of woods in her vision.

She gritted her teeth and pushed past the pain. Cognizant of how much she was bleeding, she held her hands over her wounds and ran blindly. After she put some distance between her and the crazy-ass bitch, she knelt and groped frantically along the ground, gathering dirt and mud and packing it over her wounds. She mixed the dirt with leaves and plastered them as widely over her body as she could, knowing she'd need whatever advantage she could muster.

"Smart. Be smart, Jessie," she breathed as she staggered to her feet again.

She looked frantically around, searching for some point of reference, some idea as to where she should go. But all she saw was thick woods blanketed in darkness. With the clouds and rain, there wasn't a single star visible and the moon was nowhere in sight either.

She wasn't going to outrun the psycho. But she could damn sure outsmart her.

Thrashing around the woods like a wounded animal was the very last thing she needed to do. What she needed was a good place to hide and she'd stay there until daylight when she could see where the hell she was going, and more important, see the murdering bitch when she was coming.

Quietly she crept through the dense brush, ignoring the rising panic and the urge to flee. Had it been five minutes yet? It felt like an eternity had passed.

She winced when thorns dug into her feet, but she didn't stop to pull them out. If she did, she might bleed even more, and she couldn't waste the precious seconds it would take to alleviate her discomfort. A bubble of hysteria rose in her throat. She had a shattered knee and knife wounds to her body, and she was contemplating how much time and effort it would take to remove a few thorns from her feet?

A flash of light froze her in her tracks. Had she imagined it? She stared hard, scanning the distant trees. There. Again. About three hundred yards away she saw a light bobbing through the woods.

Her heart nearly exploded out of her chest. Panic welled in her throat and she forced herself to breathe slowly, afraid to make even the slightest noise. She had to get away but she couldn't be stupid about it.

She forced herself to stand completely still as she strained her eyes to catch the direction of the light. For a moment it stopped and Jessie's heart sped up. Had her trail been picked up?

She glanced down, trying to ascertain if she was still bleeding as heavily but she couldn't see, so she gingerly patted her way down and cursed when she felt the sticky dampness of blood.

In the distance the light moved again and this time it tracked toward her in a straight line. Fearing she could be shot at any time, Jessie ducked down low and began creeping her way through the trees and bushes and the heavy ground cover. She took a course due east of her current position and then in a calculated risk she started south, moving toward, instead of away from, the killer.

If she were quiet enough they would pass each other with the bitch never being the wiser and by the time she doubled back, Jessie would have found a better hiding spot.

She hoped.

Her mind was so cluttered with panic and pain that it was hard to know if anything she thought made sense. But what she did know was that she was not going to give up, roll over, and die. She'd make that bitch trot her ass all over the thicket before the night was over.

# Chapter 15

As dawn crept through the trees, shedding pale light over a dark sky, Rick rubbed his eyes and then slipped his hand behind his neck to rub at a kink.

They didn't even know what they were looking for or if they were looking in the right area. Each time Rick's phone rang, he dreaded answering, afraid that it would be the killer, taunting him with news of Jessie's death.

But there had been no call. No news.

He and Truitt and several teams of volunteers had combed the woods starting late the night before and carrying on into the wee hours of the morning.

And nothing.

No sign of Jessie.

"Fresh batch of volunteers and the day shifters are coming on," Truitt called over his shoulder as he continued a path through the trees. "They want to meet up and discuss areas already searched and strategize the best way to cover the most ground."

Rick bared his teeth in anger and frustration. "You go. I'll keep looking."

Truitt stopped. "The hell you will. We're in this together. We're going to find her, damn it. I won't leave her out here alone. But we're searching blind. We need a better plan than this."

Rick swore but he followed Truitt out of the woods to where a makeshift parking lot in a clearing held a multitude of cars and trucks.

Bull and the chief stood next to Kim Whalen and Victor Manning. All were dressed in boots and clothing suitable for slogging through dense vegetation.

"Thanks for coming out," Truitt said as they neared the group of officers. Behind them another large group of fresh volunteers stood ready to receive instruction. Truitt was antsy and ready to go back, but he forced himself to remain calm because he was very close to losing it.

"We're glad to do it," Bull said gruffly. "She's important to you, which makes her one of our own, and we owe her for what happened." He took a deep breath and ran his hand over his head. "Hell, the son of a bitch wouldn't have targeted her if it weren't for that damn news story."

The chief nodded his grim agreement. Kim glanced between Rick and Truitt, but her gaze remained on Rick for a long moment. "Let's pull out the maps. I have an idea of where we can look next."

As they spread maps on the hood of the chief's SUV, Kim leaned over, pointing to an area they hadn't yet searched.

"My father hunts here a lot. There's a cabin here and one here. It's not an area the killer has used before. However, it's a logical place for him to eventually get to. And it's more isolated. Given that there's been no call yet, I'm guessing he doesn't want you to know where to find her, which means he'll go to greater lengths to hide the body."

At the mention of a body, Rick went rigid and his expression blackened. The ball in Truitt's gut grew to a gigantic size.

"Sorry," Kim muttered. "That was insensitive of me."

If it were someone else they were looking for, Truitt would probably be using the same language. They all knew it didn't look good for Jessie, but he couldn't make himself dwell on just how bad the situation was or that, in any other case, they'd already be assuming they were looking for a corpse.

The chief circled the points Kim had called attention to and then drew a line from those areas to their current position.

"If we take the ATVs it'll be faster but it's entirely possible we won't be able to cut through some parts because it's pretty heavy in that area," Kim continued. "We could send four-wheelers in and go the denser areas on foot."

"Thanks, Kim," Rick murmured. He put his hand on her shoulder and squeezed. "We appreciate this."

Kim smiled. "Let's get to it then."

———

Jessie woke to distant shouts of her name. It shocked her how utterly weak she was. She tried to call out, but couldn't manage more than a whisper.

She was curled into a tight ball and dug into a muddy overhang. She'd come on it by sheer chance, falling over the edge in the darkness the night before. Her strength gone, her reserves depleted, she'd dug her way into the thick mesh of brambles, covering herself with mud and leaves as she went.

It wasn't so dark anymore and dim light hovered over the ground along with a thin layer of eerie fog. She tried to push herself up but she simply wasn't strong enough to support herself.

A faint rustle reached her ears. At first she thought it was a squirrel or maybe a rabbit but it was too slow and too methodical. It sounded like human footsteps. Not very heavy ones. Slowly working their way through the woods.

She was tempted, so very tempted to roll away from her hiding place and run toward the sound, but she was too locked in fear, too traumatized to even consider leaving the one place that had seemingly thwarted a mad woman.

She closed her eyes and lay absolutely still, not that it was difficult because she was too weak to move. And it was easier to drift away, to pretend she wasn't lying on the ground slowly bleeding to death. Or that she was being hunted by a psycho who apparently thought she was the next great white hunter.

"I'm so going to kick her ass," Jessie muttered under her breath.

It made her feel better to say it and it gave her an absurd thrill to think of actually getting to do it.

The sound got closer and Jessie's panic began to rise. What if she was seen? She couldn't defend herself in this position. What if the bitch just walked up and shot her? Or knifed her to death? And here she was, lying in a ball blubbering like a sissy and hoping that no one could see her.

*If I die, damn it, I'm going to die kicking her ass.*

She dragged herself up, nearly dying with every move. Pain was constant, a bitter never-ending wave snaking through her body, coiling and ready to strike harder and longer.

She gripped a big-ass rock in one hand and curled her fingers over a club-sized piece of wood. It took every ounce of determination and sheer will to survive to push herself to a standing position.

It was then that she saw the bitch cop. Standing several feet away scanning the distance with binoculars. Curiously, her rifle was absent and she wore only a pistol in her shoulder harness. Was she playing the cop now?

Switching the rock from her left hand to her right, she took aim and threw the rock right at the back of the cop's head. Six years of softball paid off in that moment because it smacked her hard, knocking her forward to her knees.

Jessie ran. And later she'd never really know how she'd ever managed to fly across that space when her knee was such a mess. Pain crippled her but the thought of death kicked enough adrenaline back into her system that she performed the impossible.

Before Miss Batshit Crazy could react, Jessie nailed her with the piece of wood, knocking her completely to the ground so that she ate dirt. With shaking hands, Jessie yanked the pistol from her holster and backed away, her fingers glancing frantically over the stock in search of the safety. Shouldn't there be a safety? Maybe not. This one looked like one of those aim-and-fire jobbers, which was just fine with her.

As the cop picked herself up off the ground, Jessie raised the gun and leveled it at the much taller woman.

"Jessie! Oh my God, Jessie!"

"Kim, what the hell is going on?"

The jumble of voices reached Jessie, but she refused to turn her head, though the urge to run straight into Rick and Truitt's arms was so forceful that she had to jar her knee, sending a jolt of pain through her to keep her focused. Her sole concentration was on the woman in front of her. No way she could afford to divert her attention. It could cost her Rick's and Truitt's lives. It could cost her her own.

"You deserve to die, you crazy bitch," Jessie said fiercely.

Kim held up her hands and her eyes turned pleading. It was amazing how innocent Crazy could look. "Rick, Truitt, call your woman off me. I think she's lost her mind. She's obviously traumatized and has no idea what she's saying or doing."

Of all the things Jessie thought the moron would say, that wasn't it.

"Look, I'm here to help you. Help them find you." Kim motioned to where the guys stood to the side, then she turned in their direction. "She clobbered me and took my gun. Talk her down before somebody dies."

Jessie's hand shook and the numb that had settled in the night before was starting to crack.

"Jessie, honey, give me the gun. It's over now. You're okay. You're hurt. Let us take care of you."

Rick's low, reassuring voice slid over her with soul-deep comfort. But she'd seen evil in the eyes of that woman. She saw it now behind the deceptive appeal, the pretense of innocence.

But would Rick and Truitt believe her? Would they take her word against one of their own?

Truitt added his own soft plea as if he thought she'd gone completely over the edge and needed to be calmed before she jumped.

"Jessie, we're here now. Let us help you. You survived that bastard. We'll get him. I swear to you we'll nail his ass to the wall. We need to get you medical attention. You've got blood all over you and you're scaring me to death, baby. Put down the gun and let us help you."

"She's the one," Jessie said in as calm a voice as she could when she was so dangerously close to having a complete break from reality. Truitt wasn't far off if he imagined she was so very close to the edge. "She came to my apartment. She Tased me and then knocked me out. When I woke up, I was tied to a table in a hunting cabin. She smashed my knee. She cut me. So I'd bleed, so she could track the blood trail. She was going to hunt me down and kill me just like she did all the others, but I was too smart for her. Yeah, that's right, you stupid bitch. I outsmarted you. I won. And I swear to God I'm going to kick your teeth in when Rick and Truitt take you down."

It was only then that she chanced a glance at Rick and Truitt, because if they didn't believe her, if they left her alone with this woman for even a minute, she would kill Jessie or Jessie would have to kill her. Either way, someone was going to die.

Truitt and Rick looked horrified, appalled, worried, and confused. But then she saw something else. Realization. And close behind it, rage.

Truitt drew his gun and pointed it at Kim just as Rick slid his arm around Jessie and gently pried the pistol from her grip.

The very last of her strength gone, her knees buckled and she went down before Rick could catch her. Truitt's attention was diverted for the briefest of moments, and Kim reached for the pistol attached to her ankle.

She aimed for Jessie. Rick roared his denial and Jessie screamed as he covered her body with his own. A shot rang out, the sound echoing over and over in her ears.

# Chapter 16

Jessie's screams of anguish split the air. Rick tensed, unsure of who had done the shooting, Kim or Truitt. All he cared about was protecting Jessie from further harm.

"Rick, is Jessie all right?" Truitt demanded.

Rick raised his head and turned to see Kim lying on the ground a few feet away, the gun she'd aimed at Jessie a few inches from her hand.

"Call it in, Truitt. We need help. Is she alive?"

Truitt took his time walking over to where Kim lay. Still holding his gun on her, he knelt and put a finger to her neck. Then he shook his head.

Then Jessie moved in Rick's arms, her hands frantically spreading over his chest and around to his back.

"Are you all right?" she demanded weakly. "Did that crazy bitch shoot you?"

"God, yes, I'm all right," Rick choked out.

Jessie was a mess. There was blood, mud, and dirt caked with leaves covering her entire body. Her eyes were glassy with shock and with the announcement that he was okay, she seemed to completely melt down and crumble.

She began to shake violently and low moans ripped out of her throat as she clutched desperately at him. Rick eased her down long enough to tear off his jacket and wrap it around her naked body.

Truitt dropped down beside them, his hands shaking as he tried to touch Jessie. But he couldn't seem to figure out where he could without hurting her so he let them drop.

"I've called it in but we need to get her out of here. It'll be quicker if we carry her out than if we have them come in for her. A helicopter is coming to take Jessie to the hospital."

"Kick her for me," Jessie whispered.

Rick's brow wrinkled in confusion. He was sure he heard wrong. "What was that, Jessie?"

She glanced up at Truitt and tried to lift her hand to touch him. Truitt caught her fingers and lowered his head to press her palm to his lips. There was raw grief and emotion and stark fear in Truitt's eyes.

"Kick her. I told her that I'd survive so that I could kick her teeth in while you two took her down. So kick her for me, please."

Rick started to laugh. By the end he honestly didn't know if he was laughing or crying. He stood shakily to his feet and then swore at how weak he felt. Was this what love did to you?

Truitt reached gently for Jessie, sliding his arms underneath her. "This is going to hurt, baby. I'm sorry but I have to get you out of here."

"S'okay," she slurred out. "I'm just so damn happy to be alive. I can take anything."

Truitt lifted and Rick held his breath at the cry of agony that engulfed Jessie.

Tears glistened in Truitt's eyes as he held her against his chest.

"God, I'm sorry, Jessie. I'm so goddamn sorry I had to hurt you."

Jessie laid her cheek against Truitt's chest and closed her eyes.

For a moment Rick panicked and he clumsily put his fingers to her neck, relieved when he felt a faint pulse. Then he carefully pulled the jacket around her to shield as much of her body as he could.

"She's done, man," Truitt said quietly. "She hung on for as long as she could, until we could get here."

"The hell of it is, she didn't need us," Rick said as they walked past Kim's body. He stopped only long enough to send up a flare to signal their location and the location of Kim's body, and then he caught up to Truitt once more.

"No, she didn't need us," Truitt said, awe in his voice. "Not only did she survive with horrific wounds and an injured knee, but she beat the crap out of Kim and would have killed her if we hadn't shown up."

"I'm glad she didn't have to," Rick said softly. "She's been through enough without having to pull the trigger."

"Jesus Christ, Rick. Kim was the serial killer? All this time?"

Rick couldn't even wrap his brain around it. Female serial killers were rare. What motive could Kim possibly have had? It was obvious she was out of her goddamn mind, which made him even more glad that Truitt had taken her out. If she'd lived, she probably would have pled insanity, gotten a few years in a mental institution, and then been on her merry way again.

Sometimes the system sucked.

Rick stared at the woman in Truitt's arms and swallowed the knot in his throat. She was amazing. A survivor. And he loved her so damn much he felt like he was spazzing in about twelve different directions.

Love wasn't supposed to *happen*. Was it? Love was something you worked at. Worked hard at. He'd seen his parents work every day to stay together and make each other happy. But maybe love happened, and commitment was about making a relationship work *after* you fell in love.

Several police officers and a host of volunteers swarmed through the woods, led by the flare Rick had sent up. When they came upon Truitt carrying Jessie, cheers went up and echoed through the woods.

Jessie stirred and tried to lift her head. The celebration seemed to confuse and frighten her. She withdrew, burying her face in Truitt's neck and Rick quickly stepped in front of Truitt to shield her from most of it.

"Let's go," he said to Truitt. "The helicopter should be landing soon and we have to get her to the hospital."

Leaving the others to secure the crime scene, Truitt and Rick barreled through the trees and traveled the remaining distance to where the staging area for the search was formed.

As they broke through into the clearing, another round of cheers rose into the air. Two paramedics ran to take Jessie from Truitt and he reluctantly allowed them to take her and lay her on a waiting stretcher.

"ETA on the chopper is two minutes," one of the paramedics called out.

Rick and Truitt hovered over Jessie as the two medics cleaned some of the blood and mud off her arm so they could start an IV.

The chief came up behind them and pulled them both away. "What the hell went on out there? Are you really trying to tell me that Kim was some fucking serial killer? She's a good cop. She couldn't be responsible for these killings. Surely we would have known."

Truitt's face darkened. "She tried to shoot Jessie. After Rick had already disarmed her. There was no threat. But she went for her backup piece and she would have killed Jessie and Rick both if I hadn't taken the shot."

"Son of a bitch," the chief swore. "This doesn't make any god-damn sense."

"Kim was the one who pointed us to the area where Jessie was hiding," Rick said tightly. "Jessie was able to evade her last night when Kim went hunting for her. My guess is that Kim came back to look for her, hoping she'd find her before we did so she could finish the job."

The chief wiped a hand over his face and then shoved it over his hair. "It just doesn't make any goddamn sense," he repeated again.

Anger and bewilderment was etched on the chief's face and every wrinkle and line was even more predominant. They'd all gone without sleep and no one was happy that the person they'd been after for months, a maniac responsible for the gruesome murders of so many women, was one of their own.

The sound of the helicopter approaching made the men turn. The paramedics on the ground were already lifting the backboard from the stretcher and hurrying toward the landing area. Jessie was secured with two IV bags lying on her body as they transported her.

"Go," the chief said. "We'll sort this out later. I know you two will want to be with her."

The two men took off at a run, but when they got to the helicopter where Jessie was being loaded, they were told there wasn't room for even one of them.

Frustrated but not wanting to delay Jessie's departure to the hospital even for a second, they backed away.

"Come on, I'll drive," Rick said as he grabbed Truitt's arm.

# Chapter 17

Truitt paced the floor in the emergency room waiting area and checked his watch for the umpteenth time. It had been several hours and no one had been out to give them an update on Jessie.

Kirsten was at the desk demanding news right now and one of the receptionists was attempting to calm her down. Not that Kirsten seemed to care. She was ferocious. Truitt had to admire her loyalty and devotion to Jessie.

Rick was slouched in a chair by the window, his face locked in stone.

Finally one of the nurses came out and called for family of Jessie Callahan.

Rick surged from his seat and Kirsten ran from the reception desk.

They followed the nurse back and she halted outside one of the rooms that had an actual door rather than the portioned off cubicles that only had a curtain separating them from others.

"Wait here for the doctor," the nurse said. "He'll be out to speak to you in just a moment."

The nurse let herself in and Truitt rose up on tiptoe to see inside. He only got a brief glimpse of Jessie lying on a stretcher. She was surrounded by medical personnel so he couldn't even see if she was conscious or not.

Kirsten blew out her breath and leaned against the wall.

"You okay, doll?" Rick asked.

Kirsten nodded and then hastily wiped at a tear that rolled down her cheek. "She's already been through so much. The car accident was devastating. They weren't even sure she'd ever be able to walk without a cane. And now this. First she's accused of murder. Then she's kidnapped by a murderer. When does it stop? She's never done anything to anyone. She works hard. She's the best person in the world. She's just . . . good. And it's like fate is determined to shit on her."

Truitt squeezed her shoulder. "She's awfully lucky to have a friend like you. I don't want you to worry. She has us now. Rick and I are going to take good care of her. We'll see her through this. We aren't going anywhere."

Kirsten turned her tear-ravaged face up to Truitt. "You promise? I just want her to be happy."

Rick put his hand on her other shoulder. "We promise."

The door opened and a doctor, who looked to be in his forties, looked between Rick, Truitt, and Kirsten. Then he stuck his hand out to Truitt.

"I'm Dr. Anderson, the on-call orthopedic surgeon."

"Truitt Cavanaugh," Truitt said. "This is my partner Rick Broughman and Jessie's friend Kirsten. How is Jessie?"

He couldn't keep the anxiety or the impatience from his voice.

After the doctor shook Rick's and Kirsten's hands, he folded his arms over his clipboard and leaned against the wall next to the door.

"The ER physician is finishing stitching her wounds now. She lost a lot of blood but the cuts weren't deep enough to cause internal damage. What is of concern is her knee, which was already damaged by an earlier accident. To be honest with you I don't know how she managed to evade a killer. She shouldn't have been able to walk, much less run. Her kneecap is shattered. She'll be going up to surgery in a moment and we're going to try to reconstruct the bone. If that's not possible we'll have to do a full replacement."

"Will she be able to walk?" Kirsten cut in.

"Usually I'd say that depends on the patient, how successful the surgery is and how motivated the patient is to recover. But in Miss Callahan's case, I'd say without a doubt she'll likely walk, and not only walk but soon. She'll need rehabilitation and she'll use a wheelchair or crutches at first and graduate to a cane. But given just how determined this young lady seems, I fully believe she'll make a complete recovery. Will the knee ever be as good as new? No. But then she'd already sustained injury to it. But neither will it be a catastrophic injury."

"Can we see her?" Truitt interrupted.

"I don't see why not. She's been given pain medication. She's slipping in and out of consciousness. We want her to be as still as possible so she doesn't further injure her knee. It's currently immobilized until we can take her to surgery. But as soon as they're through stitching her up you can go in to see her for a few minutes before we take her up."

"Thank you," Rick said.

The doctor walked away and the three stood waiting, impatient. Truitt, unable to remain still, paced a tight perimeter, from one wall to the other, his gaze never leaving the door.

Fifteen minutes later, it opened and a nurse motioned them in. Truitt pushed off the wall and entered on the nurse's heels, Rick and Kirsten right behind him.

Truitt went to her bedside, Kirsten at his elbow, while Rick went around to the other side and carefully navigated the array of equipment.

Jessie looked completely fragile. One leg was bandaged from

knee to hip and the other was immobilized and secured in a large plastic splint. The hospital gown didn't cover much of her. Just her breasts and part of her left side. Down her right was thick bandaging where the long cut had been stitched.

She lay completely still, eyelashes resting on her cheeks. Her respirations were so light that Truitt had to lean down to reassure himself that she was breathing.

There was so much stuff everywhere, an IV in each hand, that he honest to God didn't know where he could touch her. He finally opted for cupping his hand over her head and then he leaned down to kiss her forehead.

"Jessie," he whispered achingly. "We're here, baby. You're okay now. They're going to take good care of you and then Rick and I are going to take you home."

She didn't stir.

He stroked her forehead, smoothing the hair from her eyes. For a long moment he simply stared down at her, his chest tight and his eyes burning.

Then he leaned closer so only she would hear.

"I want you to know I love you, Jessie. I've loved you since I first saw you but the idea of saying it always scared the shit out of me. I'm not afraid now. All I'm afraid of is you not being with me."

He kissed her temple and she stirred ever so lightly.

"You aren't alone anymore, Jessie. Rick and I will be here. We won't leave. We'll be waiting when you come out of surgery. We're going to be there for you during your recovery."

Her eyes opened slowly and she stared at him with sleepy, drugged eyes. But then she smiled. It was such a bone-achingly sweet smile that his heart did flip-flops in his throat.

"You're here," she whispered.

"Where else would I be?" he whispered back.

"Where's Rick?"

Rick touched her cheek, causing her to turn slowly in his direction.

"I'm here, Jessie. We both are. And Kirsten too."

Jessie glanced down the bed and smiled. "Hey, you."

The words came out quiet and pained.

"How are you feeling?" Truitt asked gently.

"Happy." It came out more as a sigh than an actual word.

It wasn't the word any of them were expecting. Truitt frowned, wondering if the drugs had turned her brain to mush.

"I'm alive," she said in a whisper. "I survived. I swore I would. Nothing else seems important right now."

"You're right about that," Rick said gruffly.

Jessie turned her gaze up to Truitt, her eyes soft and a little dull. "Did you say you loved me?"

He kissed her forehead, breathing in her scent. She smelled of old blood, dirt, and the sterile aroma of the hospital, but he savored it because it smelled of something else. Courage and life.

"I did," he softly returned. "But we'll talk more about that later when you aren't hurting so much and when you're not so drugged up."

The door opened and a nurse returned.

"Sorry folks, but we're going to take her up to surgery now. You can wait in the surgery waiting room and the doctor will come out to talk to you when the operation is over."

Kirsten pushed by Truitt and bent to kiss Jessie's cheek. "Hang in there, girlfriend. This will be over soon."

As Kirsten stepped back both Truitt and Rick leaned down at the same time and kissed her.

"Go kick some ass," Rick choked out. "Just like you did today. We'll be waiting for you when you're out."

# Chapter 18

Jessie awoke to a white, blank void. For a long moment she stared, trying to make sense of all the white space. But then as noise began to creep into her consciousness, she realized she was staring up at the ceiling and that someone was gently calling her name.

She glanced in the direction of that voice and saw a smiling woman dressed in scrubs.

"Ah, you're awake. Welcome back. Are you feeling any pain?"

If the nurse hadn't mentioned the *P* word, chances were, Jessie would have continued to float in her little dream world, but reality intruded in a rather rude, abrupt manner and pain sliced through her knee and up into her hip.

Her mouth was so dry that it felt like her lips cracked when she tried to speak. Then she realized that her throat was sore and her attempt at speech came out as a rasp. So she nodded instead. More than once so the nurse would get the idea.

The nurse fiddled with Jessie's IV and a few moments later, she floated back out to sea on a very soft cloud where there was no pain and no annoying white void.

The next time she drifted toward consciousness she heard her name again, but this time the voices were deeper and loving. She sighed and smiled dreamily.

A light chuckle made her crack her eyes open although she really didn't want to return to the reality of the wrenching pain.

Truitt and Rick stood over her bed, staring down at her, worry— and love—in their eyes.

"Hey there," Rick said. "You're awake. The nurse said you've been sleeping too long and it's time to come around. She asked us to nag you."

Jessie frowned her annoyance and Truitt grinned. "The sooner you wake up, the sooner they'll move you to your room."

"Okay."

Or so she thought she said okay. She wasn't convinced any sound actually came out, but they seemed to understand.

Rick leaned over and kissed her. Truitt slipped his fingers underneath hers and rubbed his thumb over her knuckles. It was almost as if they couldn't stand not to touch her in some way.

"Am I all right?" she asked in a creaky whisper.

"Yeah, baby, you're all right," Rick said as he kissed her temple. "You will be."

She sighed a little in relief. She was still too fuzzy to figure out just where all she hurt but they didn't look too worried, so she must not be too bad off.

She glanced down at the cast enveloping her leg and held her breath. "My knee?"

Rick and Truitt exchanged glances.

"Tell me," she croaked out.

"The orthopedic surgeon thinks you need a replacement. Because of your previous injury and the pain you already experience, he wants to discuss the option with you," Rick said.

Her mouth turned down. "Oh."

"It's not so bad," Truitt said gently. "The replacement could possibly alleviate the pain and weakness you were already having."

She squeezed her eyes shut, determined not to cry. She hadn't broken down, not even when she'd faced certain death.

"Jessie, don't cry, honey."

She opened her eyes again, but tears swam, blurring her vision. "I can't afford a knee replacement. I don't have a job. I don't have insurance. I already have medical bills from my previous surgeries. And now I'll never finish school."

She bit her lip, pissed at how defeated she sounded. She'd survived. She was alive. What else was important but that? So what if she wasn't able to walk. She could use a cane. Or crutches. Even a wheelchair. She was *alive*.

Truitt squatted beside the bed so that he was eye level with her. "Do you remember what I told you right before you went to surgery?"

After a brief hesitation she nodded. Unbidden, her gaze drifted to Rick but she jerked it back to Truitt, not wanting to make the moment awkward. It looked like she was looking to him for . . . for the same declaration. And didn't that make her twisted?

Rick leaned over, tucked a finger under her chin and gently turned her back to face him. As if he understood exactly what she'd asked for. "I love you, Jessie. I told you out in the woods but you were unconscious. I've told you in my head a million times, but this time I'm saying it out loud. To you. I love you."

This time she didn't even attempt to call back the tears. They slid in damp trails over her temples and into her hair. Truitt leaned over and kissed one away.

Then he murmured low next to her ear. "The reason I'm telling you this again is because what it means is that you aren't alone. You won't have to do this alone. You'll have us. That's right. I said us. We're going to be with you every step of the way. And you know what? We'll figure it out. You'll get your knee replacement and you'll get the therapy you need."

She glanced between the two men, afraid to hope, afraid to put to words the question burning a hole in her brain. She licked her lips and gathered her courage.

"You both are okay with . . . if . . . I mean, you won't be angry if . . ."

"If what, sweetheart?" Rick asked as he stroked her cheek with one finger.

"If I love you both," she whispered.

"Well, hell, I hope you don't just love one of us," Truitt said in a disgruntled voice. "That would be hell on a friendship, not to mention cause problems for you when neither of us refuses to let you go."

It was getting harder to concentrate as the pain in her leg became progressively stronger. She knew this was important. Perhaps the most important thing to her future. Their future. But she struggled to get the words just right.

A soft moan escaped before she could call it back.

"I'll get the nurse," Rick said grimly.

"No," Jessie said, catching at his arm as he turned to go. "Not yet. Please. I need to . . . I need to say this before . . ." Her breath huffed out, and she briefly closed her eyes as she fought a fresh surge of pain.

"Shhh," Truitt said as he stroked his palm over her forehead.

Rick turned back, his brows drawn in concern.

"I didn't say it," she said. "I asked a question, but I didn't say it. I want to say it. I love you both."

Rick's dark eyes warmed until she felt some of the pain melt away under his gaze. Truitt's hand stilled on her head, and she glanced over to see joy unfurling in his eyes. Rick took the step back to her bed and bent over to brush his lips over hers.

"I love you too, Jessie. Now will you let me call the nurse?"

"That stuff she gives me makes me go to sleep."

Truitt's smile warmed her to her toes. "That's okay, baby. We'll be there when you wake up to tell you we love you all over again."

# Chapter 19

SIX MONTHS LATER

W hy wouldn't she let us take her to her therapy session today?"
Truitt grumbled.

He leaned back in his chair and checked his watch. She should be about half done by now and he was itching to get down there to pick her up.

Rick scowled. "I don't know. She wouldn't even let us take her in. Or even let us drop her off at the door so she didn't have to walk so far from the parking lot with her cane. What the hell was that about?"

"Maybe we're getting on her nerves," Truitt muttered. "Are we too overbearing?"

Before Rick could answer, Bull stuck his head in the door of Truitt's office.

"Hey guys, I heard Jessie had her last therapy session today. How's she doing?"

"We wouldn't know," Rick said sourly. "We weren't allowed to go with her."

"Well tell her we're all rooting for her."

"Will do," Truitt said and waved as Bull withdrew.

The last six months had been long, hard months for Jessie but at the same time they'd been happy months of discovery as they charted the waters of a new and nontraditional relationship between the three of them.

The media had picked up on Jessie's amazing story of survival, and within days, a fund had been set up to help her with the cost of recovery and her eventual knee-replacement surgery.

The local university had even given her a scholarship to complete her degree and she'd taken online classes, but she planned to attend regular classes next semester.

But the best part had simply been that they were together. Jessie had come home from the hospital to Truitt's house, and there she'd stayed. Kirsten had been a constant visitor in those first weeks after Jessie's surgery, helping when Truitt and Rick had to work.

It hadn't always been easy. Jessie had nightmares and was in constant pain after her surgery. She had trouble sleeping and when she did, she battled her personal demons.

Through it all Rick and Truitt had been fiercely protective of her and they bullied her mercilessly to take proper care of herself and her knee. When they thought she pushed herself too far, they didn't hesitate to shut her down. A fact that didn't always endear them to her.

But every single day with her was a miracle. *She* was a miracle.

A lot of Kim's madness was still a mystery. An extensive investigation into her life revealed a bitter woman driven by hatred for other women. Women she considered weak and inferior. The common denominator in all of the women she'd murdered was that they had done a perceived wrong in Kim's mind. Things that had gone unnoticed in an investigation for their sheer unimportance. But to a woman steeped in insanity? They'd seemed unforgivable sins that Kim had insisted on punishing them for.

They hadn't been able to trace back a cause or even the point when she'd broken from reality. Her early years on the force had reflected a driven police officer with an unerring sense of justice.

The most likely cause, if there indeed was a driving force behind her madness, was a case she'd worked three years before when a young mother had abused and eventually killed her children only to be released on a technicality. Kim had taken the case very personally and eventually had taken a leave of absence. When she'd returned, she'd been quieter and more focused, but nothing had ever made her fellow officers believe she was anything but a damn good cop.

What had pushed her to torture and hunt innocent women? It was a question that haunted both Rick and Truitt. Maybe they'd never know. All they had was endless speculation and a lot of unanswered questions.

Tied into all of it was Kim's apparent obsession with Rick, a discovery that had baffled Rick and Truitt both. No one had picked up on her attraction to Rick, but she'd been intensely focused on him, and ironically, Kim had targeted Jessie only because of the apparent wrong she'd done to Rick when it had appeared Jessie had used Rick and Truitt as an alibi.

Jessie had simply been another woman who had committed an unforgivable sin in Kim's eyes, and Kim had set herself up as judge and executioner.

"Hey man, it's time. Let's get out of here," Rick said as he checked his watch again. "Let's go get our girl."

Truitt stood, suddenly anxious to be near Jessie again. The truth was, he wasn't over his own terror, a fact he dealt with every single day. How the hell did you ever get over nearly losing the woman you loved?

―――――――――

Jessie wrapped the towel around her neck and leaned back, her breath coming in shallow bursts. She was tired and her knee ached from the exercise regimen she'd performed, but giddy excitement coursed through her veins because today was the day she was going to surprise Rick and Truitt by walking out to them without her cane.

"How you feeling?" Carmen, her therapist, asked.

Jessie smiled. "Tired. Jubilant. Excited and nervous."

"You should be proud of yourself. You've made excellent progress in a very short time."

Jessie leaned forward to rub her knee, but Carmen sat on the stool in front of her, moved Jessie's hand, and began massaging some of the soreness away.

"I'm ready to get on with my life," Jessie said, feeling better just for saying it. "I've spent far too much time putting pieces back together and now it's time to look ahead."

Carmen smiled. "I wish all my patients were as motivated as you. But then I wouldn't have a job."

Jessie's phone pulsed, signaling a text message, and she pulled it out of her pocket. She smiled when she read the message from Kirsten.

I'm rooting for you, girlfriend. Knock 'em dead.

Jessie slid the phone back into her pocket and then took a deep breath. It was time and she didn't want to mess up her moment by having the guys come in after her.

"I'm ready," she said to Carmen.

Carmen stood and extended a hand down to Jessie, but Jessie shook her head.

"I can do it."

She pushed herself up, flexed her knee once and then put all her weight on it. Though she wasn't completely pain-free, she experienced only twinges and a dull ache when she pushed herself too hard.

She took a few experimental steps, testing her steadiness without the security of her cane. Delight fizzed through her nervous system until she was positively twitching with excitement.

"Want company on the walk out?" Carmen asked with a broad smile.

Jessie smiled back. "No. I need to do this on my own."

As Jessie made her way toward the front, the team of therapists that had worked so diligently with her gathered and started to clap. Jessie's cheeks warmed and she smiled as tears gathered in her eyes.

Joseph, one of the techs blew her a kiss and held open the door as she walked out into the midday sunshine.

As soon as her feet hit the concrete of the circle drive in front of the clinic, she looked across the parking lot to see that, indeed, Rick and Truitt were coming toward her. And they hadn't seen her yet.

She increased her pace and walked out from underneath the awning and farther away from the place she'd spent so much time in over the last few months.

She forced herself to have restraint. The very last thing she wanted was to fall on her face for her big moment. She was pleased that there was hardly a noticeable limp. Just a slower, steadier walk that would change as she gained more confidence.

For now, all that mattered was that she was taking her first steps without the aid of a walker or a cane.

Her gaze never left Rick and Truitt as they hurried toward the building. She knew the moment they saw her and realized it was her. Truitt stopped cold. Rick took two steps and then also halted.

At first they looked shocked but then slow grins spread across their faces. Truitt let out a whoop and then ran toward her. Rick's grin was no less huge but he strode behind Truitt.

When Truitt reached her, he lifted her up and spun her around until she was laughing and dizzy. Then he slowly and carefully lowered her to her feet but held on to one arm as if he was afraid she'd fall.

"What do you think?" Jessie asked.

She shook off Truitt's hand and slowly turned in a circle. When she came to a halt, Rick's eyes looked suspiciously bright and Truitt was still grinning like a maniac.

"What I think," Rick began slowly, "is that you are one incredible woman. I'm so proud of you, Jessie. You just don't know how to quit."

Jessie threw her arms around his waist and hugged him fiercely. "I couldn't have done any of this without you and Tru. I love you so much. I won't ever forget that you were with me every minute of my recovery."

As soon as she pulled away from Rick, Truitt tugged her into his side and wrapped a strong arm around her.

"What do you say we go home and you let us *show* you just how damn much we love and admire you," Truitt said.

She wrapped her arms around their waists and let them pull her close into them as they headed toward Rick's truck.

"I like that idea. A woman can never be told or shown too much how much their man—or men," she cheekily corrected, "love them."

"Damn straight," Rick growled as he leaned over to claim her mouth. "And we plan to tell you a whole hell of a lot for the next fifty years or so."

# Wanted

KARIN TABKE

*This is for all the girls who just want to have fun!*

# Chapter 1

Two things were going to change undercover cop Colin Daniels's life that day. It wasn't the blonde lip-locked around his dick or the redhead drilling her wet pussy into his face. What was going to change his life was going to gut-kick him to his knees. He was not going to see it coming and he would not recognize it when it happened, because the second thing that was going to irrevocably change his life that day was going to do its damnedest to make sure the first thing never crossed his path.

Charlie Sheen might have Adonis DNA and tiger blood, but at thirty-four, Colin had the libido of a sixteen-year-old and the stamina of a Brahman bull. Plus, he got to enjoy both with a different goddess every night. Tonight's double dessert was *almost* enough to get his mind off the call he was waiting for.

He thrust his hips into the blonde's succulent lips and dug his fingers into the sweet ass of the redhead even as his tongue thrust into another set of succulent lips. When Blondie's head bounced up and down on his dick, he slid his hand from an ass cheek and dug his fingers into her hair to slow her down. He liked his blow jobs slow, deep, and tight. The blonde moaned, cupped his balls, and reverently sucked him down to her tonsils.

He groaned, a ragged sound of pleasure. One the redhead didn't like.

Immediately, she reached behind her and tried to grab his hand away from the blonde, but Blondie stayed his hand, snarling around his dick. The redhead snarled back.

And this was exactly why, to him, variety was the spice of life.

He loved sex. Loved women. He loved all their shapes, sizes, colors, and smells. He loved that he could love them all night with no strings. He never took a woman to his place; he never stayed for breakfast at theirs. It was how he rolled.

In his line of work, commitments complicated the job—*if* he still had one.

"Bitch," the redhead hissed.

The curse along with a violent flurry of movement alerted Colin that the catfight was on. Carefully, he extracted his package and rolled, barely escaping before the redhead twisted and pounced on the little blonde.

He shook his head and yanked the redhead off Blondie despite the fact that their claws were digging into each other. Once he'd separated them, he reached for his jeans and yanked them on. He was over it.

"Now he's leaving!" Blondie screeched at Red. And the fight was on again. It was time to go. Hissing and spitting like pissed-off kittens, the women rolled off the bed to the floor.

"Girls!" he shouted. "Knock it off."

Like guilty children, they climbed back onto the bed.

"We'll play nice, Colin," Blondie said, pouting. Red nodded vigorously. To prove how serious she really was, she ran her hand along the swell of Red's hip, pulling her closer. Red arched and ran her fingers down Blondie's belly to her shaved pussy. Colin's dick reconsidered his imminent exit. The girls smiled in tandem. They reminded him of the Siamese cats in *Lady and the Tramp*. Only these pussies purred.

Encouraged by his hesitation, Red pushed Blondie roughly onto her back and spread her thighs. She looked over her shoulder at Colin and smiled an I'm-about-to-eat-the-canary smile. His dick swelled. Then she dove in, with her sweet little ass pointing right at him and her slick pink folds clenching and unclenching. It was a tempting offer.

Blondie mewed and moaned, and he knew it wasn't an act for his benefit. Red was the consummate cock and cunt tease. His cock hurt just thinking about it.

Damn women!

He grabbed a condom from his back pocket, shoved his jeans down his thighs, ripped open the foil package, and slammed the raincoat on. He pulled Red's sweet little ass toward him and dove in himself. She moaned, grinding against him. Blondie cried out as Red fucked her with her mouth and he fucked Red with his dick. He grit his teeth, closed his eyes, and let it ride.

He arched into Red and came in a harsh burst. At the same time, the "duh, duh-duh-duh" theme from *Dragnet* rang on his cell. His entire body tensed.

He was about to get an answer to the question that had been haunting him for months. Had he or hadn't he been reinstated?

He jerked out of Red's possessive pussy, grabbed his phone from his pocket, and hit the answer button. "Daniels," he said roughly.

"Looks like you used up another one of those lives of yours, Sergeant," Colin's captain said, apparently not happy with Colin's luck. No surprise there. Since Colin had joined the tristate task force four years ago, this was the third time the captain had called him to tell him he'd dodged another IA bullet with his name on it. This time it was a trumped-up charge of brutality. What the hell was he supposed to do when the bad guy resisted? Sing "Kumbaya"? Colin never pounded a bad guy who didn't deserve it. Except this time his intel had been wrong. It was the bad guy's brother. He'd said he was sorry. Wasn't enough; the dude went after his badge. Almost got it too.

Colin grinned, spanked Red's ass, and stalked toward what he thought was the bathroom.

"And a fine good evening to you too, Captain Moriarty."

"Fuck you, Daniels. I want you in my office at oh six hundred, use the back entrance, and don't tell a soul I called *or* the details of this call, including your union rep." He hung up.

Colin zipped up, slid his cell into his back pocket, and strode back into the bedroom where the panting goddesses awaited. He grinned and grabbed his shirt from the floor and shrugged it on. "Duty calls, ladies."

"No!" they cried, leaping off the bed toward him. He quickly made his exit, ignoring their pleas for him to stay.

The sun was just barely peeking over the eastern horizon when Colin strolled into a nondescript building in the Bronx, where the Federal Investigative Strike Team, or FIST, was housed. FIST was a combined task force of tenured police officers and seasoned feds in the tristate area of New York, Connecticut, and New Jersey, specifically designated to bite hunks of meat off the bones of the flourishing crime families in the area's largest cities. It wasn't just the Tony Sopranos anymore; it was the Irish, the Cubans, and the Russians. Crime in the tristate area paid big-time.

Captain M glared from his office to the left as Colin strode in whistling Dixie.

"Ah, the bulletproof prodigal son returns," Special Agent Jackson Davies said from his cubicle, giving Colin a high five.

"More like they couldn't get another sucker to deal with the devil," Colin said. FIST had several nonnegotiable requirements before a potential candidate could even be considered for a place on this highly trained and covert team: must have worked narcotics, vice, and homicide. With the exception of management, the field agents must be and remain single. No family to explain long absences to. No love interests to tug on heartstrings, and no personal commitments. Not even a goldfish. The payoff? They got to put real bad people away for a very long time. Colin lived for this shit.

Jackson nodded. "You're probably right, but make sure the next dirtbag you pound to salt is a *real* dirtbag."

Colin grinned and poured himself a cup of coffee; the only decent thing in the task-force office. "I plead the Fifth, Davies."

"Daniels, my office," the captain bellowed from his doorway.

Colin raised his cup to another agent, Teague, and the rookie, Dimarco, and strut into the captain's glass-walled office.

"Shut the goddamn door, hotshot," he growled.

Colin obliged and sprawled out in the only other chair in the room besides his captain's.

Captain Moriarty glared at him. He never had liked Colin and the feeling was mutual. Could have something to do with the fact that Colin had done his wife—before she was Moriarty's wife—six ways to sundown for just as many days. Lisa Delveccio-Moriarty was one of the few women he had gone back to for seconds, and thirds . . .

"Finally, the ladies' man will meet his match," the captain said. He shoved a manila file folder across his desk.

Colin set his coffee cup down on the floor and reached for the file. As he picked it up, Moriarty's fist slammed down on it. His intense steel blue eyes locked on Colin's. "You fuck this up, and I swear by all that is holy, I will fuck you in the ass so deep you'll be giving me a blow job."

Colin ignored the captain's threat. He got it. Got that the captain could not handle the fact that he'd screwed his wife. Got that every time Moriarty looked at him, he conjured up images of Lisa and Colin tearing up the sheets. And although Moriarty went out of his way to make Colin's life miserable, Colin got the pride thing too.

He might be a womanizer, but he wasn't a prick who rubbed his conquests in another man's face.

"Message received," Colin said not breaking his stare.

The captain sat back.

Colin opened the file to find a single photo. He picked it up and nodded. Very impressive. An odd sensation skittered through him. And . . . familiar. A woman's stunning albeit not-too-happy face stared at him in moody silence from an eight-by-ten color glossy. A lion's mane of thick golden hair haloed the classically structured face. Big green eyes stared at him from above a pert nose. And a set of glistening, full pouty lips beckoned, lips that he could envision wrapped around him—milking him one drop at a time.

Blood shot straight to his cock. It was a visceral reaction. She oozed sensuality, but something else caught him and it cooled his blood.

An angry fire burned behind the huge soulful eyes, framed by the longest, blackest lashes he'd ever seen. He felt the same fire ignite in his gut. Someone had damaged this woman. Though she'd tried to disguise it with makeup, there was a distinct scar running from the left corner of her mouth straight back to her ear. He looked up at the captain.

"Sophia Gilletti. Angelo Gilletti's very-soon-to-be ex."

"What happened to her face?"

"He cut her for talking to another man."

Colin shook his head in disgust. He may be a wham-bam-thank-you-very-much-ma'am kind of guy, but he always left his women with a smile on their faces and an orgasm or two to keep them warm. Not a scar. "Prick."

"A prick, to be sure. It's why she ran. It's why you're going to

California and bringing her here to a safe house, where she'll tell all
to the DA."

So she wasn't a crook he was supposed to bust but a witness he
needed to protect. The prospect of meeting the woman revved his
blood.

"Where's Gilletti?"

"We're not sure. He blipped off our radar four days ago. Last seen
entering Scalias's in Little Italy, he never exited. He skipped town
via the sewer system."

"Perfect place for the guy."

"He's got a million-dollar contract on her. Go get her, bring her
back here. She'll stay in the apartment upstairs, where she'll have
round-the-clock protection."

Colin looked up at his captain. "Who's going with me?"

"You're going it alone. We've put the word out that you're done
here, done as a cop, and that a warrant will be issued for your arrest.
It'll look like you're on the run. No one will think you're going to
retrieve the state's most coveted witness in history."

Something about the captain's plan didn't sit well with Colin.

The captain drilled Colin with a glare. "I'll need your badge and
your weapon." He reached down and lifted a small black duffel from
behind his desk and set it down in front of Colin. "There're one hundred rounds, two Sigs with the serial numbers filed off, a silencer,
and three thousand in marked bills. You have twenty-four hours to
get her back here before that warrant is officially executed. If it takes
you longer, you deal with the repercussions."

Colin pulled the bag toward him and inspected the contents. All
present and accounted for, just like the captain said. Colin hesitated to
hand over his badge and weapon. While FIST worked outside of the
box as a rule, this was a little too far outside. Did Moriarty hate him
so much he was setting him up? He looked back at the eight-by-ten.
The green eyes haunted him. For her, he would go. For himself, once

the mission was accomplished, he would call Moriarty out and take care of him once and for all.

"The clock is ticking, Daniels."

Colin withdrew his Glock from his shoulder hostler and slid it across the desk to his commander then pulled his badge from his wallet and placed it beside his weapon. He retrieved one of the Sigs from the duffel, loaded it, then slid it into his empty holster.

"Where is she?"

"A private residence in Lake Tahoe." The captain handed him a folded piece of paper. "She doesn't know you're coming. You'll have to convince her to return with you."

"How the hell am I supposed to do that?"

"Work that charm of yours on her."

Colin loaded the second semi and said, "She doesn't know she's going to turn state's evidence either." He looked at his captain. "Does she?"

Moriarty set his lips and shook his head. "She's running for her life. We were lucky to stumble on her whereabouts. One of the retired feds who worked to put Gilletti senior away recognized her, despite her disguise, at a gas station in Placerville, where he retired. Being the suspicious fellow he is, he followed her to Tahoe and called it in."

"So, I'm supposed to show up on her doorstep, introduce myself, and say 'I'm here to take you back to New York so you can turn state's evidence against your husband who has a hit out on you'?"

"Drive home the fact that we can protect her, and once it's over she'll be buried deep in the witness protection program."

"And you want me to do this in twenty-four hours or less?"

"There's a reason you're a sergeant," Moriarty taunted. He stood up and added, "Use whatever means necessary to convince her to talk with the DA. Gilletti is a mad dog and out of control. He's responsible for dozens of deaths in Brooklyn alone, two of which were police officers. The wife is our only hope. Get her back here."

Colin stood and looked at the address on the piece of paper, then folded it up. "Who else has this address?"

"No one but the two people in this room and the retired fed. I thanked him for the info but blew it off as no big deal."

Colin took out his lighter and burned the piece of paper, watching the ashes fall to the desk.

"Keep me posted on your movement, Daniels. I want to know where you are at all times."

That was another first. While progress reports were part of the paper trail, each one of them in the unit had full discretion on how and when progress reports in the field would be issued. Colin had never been told to give a step-by-step play-by-play. He'd never been asked to surrender his weapon or his badge either.

"I'll check in when I can," he said, then grabbed the duffel bag, hoisted it over his shoulder, and walked out of the office, then out of the building.

He stood on the curb, soaking up the warm morning sun. Despite his uneasy feeling regarding Moriarty, excitement racked through him. The feds had been after Gilletti Jr. for years. He was a nasty gangster who thought he was a rock star. They nabbed the old man a few years ago, but he died in Rikers before his trial had begun. Getting the goods on junior would be huge.

Colin grinned when he thought of the wife's big green eyes and pouty lips. Getting the goods on Sophia Gilletti was going to be his pleasure.

Colin stepped off the curb and into a careening black Lincoln gunning straight for him.

# Chapter 2

Colin leaped onto the hood in a Hollywood-stuntman move then rolled over the top of the car and off the back onto the street. He hit the ground running. Tires squealed and screeched behind him as bullets whizzed past. When he made a hard left down an alley, the car roared after him, getting so close that he leaped up to a fire escape ladder, swung his legs up, and crashed feet first through the second-floor window of an office.

A secretarial pool screamed as he dashed through their morning coffee break. He broke into a hallway, down a stairway, and hit the adjacent alley in minutes. Soon he reached the street opposite the building that housed the task force. It was oddly quiet for a midweek workday, which made him hang back. A flash of metal caught his eye. He looked up to the three-story parking garage across the street and saw someone on the top floor duck behind the concrete railing.

His heart beat like a drum in his chest. To all appearances, the offices looked like your everyday run-of-the-mill private security agency. Had his cover been blown? Had the task force headquarters been compromised?

It would not be the first time FIST HQ had been compromised. The Bronx location was the third in as many years. Even though they acted like, looked like, and spoke like a security firm, there were times when the criminals they hunted, hunted them. Both sides played an artful game of cat and mouse.

With the explosion of high-tech toys on both sides, it was becoming increasingly difficult to keep one step ahead of the bad guys. It was why Colin always had a cache of necessities nearby, one he would access as soon as he took care of the problem in front of him.

He backed into the alley and worked his way around the block and up to the top floor of the parking garage where he'd spotted the gunman. The man was now wedged between two blacked-out Suburbans. Looked government issue, but could be Mafia. Colin slid his piece from the holster and dug in the duffel for the silencer. Quietly he screwed it on and, stealthily as a tiger, he stalked the gunman.

He worked his way around the vehicles one by one, crouched, quiet, and alert. Just two cars away the Suburban closest to him moved, just enough to tell him someone was inside.

*Fuck.*

They were waiting for him. He backed up. Just as he got to the duffel, the back doors of the Suburban flew open and men poured out. Colin took off toward the stairwell. Screeching tires and the pounding of feet followed, hot on his heels. As he rounded the second level, a convertible was pulling out of a space. Colin yanked open the door, grabbed the stunned driver, and pulled him out.

"Sorry," he said, "but I need to borrow your car." He shoved the man out onto the concrete and hopped in. He downshifted, hit the gas, and took off.

The Suburban was right behind him. Colin drove through the exit-gate stop arm and made a sharp right onto the street. He shifted, blew through a red light, made a hard left and blew through another red light. The little Fiat handled beautifully, but the Suburban was still in his rearview. He needed to shake the bastards.

Colin turned right at the next street, moving against traffic, and then made another hard right into a tight alley. He lay on the gas and blasted through the chained gates at the end. He slammed the car into park, grabbed the duffel, and ran into the back of a building. He was familiar with the old trading building and knew there were numerous tunnels connecting it to several other surrounding buildings. He hurried into the bowels of the structure and headed north. As he came up two blocks away, he snatched a messenger's bike and pedaled to the Greyhound station several blocks away. Minutes later, he walked into the station, straight back to a wall of lockers. Quickly he opened the combination lock on one of them, took out one of his alias IDs, exchanged the three grand Moriarty gave him with three Gs of his own. He then retrieved an iPad, two throwaway cells, and a small leather duffel that he stuffed with his cache, turned off his personal cell phone and set it on the cash, then locked the locker. He hurried into the men's room, where he took the Sig from his holster and shoved it into the duffel Moriarty had given him, then tossed the entire bag into the trash can.

Colin had survived for so long on instinct. And right now, his instinct was screaming at him to trust no one.

Nine hours later, he was driving along Emerald Bay Road in South Lake Tahoe in a rented SUV, less than a mile from Sophia Gilletti. The flight west gave him a lot of time to think about what had to happen next. His weapons were untraceable. The iPad was registered under a dummy name, connected to a dummy e-mail he'd created on a pay-for-use public computer in Maryland. He'd paid for access to it with a prepaid Visa card. While his activity was traceable, his identity was not. He had nothing to hide from his employer, but everything to lose if the bad guys got a lock on him.

It was only early evening in the California Sierras. The clean mountain air felt good in his lungs. For the first time in a long while, Colin felt virtually alone—like he didn't have five sets of eyes watching his every move. But then he turned right on Fifteenth Street into the Keys and it happened. His antenna went up. A black SUV slowly drove by as if it were looking for a specific address.

*Shit.*

He glanced down at the GPS map. The place was a freaking maze of canals and waterways and houses. She was just ahead off Venice. In order not to look conspicuous, he kept a regular speed. As the address came into view, the hair on the back of Colin's neck stood straight up. The houses on the street were quiet, no cars in the driveways, no occupants in the yards, the interior windows covered. The only exception was the car parked across from the house that backed up to the water—the house that Sophia Gilletti was supposed to be in. Colin slowed and turned into the driveway of a house four lots down and out of view of the car. He wished he'd had time to buy a gun, but his gut told him to get to Sophia ASAP. He slipped around the back of the houses, which were connected by a long floating dock. He hurried down the dock to the back of Sophia's house.

It was hooked up to an alarm system. He opened the fuse box to shut off the electricity, but it looked like someone had beat him to it. *Shit.* Colin tried the back door. Unlocked. *Fuck.*

He entered the dark ground floor and listened. Silence. But the alluring scent of a woman caught his attention. She was here. He moved up the wooden stairway and was almost to the top when he heard a sound, not from behind him but in front of him.

Sophia slammed the lamp over the intruder's head. Not waiting to
see if she knocked him out, she ran for her life. Straight into a hard
chest. Terrified this was it, that her husband's goon had found her,
she screamed. A big hand clamped across her face. He yanked her
hard against him, pulling her down the stairway.

"I won't hurt you," a deep masculine voice whispered against her
ear. She scratched his hand and bit it at the same time.

"Jesus Christ!" he hissed. "I said, I won't hurt you."

She twisted and kicked him in the balls. He grunted in pain,
loosening his hold. She only caught sight of shocking blue eyes before
she pushed past him and ran down the stairs to the back door. There
was a Jet Ski at the end of the dock . . . If she could just get there . . .

As she ran out the door, a hard body tackled her from behind.
They went rolling down the slope onto the deck and into the shallow
water.

Sophia sputtered as she tried to get away from the blue-eyed
monster. Bullets pinged in the water around them.

He grabbed her by her hair and pulled her under the dock. "Get
the hell out of his line of fire," he cursed, dragging her farther down
the dock.

Footsteps thudded on the planks above them. Terrified, Sophia
looked at the man who held her against his chest. She almost fainted
from shock. It . . . couldn't be . . . His eyes warned her to keep quiet.
Her teeth chattered so loudly she was sure the entire lake community could hear.

Ever so slowly, he moved them down the dock away from the
footsteps thudding in the opposite direction. After what seemed like
an eternity, they reached the end. "Stay put," he commanded. Too
terrified to move, Sophia nodded. He slipped from the water. Her
instinct told her to stay, but she trusted no one. He might be there to

save her for the moment, but like everyone else, he wanted something from her, something that would get her killed. Sophia moved back down the dock to the next house. The sun was beginning to set, so if she could just slip away . . .

"I told you to stay put, damn it."

She turned around, her teeth still chattering and her body shivering so badly in the cold lake water she couldn't even tell him to go to hell. He grabbed her arms and pulled her back to the end of the dock. Carefully, he helped her from the frigid water and into a small SUV.

Moments later, they were on Emerald Bay Boulevard, heading south.

Even in the freezing cold, and with the passing of sixteen years, Sophia recognized the man driving the SUV. Looking at him now, hearing the deep timbre of his voice, she knew without a doubt it was the same man she had fantasized about each time Angelo had touched her. Colin Daniels. Her body began to shake again, but not from the cold this time. She had been a naïve sophomore; he an experienced senior, the ultimate bad boy and the fantasy of every girl, and she was sure most of the nuns, at St. John's Prep.

Sophia shivered hard as she remembered the intensity of his lovemaking. The way his fingers stroked her skin to fire. Her nipples hardened and she squirmed in her wet clothes.

He glanced at her with an indescribably complex look. Like he was supposed to know her, but couldn't quite figure out why. Anger sparked. The Lothario had no idea who she was, but he had to know she was the wife of a crime boss. The whole world knew. And just like the whole world, he was there because he wanted something from her. Just another commodity. Beginning with her parents, every person in her life had sold her out. Why not this guy too?

Sophia's eyes narrowed. He had shattered her world that night sixteen years ago, and he didn't even recognize her! Had she been so inconsequential? Just another one of his many? But she'd known that going in. It had been her choice to seduce him. Not the other way around. She'd picked him and him only for one specific purpose: to take her virginity before her parents sold her into domestic slavery to the Gilletti family.

At least Colin had done his job—quite well—and asked for nothing in return. That he had never, not once, tried to call her after she seduced him, irked her more than it should. Judging from his distant demeanor, she'd bet her life, which wasn't worth much at the moment, that if she reminded him of their all-too-brief but oh-so-hot interlude, he still wouldn't recognize her. So she'd pretend like she didn't recognize him.

"Who are you?" she demanded. "And what were you doing at my house?" Would he tell the truth?

"I'm part of a task force sent to bring you in to testify against your husband."

Sophia's heart plummeted to her lap. Angelo was a brutal man. She had run from him—the ultimate slap in the face to a man like him. Running had hurt more than his pride. If a man could not control his wife, then he could not control his business. He would not rest until she was dead. Or worse: his prisoner again. She swallowed hard. Testifying against him was the last thing she would do. "Pull over and let me out."

"We can protect you."

Panic shimmered through her digestive track. She was going to throw up. "Like the feds protected my cousin, Nicole Santi?"

"I don't know about your cousin's case, but I do know *we* can protect you."

Sophia wrapped her arms around her shaking body. "Please, let me go."

Colin reached over and touched her shoulder.

She flinched away.

"I told you, I won't hurt you," he said softly. Then reminded her, "If I hadn't shown up, you'd be dead right now."

Sophia looked straight ahead, her focus on her bleak future. She was so tired of being afraid, of wondering what new game Angelo was up to. Of running. "I'm going to be dead regardless, so why prolong it?" It was true. She held out no hope. If Angelo had found her in Tahoe, there was nowhere in the world she was safe.

Colin slowed the vehicle and turned right onto a side street, drove for a few hundred yards, then pulled down a long empty driveway before he stopped. "Hey," he said, turning toward her. She refused to look at him. But she couldn't help it. Those cobalt blue eyes of his were riveted on her. Sophia swallowed hard. She remembered the fire in them when he told her how he was going to send her to the moon. He had been one cocky senior. The same fire burned in his eyes now. But not for her. For justice.

"You cops are all the same. You don't care what price we have to pay so long as you get what you want."

He shook his head. "I care what happens to you, Sophia." Her name slid off his lips like fresh honey dripping down a beehive. Her body shivered. He smiled that smile that had done her in all those years ago. It almost worked again.

"Is kidnapping part of your repertoire?"

His smile widened as he upped his charm, her damn body warmed despite her cold wet clothing. "Consider yourself in my protective custody."

"Let me see your ID."

He leaned toward her and dug his soggy wallet out of his back pocket and handed it to her.

She took it and opened it. A New York City driver's license with his physical stats and the name Jacob Black. Her body shivered, this time in fear. He was not who he said he was.

She handed it back to him. "I'm cold, wet, and hungry." And the next time they stopped, she would be gone.

He slid the wallet back into his hip pocket and backed out of the driveway. "So am I but you don't hear me complaining."

Sophia crossed her arms and sat back in the seat. She smirked when he turned the heat on and directed the vents on her.

"So solicitous."

"I aim to please."

They drove for almost an hour in complete silence. Sophia kept coming back to the same conclusion: *If* he was really a cop, he would have told her his real name. Which meant he wasn't a cop. So, who did he work for and what did he really want with her? He pulled off into Placerville and stopped at a rental car company. "We need to switch out cars. We've been seen in this one."

"Why not kidnap one?"

"I would but that's against the law." He winked at her and Sophia felt her belly warm. Damn it.

He came around to her side of the car and opened the door. When he extended his hand, she glared at him, then looked back to his big hand. Long thick fingers with neatly trimmed nails beckoned her. She closed her eyes, remembering how they expertly stroked her. Sixteen years may have dragged by, but she remembered their one night together as if it were yesterday.

"Come on, Sophia, we don't have all night."

She shoved past him and followed him into the rental office. A few moments later after *Jacob* gave the proprietor some hush money, they drove off in a white Honda.

"Did you know that man in Tahoe?" he asked her once they were back on the road.

She had never seen him before, but that didn't mean he didn't work for her husband. She shrugged.

"Do you know where your husband is?"

She didn't, but he was going to get nothing out of her.

"Are we going to play games?"

Games? She wanted to call him out, show her hand, but she held back. Instead, she took a long, hard look at him. He looked good. More serious than he had in high school. But then, so did she. He was skyscraper tall, big boned, lean muscled, and crammed behind the steering wheel. He walked with the grace of a big cat and the arrogance of a stud. Colin Daniels was the orphaned Irish heart-throb from the wrong side of the tracks that the nuns let get away with murder, the priests slapped on the back, and the highbrow parents wagged their fingers at. He was all-state in football, baseball, and hockey. Then, he was all boy and all bad. Now he was a bad, bad man. And God help her, but even now, with her life on the line, Sophia's body was salivating. She'd die a content woman if Colin Daniels took her to the moon one more time.

She sighed like a schoolgirl.

He scowled at her, trying to read her. Tiny stress lines etched the corners of his deep blue eyes, framed by black lashes that were just shy of being too long. His nose was straight, his lips full and—she shivered—soft and could wreck shop like nobody's business. His black hair was stylishly cut but longer than she would have guessed for the cop he professed to be. His threads were fitted and looked good, soggy as they were. He snapped his fingers under her nose, jarring her out of fantasyland. Oh, hell. What had they been talking about?

"Games?" She scoffed, collecting herself. "Let's start with you telling me who you really are."

"I showed you my ID. Do you want my blood type too?"

"It could be fake."

He shot her a wounded look that speared straight to her womb. "It could be. If it is, it's fake for a reason."

"Oh."

He grinned at her and shrugged.

There was a part of Sophia that wanted to please this man on every level. That terrified her. She had tried hard in the beginning with Angelo—to please him. But nothing she wore, said, or did in or out of bed made him happy. Over time, he had turned sadistic. When she had stopped crying and begging him to stop, had turned hard and cold, had stared at him with emotionless eyes as he hurt her, he finally left her alone. But he had not broken her. She knew how it could be between a man and a woman, and for showing her that, Sophia would be eternally grateful to Colin Daniels.

"I didn't know that man in the Tahoe house, and I don't know where Angelo is."

"When we get back to New York, we'll draw him out."

"Not with me as your bait. I'm never going back to New York."

"Yeah, you are. Only you can put that piece of shit you married behind bars for the rest of his life."

"By risking mine?"

He shot her a glance then turned back to the road. "I told you, we can protect you."

"I don't want your protection. I want you to pull over in the next town and let me go."

"Do you have ID? Cash? A way to survive?"

"I'm a resourceful girl when I have to be, Mr. Black. It's what has kept me alive all these years."

He cracked a smile despite the seriousness of the conversation. His gaze raked her face, then dropped lower to her chest. She caught the excited gleam in his eyes in the dashboard lights. "I bet you are resourceful."

She stiffened at his implication. "Do you know what my husband did to me when he heard me laugh at a joke our chef made?" She didn't give him the opportunity to answer. "He cut me, then slit Roberto's throat and made me clean up the mess. So, please, do not think for one moment, I have used my body to make my life easier."

"That's not what I—"

"It doesn't matter what you think of me, Mr. Black. I'm not going to New York under any circumstances, and I'm sure as hell not going to give you or any other person information on my husband." She leaned closer and poked his hard biceps. "If you know anything about my husband at all, you know that just the fact I am alone in this car with you has put a price on your head. Anyone who aids me is dead. Anyone I speak to is dead. Now, please, let me off at the next town."

His lips tightened. When he looked at her this time, his eyes snapped. "I'm not letting you out in the next town or the one after that. Your testimony is vital. So is your life." He looked back at the road. "I have a very special skill set that when applied takes no prisoners. I will protect you, with my own life if necessary."

Sophia swallowed hard. He sounded so sure. She was glad he was on her side. But that didn't change anything. "I'm not driving to New York with you."

He let out a frustrated breath. "My original plan was to fly back tonight, but with no ID, you'll never make it through airport security, so we're going to drive." Glancing at her he said, "I'll make a deal with you, if I can't convince you to turn state's evidence by the time we get to Pennsylvania, then I'll give you the rest of my cash and you're free to go."

Sophia contemplated his offer. That was at least a four- to five-day drive if they turned east right now. At least ninety-six hours to slip away. She didn't hesitate. "Deal."

He reached over and extended his hand. Sophia took it this time. When his fingers wrapped around her, they both felt the jolt of electricity that zapped between them.

He released her hand, cursing under his breath.

Sophia was too much of a lady to put into words how she felt.

Just as the sun began to rise, they pulled off Highway 5 into a small rural town, and drove east for several miles, until he finally pulled into an obscure hotel parking lot off the main drag.

"Oh, great, a roach motel."

"It's better than floating in Lake Tahoe."

Touché.

Colin dragged her in behind him when he registered for a room, requesting one in the far back, away from the casual observer. He wasn't taking any chances that the rental manager in Placerville would keep his mouth shut if Gilletti's men spotted his SUV and came knocking on his door. He'd told the guy to put it in the small fleet garage. For everyone's sake, Colin prayed he had. Because if he hadn't, Colin knew once they got the info out of rental guy, they'd whack him.

The woman at the counter gave Colin a slow, thorough once-over, completely ignoring the fact that Sophia was standing right beside him. As she slid the key card across the counter, she smiled and said, "If you need *anything* at all, Mr. Black, come see me. I'm here 'til noon."

Colin winked at her. Sophia gaped at the woman's audacity.

Once they were in the cramped one bedroom, he turned the dead bolts and then chained the lock. He turned to her and nodded toward the bathroom. "We have three hours tops before we have to move. Now strip and give me your clothes. I'm going to make that cougar at the front desk an offer she can't refuse."

"Oh, I'm sure you will," Sophia said, then looked at the pitiful queen-sized bed that looked like a half-pipe, the center was so caved in, then looked back to Colin. "I'm sure she'll be more than happy to put you up at her place for the night."

"Probably safer there, all things considered. But you're stuck with me right there in that bed for the duration."

Vehemently, Sophia shook her head and backed up toward the door. Lord help her if she was that close to him for one hour, much less three. "I'm afraid that won't work for me."

"I'm not sleeping on the floor or in the tub."

"But—"

"Look, lady, I saved your life, and you're acting like I'm a rapist. I'm an adult, you're an adult. It's not the best of situations but we'll make the most of it. Now, strip."

Sophia dug in. She was being unreasonable. She knew it. And she knew why. It supremely bothered her that, having spent the last few hours sitting less than a foot away from him, he still did not recognize her! Was she that forgettable?

"Is it something I said, or do you always act like a spoiled two-year-old when a man saves your life?"

"I didn't ask you to save my life!" How stupid did that sound?

"At the very least, a thank-you would be in order."

Her eyes narrowed, but her body warmed. "At the very least? What did you have in mind for the very most?"

He grinned. "I could think of a few things." Her nipples stiffened.

"I hardly know you!"

He strut toward her, his eyes blazing. Her eyes dipped to the bulge in his jeans.

"Hardly."

Sophia swallowed hard when he reached out and swept her mangled hair from her shoulder. He lowered his lips to hers. Her heart pounded in her chest. He was going to kiss her.

"I know you're afraid, Sophia. I would be too. But I need you to trust me. I won't let anything happen to you on my watch." He stood back.

Her heart stopped. Embarrassment flushed her cheeks.

"Now strip."

Mortified, she nodded, hurried into the bathroom, shut the door, and shucked the dirty clothes. She opened the door slightly and dropped her damp clothes, including her bra and panties, onto the floor.

Then she shut the door and locked it. For a long time she stood with her back against it, trying very hard to regulate her breathing. A myriad of emotions and sensations ran a relay race inside of her. Yes, she was terrified Angelo would hunt her down. Terrified that he would exact a slow, excruciating death from her for embarrassing him, and then force her to witness him do the same thing to Colin.

Colin. Lord help her. When she thought he was going to kiss her she melted like an ice cube on a hot griddle. She wanted him. She wanted to experience the sublimity of him again. For sixteen years she had held on to that memory. Maybe it had been blown out of proportion in her imagination. Maybe she had created a fantasy to carry her through the terrible years, a beacon of hope that not all men were sadistic pigs and that sex wasn't meant to hurt. Maybe she was a lunatic! Sophia turned the shower on as hot as it would go. Maybe she needed meds or a shrink—or both. Maybe she just wanted to get laid by a man she trusted not to hurt her. Or maybe, a woman scorned, she wanted some payback.

Sophia debated the entire time she was in the shower whether to silently seduce Colin Daniels and make him so crazy for her that he would get down on his knees and beg her to make love, or to just turn the hot water to cold and forget about it.

# Chapter 3

Colin paced outside the hotel room door. He did not want to go in. If he did, he was not going to be able to keep his hands off the woman inside. The minute she spoke in the car, her soft husky voice stirred his dick and his memories. Maria. His graduation party. She had come to him like an angel from heaven and given herself to him. He took it. All of it. Repeatedly.

He still remembered the feel of her soft skin, her full breasts, her sweet virgin pussy. The way it clung hungrily to his dick.

*Fuck!*

He swiped his hand across his face. He wanted that again. And it pissed him off that she didn't remember him. How the hell did a girl forget her first time?

He had almost kissed her. Whether she remembered or not, she wanted it. He could see the spike of her pulse in her jugular. The way her nostrils flared and her lips parted. Her nipples had hardened and it was not cold in the room.

Keeping it professional was proving to be damn near impossible.

She was damn vulnerable. Scared to death. And while he might be a lot of things, he wasn't the kind of guy to take advantage of a vulnerable woman. He wasn't going to remind her about that night either. It could complicate things. And Uncomplicated was his middle name.

Didn't mean he didn't want to sink balls deep into her.

He sucked in a breath and exhaled. For both of their sakes, he was just going to have to do a better job of keeping it cool, and of keeping his dick on a leash.

He slid the key card into the lock, pushed open the door, and locked it behind him. He turned into the room and groaned. His body jolted painfully, as if he had been struck by a Mack truck.

He put his tongue back in his mouth as she emerged all hot and dewy from the bathroom. He tamped down the immediate urge to throw Sophia Gilletti onto the bed and sink so far into her he'd be lost for days. All he had was a towel wrapped around him. After he called in his change of plans to Moriarty, he had barely escaped the cougar's lascivious claws when he'd stripped and handed over his and Sophia's clothes. He didn't want to think about what she was doing to them. But the same lust that induced her now induced him. He wanted the woman standing in front of him in a real bad way.

All Sophia had on was a thin damp towel that hugged her sweet curves like a second skin. "Jesus, can you cover up?"

She turned those wicked eyes up to his and smiled. His dick flinched against his thigh. This was turning into a really bad idea. "I'm not a genie. I can't blink and make this towel larger," she said, then looked at his towel that was beginning to rise. "I could borrow yours."

Colin set his jaw, mentally commanding the devil between his legs to mind his manners. "Do you really want it?" he heard his raspy voice ask.

Her huge eyes stared at him, unblinking. She swallowed. He watched the slow undulation of her throat, imagining his lips pressed there. His jaw dropped when she squeaked out the word, "Yes."

His dick sprang against the cotton, the friction excruciating. He hissed in a breath. *Jesus.* What was her game? Colin stepped toward her. Her big eyes widened, unsure. He struggled to regulate his suddenly shallow breathing and reached for her, not, he told himself, for sex, but to reassure her she was safe. As much as he wanted to, he reminded himself he wasn't a complete dog, and would not take advantage of her vulnerable state.

She shook her head and backed up against the wall. Fear flashed in her eyes. He stopped and dropped his hand. "I'm not like Angelo," he said softly. "I won't hurt you."

Tears rose in her eyes. She nodded, and they tracked down her cheeks. Colin had always considered himself a compassionate guy. But what he felt at that moment for the woman standing six inches away from him was more than compassion. A fierce protectiveness reared its head in his gut. Violent in nature, willing to kill anyone who dared hurt her.

He touched a finger to her cheek and caught a tear, then traced it along the scar on her face. "When I meet up with your husband, I'll kill him for that."

She looked up at him, her eyes pools of hurt, fear, and—a raw need he understood.

"What do you want from me?" he softly asked.

"My freedom."

His chest hurt at just the thought of Angelo or one of his goombahs hurting her. "I can't give you that, Sophia." Her name slid off his tongue like a caress. She was an old soul, kindred somehow to his. He shook his head and these ridiculous emotions from him. His fingers dropped to her dewy shoulder. Her body quaked violently.

He stepped away, wondering what kind of animal instilled such fear in a woman. She needed to know she had nothing to fear from him. He'd keep his hands to himself, but he'd be damned if he was going to go all altar boy on her. He was what he was, and he liked what he liked, and maybe he could get her to loosen up just a little. He strode past her into the bathroom. He dropped the towel and said over his shoulder as he stepped into the shower, "I'm going to be watching you."

And he knew she was watching him. He turned and fully faced her, every inch of him clearly visible through the glass shower doors. He watched her eyes drop to his resurging erection, then rise to his gaze. He turned the shower on, the hard spray of cold water hitting him like a glass wall. His muscles flexed; his dick flared. He fought for composure as the water turned warm, spraying the head of his dick. "And if you know what's good for you, you'll be wrapped up like a cocoon in that bedspread and asleep before I get out of here."

But she didn't move. Didn't so much as blink. For a long, drawn-out minute their eyes locked, neither looking away. He reached for the soap, and, not taking his eyes off hers, he worked up a lather between his hands. Steam frosted the glass, so he swiped his hand across the door in a wide swath. He smiled and slowly began to work the lather into his chest, down his belly, then lower . . . Sophia's eyes widened. He watched the heat rise in her cheeks.

His hands slipped around his rock-hard dick. His body flinched in his grasp. His eyes narrowed as he slowly began to stroke himself. Sophia's big pouty lips parted, and then her gaze dropped to his stroking hand. She swallowed hard and shut the door.

———————

Sophia tossed the nasty bedspread from the bed and ripped the blanket off and wrapped herself so tightly in it she could barely breathe. Her heart was beating so fast she couldn't swallow. My God! Why had she done that? He must think she was a—She buried her head in the pillow, reached over to the lamp and turned it off. Embarrassment over her boldness consumed her. She wasn't like that!

*Like what?* her alter ego demanded.

Like that horrible woman at the front desk! A sex-starved hussy!

*Pah!*

Moments later, the bathroom door opened. Sophia prayed the bed would open up and swallow her.

The bed dipped with his weight. He stretched out and the curve of the mattress rolled him on top of her. Sophia stiffened. He pushed away from her but she could still feel the tension in his body. It matched hers. She squeezed her eyes shut, trying to ignore his warm breath on her neck. She squirmed and attempted to burrow deeper into the sheets. Her bottom brushed against something hard. Her eyes popped open.

"Jesus," he groaned. "Stop moving."

"I can't get comfortable."

"You're making me damned uncomfortable."

Sophia could not help a smile. "A small price to pay for kidnapping me."

He moved closer and pressed his body against hers. "I'm not kidnapping you."

She made the mistake of turning around to face him. Her chest smashed into his. The sheet separating them slid across her sensitive nipples. She gasped, arching her back.

"Bad move," he said hoarsely. Pressing her back into the mattress, his lips swept hers in a deep, feral kiss.

Sophia's body lit up on sensory overload. She tried to pull her arms out of the tangle of sheet wrapped around her, but it was like a straightjacket and she couldn't. Colin tore his lips away, his hot breath fanned her swollen lips. "I'm not going to apologize for that, Sophia. But damn it, it won't happen again."

He hauled himself off the bed, grabbed a pillow, and dropped down on the comforter she had tossed on the floor. "Go to sleep. I'm waking you in two and a half hours."

Sophia stared at the ceiling for what seemed like hours, trying to calm the storm that swept through her body. Why did he get to make the rules? Why couldn't she? She wanted him. It was obvious he wanted the same thing. Did she just have to flat-out demand it?

Maybe she would.

---

She woke to Colin's warm breath against her cheek. "Wake up, Sophia," he whispered. "We need to get out of here."

Her eyes flashed open and her heart rate skyrocketed. Angelo?

"You're safe. We just need to keep moving," he reassured her.

She rolled back to face the wall and nodded. The blanket had fallen away from her sometime during her sleep and she realized she was bare-ass naked. As she moved to the edge of the bed, his finger touched the small of her back. "What's this?" he asked roughly.

Her entire body stiffened as he traced his fingers across the mutilated skin. "My brand," she bit out, then walked with her chin up into the bathroom and quietly shut the door behind her. She flinched when she heard him punch the wall. But she wasn't afraid. Colin's violence was different from Angelo's. Colin's brand of violence would never be turned on her. He was not that kind of man. Part of her heart melted a little bit more for him.

When she emerged, Colin was dressed and angry. He pointed to the bed. "Your clothes." He turned away while she quickly dressed. Just as they were opening the door, the room phone rang. Sophia's heart lurched against her rib cage. Colin put his finger to his lips and quietly lifted the receiver and put it to his ear. She heard a woman's raspy voice then the phone went dead.

Colin set the phone down on the cradle and looked at her. Her blood ran cold. "They're out front, where I parked the car. That was Ruby, the cougar. Her red Firebird is parked behind the office with the keys in it. We're going to walk very slowly toward it."

Colin grabbed his leather bag and cracked the door open. He held his hand out to her. She took it and they slipped out into the blinding sunshine. Sticking close to the rooms, they passed a housekeeping cart and an open door. The Firebird was in view, fifty yards away.

The prowling sound of a car turned the corner behind them. Colin pushed Sophia back, into the open door, startling the maid. *"Por favor, señorita, el esposo de mi hermana es muy malo y en busca de ella. Por favor, vamos a quedarnos aquí hasta que pasa,"* Colin said urgently as he pulled out a wad of bills and shoved them in her apron pocket. The sound of slamming car doors preceded heavy footsteps.

*"Por favor,"* Colin said as he pushed Sophia into the bathroom. He left the door partially open to make the room look completely inconspicuous.

"Where's the people from the room next door?" a rough-sounding Guido asked the maid.

*"No habla Ingles,"* she said.

The maid screamed when he smacked her. Sophia flinched hard against Colin's rigid body. "A *hombre* and a *señora. Donde?*"

*"Se fueron en un taxi,"* she lied.

"What taxi?"

"Los Banos taxi," she cried.

He punched her again for good measure. Sophia's heart broke for the brave woman.

When the car doors slammed shut, Sophia broke free from Colin and went to the maid. She was wiping the blood from her broken nose. "I'm so sorry," Sophia said, helping her up.

"It's okay, it's okay," the maid said. "Those motherfuckers can go to hell."

Sophia's jaw dropped and the maid grinned a toothless grin. "I lived with an abusive man for ten years before I shot his ass. I should have done it sooner."

Colin shook his head and handed her more cash. "What's your name? I'll send more."

"Berta Martinez. Ruby'll know how to get in touch with me.

Now go before those *tontos* come back when they realize there is no
Los Banos taxi."

"Berta, we owe you big-time," Colin said, kissing her forehead
then grabbing Sophia's hand. He peeked out into the parking lot.
Clear. "C'mon." He pulled her behind him to the dilapidated circa
1980 Firebird. They hopped in, Colin turned the key, and it rumbled
to life. "Duck down," he said as he slipped on his sunglasses and the
cowboy hat he'd grabbed from off the backseat.

"It's the same guys and the same car parked in front of your place in
Tahoe," Colin said as he gave the car some gas and turned right on what
she knew was the frontage road. Long, drawn-out moments passed as
Sophia tried to regulate her erratic breathing. She was terrified.

"You can get up now," he finally said.

She sat up and took deep, cleansing breaths.

Colin reached over and squeezed her hand. "I said I would protect you."

She didn't look at him, afraid she'd break down. She pulled her
hand away, wanting to believe him, but she knew Angelo too well.
He would not stop until he had her back. Not because he loved her,
but because she was a possession, and as his, his pride could not take
the hit that she was running from him. "How did they find us?"

"I'm guessing they beat the info out of the rental guy in Placerville until he gave them the GPS coordinates. Then followed us on
their laptop."

"But how did they know he had rented you the car?"

"The SUV I dumped had a GPS chip in it too and they got lucky
finding the place at the Tahoe airport I rented it from. Might damn
well be the same place they rented theirs from."

"Where are we going now?"

"San Francisco airport. I'm going to dump Ruby's ride, borrow a
car from long-term parking, then drive to San Jose airport, dump it,

and rent a chopper to get us as far from California as possible, then find another ride and head east."

"They'll find us." They always found their target.

He reached over and squeezed her hand. "They'll have to catch us first."

Sophia pulled her hand to her lap and stared out the window. The nondescript landscape sped by, and so did her life. She never should have left Angelo. Because she had, people were dying. More people would die. And when he got his hands on her, he would make her pay in slow, painful increments.

"Why did you marry Gilletti?" Colin asked out of the blue.

"He made my father an offer he couldn't refuse."

"Which was?"

"He told him if he didn't hand me over, he'd cut my mother up piece by piece until there was nothing left of her. He gave my father three days to say yes, or else."

Colin's knuckles turned white as he grasped the steering wheel. "I would have killed the bastard on the spot."

"Daddy didn't know I overheard the conversation. I went to Angelo on the morning of the third day and told him I would marry him when I graduated high school."

Colin shook his head and looked at her, then back to the road. "The obvious aside, why you?"

Sophia smiled at the compliment. "The Gilletti family needed a front to launder their dirty money. My father's investment firm was the perfect foil."

"You're a brave daughter, Sophia. How did your folks take the news?"

"It was one of those 'should I jump with joy or cry in misery?' moments. It didn't matter. While my father vacillated about taking a bullet for me, I didn't. They died last year within three months of each other. So with no worries Angelo would hurt them, I took off. Little did I know, I could never really leave."

"You did leave, and I swear to you, he won't get near you ever again."

"Because of me, that poor man in Placerville is most likely dead. The maid has a broken nose, and God only knows what will happen to Ruby."

Colin grinned. "My money's on Ruby. She's got a shotgun under that counter aimed right at their balls."

"Why was she so helpful?" Sophia asked, hating herself for sounding jealous.

Colin grinned. "Oh, I had something she wanted and she had something I wanted."

"You did not!"

He threw his head back and laughed. "Not that. I told her I could fix things. Turns out she has a son with some legal issues. I'll see what I can do when we get back."

"But we're in California."

"The long arm of the law knows no boundaries." He pointed to the floor in front of her seat. "Reach under there and see what she left me."

Sophia felt under the seat and found a cloth bag. It was heavy when she pulled it out. "Open it," he said. She did and withdrew a handgun and two boxes of ammo and several loaded magazines.

"Nice job, Ruby. I owe you big-time."

"I can imagine what she really wanted in trade," Sophia sniffed, putting the gun and ammo back into the bag, then under the seat.

"Jealous?" he asked, smiling.

"*Pfft.* I hardly know you."

"I feel like I know you." He looked at her with a smile. "Maybe a different life?"

Sophia's blood warmed. She almost told him they had more than met but she hesitated. She wanted him to tell her the truth about who he really was before she came clean with him. "What about you? Where did you grow up?"

"Never knew my dad, and my mom—she had a few issues. She died when I was nine. Oddly, life got better. I grew up in several foster homes, mostly in Queens. They were stable. I tried to stay out of trouble. But the dye had been cast. I was used to moving around, a different adventure, good or bad, each day."

"Where did you go to school?"

"I started in public schools, but my get-out-of-jail-free card was my athleticism. By the time I hit high school, the local catholic high school was looking to build their sports programs. I knew if I didn't hunker down and stay put, my luck was going to run out. They made me an offer I couldn't refuse. I graduated from St. John's Prep in Astoria."

Sophia swallowed hard. It was the night he graduated that she had cut him from the herd and had her way with him.

"Did you go to college?"

He shook his head and grinned. "Nope, school never was my thing. The day after I graduated, I shipped out to Parris Island and gave the USMC the next six years of my life. Then went to work for the NYPD."

"You said you were part of a task force."

"That came later. But, yes. We do good work. Putting your husband away is going to be a crown jewel."

Sophia sat silent for a long time, processing over and over in her brain the fact that he'd shipped off to boot camp the morning after he'd changed her world forever. He hadn't written or called, but was it because he hadn't been able to, as opposed to didn't want to? He hadn't even known her as Sophia. In high school, she went by Maria. Maria Castavettes. Sophia was her middle name. Angelo said Maria made him think of his mother, so he started calling her Sophia. And she had been a brunette. She'd gone blond years ago, hoping to make

Angelo happy. He said she looked like a two-bit whore. Out of spite, she went two shades lighter.

"Have you ever been married?" she asked, wishing as soon as the words left her mouth she could take them back.

"Hell no!"

Her back stiffened. "What's wrong with marriage?"

"First of all, you're the last person I would expect defending that institution, but in answer to your question, my work doesn't allow for that kind of commitment."

"Bull! You're just using that as an excuse."

He grinned at her. "I'm not good at planting roots. I move around."

"Another excuse. What's the real reason?"

"I like variety."

"The spice of life. I should give it a try. But I'll never marry again."

"After what you've endured, I can't blame you."

"It doesn't mean that I'm opposed to a relationship, just all on my terms."

He shivered. "The dreaded *R* word."

"So it's sex to go for you?"

He turned those deep blue eyes on her and smiled a sizzling smile. "Very *good* sex to go."

"Hmm, you seem pretty cocky."

"You saw how cocky I am."

Sophia's face reddened. He smiled again. "I like it when you blush like that. Not enough women do."

Damn him. He was reeling her in so easily she hadn't realized he'd hooked her. And suddenly it didn't matter. What mattered was the here and now. Because with her luck and Angelo's cunning there wasn't going to be a tomorrow. "I'm going to take a page from your spice book. I want to live before I die," she said softly. Then with more conviction, "I want to live today like there's no tomorrow." She turned in the seat and looked directly at him. "Do you find me attractive?"

"You know I do." He turned that lethal smile on her. "Do you find me attractive?"

"Very much so. So much so, I want to have sex with you." Colin coughed and looked at her like she had just sprouted a third eye. "*Would* you have sex with me?" she asked him as if she were asking him to pass the peas.

He coughed again and looked at her, this time his face reddened. "*What?*"

"I didn't stutter."

"I—No. No! Not because I don't want to, but—because, I'm on the job here."

"So?"

He shook his head. "I can't. I would feel like I was taking advantage of you in a vulnerable state."

Sophia laughed so hard her cheeks hurt. She laughed even harder when he narrowed his eyes. She doubled over, unable to control herself. "I can't believe that the Lucky Irishman just said that."

He stiffened. "Where did you hear that name?"

Sophia hiccoughed and shook her head. "I went to St John's too. I watched you walk all over campus with a different girl every day, sometimes two or three different ones in the same day. So don't lay that guilt bull on me."

"Take it any way you want it."

"I will." She sat back smiling, playing off the most embarrassing rejection of her life. "No big deal. I'll find someone else."

"For what?" he asked incredulously.

"For spicy sex." Though the thought of sex with anyone other than Colin held no interest.

"We're on the run here. Why do you want sex all of a sudden? And why with anyone who'll oblige you?"

"It's not all of a sudden. And not just any random guy with a willing penis will do. Before my husband, there was only one man.

It was"—her voice choked—"perfect. I want that again. For more than ten years I have lived in a prison with a sadistic jailer. Now, while I'm free, I want to live like I was dying, which in effect, I am. I want sex on my terms before I head up to the big cloud in the sky."

"You're not going to die!"

"We all die, Colin."

He gritted his teeth and looked sideways at her. "You're not going to die on my watch."

She shrugged. "You don't know that for sure."

"I haven't lost one yet. You're not going to be the first."

"I'm just a job." She bit her lip, hating that she had just said that. Of course, she was just a job. Why would she be more? He didn't remember her, and even if he did, so what? They had sex, once, over a decade ago.

"I take my job very seriously."

"I can see that."

For the next hour, they drove in silence. "I'm hungry," she said.

He pulled off at the next exit and drove through a fast-food joint and ordered enough food to feed five people. And they were off again. They hit the San Francisco airport and switched cars without incident. They did the same in San Jose, but hit a snag. A chopper would not be available for the distance they wanted to travel until early the next morning.

Sophia could barely keep her eyes open and Colin was showing signs of fatigue as well. "Let's get a room, then come back in the morning."

He pulled into a much nicer hotel chain. Still one bed, but she didn't care. Sophia fell flat on her face on the king-sized bed and there she lay until her bladder woke her several hours later.

# Chapter 4

After waking to a full bladder and very naughty thoughts of what she would like to do to the man sleeping next to her, Sophia hurried into the bathroom and stripped. The cold shower didn't help cool her physically or mentally. There was only one thing that would do that, and that specific provider wasn't interested. Yet. She smiled and turned the water to hot.

She'd just have to make him an offer he couldn't refuse. Colin Daniels may not want to satisfy her for his noble reasons, which she thought was an admirable trait in a man, but damn if she cared about them at the moment. Her body ached for him. Every female part of her had been simmering since she walked out of the shower last night. She was more than capable of satisfying herself, and doing it in front of Colin would be the ultimate erotic high. She looked down at the dark, downy triangle between her thighs and decided to get with the times. She grabbed his razor from the vanity and got to work. A half hour later, wrapped in a thick terry cloth hotel robe, she emerged from the bathroom squeaky clean, with her hair dried and a body as smooth as a baby's butt.

Her breath hitched in her chest to find Colin's hooded blue eyes fixed on her. He lay on his back with his hands locked beneath his head. He wore only black boxer briefs and either he had a morning erection or he was happy to see her. Sophia ignored it. As much as she would like to straddle the impressive stud, she had other plans. Besides, she would not beg him for sex, and even if he changed his mind, she had her pride. But she wasn't above making him regret it.

She smiled. Holding his stare, she slowly pulled one end of the robe tie loose. His left brow rose in interest. She responded by letting the belt fall away. The robe opened slightly, exposing the fact she wasn't wearing her bra or panties. His other brow cocked. Sophia's smile deepened as she shrugged off the robe. It fell in a muffled heap around her ankles. Colin's sharp intake of breath followed it.

With one foot, she kicked the robe away. His hot gaze raked her from head to toe and then back again. Heat infused every inch of her.

"You don't fight fair, Sophia," he said hoarsely.

Acting as if she had not heard him, she ran her fingers through her long hair and shook it, then lay down beside Colin. She rolled over onto her belly, propped her chin on her hands, gazed deeply into his eyes, and asked, "So, is room service an option?"

His cobalt eyes burned hotly. He reached out to touch her but fisted his hand and retracted. Sophia smiled inwardly. She was just getting started. Languidly, she rolled over onto her back, and her breasts bobbed just under his nose. His breath hitched.

Innocently turning to look at him, trying to quell the shimmers of desire running through her, Sophia said, "So, Colin, if you didn't feel so guilty, and hypothetically, let's say you took me up on my offer, what would you do to me?"

She felt him swell beside her. She stuck her right index finger into her mouth and sucked, then traced the moist tip down the hard path of his six-pack abs, stopping just above the elastic band of his briefs. "Hypothetically speaking, would you just take me like Tarzan or"—she cocked her head to the side and smiled at his obvious discomfort—"or would you make slow, sweet love to me?"

He rolled over and moved into her, but not close enough that their bodies touched. "Hypothetically? The first thing I'd do is spank that smart little ass of yours just for thinking of looking for another man to satisfy you." This time *her* breath hitched. He lowered his lips above a tight nipple and blew. Sophia squirmed so that the sensitive tip brushed his chin. Body parts began to melt. She squeezed her eyes shut, then slowly opened them.

He kept talking. "Then I'd start at your toes, and lick, suck, and kiss my way up your legs, to your thighs . . ." He closed his eyes and inhaled. "Mmm, yes, then to that sweet, smooth pussy of yours." He moved slowly down her body, his hot breath singeing her in its wake. He stopped above her shaved mons. He opened his eyes and looked up at her. "Did you do that just for me, Sophia?"

She swallowed and nodded, wondering when she had lost control.

"Thank you," he breathed against her lips. "Spread your legs."

She did before he finished his sentence.

"God, you are gorgeous," he said roughly. He dipped his nose lower. "And so wet for me."

His breath caressed her sensitive folds. Sophia closed her eyes, parted her lips, and grabbed the sheets, twisting the fabric in her fists until she hurt. The tension in her body was so thick she was afraid she would snap in half.

"Hypothetically"—he breathed—"before I sunk my cock into this sweet, wet pussy, I'd make you beg for it, Sophia. Beg until you couldn't stand it." He traced his lips along the curve of her hip. Sophia expelled a long breath, as her body rose off the sheets.

She swallowed hard and rasped, "No touching . . ."

"I bet you taste as warm and sweet as you smell." His nose lowered to her thighs and he inhaled. "I'd make you come with my lips, sucking your stiff little clit until it exploded in my mouth." Sophia moaned and arched, pulling the sheet loose.

He blew on her pussy. Sophia moaned again and, unable to stop herself, she let go of the sheets and slid her fingers down to her sweltering mons.

Sophia clenched her jaw as her pussy clenched against her fingertips. Dear lord, he was making her forget—everything. She closed her eyes and lay back on the sheets, and imagined it was his hands on her.

"Oh, you are selfish, Sofia. So, so, selfish," he crooned. "Keeping all of that sweetness for yourself."

Slowly she stroked her stiffened clitoris. Thick waves of sensation caught her by surprise.

"If that were my hand, I'd slide my finger so deep into your dewy cunt, you would snap."

Sophia's breath caught in her throat. Her body was on fire. She wanted him to do everything he said he would do. And more. But she would not beg. She arched her back, spread her thighs, and slid her middle finger into her vagina. Her lips parted. "Ohhh—" she moaned.

His breath was warmer, harsher, faster against her thighs. "That's it, Sophia," he urged. "In and out, nice and slow. Imagine it's me inside of you." She thrashed against her hand, wishing it *was* him. *Wanting* it to be him. Her eyes opened as a wave of sensation crashed through her. He rose up and pressed his lips to hers, stifling her cries. Her body melted into a liquid pool of want.

Only his lips touched hers. He clasped the sheets beside her. Warm and soft, his hands pushed hers wide open, taking what he wanted with or without her permission. His tongue swirled across hers as he angled his head for maximum fit. She rose against him, wanting him to take all of her. His tongue slid and thrust against hers, mimicking the cadence of her hand. He sucked her bottom lip into his mouth then thrust his tongue into her. Caught in a wild whirlwind of chaotic passion, it swirled around her in fragmented pieces, the connection the complete unity of their bodies.

She raised against him, pressing her breasts into his chest, her finger deeper inside, her cadence faster, harder. His tongue plundered her mouth in slow, tortuous thrusts.

She tore her lips from his, gasping for breath. "Colin," she gasped. "Make the ache stop."

"I want to watch you do it," he said roughly, moving down between her thighs. He was on the end of the bed, looking up at her through her thighs. She wanted to throw her head back and close her eyes, but his gaze held hers. He blew on her. When she undulated, her hand touched his lips. "Do it, Sophie. Come while I watch."

Between her fingers, Colin pressed his lips to her clit. And she launched. Like the space shuttle on liftoff, she hurtled through the air at eight hundred miles an hour, straight toward the moon and stars. She could not take her eyes off him. Off the erotic vision of him between her legs, his full lips glistening with her juice, liplocked on her clitoris, savoring her as if she were a gourmet meal. Never had she experienced such exposure or such a raw, aching need for a man—no, not just any man, a need for *this* man—to finish what she had so shockingly started.

She dug her free hand into his thick hair, and arched. "Colin," she gasped, as the first wave hit. His lips tightened, his tongue flicked. She thrashed her hips, pulled his hair, cried out for more. He gently shook his head, not releasing her swollen clit. Another wave slammed into her, followed by another, as his lips sucked, and pulled and sucked and pulled, pushing her higher and higher, and higher—until the waves hit so fiercely, they crashed into each other and she fell to pieces.

Colin could not remember witnessing anything as damn sexy as
Sophia Gilletti coming on her hand and his mouth. Her long, tanned
legs twitched, and her chest heaved as she tried unsuccessfully to
catch her breath. Her hand was still pressed between her thighs, as if
she could control the spasms that shivered through her. He kissed the
top of it and crawled over her, careful not to touch. His gaze swept
over her perky tits, the pink nipples puckered, begging him for attention. Unable to resist, he licked one. Sophia moaned. His heavy cock
flinched against her thigh. She bit her bottom lip and moaned again.
Her eyes were screwed shut, her pouty lips damp, her nostrils flared.

God Almighty, he wanted to sink into her. He literally ached for
her. Every inch of him, most especially the throbbing length between
his legs. He wanted to do all kinds of naughty things to her, but
mostly he wanted to make slow, passionate love to her. She deserved
that.

Colin shook his head, confused by his thoughts and the uncomfortable emotions that spurred them. Making love? What the hell
did that mean? He was a sport fucker. Good Time Charlie. The guy
who didn't do breakfast. The guy every girl could count on to be gone
in the morning. And yet, here he was, two mornings later.

He rolled away and sat on the edge of the bed, raking his fingers
through his hair. Two mornings later because he was doing his job,
he reminded himself. He looked over his shoulder to find Sophia
staring at him with sated, hooded eyes.

He couldn't help a smile. "Did you enjoy that?"

"Hypothetically, yes."

He threw his head back and laughed. He stood and was careful
not to turn toward her. He'd give her a black eye if he did. "I'm going
to jump in the shower. We need to get on the road."

"It's still dark outside!"

"We need to keep moving, Sophia."

She sat up and crawled on the bed toward him. Her full breasts swayed in sync with her sweet ass. His dick swelled. "Damn it, woman. I'm not made of concrete."

She sat back on her knees and looked at him with a total feline smile. "I invited you to make love to me, Colin. You passed. Now suffer the consequences."

"It's not that I don't want—"

"The reason isn't important," she interrupted. "The outcome is the same." She leaned toward him. "But I'm afraid you have unleashed a sleeping tiger. I want more of that, with or without you."

Colin scowled. "Is that all it is to you? Sex?"

It was her time to laugh. He didn't like it. "Oh my God! Are you serious? Colin! Did you just really say that?"

"I meant, will any cock do?"

She smiled that tigress-on-the-prowl smile again. His blood warmed as her gaze dropped to his thickening cock. She was playing with fire. He could change his mind . . .

"Oh, dear lord, no. Not any cock." She reached out and stroked the dewy head of his, all the way down to his balls. Colin hissed in a breath. "Only a cock as glorious as this."

He wrapped his hand around her fingers and squeezed. He shut his eyes and clamped his jaw tight. When she began to slowly move her hand up and down, he nearly came. He squeezed her hand tighter in an effort to stop her, but it only stoked his fire.

"Soph—"

She pulled him gently toward her and rose up on her knees, sliding her tits against his chest. Colin sucked in a deep breath. He was so damn close to losing all control. She kissed his neck, then behind his ear. His muscles tightened as he wrapped an arm around her waist, pulling her tighter against him. "While you're in the shower, can I order room service?"

"What?" he asked not believing she would—

"Can I order room service?"

Colin closed his eyes and exhaled. He peeled her fingers off his dick and blue balls. When he looked at her, he saw the laughter in her eyes. She was having too much fun at his expense. "Have at it, but tell them to leave the tray outside," he bit out as he grabbed his bag, then strode into the bathroom, slamming the door behind him.

"Do you want anything?" she asked laughing.

"Coffee and a blow job!"

"Hah, I'll see if that's on the menu!"

Despite his blue balls and stiff cock, Colin grinned, shaking his head. Who knew the runaway Mafia wife was so plucky? It was a shame their road trip would ultimately end. He was still smiling when he exited the shower. He wrapped a towel around his waist, grabbed Ruby's handgun from the leather bag, slid it down between the small of his back and the towel, not taking any chances there was a room-service glitch. He took another towel to his hair, and as he was drying it, walked out of the bathroom. "Sophia, we need to—" He froze in his tracks as the blood drained from his body.

They had company.

# Chapter 5

Colin had been trained for situations exactly like this, which is the only reason he remained outwardly calm. Inside, he was pissed he had taken his eyes off Sophia for one minute. This was his fault, damn it!

A mountain of a man held Sophia in a one-handed chokehold. With his other hand, he dug a modified P90 into her temple. She was ghost white, naked, and from the looks of her, about to faint.

"The boss ain't gonna be happy when he finds out you been dipping into the family assets," Guido said.

Colin shrugged it off like it was no big deal, wondering where Guido's partner was. Probably waiting outside with the car running. "We both know you won't pull that trigger," Colin said. "So I guess the question is, are you going to make a break with just the girl or are you going to try and be a cowboy and take me with you for the extra Brownie points?"

Guido nodded and pointed the mini machine gun at Colin's chest then lowered it to his dick. "We got room for you." He pulled the trigger just as Sophia dropped to the floor, elbowing Guido in the balls on her way down. It was enough to throw his aim off. Colin pulled the Glock and capped off a single round, hitting the guy right between the eyes. Guido's three-hundred-pound body buckled to its knees, then toppled forward. Sophia screamed and rushed to Colin. He pulled her behind him and leveled the barrel at the unmoving heap on the floor.

"Get dressed," Colin said as he grabbed the P90 out of Guido's hand and rifled through his pockets for another magazine. Jackpot! One fifty-rounder. He kept the P90 out and stuffed his gun and the magazine into the duffel bag.

Sophie dressed in a rush with Colin right behind her. Together they dragged the dead assassin into the bathroom, hoisted him into the tub, and tossed all of the towels on top of him. Colin grabbed his duffel bag and Sophia's hand, then moved toward the door. Cracking it open, he looked down the long hallway before he pulled Sophia out and toward the stairs. They went up two flights. Urgency gripped him. If the other half of Guido's team wasn't already looking for him, he would be soon, probably via the service elevator.

"Back down the stairs to the lobby floor," Colin said evenly. He kept his voice level, his movements precise, and his breathing even, hoping to keep Sophia calm. If she lost it, they'd be in big trouble.

Sophia followed silently. At such an early hour the lobby was graveyard quiet. Colin pulled Sophia along and into the ladies' room. After he made sure they were alone, he pulled out the throwaway cell phones. She gasped when he smashed them against the counter and then did the same thing with his iPad. "Why did you do that?" she asked as he scooped up the pieces and dumped them into the trash can.

"I used the iPad to search for the helo charter, and while you were taking a shower, I used one of the throwaways to alert my team we were on the run and not going to be back into New York for a few days."

Her jaw dropped. "You can't be serious. You think—?"

"Someone traced it."

"But how? How would Angelo be able to do something like that?"

"I don't know, but he found us. I'm not taking any chances."

He took her hand and started for the door. As he poked his head out to clear the area, Guido's twin strode boldly into the lobby. Colin pushed her back. "We've got company."

It didn't take long for the ladies' room door to slowly open.

Colin sat hunched in the last stall on the toilet seat with Sophia trembling violently behind him. Cautious footsteps approached, followed by the quiet whoosh of each metal stall door being carefully opened and then closed. The footsteps halted at the stall next to theirs. Sophia's heart slammed against his back. Colin carefully adjusted his aim. He knew what was coming next. He opened the automatic.

The body on the other side dropped to the floor with a controlled thud. Colin followed the bad guy's fall with a steady stream of rounds. Grunts and cursing preceded a splatter of rounds from the other side of the door. Colin pushed Sophia against the wall as he made himself a bigger target, shielding her.

It was all over in seconds.

A widening pool of blood spread toward them on the tile floor. Colin kept the barrel pointed at the target and kicked open the door. The guy was flat on his back and full of holes. Colin grabbed the duffel and stuffed the dead guy's weapon into it, then stuffed in his own. He grabbed Sophia up into his arms. "Don't look," he said, then carried her over the body, let her down, and hurried toward the door.

They slipped out the front doors just as hotel security poured in. They were in the car and on the road just as the first siren echoed in the distance. He didn't say a word, he just drove.

When he was sure they were not being followed, he looked at Sophia's ashen face. "What happened in the room?"

She swallowed hard and shook her head. "I—I was just getting ready to call room service when the door flew open. He had a key and bolt cutters. He—he just cut right through the chain lock. I screamed and ran for the bathroom but he tackled me—" Her voice cracked, tears welled. "I didn't know what to do, Colin. I was so afraid he was going to kill us both! Then that second man in the bathroom. I thought I was going to die!"

Colin reached over and grabbed her shaking hands. He winced at a sharp, abrupt burn in his biceps. He'd been hit, damn it. "Sweetheart," he softly said, squeezing her hands. "I told you I'd protect you. I won't let you out of my sight again. From this moment forward, until we hit New York, we're going to be joined at the hip."

Wide-eyed she looked over at him. "I'm so scared. I—Oh my God, you're bleeding!"

The bullet wound was nothing. Getting Sophia to a safe place was all he cared about. "I'm fine."

She shook her head and ripped the sleeve off her shirt. "Pull over."

"I said I'm fine."

"Pull over, now!"

Exasperated but unwilling to freak her out any more than she had been, Colin pulled over onto the shoulder.

"Take your shirt off."

He opened his mouth to argue, but the stubborn set of her jaw and the glare in her green eyes stopped his protest. He unhooked his seat belt, unbuttoned his shirt and pulled it off. He looked down at the hole at the top part of his biceps. The bullet had gone clean through. He'd survived worse with no medical attention.

"That's more than a graze, Colin! You need medical attention," she said nervously. Her voice shaking with emotion.

"That's not going to happen."

She ignored him. She wound the fabric around his arm, tying it snugly. "That should help stem the blood flow. But we need to get that cleaned up before you get an infection."

"Yes, Nurse Ratched." Colin shrugged his shirt on and started to button it when she slapped his hands away. "I'm not a two-year-old," he growled as she buttoned him up.

"No, you're more like a three-year-old." When she had finished, he cocked a brow and asked, "Can we go now?"

"Yes."

They needed to hole up somewhere safe, somewhere he could get his bearings, somewhere he could give Sophia a few survival lessons. He hit the gas and asked her, "Have you ever shot a gun?"

"No."

"You're going to learn."

Colin didn't go back to San Jose's Mineta International Airport for the helicopter ride. He was taking no chances. He drove south toward Monterey, where he had an old buddy. Evan "Cappy" O'Malley was only eight years Colin's senior, but he was a marine who had done numerous tours in Iraq and Afghanistan and had lived to talk about it.

When Colin turned off on the Cannery Row exit, he felt Sophia's eyes on him. He touched her knee and squeezed it. She pulled away. She had not said a word since she'd bandaged him up. He knew she was upset. Scared and angry. But what bothered him most was the way she withdrew from him. Each time he glanced over at her, she was staring straight ahead, in a near catatonic state.

"Sophia?" he softly said. "Talk to me."

She shook her head. "What is there to talk about? We're running from a man who has eyes and ears everywhere. We were almost killed back there. You're wounded. He's going to get one or both of us." She looked at him, her eyes dull and hopeless. "What do you want me to say about that?"

"I want you to trust me. I gave you my word, Sophia. I'll protect you."

"Like you did in the hotel room?" she blurted.

Her words cut him to the quick. He'd fucked up. He wouldn't again. But he couldn't help the defensiveness that leaked into his voice. "You're here, and alive. What more do you want?"

"I want to stop running! I want to stop being afraid! I want to live, Colin, but not like this!"

He didn't blame her, this was no way for anyone to live. "Trust me, Sophia. It will all be over soon."

She slumped back into the seat and stared out the window as she had before. "It will never be over for me."

―――――――

Sophia sat quietly and watched Colin go into a convenience store and emerge a few minutes later with a plastic bag. The bloodstain on his shirt had widened. He hopped back into the car, pulled out of the parking lot, and headed toward Cannery Row. He reached into the bag and handed her a cell phone. "It's a throwaway. The only number you're going to call, and only if you need to, is mine." He pulled out another throwaway. "Go ahead and program them in."

As Sophia did, she asked, "Did you get something for your wound?"

"Yeah."

"Where are we going?"

"To a safe place."

No place was safe for her. But she kept that to herself. Trying to convince Colin that Angelo would eventually get them only pissed him off. And she didn't want to piss him off. He had put his life on the line to protect her. She had been terrified this morning, but he had kept her calm, reassuring her they would make it. In her heart of hearts, she believed that if anyone could keep her safe, it was Colin.

Thirty minutes later, they pulled up to a double-studded wooden gate, with the image of a large horse head, like a chess piece, carved into it. It was very similar if not the exact same design as the tattoo that ran down Colin's right side.

Colin took his cell and punched in a number. "Sergeant Daniels requesting permission to enter, sir." He spoke in the clipped respectful tone of a subordinate speaking to a superior officer.

A moment later, the gates rattled, then slowly opened. Colin gave the car some gas and entered what Sophia could only describe as a psychedelic jungle. Overgrown palms and ferns, dotted with bright blooming bushes and plants she had seen only in magazines grew in a crazy kaleidoscope of colors, textures, and fragrances. Wind chimes, garden gnomes, and lawn jockeys peeked out from between brightly colored planters that were peppered throughout the yard with no thought given to strategic placement. But somehow, it all worked. At the end of the gravel driveway was a sprawling hacienda. And standing on the front porch with a rifle slung over his shoulder and two mastiffs drooling at his feet was a man who looked like he should be sitting on a street corner with a cup, begging for his next drink.

"My captain," Colin said, shaking his head, a smile splitting his face. He pulled right up to the porch and put the car in Park. "Stay here." He slid out. The massive dogs began to bark. A sharp command from the captain shut them up.

Colin saluted the man. Something caught in Sophia's throat, and her belly rolled. The hot sting of tears distorted her view. Angrily, she swiped at her eyes. She did not want to have such tender feelings for Colin. Being hot for him was one thing. But at every turn he proved he was a man worthy of any woman's love. She shook her head. Love? She did not know what it meant anymore. She didn't even try to figure it out.

The captain said something gruffly, and Colin embraced him. Then heads together, they spoke urgently. The captain nodded, then went inside. Colin came around to her door and opened it. He extended his hand and said, "Come on, Sophia. No one will find us here."

She let out a long breath she had not realized she was holding and took his hand. The captain was nowhere to be found when they entered the airy, open house. "Captain O'Malley is the shy type. He thinks it's better you don't get a good look at him. I told him he was a dick, but he insisted we have the run of the bottom floor."

"Is it because he doesn't want me to know what he looks like?"

Colin shrugged. "I stopped trying to figure him out years ago. I just know we can trust him and he's going to get us to New York."

"He's driving to New York with us?" She was praying he was not.

"Sweetheart, we're flying."

"How? I don't have ID?"

"Captain O'Malley is a man of many talents, with many toys. One of them flies."

Sophia should have been excited by the prospect, but she wasn't. Flying meant going to New York sooner rather than later, and she wasn't planning to go at all. Not if she wanted to celebrate her next birthday.

"When are we leaving?"

"Tomorrow morning."

She swallowed hard and nodded. If she was going to make her escape, she was going to have to do it tonight. No way in hell was she getting on that plane.

# Chapter 6

Colin showed Sophia to a large, comfortable bedroom at the end of a long hallway. It was decorated to reflect the landscape outside; a hodgepodge of fabrics, wandering textures, and exotic colors framed an eclectic grouping of furniture that all somehow worked. Peeking into the large bathroom, she almost drooled over the huge sunken tub. Colin stepped in behind her and she jerked in surprise.

"Remember what I said? Joined at the hip."

Sophia shivered. His warm breath caressed her neck just as his body heat pulsed behind her. "I think we can part long enough to bathe." She wanted some private time to figure out how she was going to get away from Colin. Her belly did a slow roll. Leaving him was not going to be easy.

"I'll scrub your back." He brushed her long hair from her shoulder and pressed his lips just behind her ear. Gooseflesh erupted along her skin. She wanted to close her eyes, lean back into his hard chest, and let him hold her for the rest of the night. But she had to go.

He slipped his arms around her and pulled her back against his chest just as she wished. His lips trailed along her ear.

Her knees shook when his tongue slid languorously around the shell of her ear. He sucked in her earlobe. Her nipples stiffened. She closed her eyes and let herself forget for just a few minutes. After all, they were safe and both consenting adults. And wasn't she entitled to a little pleasure after all they had been through?

His fingers traced around her aching nipples, then one at a time he plucked them as his tongue swirled along the shell of her ear. Sophia moaned, arching against him. Everything about this man excited her. He was dangerous, passionate, and knew exactly what her body craved.

"I won't let anything happen to you, Sophie. I swear on my life," he said huskily.

His words brought her back to the here and now. Reality.

She turned in his arms and looked up into his intense blue eyes. It took her a moment to compose herself so that she could speak without her voice cracking with emotion. She believed Colin, but she could not make the same vow. "I wish I could promise you the same. Even if Angelo goes to prison, he won't rest until one of his thugs brings your head to him on a platter. And you know he can do it from prison."

"Let me worry about that," he said, lowering his lips to hers. She welcomed the kiss. She welcomed the comfort he gave. She welcomed all that Colin Daniels had to give, but with one exception. She would not allow him to forfeit his life. That she would not take. If she went back to New York with Colin, Angelo would kill him.

Her heart ached at just the thought of losing him. She gasped as the sudden realization that she loved him slammed into her heart. She had always loved him. That night he made love to her, she fell in love with him. He had been so gentle, so loving, so reverent. He had made the terrible years after, bearable. It was her dreams of him that had pushed her to get out of bed in the morning. The fantasy of what could be between a man and woman. Not the violence of Angelo or the weakness of her father.

She would not thank him by leading Angelo to him.

His lips grew more demanding and the emotional hooks he'd already imbedded into her heart sank deeper. She could give in to what they both wanted. A single night of passion. Maybe one that would carry her through another ten years? Or would it destroy rather than save her? Prove fatal to her heart?

She craved him, but losing herself to him on all levels would only make a bad situation worse. Fear trumped her craving. Fear of wanting more. Fear for his life. Fear of falling deeper in love with a man she would already die for.

She tore her lips from his. "Colin, we need to clean up your arm."

"Don't worry about me. The captain's going to stitch me up," he said, trying to recapture her lips.

She turned away, not brave enough to look him in the eye, afraid of what he might see.

"Stop avoiding me, Sophie."

She swallowed and looked up at him, forcing a soft smile. "I'm not, I'm just nervous."

He looked past her to the tub. "A good soak might help relax you," he said, grinning as if he had plans for something else that would relax her too. "Fill that monstrosity. I'll be in the bedroom getting fixed up."

He left her then. And took all the warmth with him. Feeling an odd sense of emptiness, she pushed runaway plans from her thoughts. She would think of them later. Sophia turned her attention to the large room. As bathrooms went, this one was a slice of heaven. The huge spa-sized sunken tub was smack-dab in the middle of the room, with two walk-up steps. Nearby, a carved stone oversized shower with two heads, a triple Italian stone vanity, a commode, bidet, and a large baker's-type rack with big fluffy folded towels and all kinds of lotions, bath salts, and oils. How odd, she thought, that a single military man would have all the necessities of a lady's bath. Maybe there was more to the captain than met the eye.

There was only one aspect of the bathroom Sophia didn't care for. While there were high skylights, there was no way out except back through the bedroom. But that meant no one could come in either. No one but Colin. That meant she was safe. For now.

She quietly shut the door and turned the two waterfall faucets on full blast. She took her time selecting bath salts and oils. She set them on the edge of the tub, then took out two big fluffy towels and nearly squealed with delight when she opened the single drawer beneath and found a folded white one-piece terry cloth patio dress. She pulled it out, hoping the captain would not mind her borrowing it while she was there. She needed to wash her clothes. And, she exhaled nervously, while Colin was asleep tonight, she'd slip out the window and take off to parts unknown. If she didn't know where she was going, how could Angelo track her? She would take some of Colin's cash and lay low for as long as she could, then start moving.

Eventually, she'd land somewhere, make a few bucks waiting tables, then move on again. She accepted that as long as Angelo was alive, she would never be safe. She also accepted that as long as she and Colin were not connected, he would live.

When the mini swimming pool was half-full, Sophia stripped, clipped her hair up with several bobby pins she'd found in the vanity drawer, and sunk into the steamy, velvety water. Ohhh, that felt sooo good. She submerged herself up to her neck and savored the exquisite simple pleasure of a bath. Resting her head on the curved marble cutout made just for that reason, she turned the pulsing jets on and liquefied more. Her muscles were so tense they ached. The pulsing jets pounded and rolled against her stiff body, loosening the tension one inch at a time. What she would not give for a full-body massage.

"You look content, Sophia." Colin's deep voice sounded from less than a foot away. She opened her eyes and caught her breath. He wore only his jeans. His defined chest and abdominal muscles shimmered in the humidity of the room. The thick muscles in his arms and shoulders rippled with the slightest movement. The dark horse tattoo along his right side made sense now. It was his Company insignia.

She looked at his right biceps and was impressed by the neat row of stitches across it. She noticed he had another scar about four inches long that ran along the inside of his left biceps, and another one just like it farther down his forearm. She pointed to them. "How did you get those?"

"Knife fight in Fallujah."

For the first time, Sophia saw Colin as the survivor he was. His childhood, high school, the marines, hand–to–hand combat in a foreign country, the task force. He had the scars to prove he had engaged and walked away the victor. Could he win against Angelo? A spark of hope lit up in her heart. If anyone could, it was Colin. "I'm glad you won."

"I always win," he said. No arrogance, just fact.

He pulled off his jeans, leaving only his boxer briefs between them. He stepped up one step, then the other. Sophia's belly did a slow flip-flop. She moved across the tub out of harm's way. "What are you doing? You can't get your arm wet!"

He grinned that boyish grin that got her every time. He shucked his underwear and stepped into the tub and then sank down into the frothy bubbles. "Come here," he said hoarsely, catching her eyes with his hot gaze.

She shook her head and moved around the perimeter away from him. "No, Colin. No more."

"You asked me to make love to you. What better place than right here?"

She grinned but held firm to her resolve. It was going to be hard enough saying a silent good-bye as it was. "I asked you to have sex with me. Not make love. And that was before—"

Lightning quick, he struck out a hand and grabbed her wrist. She squealed as he pulled her toward him. Her bottom moved helplessly in the warm oiled water.

"Would you believe me if I told you that in all the years I have been sexually active, I have only made love to one woman, one time?"

"That's a lie! You've had sex with every girl at St. John's and probably every woman in New York!"

"Except one."

Sophia stopped fighting him, her curiosity piqued. "So you're saying for you there is a difference between having sex and making love?"

"Isn't there for you?"

"Well, yes, but I didn't think—"

"The caveman could distinguish between the two acts?"

She shrugged. "Something like that."

He drew her into the circle of his arms. "There's a lot more to me than meets the eye." Her bottom slid up his thighs and his very thick, very rigid cock speared the inside of her thigh.

She caught her breath. If she just moved an inch or two to the left, he would be inside of her. "Yes, there"—she swallowed hard trying to breath normally—"certainly is."

His hands locked behind her waist as he pulled her even closer to him. Sophia grabbed his shoulders, pushing him away as she arched, resisting.

"You have amazing tits," he groaned, catching a taut nipple in his mouth.

The delicious sensation sent shock waves straight to her pussy. "Oh." She gasped, not knowing what else to say. Her entire body lit up in a torrent of flames.

His hands slid down her slick back, his fingers grasping her butt cheeks. He moved his hips and his cock popped up between them.

As Colin captured the other nipple he hoarsely said, "Touch me, Sophie."

The ache in his voice was too much to resist. Sophia opened her eyes and stared into his deep blue ones. Her right hand slid down his hard, slick chest, down his belly to his hip. When she touched the wide tip of his cock, he hissed in a breath and flexed against her palm. She traced her fingertip around the head, then just below it. He thrust against her. Yet she didn't fully touch him. She traced her fingers down the pulsing vein on the underside of his shaft and gently cupped his balls.

"You're a prick tease, Sophia," he growled before he devoured her nipple.

The passion of his possessive action stirred her primal woman. He tightened his grip on her derrière, pressing her fully against his hips. Sophia threw her head back and grasped his straining cock and slowly began to pump him.

She wondered what it would be like to make love to his cock again. She didn't think of the ways Angelo demeaned her when he forced her to touch him in ways she didn't want to. Colin was nothing like Angelo. He enjoyed pleasing her. Making her feel as if she were the only woman in his world.

His big hands slid around to her breasts, cupping them as his lips suckled her. Her entire body loosened, and Sophia let herself go with it. She wanted this night. She would kill for one hundred more, but she knew she could only have this one. It would have to be enough. She took Colin into both of her hands and in slow, deliberate strokes, she worked him into such a lather his hips bucked against her. His breathing became labored. Abruptly Sophia move away from him. She shut the faucets off and turned to him. His skin flushed red, his chest rose and fell in short, shallow turns. "Sit on the seat," she hoarsely said pointing to the seat carved into the marble.

He eyed her skeptically but did as she said. Only his legs and ass were in the water, and that glorious erection of his shimmered hotly like an obelisk rising from the seven seas. She moved toward him and sat up on her knees. "I owe you for last night," she teased, then licked a wide swath around the head of his dick. His hips rose. She pushed him back into the seat. And then went down on him.

---

Colin's body stiffened as she took his cock all the way down to her tonsils. His fingers dug into her silky soft hair. God, he loved the way she sucked him. Like she was worshiping him. Slow, deep, reverent. Her hands stroked, cupping his balls gently. Her tongue was lethal the way it flicked and rolled around his head. He was so fucking stiff, he was literally in pain. He wanted inside of her so bad he wasn't sure what he would do if she said no.

Her head moved up and down, her tongue licking him like a melting ice-cream cone on a hot summer day. Her lips were locked, soft and succulent, clamped around him as if he were her last meal. Her hands wrapped around him as she sucked. Slow, deep, up and down. "Jesus Christ." He was coming as quick as a sixteen-year-old. Her lips tightened and her hands again cupped his balls. His fingers tightened around her head, his hips thrust in and out of her mouth. "Sophia!" he cried out as he came in a violent burst in her mouth. She hung on, and with those luscious lips of hers, she sucked every ounce of cum from his balls.

Colin's chest rose and fell in short, shallow dips as he reached out his arms and hung on to the edge of the tub. He slumped back against the marble side. He could not take his eyes off Sophia's pink little tongue darting and licking the last vestiges of his ejaculation from his still very hard cock. Just the sight of her kept him hard. Her lips were so red, lush, and soft. Her slender fingers stroked him. Her nails were short but neat, with a clear coat of polish on them. Her skin was as flushed as her lips, smooth and sultry from the humidity and the oil. The urge to fuck her was so overwhelming, he swelled in her hand.

"You are evil," he moaned, pulling her up into his lap. Slipping his arms around her, he nuzzled her neck. Her pulse beat wildly against his lips. Loosing his fingers in her wild mass of hair, he pulled back just enough to kiss her, not caring that she just swallowed what she swallowed. Her lips—soft, willing, inviting—parted for his. He lost himself in her. She turned into him, her skin sliding against his. Every lush curve of her body imprinted itself on his skin. He was losing himself to her, and he didn't know how to stop it. "That was amazing," he said softly.

She smiled against his lips. "I'm glad you enjoyed it. That was my inaugural blow job."

"What?" He didn't believe it. Surely, she and her husband . . .

"Angelo left that to his whores. I was happy to let him." She wrapped her arms around his neck and rubbed her hot tits against his chest. "I'm sure you've had better, but I'm glad I didn't disappoint you."

He tightened his arms around her. "I'm not going to lie to you and say I've never had a blow job before, but I can honestly say, no woman has ever made it into such—art."

She smacked him and wiggled out of his lap and slid across the huge tub to the other side. She picked up a big sponge and poured bath oil onto it. The way she was sitting, she was exposed tits up. She smeared the sponge across her full tits. Her nipples stiffened. So did his dick. "Sophia," he said hoarsely. Her big green eyes looked up at him trustingly. He swallowed hard. Her life was literally in his hands. A rush of emotion so foreign to him that it felt like a kick to the gut took him so completely by surprise he could not speak. It wasn't just him protecting her because it was his job, it was more than that. Much, much more. So much more that he could not define it. He didn't want to. It scared the shit out of him.

"Colin?" she asked, looking concerned.

He shook his head and collected himself. He smiled, covering his momentary nose dive into sentimentality.

God help him, but he wanted a future with one woman—*this* woman. Yes, damn it. *This* woman. The *only* woman. The realization was emancipating and terrifying at the same time. He didn't want to feel what he felt. It was complicated with his work, and he needed time for the emotions to settle—they were so damn new and un-expected. "I'm going to fuck you proper." He sunk into the tub and moved toward her. "Then, I'm going to make love to you like you've never been made love to before."

He watched her process his words, then decide if she was going to play coy or— She shook her head as her eyes filled with tears. Christ. What had he done now?

"Colin, I—" She looked down at her hand holding the sponge. A tear plopped on her breast. "I don't want this. I mean—" She looked up at him. "I do. But I'm afraid I'll—"

He shushed her with a finger to her lips. He knew what she was going to say. Sex would complicate things. Why did it for women but not men? Or at least, not him? Well, the first time it complicated things for him. What he felt as he held her in his arms all those years ago scared him witless. He had run. Far and fast. He traced a finger across her right breast. "I won't hold it against you for whatever you feel for me, Sophie."

Her cheeks reddened, and her eyes flashed. "Because while I may have feelings for you, and sex or making love will most likely make me feel more, it's okay because you're a fucking emotional retard?"

Colin blanched at her outburst. "I have feelings too, you know." Feelings that, if he admitted them, would change everything in his life. Looking down the barrel of gun? No sweat. Telling Sophia he loved her? Terrifying.

"What exactly are your feelings for me, Colin?"

He wanted to say the words but he chickened out. "I'm attracted to you."

"You're attracted to anything with a vagina and tits!"

"That's not true!"

"Oh, I'm sorry, how careless of me. You're attracted to anything with a vagina, tits, and shit for brains." She threw the sponge at him and climbed out of the tub.

He could not help but admire how her flushed skin glistened, and how sleek and fuckable her lush body looked. She turned a hot gaze on him. He grinned at her. "You're impossible!" she shrieked.

She grabbed a towel and wrapped it around her body and stomped from the bathroom.

# Chapter 7

Knowing he had to fix what he just broke, Colin stepped dripping wet from the tub and strode naked into the bedroom. Wrapped tightly in her towel as if it would protect her from the world, Sophia sat in a rattan peacock chair near the window. She turned her head and stared daggers at him. He knew why she was mad, and knew he was a coward for not professing his feelings. He knew how to fix it, but he just could not quite pull the trigger. What if he was just caught up in the heat of the moment? His stomach did a slow roll. He raked his fingers through his hair and looked sheepishly at her. "Does this mean we're not having sex now?"

She pounced with the swiftness of a tiger. The velocity of her hit sent him sprawling back against the small table behind him. She screamed, snarled, punched, and kicked him.

Colin tried to wrap his arms around her to stop her attack but the oil on her body made her as slippery as a seal. She kicked his instep. He lost his balance and they went tumbling onto the floor. Colin turned to take the brunt of the fall, but even though they landed on a soft alpaca throw, the hit jarred his stitches. It hurt like hell.

"You are a miserable excuse for a man!" Sophia railed. "My husband was more of gentleman than you!" She pummeled his chest.

Colin didn't like what she was saying but he liked the way she way saying it. It was better than the weepy emotional scaredy-cat she'd been. Grinning, he rolled over onto her. Her eyes widened when his thickening cock speared the inside of her thigh. Oh, hell, he was so close. Her skin was so slick that if she moved so much as an inch he would be inside of her.

Colin swallowed hard and, just for the sheer pleasure of ruffling her feathers more, he said, "So that's a no?"

"Argh! You are impossible!" She strained against him. Her nipples were hard as pebbles against his chest, her skin had warmed, and she was trembling. He lowered his nose to her neck and inhaled. "I yam what I yam."

She made a choking noise and he kissed the pulse in her jugular despite the way she strained against him. "And what I am is sorry for hurting your feelings."

"Colin," she hissed. Didn't matter. He could feel her body call to his. She wanted him just as he much as he wanted her.

"Sophia," he answered, kissing her behind the ear. Tenderness was an unfamiliar feeling blooming in his chest.

She raised her knee again. He blocked it with his own. The action thrust his hips higher between her legs. Tenderness gave way to primal heat.

The head of his cock tapped into her slick folds. Sophia's eyes widened and her body gripped him. He clenched his jaw so hard he was afraid he'd break his teeth. Her body sizzled and pulsed around his cock with such intensity that he could not—

She shifted and—Ah, Jesus. He slid another inch into her. They both gasped, but still she pushed him away. "For the love of God, Sophia," he rasped. "Let me in."

She inhaled sharply, pushing at his shoulders while her hips moved upward and her pussy lured him in deeper. She was giving mixed messages. He was but a mere man and she the almighty, all-powerful woman. Her velvety muscles clenched and unclenched around his throbbing cock, seducing him in the way only a woman's body could.

He was on the verge of a compete meltdown. Perspiration beaded on his forehead. He did not move, not even a flinch. Their bodies were as rigid as steel beams. It was all Colin could do not to sink balls deep into her. Her body was so slick with oil, each time she inhaled he slipped a little deeper into her, and with each exhale she pushed him back. He thrust, she parried. He dug his fingers into her hair and rested his forehead against hers. The slight movement took him another inch deeper into her.

He squeezed his eyes shut, clamped his jaw tight, and fought his body's natural inclination to move deeper into her and mate. Her warm body trembled beneath him. Her breathing was fast and furious. He opened his eyes and stared into her big green eyes; only then did he realize they were shimmering with tears.

The sight broke him. He did not want to hurt her. Would never intentionally make her cry. He was acting like a cad. He knew he could beguile his way into her, but that was not how he wanted her. He kissed her on the lips and said, "I'm sorry."

Gently, he moved away from her.

"No, Colin, stay," she whispered. Instead of pushing him away again, her hands suddenly clung to him.

His chest hurt. That crazy feeling he felt in the bathtub was back. "Are you sure?"

She nodded and smiled though her tears.

"Don't cry, sweetheart." He kissed her tears away and, as he did, he slid into her. It was the most sublime moment of his life.

Sophia had spent more than a decade longing for Colin. A decade of dreaming and wondering if it had all been just a schoolgirl's fantasy spun out of control. Now that dream had come full circle. It was the fantasy lived out, but even better. His fingers traced her eyes, her cheeks, her nose, and her lips as he allowed her body to accommodate his length and width. When he rocked into her, she gasped and arched. Dear Lord, that felt so damn good.

Sophia wrapped her arms around his neck. "Colin," she breathed as he began to gently rock into her. She didn't want gentle; she wanted hot, fast, and urgent. Then she wanted slow, agonizing, and deep. "That feels so good."

His lips melted into hers as his hips thrust slowly, deeply, wantonly. She opened her body, mind, and soul to him. There was nothing she would not give Colin Daniels at that moment. Even her life. He made her feel like no man had in over ten years. He was just as deep, just as reverent, just as gentle. Tears burned her eyes. *Oh, Colin, why couldn't it have been you?*

"It is me, sweetheart, here and now. I'm all yours," he whispered against her lips.

Her cheeks flamed. Oh my God, she had actually spoken her thoughts out loud!

"Yes," she said. "Here and now." Because there would be no tomorrow.

He pushed her hard, then soft, then fast, then slow. Each time he rocked her to the edge of oblivion, he pulled her back only to thrust her to the edge and yank her back again. His hips ground and thrust, gave then took. Sophia became delirious with the need to climax, but each time she was about to scream from the mountaintops, Colin slowed, only to build her up again, the next time more potent. Finally, she thrashed and cried and begged him to let her go. When he did, Sophia shot straight to the stars, where she exploded into a million shimmering shards of sensation. She hung suspended as the fire burst into another fire, then another, higher and higher like the fireworks on the Fourth of July. When the last burst exploded, Colin shot up beside her, his body convulsing and the fire burning him up inside, just as hers had. And then, together, they began their soulful descent back to earth.

They crashed hard. Together they lay spent, barely able to breathe a steady cadence, knowing their lives had just been irrevocably changed forever.

Long, saturated moments passed before Colin lifted her up into his arms and laid her on the big comfortable bed. He climbed in beside her and pulled her into his arms. For a long time they lay, limbs entangled, listening to the crash of the waves outside the window. Sophia's body still shimmered from the intensity of Colin's lovemaking.

She closed her eyes and licked her lips, imagining him taking her again, and again, and again. She sighed as his lips kissed a hard nipple and his big hand slid down her belly to her smooth mound. He rubbed the tip of his index finger around her straining clit. Sophia moaned as small bursts of sensation electrified her.

"You are so dewy and ripe," Colin whispered against her nipple. "Like a juicy peach." His finger sunk into her pussy. She moaned as her liquid muscles wrapped lovingly around him. "So swollen." He nipped her nipple. She gasped. "So receptive." His lips trailed down her belly to her hip, where he nibbled, then licked a long swath across her shaved pubis and around her sensitive clit. He slid his finger from her and pressed his lips to her weeping labia. "So succulent." He lapped her slit, rolling his tongue in and around her.

Sophia's body was so turned on, she wanted him everywhere. She cupped her breasts and tugged her nipples. She moaned when he slid another finger deep into her. His lips teased her sensitive clitoris, driving her insane with slow, torturous swirls as his fingers thrust in and out of her and his free hand cupped one of her breasts.

Sophia reached down and pulled his hand to her lips to suck his index finger. He moaned and moved hotly against her.

In slow, undulating swirls, Sophia moved her hips to the cadence of Colin's lips and fingers. He vibrated his fingers inside of her, tapping a spot so sweet and so responsive she shuddered each time he did. He removed one slick finger, slipped it between her ass cheeks, and pressed against her opening there. Not realizing that spot was so sensitive, she moaned. In response, his lips clamped onto her clit just as his finger tapped her sweet spot with deep, quick thrusts. It sent her reeling. He brought her to the edge, then shoved her over it.

She screamed as she fell into a shattering orgasm. She gaped for air like a beached fish. Her body had slickened with sultry perspiration, and her limbs once again became noodle-limp as each orgasmic wave hit her sensitive shores. No sooner had her body stopped convulsing than Colin turned her over and pulled her up to all fours. He wrapped an arm around her belly and slid his thick cock into her. Sophia hung suspended in a time warp of sensation overload. Every part of her thrummed. He filled her so completely, she could not move. And, oh God, each time he hit that sweet spot dead-on, her entire body melted like butter in the sun.

When he began to rock into her, Sophia nearly wept because the passion he evoked from her was so extreme. He moved back and grabbed the cradle of her hips, then arched his body, thrusting high and deep. Sophia muffled a scream, the pleasure so intense she was moved to tears.

She pushed back, grinding on him, and he rotated his hips, grinding into her. Their connection was so completely sublime she could not imagine ever experiencing it again. So she didn't. She reveled in the moment as he moved deep, hot, and long inside of her, his rhythm in perfect time with hers.

"Colin!" She gasped as she came in one long, grinding orgasm, the intensity almost too much to bear. She screamed, thrashing against him, as if she were impaled. He moved so fast in and out of her she felt as if she were going to fall off the face of the earth.

His body tensed. "My God, Sophia," he groaned. His hips trembled and then, as she had before him, Colin came in a wild torrential explosion.

She collapsed beneath him, unable to hold herself up, her limbs like putty.

He fell atop her and, still connected, they drifted into an exhausted sleep.

***

Still on her belly, Sophia awoke to a warm wet cloth between her legs. Her pussy was sore, but damn if she didn't want him inside of her again. He swept her wild mass of hair from her back and shoulders, his big hand leaving warm tingles in its wake. When he dripped warm oil down her back, Sophia moaned, pressing her sensitive pussy against the soft comforter. She dug her fingers into the smooth fabric, anticipating another wild sensual romp with the master of ceremonies. Beginning at her shoulders, he kneaded and rubbed the oil into her tired muscles. His strong fingers dug into her flesh, loosening the knots, then smoothing them. He rubbed her back, her arms, her hands, and her fingers. He avoided her hips and between her thighs, making her burn with want. When he slid his fingers across her ass cheeks, she rose against his hand, begging for more.

His lips pressed against the small of her back as he slipped his fingers between her cheeks, then out and then between again, this time deeper. The first time he brushed his fingertip across her anus, she stiffened in surprise and embarrassment. "Relax, love," he crooned. "Relax." The second time, he swirled his finger around the sensitive spot, she popped her bottom up. The third time, he pressed more firmly and nipped her cheek with his teeth. She had never let another man touch her like that. Only Colin. She moaned, a willing partner, enjoying the new sexy sensation, anxious to see how far he would go and how exciting it would feel.

She pressed her knees into the comforter, giving him more access, letting him know she was game. "That's a girl." He continued rubbing her anus. Sophia moaned, pressing her bottom against the pressure. His lips trailed along her cheeks, kissing, nipping, licking. The slickness of the oil coupled with the strange but erotic feeling of Colin's finger swirling around her anus caught her off guard. She gasped in a breath and pushed back into his fingertip. His tongue slid between her ass cheeks as his fingertip tapped gently into her opening. Sophia swallowed hard and tightened up.

"Relax, Sophie," he crooned. Gently, he turned her over onto her back and pressed her thighs open. He slid his thick middle finger deep into her dripping, clenching pussy, as his tongue slid back and forth across her sensitive clit. The tip of his finger rubbed her anus, pressing gently for entry.

Sophia dug her fingers into his hair and let her thighs loosen and fall open. She'd never thought of doing such a thing, but with Colin it seemed like the most natural thing to do. His finger gently, persistently teased her to total relaxation. "I want to take you to places you've never gone before."

And she wanted to go there with him. Only him. Sophia closed her eyes completely, losing herself in the eroticism of the act. With one finger inserted deep into her pussy, the other in her anus, and his lips locked around her clit, teasing and taunting it to the point of shattering, he breathed, "You okay?"

Sophia opened her mouth to answer, but he began to gently rock into her with a slow, steady cadence. Her clit pulsated. He hit her

G-spot and some other spot in her anus she had no name for. The combination of sensations was so overwhelming, and felt so damn good, her body could not process the overstimulation.

"God, yessss," she crooned. He pushed her higher, then higher again, so high she lost sight of earth. So high she could not breathe, so high she felt as if she had indeed died and gone to heaven. No modesty, no inhibitions, just pure, unadulterated passion with a man she barely knew but felt she had known a lifetime. And then, her entire body liquefied as if it came apart all around her. Sophia screamed as her clit, pussy, and anus convulsed as one, then fell apart. In a wild spiral, she twisted, turned, and undulated as lightning repeatedly struck every erogenous zone in her body.

And in her spiral, he pushed her higher, into the moon, sun, and the stars, before she crashed. Sophia lay broken, heaving, gasping for air as her body twitched and trembled, the convulsions crashing into her, multiple orgasms licking her nerve endings raw. Then Colin sunk his hot, thick cock so far into her, she felt him hit the tip of her womb and she shattered all over again.

His lips took hers, his tongue tangling with hers as he thrust into her with an urgency that belied the act. It was full of emotion. Of a need so deep and profound, it transcended his body into hers. His head might deny what his body professed, but Sophia knew he cared for her, more deeply than he admitted.

Just as another wave slammed into her, his body strained, jerked, and he released inside of her with such an explosion she felt his warm seed fill her. His slick body collapsed against hers, and they stared at each other in wonder and awe, as they struggled to gain a sense of what had just happened.

Colin rolled over, pulling her in to his arms, his body trembling in time with hers.

They lay unmoving except for their bodies struggling to regain normalcy. But even hours later, as the sun sank into the churning

Pacific, their bodies still entwined, Sophia knew nothing would ever be normal for her again.

"Colin?" Sophia whispered.

"Hmmm," he answered lazily.

"Tell me about the one woman you made love to." She didn't know why she asked, especially after all that had happened between them in the last few hours, but her female curiousity got the better of her. She wanted to know if he still had feelings for her, even though it was none of her business.

He lifted his tousled head from where he'd been resting between her breasts and looked at her with hooded, laconic eyes. He smiled and kissed a nipple. "Her name was Cinderella."

Sophia stiffened. "Cinderella?"

"Uh-huh. That's how I think of her. She left me after we made love, without even a glass slipper to cherish the memory. I never saw her again."

Jealousy prickled her heart. "Did she go to St. John's?"

He kissed the other nipple, then licked it. It immediately perked up. "Yes." He looked into her eyes and smiled that cat-that-ate-the-canary smile. "What about you, Sophia? Any long-lost loves?"

She set her jaw, wanting to tell him everything, but she hesitated. He'd think she was foolish and she'd get really pissed when he wouldn't remember. She should just leave it alone. But she didn't. "There was a boy in high school."

"What happened?"

"Angelo happened. But even if he hadn't, the boy barely knew I existed."

His lips trailed along the pulsing vein in her neck to her chin. "Oh, I doubt that. You are a hard girl to forget."

Sophia stiffened. "Not when he had a thousand girls throwing their panties at him."

He chuckled. "You think so?"

His hand slid down her belly to her warm mound. Sophia tried to ignore the eruption of sensation. "Did you—have feelings for Cinderella?"

He slid his finger around her slick folds and her body immediately salivated for him. "Jesus, Sophia. Your pussy is insatiable."

"Only for you." Aware that he'd avoided answering her question, she pushed him onto his back. She nipped his nipple, then sucked it. She looked down at his intense gaze. "Did you have feelings for Cinderella?" she asked more forcefully.

"Yes."

"What kind of feelings?" she asked, jealous of a ghost.

She felt his cock thicken against her thigh. She raised a brow and cocked her head.

He grinned. "Those kind of feelings. And, the kind of feelings you have for someone who is pure of heart and who gives themselves to you selflessly."

Sophia was dumbstruck by his words. Was this Colin Daniels speaking? Her shock must have shown on her face. "I'm not a complete Neanderthal, Sophia. Of course it took me a long time to realize just how special she was."

Pain flashed through her. *Be careful what you ask for, Sophia, you might get it.*

His hands ran down her back to her ass. "Did anyone ever tell you how special you are?" She shook her head. He reached up and kissed a petulant nipple. "How brave and generous you are?" He suckled her nipple deep into his mouth and tongued it. Then he pulled her lips down to his. "How fucking hot you are?" His cock thickened against the inside of her thighs. He rolled her over and slid into her. "How fucking tight you are?" Sophia closed her eyes and surrendered to him. "How sweet your pussy is?"

"No," she whispered.

He cupped her breasts, pushing them together, sucking one nipple, then another. "God, I love your tits."

*I love you, Colin.*

"I love the way your body responds to me." He slowly undulated against her. "How you let yourself go. So trusting. So sensitive." He thrust deeper into her. "So greedy for more."

Emotion swelled with the fierceness of a tsunami in her chest. It threatened to wreck her entire world. Colin Daniels tried to come off as a womanizer of the highest order, but he was a man who felt deep. She loved him more for it, even though he didn't love her. Sophia wrapped her arms around his neck and pulled him tightly to her. "Colin," she cried. "I'm afraid."

"Shhh, sweetheart. I will stand by you every step of the way."

And if it were against any other man than Angelo Gilletti, she'd let him. "Make love to me, Colin, like there is no tomorrow."

# Chapter 8

Colin woke to an empty bed. At first, he thought Sophia was just in the bathroom, but when he realized the sheets beside him were cold, he jackknifed to a sitting position. The room was completely dark. He fumbled around for a light. Finding a lamp on the nightstand, he turned it on. Her clean clothes were gone!

He leapt from the bed and ran down the hall to the kitchen. Empty. The entire first floor was vacant. He ran upstairs, and before he got to the captain's room, his two mastiffs were furiously barking.

"Captain!" Colin said. "Tell me Sophia is in there with you!"

The door jerked open and the captain was shrugging on a shirt, taking earphones out of his ears. "Huh?"

"Sophia? Is she in there?"

"Hell no!" He held up the earphones. Colin could hear music blaring. "I had to put these on because you two were so damn loud last night."

Panic tore through him. "She's gone, damn it!"

The captain laughed and pointed at Colin's half-hard cock. "You probably scared her away with that monster pecker."

He had to find her! "I'm getting dressed. I'm going to look for her. I won't say no to help."

Colin raced down the stairs to get dressed. The captain called after him. "Did you put a GPS in her with your dick? Otherwise, only pure luck will help you find her."

"I'm feeling lucky tonight," Colin called back to him and ran to the bedroom. Why had she flown? Did she not trust that he would protect her? As he came out of the room two minutes later, the captain had both of his dogs leashed.

"Spartacus and Caesar have the two best noses in this county. Grab something with her scent on it. The boys will find her."

Colin ran back into the bedroom and grabbed the towel Sophia had used and ran back to the captain. He let both of the drooling dogs sniff then said, "Find it, boys. Find the girl!"

They put their noses to the air, then to the ground. They picked up her scent and went straight into the bedroom, then to the big bay window, and through it. Colin followed the captain through, and they were hot on her trail. The dogs kept their noses diligently to the ground in a crazy, haphazard trail. It was apparent Sophia had no clue where she was going. Twice she ended up at a dead end. And twice she crossed the road to the beach and ran through the water. But the mastiffs picked her scent back up. Almost two miles down the road, the dogs began to get excited. They led him to a van parked at the end of a dark driveway of a house that looked as if the occupants were on an extended stay.

"Call the dogs off, Cappy. I'll finish," Colin said, striding angrily toward the van.

Cappy backed off about fifty yards. Colin tried all of the doors. They were locked. Frustrated, Colin shook the van. "Sophia, unlock the door!"

Silence.

Fine.

Colin pressed his fingers up and around each of the wheel wells, hoping to find a hidden key. No luck. He felt around the fender. Nothing. He lifted the hood of the vintage van and felt around the inside lip of the hood. Nothing. But she didn't have to know that.

"I found a key, Sophia."

Nothing.

Damn stubborn woman! Didn't she know she was in danger running alone? "Unlock the door. *Now.*"

Finally some movement. She moved up to the driver's seat, where he was standing. She rolled the window down a few inches. Tears stained her red puffy eyes. His heart broke for her. But more than that, euphoria swept through him. He would never let her go. Not now, not when he had just found her again. "Sophia."

She shook her head. "No, Colin. I'm not going back there!"

"Open the door."

She sniffed hard and jerked it open. "You can't force me."

"I won't force you."

Her head jerked back. "You won't?"

"No. I won't. But I want you to tell me why you don't believe I can protect you."

She swiped her shirtsleeve across her runny nose. "I trust you! I know you would die protecting me! But I'll never be able to live with him alive. And Colin"—she grabbed his shirt—"Angelo will get you. I care too much about you to let that happen."

"I care too much about you to let him hurt you. Or to let you run from me just because you're afraid."

"You don't understand! As long as he's alive, we're both dead!" She sniffed and dropped her bomb. "I'm not testifying. I'm going back to him."

Rage and terror swept though him. No! She would not go back

to him. Never! Gilletti would destroy her. Colin would never allow that. "Sophia," he calmly said, taking her face into his hands. He looked earnestly into her terrified green eyes. "Listen to me. You will never be able to live until you are free of Angelo. The only way to do that is to put him in prison."

"He'll kill us both."

"Do you have so little faith in me?"

"I know Angelo."

"And I know you."

"No, you—"

"Yes." Colin looked at her and said softly, "I once knew a brave girl who took on the biggest, baddest guy in town to save the people she loved. But before she sold herself to the devil, she gave herself to a man who didn't deserve her. A man who never forgot her or the one night they spent together." He smoothed the wisps of hair from her cheeks. "I went looking for you, Cinderella, but you were gone. Then I had no choice but to ship out."

His words knocked the breath from her chest. He knew! He went looking for her? Sophia's heart thudded like a kettledrum in her chest. Her eyes stung with fresh tears. "You . . . remembered?"

He kissed her damp cheeks. "How could I forget?" He kissed her nose and her lips. "And now that I've found you, Maria Sophia Castavettes, you want me to walk away?"

"I—Oh, Colin. I'm so afraid."

"Trust me, please."

She took a leap of faith, and threw her arms around his neck and clung to him. "I do, Colin. I do."

———

Several hours later, they were headed for New York City on Captain O'Malley's private plane, piloted by none other than the captain himself. Colin called the DA's direct line, brought him up to speed, and discussed when and where to meet. He made it clear that the DA was not to inform anyone of their meeting time or place. No one. Colin was taking no chances.

Sophia slept for most of the flight. An hour out, Colin roused her.

"Cinderella," he said with a smile, "I need to talk to you about a few things before we land."

She rubbed the sleep from her eyes and nodded. He handed her one of the cell phones. "Put this in your pocket and keep it on vibrate in case we get separated."

"Separated?"

"I'm going to handcuff you to me the minute I get within reach of a set, but just in case, take it."

Reluctantly she did. "We're meeting the DA in his office. I told him four hours, but we're going to be there in less than two."

# Chapter 9

In three hours, Sophia destroyed what had taken the Gilletti family decades to build. She promised to back her incriminating declaration with documents, bank account numbers, and names. The DA was dancing on his desk with glee.

Colin sat silent for almost the entire three hours, his pride and admiration for Sophia growing with each minute. She was the bravest woman he knew. And she was his. His stomach did weird rolls and flops each time he thought about how deeply he felt for her. In the three hours he sat beside Sophia, he had mentally rearranged his life so that he could have one with her.

When they were finished, Colin stood. "If you've got everything you need for now, I'll be taking Sophia to a safe house."

"We'll be issuing a warrant for Gilletti's arrest within the hour," the DA said.

"His lawyers will have him out before you fingerprint him," Colin said. He took Sophia's hand and gave her a reassuring smile. She looked exhausted. Hell, he was surprised she was still standing after all she had been through. He pulled her against him. "I'm taking Sophia off the grid. No known safe houses."

"Do you think that's wise?"

"Someone has been spoon-feeding Gilletti information. I don't trust anyone." And when he found the leak he was going to plug it. Permanently.

"If you need protection, my office can provide it."

Colin shook his head. "With what, a couple of DA investigators?"

"They're all former or retired law enforcement. I had my secretary contact two of them right after your arrival. They're arranging a safe haven as we speak."

Sophia stiffened beside him. Colin was furious. "That wasn't part of our deal, damn you! Not knowing where the leak is, Gilletti has had time to set an ambush. We're fucked."

Sophia squeezed his hand. "Maybe we should trust him, Colin."

Colin took her face into his hands and said, "Right now there are only two people in this world I trust: me and you, period. Thanks for nothing, Mr. Ross, but we'll go it alone." Colin took Sophia's hand and led her from the office into the outer lobby and down the hall, his senses on high alert. Near the elevators, he could see a man in a suit, apparently waiting for the elevator, but when the doors opened and then closed, he didn't get on. Before the man could turn around to see the two of them, Colin pushed Sophia ahead of him into an office. "Don't question anything I tell you, just do it. Okay?" Colin said.

"I will," Sophia said, her voice trembling.

It killed him that she was so afraid. It killed him that he had forced her here. He should have let her go.

"May I help you?" a clerk asked from behind a counter.

"No," Colin said.

"Did you two want to get married?" she asked.

"What?" they answered in unison.

The gnome of a woman smiled. "We're temporarily issuing marriage licenses out of this office while the city clerk's offices are being painted. Did you want a marriage license?"

"Oh, hell no!" Colin quickly assured her. Maybe too quickly. Sophia elbowed him in the ribs. "I mean, not today. Is there a fire exit from inside of here?"

"Well, yes, but you'd have to—"

"Where is it?" Colin was getting antsy. It was too quiet out in the hallway.

"Well . . . through that office." The clerk pointed to a door on the other side of the counter. Colin had already scanned the room and found no access through the counter. Scooping Sophia up into his arms, he slid her across the counter and then jumped over it himself.

"Thank you, ma'am." They hurried through the door and into a small corridor with a window, unisex bathroom, and a door with an Exit sign above it.

Colin hurried to the door, dragging Sophia along with him. "If I'm right, we don't have much time. In fact, we may already be out of time."

"Do you have a plan?"

"My plan is the same as it was in the beginning: to protect your life." Colin opened the door to the stairwell and they began a quick descent. "When we get outside, I'll find us a car. I'll bet my retirement your husband is on his way."

"Pray he isn't," Sophia said, then with a shaky hand, made the sign of the cross.

At the bottom of the stairs, they halted momentarily. If they went through the door the alarm would sound. Colin looked down at her heeled shoes.

"You can't run in those. Take them off," he said.

"And go barefoot?"

"Yes."

He caught her up into his arms and looked deep into her misty emerald eyes. "I love you, Sophia. We're going to get through this. I promise." He kissed her hard, then looked at the fire exit. "I don't know what's on the other side of that door. Whatever it is, we may not have much time to think or figure things out. When I say *go* or *jump* or whatever the hell I say, you need to be ready to just do it."

"I trust you, Colin." She grabbed his chin and brought his lips down to hers and said, "I love you. We're going to get through this. I promise." She kissed him hard then pulled away. "I'm ready when you are."

"Let's go."

Sophia kicked her shoes off and grabbed them. Colin slammed the door open. The alarm immediately began to wail. They bolted toward the parking lot. Colin quickly scanned the perimeters into the interior, searching for a moving vehicle to commandeer. Two rows up he saw a man, his arms full of files and a briefcase, making his way toward a car. Some schmuck public defense attorney, he thought. He grabbed Sophia's hand. "C'mon." And headed in his direction. From the corner of his eye, Colin saw a black SUV with dark tinted windows rolling their way.

"Fuck!"

"Is it Angelo?" Sophia cried. Her body was shaking so hard she could barely keep step with him.

"Keep moving!" He urged her forward. The SUV was quickly moving toward them, and while they gained on the schmuck, he didn't seem any closer to his vehicle than when Colin first spotted him. However, he still remained their most viable option. Whoever was driving the SUV had already figured out Colin's plan and was bearing down on them. Clearing the last row of parked cars, Colin turned them to the right, away from the encroaching SUV and toward their hopeful getaway.

"It's getting closer!" Sophia shouted as she realized what was happening.

"Your car! Which one is your car?" Colin shouted as he spun the man around.

"I beg your . . . ?"

"I don't have any fucking time for this!" Colin shouted. "I'm a cop! I need your car!"

"Are you going to take my car? Like they do in the movies?" the idiot asked.

"Your car, damn it!" The low rumble of the SUV was almost upon them. Colin snatched the car keys from the man and hit the unlock button. A low chirp answered.

Colin ran toward it.

"The red minivan, right there," the owner shouted.

"You need to go!" Sophia yelled at the man, pushing him in the opposite direction of the oncoming SUV. "Run, quickly! Don't stay here, go now!"

"Sophia!" Colin shouted. "Get over here!"

Colin turned back to get her. She shoved the man back when he refused to run and turned into the driveway. And in that hesitation, it was too late for both of them. Sophia cleared the racing SUV but the willing Samaritan was not as lucky.

"Sophia!" Colin screamed as his view of her was blocked by the SUV pulling just past her. Shots rang out from the front window, dotting the minivan. Colin took cover behind the rear wheel and drew his weapon. Just as quickly as it had appeared, the SUV was in reverse making a quick getaway with Sophia inside.

Colin's heart pounded like a sledgehammer against his rib cage. He jumped in the van and fired it up. He quickly maneuvered the box on wheels and was soon right behind the SUV. They raced out of the parking lot and onto the city streets.

———————

Sophia's heart rammed high in her throat, making breathing difficult. But she would not show Angelo fear. He fed off it. He shoved her against the window.

Her husband's dark features twisted with rage. "Sit still or I kill you right here!" he screamed.

She kicked him in the shin. He backhanded her. She slapped him. Under any other circumstances, she would have laughed at his stunned face. "I'm not afraid of you, Angelo!"

He laughed and raised his hand again. She slapped it away.

"Your brief independence has changed you. Or was it that cop you were fucking?"

"Fuck you, Angelo. You can kill me, but I gave the DA everything, including the safe-deposit boxes with all your dirty little secrets stashed away."

"A wife cannot testify against her husband."

"I'll have our sham of a marriage annulled. I was never your *wife*. I was your money-laundering hookup."

The vehicle swerved, throwing Sophia against the man she would kill with her own two hands if given the opportunity.

Angelo shoved her off him and looked out the back window. "Is that your boyfriend back there? Is that the man you've been fucking?" He sneered.

"At least he's a real man and with a real cock." Sophia spoke loud enough for Angelo's henchmen in the front seats to hear her. She turned the screws. "He's so big your prize stallion would be embarrassed to stand next to him. And he can fuck all night long! All. Night. Long! Angelo!"

The back end of the SUV lurched to the right from the impact of the minivan slamming into it on the left rear fender. The driver struggled to right the vehicle and managed to drive out of the skid. The impact momentarily freed Sophia, who was still holding her heels in her hands. Jumping up from the seat, she swung the left with a wild backhand, striking Angelo just below his right eye. Swinging her right hand with equal vengeance, Sophia struck the driver in his right cheek.

Angelo grabbed her left arm and pulled her back against him. Like a snake on hot asphalt, Sophia recoiled and struck him again with her heel, this time *in* the right eye. He screamed, grabbing at it. She went after the driver again, but the front passenger had turned. He shoved her back into her seat. The driver swerved as they were hit again.

———

Struggling to keep pace with the fleeing SUV, Colin continued to gain ground for another assault. He didn't want to think of what Sophia was enduring inside. All he could think of was stopping the SUV and getting her out of there, and then blowing Angelo Gilletti's fucking brains out.

He punched the gas pedal. This time the van struck home, the impact pushing the SUV into the curb. The velocity pushed the back of the vehicle into the air, causing it to flip onto its side. It skidded along the sidewalk for a short distance, coming to rest on an empty bus-stop bench and canopy.

Colin came to a skidding sideways stop. He leapt from the vehicle and rushed to the driver's door. When a head popped up like a ground squirrel on the prairie, Colin put a bullet in it, dropping him back inside. He quickly moved to the front of the vehicle to get a better view. Cautiously, he cleared the front end, where he found the front passenger had been launched through the windshield and onto the pavement. He heard the back doors slam open and Sophia's screams.

Angelo crawled out, dragging Sophia by her hair. He pushed her in front of his big body, using her as a human shield. Angelo waved a gun wildly around her head.

"Come near us and she's dead."

Colin carefully took aim but the shot was impossible.

"Let her go, Angelo! It's all over," Colin yelled, walking toward him, his gun aimed at Angelo's head.

Colin caught Sophia's eyes. He quickly dropped his, then looked back a her. She nodded in understanding.

"I want a car! You have five minutes or I blow her fucking brains out."

"It's over, Gilletti! See it for what it is. It's done."

"It's not done until I say it's done!" Gilletti screamed. His head swiveled, searching for an exit, a way out. "Four minutes," he shouted.

"The police are right behind me. Let Sophia go."

"I will never let her go! She is mine!" Gilletti roared, raising the gun to her head. Sophia dropped.

Colin pulled the trigger. The bullet hit Angelo in the right shoulder, twisting him back to one side. He tried to raise his gun but his shoulder wasn't responding. Reaching across his body with his left hand, he took the gun from his right hand. Colin pulled the trigger again. A fatal last round, center mass. The impact flung Angelo backward to the ground.

Sophia jumped up off the ground and ran to Colin. He grabbed her into his arms and squeezed her so hard, he was afraid he would break her ribs.

"Oh God, Colin, it's over! It's finally over."

He hugged her tighter, burying his nose into her soft hair, inhaling the sweet scent that was unique to her. He had never been so happy, scared, relieved, and terrified all at once. But trumping those emotions was the burgeoning love he felt for the brave woman in his arms.

She looked up at him, her face the most beautiful sight to his eyes. She pulled his head down to her lips and kissed him.

"I love you, I love you, I love you!" Sophia said.

He grinned and pulled away from her, but kept her in the circle of his arms. "What do you say after we give our statements here, we go back and pay that clerk a visit?"

Sophia's eyes widened to the size of saucers. "Colin Daniels, are you asking me to marry you?"

"I yam."

She threw her head back and laughed. "I will!"

# Taking the Heat

SYLVIA DAY

*This one is dedicated to Cindy Hwang.*
*I love writing novellas.*
*Thank you, Cindy, for breaking the dry spell.*

## ACKNOWLEDGMENTS

My gratitude goes to Cynthia D'Alba, who critiqued this story for me in the midst of celebrating her first sale. Now that's a friend!

And hugs to my dear friends Maya Banks and Karin Tabke. It's an honor to share a book with you both. I'm ready for our next retreat, ladies!

# Chapter 1

Two explosions rocked Deputy U.S. Marshal Brian Simmons on August 15 at 4:32 in the afternoon: the first was the sight of his perennial wet dream, Layla Creed; the second was the detonation of a launched grenade.

Brian heard the whistling of the approaching explosive a second before the projectile hit one of three Chevy Suburbans waiting to transport Layla from a safe house to the Baltimore/Washington airport. Lunging forward, he tackled her to the ground, shielding her with his body with only seconds to spare.

The blast radiated from the point of impact, sending a surge of heat roiling over them. The shock wave jolted her slender body and he curled around her, clutching her tightly. The ringing in his ears was deafening, dulling the sound of Layla's screams. But he felt them. Felt them vibrate against him.

Shrapnel rained down. Fire licked at the soles of his shoes. He scrambled to his feet, pulling her up and hauling her back into the apartment building. His ears felt as if they were stuffed with cotton, his focus narrowed by the instinctive need to get Layla to safety.

*Layla.*

Withdrawing his service weapon, Brian steered her with a firm grip on her elbow. They bypassed the elevator and slipped into the stairwell. He glanced up, momentarily considering the viability of returning to the room she'd occupied the night before. Then, he pulled her down toward the subterranean garage.

The safe house had been compromised. At least two deputies had lost their lives, one of whom was a friend he'd known for years. He wasn't certain who he could trust, and with Layla in the crosshairs, he wasn't taking any chances. Hard-driving possessiveness pushed him forward. She kept up; her fingers linked tightly with his as they thundered down the stairs.

They burst through the metal stairwell door into the garage. A forest green Honda was backing out of a parking spot to their left and Brian stepped behind it, withdrawing his badge and identification from his pocket.

He met the gaze of the female driver who gaped at him through her rearview mirror. "I need you to get out of the car, ma'am."

A harried-looking brunette climbed out from behind the wheel, her widened eyes on his Glock. She held both hands up, her purse dangling from the bent crook of her elbow.

He holstered his weapon and handed her his business card. "Call that number and they'll get you squared away."

Grim-faced, Layla slid into the passenger seat without prompting.

Brian was pulling out of the garage when the wail of sirens announced the arrival of the local authorities and fire engines. He could see the black plume of smoke as he hit the freeway on-ramp.

# Chapter 2

Layla gripped the edge of the Honda's passenger-seat cushion and glanced at the man she hadn't seen in the flesh in five long years. He looked different than he did in her dreams. Harder. Leaner. Still dangerous. A person would have to be nursing a death wish to face off with Brian Simmons.

Which hadn't stopped her from giving him her virginity . . .

"Are you hurt?" He glanced at her, cutting straight through her with his crystalline green eyes.

"No. Wh-what about—" She cleared her dry, aching throat. "Sam? The others?"

He shook his head.

Jesus. Her stomach knotted so tightly she thought she might be sick. Sam Palmer had become a friend over the last three years she'd spent in the Witness Security Program. Beyond his job, the inspector had become her lone tie to reality. His monthly phone calls to check up on her had become the only reminder that she was still Layla Creed underneath her assumed identity of Layla Cunningham.

She used to live a normal life. She used to live in the same town she'd been born in and have friends who knew her well enough to put up with her pining over the man sitting just inches away from her now. She'd lost it all that fateful weekend she partied in Tijuana, trying to prove to herself that she was truly over Brian Simmons.

Pulling a cell phone out of his pocket, Brian hit a speed-dial button.

"We're hot," he said without preamble to whoever answered the phone. "They hit the convoy with a fucking grenade launcher."

In the midst of a nightmare, Brian's low-pitched and faintly husky voice was soothingly familiar. She dreamed of that voice, remembered it groaning with pleasure and biting out raw, heated sexual words. He was a vocal lover and his openness made her shameless. She'd had no inhibitions with him, no reservations or hesitation. Nothing to shield her heart from a man who lived to be in the line of fire.

He could have died today, right in front of her. The biggest nightmare of all.

"No," he went on. "I'll have to get her out of town another way . . . I can't do that either. Someone leaked the safe house. I don't know who to trust . . . I can guarantee she had nothing to do with word getting out . . . It's Layla, Jim. Yeah, *that* Layla. Listen—I need a favor. Take everything you need out of the Bronco, toss what body armor and camping gear you can spare in the back, and head over to the gas station on Main and Seventh. Leave the keys in the ashtray and go for a walk . . . Thanks, man. I owe you."

He ended the call.

Layla blinked through her tears. She didn't ask any questions. If there was anyone on earth she trusted with her life it was Brian. It was the way he took care of his own hide that had led to their breakup.

They pulled into a retail store parking lot. He took a spot in the very back, near the garden center, and dropped the keys in the ashtray and closed it. Then he popped the battery out of his cell phone and tossed the separate pieces on the backseat. As if on cue, Layla's cell began to ring. She wriggled it out of the small backpack-style purse she wore and handed it to Brian, who waited with his hand held out.

As he disassembled her phone, he said, "There's a bank inside. We both need to pull out the maximum amount we can from the ATM. When we leave, we'll be traveling on cash to California—gas, food, lodging, the works—and we won't be able to pull out more. We'll need to grab clothes and toiletries while we're inside, and we need to be quick."

She nodded, briefly examining the crushed sunglasses in her bag before discarding them in the center console. "Are we hiding from the good guys, too?"

"For now." He tossed her phone onto the rear seat beside his. "Let's go."

Layla climbed out of the car with a racing heart. Her palms were damp and her breathing shallow. When she rounded the trunk, he caught her by the hand and set off at a brisk pace. They entered the store and it felt like every eye was on them. Her ears were still ringing, whether from the explosion or her own thundering blood, she didn't know. Her grip on him tightened.

Giving her a reassuring squeeze, Brian leaned in close. She saw the words on his lips more than heard them. "It's okay, baby. I've got you."

He'd said the same thing to her while she'd quaked with her first orgasm, his breath humid against the slick folds of her pussy. A shiver accompanied the memory, still so vivid despite the years that had passed. He pulled free of her grasp and draped his arm over her shoulders, careful to keep the loose tail of his unbuttoned flannel shirt over his holster.

"You're in shock," he murmured with his lips to her ear, sending another tremor through her body. "Just hang on to me."

The warmth of his leanly muscled frame sank into her side and she soaked it up, her arm wrapping around his waist. He wore Dr. Martens and loose-fitting jeans with a super-soft white jersey T-shirt. His green, tan, and aqua flannel was so attractive she would have stolen it if they were still together.

Brian got a shopping cart and led her through the store with swift efficiency, thinking of everything from underwear and tooth-brushes to disposable cell phones and two small wheeled suitcases. They separated briefly, standing across the aisle from one another while she grabbed clothes and he picked up razors. They were in the checkout line in less than twenty minutes. The ATM was next, where they withdrew a collective fifteen hundred dollars. They exited out the front entrance instead of through the garden center, and he stopped by a bench near the main doors to cram most of the clothes in one carry-on and the rest of the items in the other.

"We're going to cross the street to that convenience store." He reached for the packed bags, but paused, studying her. Whatever he saw caused him to straighten and reach for her. He cupped her nape in one hand, her hip in the other, and pulled her close. Their fore-heads touched. "You're being so brave, baby. I'm proud of you."

Her eyes stung. "I'm not a little girl anymore, Brian."

"Believe me, Layla. I know that." Releasing her, he dug two base-ball caps out of the bag and slid one onto her head. His fingers sifted through the dark tresses draped over her shoulders, as if he couldn't help himself. "When we get to the car, I want you to change your shirt and tie up your hair."

"Okay."

He grabbed the bags and set off, heading in the opposite direction of the Civic he'd commandeered. They made their way across the street, his stride smooth and easy, but she knew he was sharply focused on their surroundings. He was always alert, but he was inclined to be hypervigilant with her. Not just because she was a protected witness, but because she was his best friend's younger sister and the woman he'd once loved.

He walked directly to a beat-up Bronco parked off to the side of the convenience store and tossed the bags through the lowered rear window. "Hop in."

When he slid behind the driver's seat, he handed her a body armor vest he'd pulled out of the cargo space.

They were back on I-70 in less than five minutes.

Brian took the cap off his head and tossed it on the floorboard behind Layla's seat. She was already pulling her Henley off, as comfortable in her own skin as any woman had a right to be. As she bared a teal-colored lace bra that perfectly matched her irises, he could barely keep his eyes on the road.

"So the guy whose car this is," she began. "A deputy? Or a SEAL?"

"Can't he just be a civilian?"

"Not with you. You live and breathe the job—on duty and off."

Which was why she'd left him. "Deputy."

She dug into the plastic bag of clothes he'd set between her feet. "What do we do now?"

Now that they were on the move, his tension eased up a fraction, although he knew he wouldn't be fully relaxed until after Layla testified. Looking over, he saw the bullet-hole scar on her back and the rapidly bruising flesh on her elbows from when he'd tackled her to the ground. His teeth grit again. "We're going to drive straight through to San Diego. Fourteen hours a day on the road will get you there on time. I know that's not going to give you much opportunity to go over your testimony with the assistant U.S. attorney."

"Well . . ." She exhaled harshly and straightened. "Missing witness prep is better than death."

Fucking understatement of the year, but so like her. The daughter and sister of Navy SEALs, she'd been raised to be a straight shooter. The day she'd turned eighteen she had marched right up to him at her birthday party and tossed a gauntlet at his feet—*Teasing's over, Bri. Put out or get shut out. I'm not hurting for dates.*

Prior to that day, he'd told himself to wait a little longer. Let her go to college, spread her wings. He knew once he had her, their future together would be cemented for both of them. She'd be his and he would be hers 'til death parted them.

But faced with the possibility of seeing her with other guys, laughing and playing and fucking other guys . . .

His hands tightened on the steering wheel. "Tell me what happened."

She glanced at him, then yanked a new shirt over her head. She slid the vest on over it with impatient but practiced movements. "What are you talking about?"

"Tell me how you got into this mess."

Sitting back, she put her seat belt on. "Steph and I headed down to Rosarito and Tijuana for spring break. She hooked up with this dude she met at Papas and Beer, and since she was drunk and hellbent on getting it on with him, I had to stick with her. I wasn't going to let her take off with some strange guy all by herself. So he rounded up a friend of his and we climbed into a Camaro and headed back up to TJ."

Fighting to relax his tautened jaw, he bit out, "You fucking know better!"

"What's the problem, Deputy? Living dangerously only applies to you?"

"Don't even try to compare reckless partying with the job I do."

Layla stared out the passenger-side window, frustration vibrating from her slim body. Her feelings about what he did for a living had broken them apart. He understood that losing her father and brother had set her against the military, so he'd finished out his naval service and arranged to stay stateside by joining the Marshals Service. She hadn't liked it, but she'd tolerated it. Until he joined the Shadow Stalkers.

"Go on," he said tightly.

"Why? So you can get your kicks out of treating me like a kid?"

"Layla." He shoved a hand through his hair. "I can't help how I react when you're in danger."

She glanced at him with those cool eyes that turned him inside out. "Now you know how it feels."

Brian took the hit. He'd made the worst mistake of his life thinking she'd come around eventually and take him just as he was. Instead she'd been shot and absorbed into WITSEC before he knew what hit him. It was the worst irony that she'd joined his world, and instead of bringing them closer together, it had taken her further away from him than ever.

"We made it back to TJ," she continued. "We were near the border—not too far from that town square with the mechanical bull—when we slowed for a turn. These two guys stepped out of the shadows and lit us up. It seemed like we were getting shot at from all sides. The guy who'd joined us at the last minute fell out of the passenger side and I squeezed out after him. That's when I got hit. He did, too. He threw himself over me, but I think they wanted him alive, because they stopped firing. I think he knew they'd stop for him and that's why he did it. To save me . . ."

Her voice had softened with every word until the last was hard for him to catch.

"He was the undercover DEA agent? Sandoval?"

Layla nodded. "Ricardo Sandoval. Although I didn't know that until later. The gunman standing above us . . . I remember looking up at him over the barrel of a semiautomatic and seeing a sick glee on his face."

"Angel Martinez." It was her testimony against Martinez—one of the cartel's most prominent lieutenants—that endangered her life.

They would not have risked the offensive they'd taken today, on American soil, for anyone less.

"Yes. Martinez. Agent Sandoval swung at his thigh with a knife he had. Blood spurted everywhere and Martinez dropped like a ton of bricks. The other shooter started firing again, but the shots were wild. It was chaos with Martinez hollering. Sandoval dragged me around the back of the Camaro and into an alley that emptied into another street. Some guys speaking English were partying nearby. I screamed at them for help. They turned out to be marines from Pendleton and they got us back to the border. Agent Sandoval d-died later that night."

Sandoval's murder had been nationwide news when it broke—the blatant attack had hit a nerve first struck by Enrique Camarena's torture and killing by the same cartel. Layla had been the "unidenti-fied witness" referenced in the reports. Although Brian had heard the story before, listening to Layla tell it, hearing her voice crack and tremble as she spoke . . . Fuck it all, she should have been with him, *would* have been, if he hadn't been so goddamn stubborn.

"You still have nightmares, baby?" he asked quietly.

She looked at him, brushing her wind-whipped hair out of her face. "How did you know?"

"I know you." He reached out and caught up her hand. "You hold your pain close to the chest."

Her gaze dropped to their joined hands. "So do you," she said quietly.

Brian didn't know if she was referring to her brother Jacob's death or their breakup. "Sometimes."

"I've seen you laugh and I've seen you spitting mad, but I've never seen you cry." She pulled away. "When I told you we were over, you didn't even blink. I should have seen that coming. I was too young and naïve, I guess."

His fist clenched, his palm aching from the loss of her touch. His damn pride had gotten in the way before, and it was clogging his throat now, preventing him from saying words that would slice him open if she threw them back in his face.

Still, he had to say, "You knew what you meant to me, Layla."

"I knew it wasn't enough. We had Jacob and great sex in common. That was it."

"Bullshit." He checked his mirrors for the millionth time, canvassing for trackers. "The sex was great because we had something special."

"Then why didn't you come after me when I left?"

There it was. Colossal fucking mistake number one. "I thought you needed a little time to cool off."

"No," she argued, setting her elbow on the windowsill and her head in her hand. "You thought I needed to grow up. That I'd eventually see things your way, which just goes to show what a mistake we were. I'm always going to be Jacob's kid sister to you. I grew tits and reached the age of consent, but you were never going to treat me as a woman who deserved a say."

"You're starting to piss me off."

"Hitting too close to home?" she taunted, with a sly smile that made his dick hard.

"No, sweetheart. You're way off base." At least in regard to the way he felt about her. Yeah, the sex between them had always been white-hot—in that aspect of their relationship, they'd never had any trouble—but he loved her, too. So much it ate at him. There were times in the last few years when he'd been half-insane with the need to see her and hear her voice, to hold her and feel her hands on him.

Silence fell between them, thick with all the things that needed to be said. With every mile that passed, he was taking her closer to the point where he'd lose her again. Once she testified, she'd get sucked back into WITSEC. A new identity, new location and occupation, a new inspector to check on her. He had three days to clear things up and fix everything that was fucked up between them.

Three days to remind her of how good they were together. She was a captive audience, with no one around to screw things up for him.

Except himself. Unfortunately, he could do that well enough on his own.

Time was racing away from him, but that didn't stop him from sitting there with his jaw locked shut and his gut churning. Scared shitless by the possibility that she was over him by now. She had grown up since he'd let her walk away, while he was the same guy he'd been before—rough around the edges and unable to say how he really felt about the most important thing in his world.

# Chapter 3

'm going to head over to the diner and get us something to eat."

Layla arched a brow at the brooding, impossibly sexy man standing by the motel room door.

*One* motel room. With *one* king-sized bed.

Outside in the parking lot, there were so few cars or rooms with lights on that it was obvious the motel had a room available with two beds.

He met her gaze with a defiant scowl, knowing damn well what she was thinking. "What do you want?"

"Looks like you already made that decision for me," she shot back dryly.

"To eat," he grated.

Him, for starters. But she wasn't going to let him off easy. He could have at least been subtle enough to get two beds, even if she was a sure thing.

They both knew they wouldn't be able to keep their hands off each other when they were alone. Especially not while they were getting stripped down for showers and there was a bed nearby. In their present situation, while they were on the run and people they'd respected had paid with their lives, they were going to need each other more than ever. And time was so short. She had less than seventy-two hours with the man she'd loved for as long as she could remember.

She toed off her running shoes and pulled her shirt over her head. When she heard him inhale sharply, she hid a smile in the folds of the cotton. "A cheeseburger and fries would be great, with an unsweetened iced tea. I'm going to grab a shower while you're out. And don't forget to order a cot from the front desk. It's too bad they were sold out of double-bed rooms. Those rickety rollaways are especially uncomfortable for men your size."

The door closed behind him with more force than necessary.

Laughing softly, Layla propped one of the suitcases open on the luggage rack she pulled out of the closet. She paused in the act of digging a razor out, her gaze caught by a box of condoms and personal lubricant. She whistled.

She knew him. Knew how he worked.

Brian Simmons was arrogant and well aware that he was her weak spot, but getting her into bed wasn't about getting laid. If sex was all he was after, he could pick up someone at the diner. If he set his mind to it, he could have a woman against a wall before his food got cold. He was hot as hell and radiated dark sex appeal, but what really drew the chicks like flies was the dangerous remoteness about him. Brian was a real-life American antihero and he was impossible to pin down, which only made women want to try harder. God knew she'd tried.

But the same couldn't be said in reverse—Brian knew how to get to her. He knew how to strip her defenses until she was wide open to him, and that's certainly what he'd been thinking about when he was picking up such optimistic items. The pleasure wasn't the goal; it was a means to an end.

Her consolation was that when she was laid bare, he willingly opened himself to her in return. In bed, inside her, was the one place where he gave her all of himself. She wished he would take those risks with her in the real world. That's all she'd ever wanted.

Tossing the condoms on the bed and the lube in the nightstand drawer, Layla headed into the bathroom and closed the door. With the click of the latch, her shoulders drooped, taking her by surprise. Her chest grew tight, the moment of privacy revealing how vulnerable she really was, something she'd suppressed all afternoon without realizing it. Grief and regret rushed over her like an avalanche. She stumbled into the shower stall, her head bowing beneath the hastily turned on water. Tears flowed. Her chest shook with sobs. Gripping her lower lip in her teeth, she stemmed the sounds that would have betrayed her fragility.

It would be so easy to turn to Brian, to fall apart on him and take the comfort he would give her without reproach or hesitation. But they both needed her to be strong now. She couldn't distract him. He was one man transporting a witness who was supposed to have a half dozen of the Marshals Services's top deputies keeping her safe. Shadow Stalkers they were called. Special ops deputies who most often hailed from military special forces like Brian did.

It was his acceptance into the Shadow Stalkers that had broken them apart. After losing her father and brother to military service, she'd been determined not to lose Brian, too. He'd led her to believe that leaving the Navy was a new road for him, but it hadn't been a safer road; not after he volunteered to be a Shadow Stalker. She couldn't forgive him for what she'd thought at the time was a monumental deception and callous disregard for her concerns.

When she returned to the bedroom, Brian was back. The room smelled like tasty greasy food and he was glaring at the turned off television with his hands on his hips. He'd ditched his shoes and his flannel, leaving him in jeans and a fitted T-shirt, with his holster strapped around his shoulders.

Layla paused midstep, her uplifted hands stilling in the act of scrubbing her hair dry with a towel.

It struck her abruptly: she felt safe.

He couldn't know what that meant to her. Feeling safe was a comfort she'd thought she'd lost forever that night in Mexico. And yet the sight of him, so strong and confident, so determined, made her feel like nothing could get to her. Anyone who wanted her would have to get through Brian first and she couldn't see that happening.

He gestured at the condoms in the middle of the mattress, his green eyes hard as jade. "Contrary to what you might think, I wasn't planning on fucking you tonight."

"I could tell."

"Smart ass." He rubbed the back of his neck. "I don't want you sleeping alone tonight. You've had a rough day. The inspector you've been talking to for years died in front of you. I know you, sweetheart. You can't just shrug that off. You're hurting and you're bottling it up."

Her throat tightened and she shook her head, warning him away from a topic that would lead to more tears.

He stepped closer. "I want to hold you, keep you warm, make sure you feel safe. I'm not going to let anything happen to you, Layla."

She swallowed hard. "I know. Right now, that's the only thing I know for sure."

Before she knew it, she was in his arms, held tight against him. Burying her face in the soft cotton jersey of his shirt, Layla breathed him in—the warm, clean scent of virile male. Brian wasn't a cologne kind of guy; just soap, antiperspirant, and natural pheromones, which did a number on her every time. Her reaction to him was instinctual and primal, as if she'd been hardwired to seek out this one man, the only one who made her feel as if she was right where she was supposed to be.

Layla dropped the towel in her hand. Her hands fisted at his waist, gripping both his shirt and belt loops. As always, she felt like she was hanging on to him with a death grip, trying to stave off the inevitable separation. Even when he'd been hers, she'd never really felt like she had all of him. His job owned him first and foremost, and eventually she'd realized that if she made him leave it behind, the loss would alter him in a fundamental way. She couldn't ask that of him. He had to make that decision for himself.

And he had.

The job won.

Exhaling in a rush, she released him and stepped back. His arms fell away reluctantly, loosening the towel she'd secured around her torso with a tuck between her breasts. She barely caught it before it parted and fell. Brian sucked in a sharp breath and turned away, displaying a restraint she wouldn't have expected from the Brian of old.

"You need to eat." He dug into a large bag and pulled out a foam container. He peeked inside it, then grabbed a napkin and some plastic utensils.

Layla watched as he set a rudimentary place setting for her at a small round table by the window. The blackout drapes were drawn tightly together, shielding them from view of any passersby. She grabbed a fresh change of clothes and donned them in the steamy bathroom before sitting down to eat.

"What did you get?" she asked.

"Burger. Same as you."

She chewed a fry thoughtfully, her gaze moving to the bed and the condom box.

"They were near the razors," he muttered. "I didn't go out of my way looking for them."

Layla managed to repress the smile wanting to escape. His surly moods always brought her amusement. He was the type of guy for whom most everything just rolled off his back. The only thing capable of knocking him off his game was her. "God bless stores with convenient layouts."

He growled and ripped off a bite from a burger that was easily twice the size of the one she had. Brian wasn't a fan of breakfast, but he more than made up for it with the amount of food he ate the rest of the day.

"Aren't you going to join me?" she asked sweetly.

His gaze narrowed suspiciously, but he snatched up his food and came over, pulling out the chair opposite her and sinking into it with movements that were inherently graceful. She'd always loved to watch him in motion, loved to watch the way his muscles bunched and lengthened with sleek fluidity.

"You look great, Bri." Her voice was low and warm, prompting her to take a quick drink of her soda to cover the slip. Letting him know she still loved him would be a mistake. They had even less of a future now than they'd had before.

He stilled midchew. Swallowing, he said, "Thanks. So do you."

She offered a shy smile and resumed eating.

"So . . ." he began. "What have you been doing the last few years? Have you been in Maryland the whole time?"

"Pretty much."

"Do you like it?"

She shrugged. "It's all right. Nothing like SoCal."

"No," he agreed. "Are you still studying interior design?"

She shook her head. She hesitated, then took a deep breath before elaborating. "Criminal justice."

His brows rose and he studied her over the lip of his cup. She knew he was thinking of how big a change that was. He might even be wondering if it might tie into his and Jacob's former plans to start their own private security firm. Their dream wasn't one she had shared beyond her anticipation of having the guys home more often, but she'd grown to love it since joining WITSEC. In a way, it kept her connected to Brian and her brother.

"Are you happy, Layla?" he asked softly.

"I'm not *un*happy."

"Are you seeing anyone?"

Layla washed her food down with a leisurely draw on her straw. "Shouldn't you have asked that before you bought the condoms?"

"Damn it." Brian dropped his half-eaten burger onto his fries. "You're not going to let it go, are you?"

"Sure. I'll drop it."

"Thank you." He shoved three fries into a pile of ketchup, then pushed them into his mouth.

"But about the lube—" She blinked innocently when he erupted into coughing. "You gotta admit, that's pretty personal. And ambitious. It's one thing to rekindle a little fun in the sack, but anal sex, Bri? I'm sure you've known women who serve that on the main menu, but that's a chef's table item for me."

*"Layla."* He pushed back and stood.

"You really should eat," she admonished. "You've got to keep up your strength. We're on the run after all, and you've got some serious mattress gymnastics planned."

"Fuck it."

"Yeah, I got that from the lube—"

"Shut up." He walked to the bed, grabbed the box of condoms, and tossed them across the room into the trash can. Digging into the suitcase carrying the toiletries, he searched for the personal lubricant.

She watched him. She ate her burger and fries. And she got hotter by the minute. He was seething, so damn passionate in his aggravation and embarrassment. She'd rarely seen him like this out of bed.

"Where is it?" he barked.

"If I promise to be a good girl and stop picking at you, will you come back and eat?"

"Don't patronize me!"

"I'm sorry."

He held up a hand to ward off any further words.

"Really," she pressed. "Can I help it if I want to see if I can still get under your skin?"

"As if you ever got out from under it." He pointed an accusing finger at her. "Don't look so damned shocked! I'm not the one who split us up."

"Aren't you?"

"No, damn it. I'm not. I was in it for the long haul."

Layla shook her head, her own ire rising. "'Til death do us part doesn't add up to much when you can be dead any minute."

"Don't." He stalked closer, vibrating with all the emotions he was usually so adept at leashing. "It's five years later, baby. I'm still breathing."

"Only because we're not together. If you haven't noticed, men don't live long around me."

Brian stopped two steps away. "You can't be serious."

She shrugged and closed the lid of her box, her appetite gone. "Your food's getting cold."

"If you're a death sentence, that meal on the table isn't the last thing I want to eat."

Standing, she went to move around him.

He caught her arm.

"I'm tired," she lied, achingly conscious of his grip and proximity. The top of her head was level with his shoulder. She wanted to turn into him and hold him again. Fear held her back. The fear that she wouldn't have the strength to part from him again when the time came, which was only a couple days away.

Pressing a quick, hard kiss to her forehead, he released her.

She brushed her teeth, then climbed into bed. Brian gathered up what he needed and headed into the bathroom to shower. She feigned sleep when he slipped between the sheets and curled up behind her. Soaking up his warmth and the comfort of his embrace, she finally shut off the horrible images in her mind and drifted off.

# Chapter 4

Layla's soft cry of distress woke Brian a moment before she jerked violently in his arms.

"Baby," he murmured, jostling her carefully. "Wake up. It's okay."

Her short nails dug into the forearm he had draped over her waist. She gasped and turned into his chest, burying her face against his bare skin.

"It's okay," he said again, running his hands up and down her spine to soothe her trembling. "I've got you."

She pushed him to his back and climbed over him, clinging to his torso like a crab.

"Wanna talk about it?" he asked quietly, glancing at the clock on the nightstand. It was just past two in the morning.

"No," she mumbled into the crook of his neck. "Just hold me."

"Always." He hugged her tight.

Wriggling over him, Layla got more comfortable. The position notched her pussy directly over his cock, the heat of her flesh burning through her boy-short underwear and his boxer briefs. His dick responded despite his strenuous efforts to keep it in check. When it came to Layla, he'd never been able to control his reactions to her— bodily or otherwise.

He knew the moment she became aware of his hard-on. She tensed slightly, her breathing hitching a moment, before continuing with a cautious tempo that was obviously considered.

"Ignore that," he said.

Instead, she rolled her hips, stroking herself with the hard length of his cock. With her lips to his skin, she whispered, "It's too big to ignore."

Her tongue flicked over his throat and he cursed, his body tightening.

"Layla . . ." he warned.

Her hands slid down the sides of his chest to his waist. "Here's a tip, tough guy: You're about to get laid."

*Christ.* Brian's eyes squeezed shut. He wanted her so badly his teeth ached with it, but adrenalized by a nightmare wasn't the state of mind he wanted her in when they finally went at each other.

But Layla wasn't the kind of woman to be deterred, especially when it came to sex. And when she slid down his body and her teeth scraped lightly over the flat disk of his nipple, Brian lost the will to deny her.

Her tongue licked over the sensitive flesh and he jolted with a grunt.

"Watch it, baby," he growled. "You know what it's like with me when it's been a while since I've had you."

She wouldn't have forgotten. He'd sometimes been overseas on a mission for months at a time. When he came home to her, she knew to have a cleared schedule and the kitchen stocked, because they wouldn't be leaving his house for days.

"God, you're sexy, Brian," she said with a low moan and unmistakable note of resentment. "I get wet and needy just looking at you."

And he was apparently going to pay for that. The way she reached between them and squeezed his erection wasn't tender or tentative. It was firm and demanding. The stroke of her palm up and down was quick and forceful.

"Just thinking about you does it for me," he said gruffly, startled when she lifted off him and slid out of bed.

"Get naked."

Her sharp order had his blood raging. She'd been a virgin the first time he'd had her and that first encounter had set the tone for their sexual relationship—he led, she followed. That was the way he liked it—and she as well—but he was more than willing to let her have some fun. Shit, he was *very* willing. "Bring it on, baby."

As he lifted his hips and pushed off his boxer briefs, Brian heard her undressing. The lamp on the nightstand rattled as she bumped into it, but she was too focused to complain. Focused on him. On fucking him.

He'd never seen her like this. When it came to Layla, he was easily seduced. A heated glance or a coaxing, *"Brian, honey . . ."* was all the encouragement he required to have a rock-hard dick and a spurring impatience to find some privacy. But right now, she was running the show and going full throttle, and he was going to let her—for a little while—and just enjoy the ride.

Layla returned to him in a rush of silken limbs and warm, soft woman. *His* woman. The only thing in the world he'd ever felt truly belonged to him. And he'd let her walk away. Because he had shit for brains. No man in his right mind would have let that happen.

He tried to catch her, to kiss her, but she was sliding lower, her beautiful perfect tits caressing his abdomen the whole way down. Reaching up, Brian fisted each side of his pillow, wishing the light was on so he could watch her suck him. There was something in her eyes when she gave him head, a softness and vulnerability that flayed him open. They *connected* when they were intimate with each other, in a way he'd never known was possible until she had shown him. He couldn't explain it—the way her pleasure became his own, the way his joy made her happy, the way the need to touch and taste became as necessary as breathing. He just knew that he'd lost the ability to be happy when he lost her, that he had stopping living and just barely managed to make it through each day without her.

She gripped his throbbing cock in her hand, her slender fingers not quite able to surround him. Her partial clasp was a torture all its own and he groaned, so thick and sensitive he knew he wasn't going to last long. She pumped him a few times with her fist, priming him, bringing the first drops of pre-cum to the tip. The moment her tongue licked across the engorged crest, he cursed.

"I'll let you play, sweetheart," he bit out, as her breath blew hot over the dampness she'd left behind. "But now's not the time to tease."

Her fingers massaged his balls, gently tugging at their tautened weight. "You're the one who says it's no fun when you rush."

"Who's rushing?" Gripping her by the hair, he arched his hips and nudged her lips with the crown of his dick. "I'll be fucking you 'til sunrise."

Brian felt the little shiver that moved through her. Once they took the edge off, they'd settle in for a slow, deep ride. She knew how it would be. The intensity. The intimacy. The unbearable pleasure. He couldn't wait to get there. He'd been dying in slow degrees ever since she took that away from him.

She touched the back of his thigh. "Spread your legs and bend this knee. Let me get comfortable."

"You won't be down there long enough to get uncomfortable. You're just going to ease me back a bit, so I don't bruise your tight little pussy on our first go-round."

He swore he could feel her smile. And then her sassy mouth was engulfing him and his head pressed back into the pillow, his gut knotting from the heated pleasure. "Fuck, yeah."

Layla took him deeper, her mouth so hot and tight he spurted a wash of pre-cum over her wicked fluttering tongue. She moaned and swallowed, sucking hungrily for more.

"That's it, baby," he said hoarsely. "Suck my dick . . . *Ah*, God."

Eyes closed and teeth clenched tight, Brian's mind spun from how damn good it felt. Her head lifted and lowered, her lips sliding slickly up and down, her fist pumping him at the root. As if she was starved for the taste of him.

The pressure in his balls increased when her mouth drew hard on his cockhead. Her fingers left his scrotum, sliding lower, the pads of her index and middle finger stroking over the pucker of his ass.

He tensed in surprise. Her hand withdrew, her lips curving around his cock.

"Witch," he hissed.

Layla's tongue swirled around the sensitive crest, making his teeth grind. His spine was rigid with the need to come, his stomach so taut he felt like he couldn't move. Shit, he didn't *want* to move. If he could hang on to the edge forever, so damn ready but still able to hold off, he would. There was nothing in the world like the pleasure she could give him or the love he felt in every touch, kiss, and moan she gave up to him.

"So good." He groaned. "You suck me so fucking good . . ."

Her fingers returned between his parted legs, once again teasing the tight ring of muscle, her touch now slickened with what he quickly realized was the missing lube. Her head rose and fell faster, her mouth working his aching cock in what he was sure was a deliberate attempt to distract him from the pressure for entry she was applying.

"Layla, baby, what are you doing?"

She released him with a pop. "You bought the lube; you can't tell me you didn't want some anal play."

She knew damn well *his* ass wasn't what he'd had in mind, just as he knew that this was his punishment for excessive optimism in buying the lube to begin with. Neither of which mattered, because he'd always give Layla anything she needed.

Brian pushed out, as he'd taught her to do when accepting his cock in her rear, and the slim tip of one finger slipped inside him. Instantly, sweat misted his skin. He forced himself to relax, to give her no resistance while she explored a new aspect of their lovemaking.

Chest heaving, he absorbed the feeling of penetration and the vulnerability that came with it. Layla took his cock in her mouth again, sucking the head with delicate pulls, her finger pulling out and then pushing back in.

"Ah, Christ." His neck corded tight with strain. His thighs began to quiver.

He gasped when she pushed a second finger inside him, the slight burn sending a violent shudder through his frame. She rose to her knees, her hair falling over his hips, her mouth sucking in a greedy, demanding tempo. Her fingers moved in and out, fucking his ass.

"Damn it, Layla. You're shredding me." The shock and instinctive recoil he felt was tempered because it was Layla who touched him. She was already so deep inside him, so much a part of him, that ceding the intimacy to her was a natural extension of that connection. It also felt surprisingly good. Without conscious thought, both of his knees fell wide, encouraging more forceful thrusts of her hand.

"I'm going to kill whoever taught you this," he bit out. "String him up and castrate the motherfucker. Ah . . . shit, baby. I'm gonna come. Slow down."

The sounds filling the room—her vibrating moans and his tortured growls, the voracious suckling and the rhythmic thudding connection of her knuckles to the lower curve of his buttocks—were driving him insane. His dick was so hard it hurt, his balls drawn up tight and full. She owned him, possessed him completely, and he felt his surrender burn through him like a fever.

"I'm gonna come hard," he warned hoarsely. "Ease up, baby. Now. *Ah . . . fuck!*"

She'd found his prostate. Rubbing the gland swift and hard, she threw him over the edge.

Mindless with the savage, wrenching pleasure, Brian cried out and climaxed violently, his hands in her hair, his hips bucking. His head slammed back into the pillows, his eyes and jaw squeezed shut, his spine so stiff he thought it might break.

He pumped her mouth full and couldn't stop, years of pent-up lust and longing exploding from his aching dick with a force that felt ripped from his vitals. Her hungry moans made his head thrash; her greedy swallows barely kept up. Her evil fingers still worked his ass, coaxing every drop from him until he collapsed into the mattress.

Dripping with sweat, he forced his cramped fingers to release their grip on her hair. She gave one last hard suck, then straightened. In a distant part of his ecstasy-dazed mind, he heard her pad to the bathroom and run the sink. That short distance between them was too much. He needed her next to him, with him, where he could hold on to her and never let go again.

"Leave the light on when you come out," he said gruffly. "Keep the door cracked."

Layla stepped into view a moment later, naked and flushed and so damn beautiful his heart thudded painfully in his chest. His dick twitched, a response that shouldn't have been possible after the orgasm that just shattered him, but wasn't totally unexpected with her. He'd been built for her, designed to please her. As long as her hot little body was hungry for cock, his body was ready to give it to her.

"Come here." His arms lifted to embrace her. "Kiss me."

She draped her body over his. The moment their lips touched, Brian rolled her beneath him, his head angling to form a tighter seal. His tongue thrust in slow and easy, stroking alongside hers, gliding over the soft recesses. She quivered and moaned, surrendering, her body going lax and pliant beneath his. He pushed a thigh between hers, finding her pussy slick and swollen. She'd always gotten off on his pleasure. Because she loved him. He knew she loved him still or she couldn't have touched him so intimately. But that didn't mean she loved him like she used to, with her heart and soul, and not just because of fond memories and the connection they'd shared through Jacob.

Lifting from her, he bent his head and caught a hard, peaked nipple in his mouth. He groaned at the feel of her on his tongue, the joy of having her close, the relief from the constant ache he'd lived with the last five years of his life.

===

Layla bit her lip and whimpered as Brian's tongue curled around the tip of her breast. The vibrations of his groan sent ripples of sensation skipping across her nerves. She arched her spine, fisting her hands in the bottom sheet. His skin was hot and damp to the touch, his scent sifting through her mind like intoxicating smoke.

From the time she was sixteen, she'd been drawn to his clean masculine smell. Her primal attraction to him had ultimately exposed her love to her brother. Jacob had caught her sleeping in one of Brian's shirts and he tore her a new one. It was Brian who told him to lay off, waving her thievery aside as if it was just aggravating kid sister shit. But he'd shot her a look that gave him away, a look that revealed a tempered hunger that made her ache. She'd known then that he was aware of her the way she wanted him to be—as a woman.

The next two years of waiting to turn eighteen had seemed endless. Just as the last five had.

"Brian." She touched his broad shoulders, stroking over the lean flexing muscles with a soft hum of delight.

He bit lightly on her nipple, the tip elongated by his suckling. Nuzzling his way across her chest, he paid the same focused attention to her other breast, plumping the swollen flesh with his large callused hand. She was barely a handful, but he worshipped her tits as if they were the best pair on the planet.

"You're so beautiful," he praised, squeezing her hip before sliding lower. "I've dreamed of having you like this again . . . hungered for it until it gnawed at me. Your body is like food and water to me, Layla. I can't live without it."

She closed her eyes, fighting back tears and words she couldn't afford to say.

When he slid between her thighs, she opened to him as he'd opened to her. Not just to take pleasure, but to give it. Knowing the sounds she made, her unrestrained reactions to his touch soothed something ferocious inside him.

Brian draped her leg over his shoulder, his lips kissing their way down her inner thigh to the tender flesh clenching in emptiness. She'd felt empty for so long. So lonely and alone.

She had walked away from him because she'd needed to be the one that left, instead of the one that was always left behind. She knew she couldn't survive another official car pulling up to her house, carrying men bearing the news that someone else she loved was gone forever. She had cut the tie first, but she'd paid the price. She was still paying it.

He pressed a soft kiss to her clit, then massaged it with the pointed tip of his tongue.

"Later," she said, staying him.

His head lifted, his gaze meeting hers. His smile was wolfish, but it faded. Whatever he saw on her face, he knew what she needed.

He came over her in a rippling display of gorgeously delineated biceps, washboard abs, and long thick cock. Biting her lip, she slung one leg over his hip, wanting him inside her more than she wanted to live to see another day. A soft sound escaped her when she felt the wide crest part the slick folds of her pussy.

"Shh, baby. I've got you." Brian cupped her buttock, canting her slightly, making it easier for her to take the first hard inch.

Heat flared across skin, flushing her.

"So pretty," he murmured, pushing deeper. "I love the way you blush when I slide into you. And, God . . . I fucking love the way you feel. So tight and hot. So slick. Your cunt gets so wet for me."

She lifted her hips, needing faster and deeper. "Hurry."

His gaze was on her face, tender and searching. "Didn't we already talk about rushing?"

"I need you in me. You can slow down once you're there."

"You're tight as a virgin, Layla." He slid a fraction deeper, his eyes darkening as her pussy rippled greedily. "You feel like you did the first time I had you."

Turning her head, she pressed her hot cheek into the cool pillowcase. She'd tried starting a relationship with someone else, gave it her best shot and stayed with great guys longer than she should have. But after a couple years of trying her damnedest, she'd given up. She was hurting men who didn't deserve to be hurt and she was hurting herself.

Brian caught her face in both hands. "Open your eyes, Layla."

Her neck arched as he withdrew a little bit, then pushed deeper.

"Look at me," he coaxed. "Let me watch you take my cock."

Her lids lifted. She watched him, too. Watched his skin tighten over his cheekbones, watched the pleasure cross his face like the sweetest agony. He worked into her with slow easy drives, holding her gaze as the connection deepened. Tugging him closer with her legs, Layla lifted as he bore down, the pleasure hot and drugging.

The leisurely penetration felt like a deep inner massage and she moaned. "Brian, please . . ."

His tongue followed the curve of his lower lip, his look so fiercely sexual she trembled with the force of her desire. "There," he purred, rolling his hips and pushing home. He stroked in and out, then pushed his torso upright. "You've got all of me."

God, how she wished that was true.

With her legs draped over his thighs, Brian looked down between them. "I've dreamed of this. Dreamed of filling you again. So many damn times."

His thick cock pulled free to the crest. The vein-corded length pushed back into her, stretching her deliciously. His raw, serrated groan of pleasure made her come.

"Oh!" She trembled violently as the climax hit her. *"Brian."*

"Yeah," he growled, holding her hips and pounding through her orgasm, driving deep and hard. His head bent to her breast, his mouth surrounding an aching nipple and working it with his tongue, his hands keeping her still as his cock shafted her convulsing pussy with savage hunger.

She clung to his wrists and fought for breath, the mattress squeaking under the ferocity of his thrusts, her body quaking with the violence of her pleasure.

"Me, too, baby." He gasped. "Ah, shit . . . me, too."

He crushed her against him, his hips grinding against hers as he emptied his seed deep inside her.

"Layla." He gripped the sides of her head and rubbed his cheek against hers. *"Layla."*

Closing her stinging eyes, she held on as tightly as she could.

# Chapter 5

Showered, dressed, and standing over the bed, Brian woke Layla with a gentle tug on her ear with his teeth.

"Put it away, stallion," she muttered, clutching tighter at the pillow in her arms.

He laughed, his love for her a purring beast in his chest. "I've got a hot bath waiting for you. I'm going to grab something to go from the diner, make a couple calls, then gas up the truck. I should be back in about thirty minutes, then we've got to hit the road."

"What time is it?"

"Seven thirty."

"Oh, man . . ."

He smacked her ass through the sheets. She'd never been a morning person. On nights like the one behind them, she usually didn't roll out of bed until after noon. "You can sleep in the car."

"How can you be awake right now?" she groused. "I'm dead."

"Sex with you is invigorating. You keep me going."

"Don't remind me."

For all her complaints, when he pulled the sheet back and trailed his lips along the curve of her back, she moaned with pleasure and arched into the contact. The bruises on her elbows were darker than they'd been the day before, reminding him of how fragile she was.

"Be a good girl," he whispered against her skin, "and I'll reward you later."

One bloodshot eye opened and glared at him. "You owe me."

"I'll pay. Gladly." Brian straightened and backed away from the temptation her sleep-soft naked body presented. He'd fucked her for hours, finally managing to pull away from her when sunlight peeked around the edges of the blackout drapes. But he still had so many nights to make up for. He'd had little appetite for sex since she left him and it felt as if every hunger that had been dammed up behind his heartache was breaking loose. "Don't forget to pack the lube."

She held up a hand, revealing the bottle clutched in her fist.

The smile on his face fled the moment he left the room. Before he walked away, he made certain the latch was firmly engaged. The morning was cool and gray, with a slight nip in the air. With a baseball cap pulled down low over his forehead, he kept a careful surveillance of his surroundings. He took a weed-riddled path through a copse of trees to the strip mall up the road, where he'd parked the Bronco. There, he bought a newspaper from a coin-operated stand in front of a grocery store and looked for any signs that the vehicle had been staked out. Digging one of the disposable cell phones out of his pocket, he called Jim.

"Hey," the deputy answered. "You all right?"

"So far. How are things on your end?"

"They're not looking at me for anything, so you're still clean with the car. But you're the lead person of interest, of course. Your mug has been sent to every law enforcement agency across the country. The heat is on, my man."

"I can take it." He'd expected it. He had survived the blast and taken off with the witness. To call that suspicious would be an understatement. "Thanks, Jim."

"Take care. I won't breathe easy until you get to San Diego."

"You and me both."

Brian ended the call and dismantled the phone. Then he pulled out another one and called the assistant U.S. attorney in San Diego to assure her that Layla Creed would appear on the witness stand as scheduled. He made the call short and to the point, despite the groggy AUSA's valiant efforts to get more details out of him. He took that phone apart, too, and as he passed a parked pickup truck, he tossed the pieces in the bed. Then he drove the Bronco to a gas station and back to the motel, where he grabbed some foil-wrapped breakfast burritos and coffee from the adjacent diner.

When he returned to the room, he found Layla packed up, bathed and dressed, and falling asleep at the small table under the window. He loaded the suitcases into the truck, then came back for her.

"Ready?" he asked.

"Yep." She pushed to her feet, slapped a hat on her head, and set her hand in his. She'd pulled her dark hair back into a ponytail, showing off the slender neck he loved to run his lips over. She wore jeans and a T-shirt with body armor over the shirt, and his flannel from the day before over that. Call him a caveman, but he loved the idea of her wearing his scent. Loved that she'd always wanted to and still did.

He'd backed into the parking spot in front of the motel room and left the passenger door open. Keeping Layla between the vehicle and himself, he escorted her to the car, then rounded the back end of the Bronco and climbed behind the wheel. He headed straight for the highway.

"Thanks for this," she said, referring to the unzipped sleeping bag he'd set on the floorboard. She dragged it up to her neck and snuggled into it.

"Recline the seat. Take a nap. If you're hungry, there are egg, bacon, and salsa burritos in the bag. Coffee with way too much cream and sugar—just the way you like it—is right here."

Instead of looking at the cup he pointed to, Layla kept on looking at him. "Are you okay?"

He took a sip of his overly hot black coffee. "After last night? I'm better than okay. I haven't felt this good in years."

"Liar." Her exhale was audible. "What is this going to do to your career, Bri? How much trouble are you going to get into for this?"

"I'm not worried about it." Not absolutely true, but mostly so. He'd invested a lot in his job. Shit, he had lost her over it. But that old argument between them had been about *his* life being on the line. Now, they were talking about hers. There wasn't anything he wouldn't sacrifice to keep her safe.

"I am."

"Don't be." He glanced at her. "The only thing you need to be concerned with is following my directions."

She nodded, but still looked troubled. He wasn't worried about her making his job harder. She knew the drill and she was an intelligent woman. She might give him a hard time about everything else, but when it came to his job and her safety, she'd do what needed to be done.

Silence followed, but when he looked at her, she was still watching him.

"Tell me about your dream last night," he said.

She shook her head. "It was morbid."

"I don't care. It might do you good to talk it out."

"I doubt it." Her lashes lowered over her eyes. "Just remember you asked for it."

With a sigh, she began. "You died in the car bombing. Everyone died except for me, and I was screaming at your corpse, telling you I'd known it would happen. That I knew you'd leave me behind. I was so mad that out of all people to be the sole survivor, it had to be me."

"Jesus," he breathed, feeling like he'd been punched in the gut.

"I'm sure I had that dream because I was so damn happy to see you yesterday. I stepped out of the safe house and saw you and . . ." Her eyes fully closed on a harsh exhale. "I was too happy. You were running toward me and I thought it was for a different reason at first.

Then, everything blew up and you hit the ground face-first at my feet. And I couldn't cry about it, because I was too pissed off at you."

Brian rolled his shoulders back, remembering the wounded animal noise she'd made while asleep.

"As you can see, I have issues," she muttered, snuggling deeper into the sleeping bag.

Layla may have been ticked off at him in her dream, but the way she'd externalized her emotions wasn't with anger. She had reached for him and held on as if she would never let go. Then she'd seduced him. Shredded him. Stripped him down to nothing but his need for her.

"It's okay to be pissed off at me, baby," he said. "I'm pissed off at myself. I shouldn't have let you walk away."

"It was for the best. We were both strong enough to break it off when we needed to."

"Stubbornness isn't strength. It's fucking stupid. Living miserably without each other is stupid."

"Have you been miserable, Bri?" She was looking at him again; he could feel it. "You asked me if I had anyone in my life, but you never said if *you* did."

Glancing at her, he said, "You know better than to ask me that."

"Because it'll just make me jealous? I'll get over it." Her face gave nothing away. That was new for her. She'd once been so expressive, so open. But she'd been innocent then and life had dealt her some painful blows.

"There's nothing to get over."

"Still lovin' and leavin' 'em?"

He caught her gaze and held it. "No."

Her lush mouth twisted wryly. "Sorry. Fuckin' and leavin' 'em?"

"No, damn it."

"Fine. Don't tell me. But don't expect to interrogate me. It goes both ways, Bri."

"Really?" he said grimly, his muscles hard with building anger and barely tempered jealousy. "Did you save your body for me, baby? Did you think of me at night and get yourself off? Were your fingers—maybe some toys—the only things to fuck that sweet, hot cunt of yours, because damned if you'd let another man touch what's mine?"

"Ha!" She straightened. "As if you spent the last five years jacking off to memories of me. Jacob told me all about you, Bri. Tried to warn me off of crushing on you with stories of your many, many conquests. You can't keep it in your pants."

"Did those stories make you hot?" he purred, pissed off that she didn't give him the credit he damn well deserved. "You sure asked about them often enough."

"Fuck you."

"Only you."

Layla shut up, her open mouth snapping closed. She glared at him.

"Say you don't believe me," he coaxed darkly, reaching between his legs to rub his palm over his cock.

"You're a crazy-assed motherfucker if you're serious." Her voice was clipped and hard. "You sure found it easy enough to let my golden pussy get away."

"Letting you go was a lot of things, but easy sure as hell wasn't one of them."

"At what point did you realize you'd made a mistake?"

He breathed in and out carefully, trying to rein in his temper. "The instant before you walked out the door. I knew I couldn't live without you."

"But you did. For two years before that trip to Mexico screwed up my life." She sat up and reached for her coffee.

"We hooked up before you had a chance to grow up. I felt like I'd pulled you straight out of high school into a marriage-like situation and you hadn't had the opportunity to get your bearings or really figure out what you wanted."

"Always trying to make all the decisions for me, because I'm just a kid."

"What the fuck? I tore my heart out giving you the opportunity to make all the decisions you wanted."

"And who made the decision that I needed those opportunities?" Putting the coffee down, she dug into the bag for a burrito and dropped it into his lap, then grabbed one for herself.

"I'm not hungry."

"I decided you are. Eat."

Brian cursed under his breath.

"I knew what I wanted, Bri—*you*. I knew there wasn't another man in the world for me. I didn't want to check out the scenery or waste time that could be spent with you."

"Then why did you leave?" Keeping one hand on the wheel, he used his teeth to rip the foil wrapping off the burrito.

"You know why."

"And you knew what I did for a living when we started."

"You lied to me when you joined the Marshals Service."

"Bullshit."

"You never said anything about volunteering for the Shadow Stalkers!" She tore a chunk out of the burrito with violent gusto.

"I was qualified."

She chewed angrily, then washed down her food with a large swallow of coffee. "You were also qualified as a security expert."

He put the burrito down. Starting his own firm had been a dream he'd shared with Jacob. After his best friend died, Brian felt as if the dream had died, too. He couldn't imagine going forward with the endeavor without Jacob on board. "Things changed."

"*You* didn't. You're an adrenaline junkie with a hero complex."

"And a big dick," he lashed out, stung. "Don't forget that."

Her gaze bore into him. "Truth hurts, doesn't it?"

"Your pussy doesn't seem to mind."

She flipped him off and resumed eating, canting her body toward the window.

He'd wanted to at least have a dialogue about his work with the Marshals Service Special Operations Group before she tossed out her ultimatum, but she'd said the discussion should have been held *before* he volunteered for SOG and she wasn't staying with a guy who had a death wish.

"What about *your* painful truths, Layla? Your fear of abandonment kept you from trusting me. You were always laying out ultimatums, with the proof of whether or not I loved you hanging in the balance. You were always waiting for some excuse to say I wasn't going to stick around after all."

"And you gave it to me, didn't you?"

"Look for something hard enough, you find it, whether it's really there or not."

Shrugging, she said, "People have baggage. When you love someone, you deal with it."

"I was dealing with yours. You're the one who couldn't deal with mine."

"You know what?" Layla pivoted on the seat to face him. "I don't know why we're talking about this. It really boils down to the fact that our personal issues conflict. What you require to be happy is exactly what makes me unhappy and vice versa."

"And the fact that I need you and you need me?" he challenged. "What about that?"

"What about it? In forty-eight hours or so, I'm going to disappear and you're going to face whatever the hell you're going to face for going rogue with a witness." With a sigh, she faced forward again. "We've been trumped by fate, Bri. Consider it a blessing. God knows we're too stupid to stay away from something that'll never work."

Maybe, he thought savagely. But stupid or not, he wasn't giving her up again without a fight.

# Chapter 6

They holed up for the night in Joplin, Missouri. The motel Brian chose was cheap and in need of serious updating, but Layla was so relieved to get off her ass that she didn't care. She stumbled into the room and collapsed on the bed face-first, pointing her toes to stretch out her legs.

She heard Brian bring the suitcases in and sighed with gratitude, eager to take a hot shower.

"What do you want for dinner?" he asked, his hand wrapping around her ankle and squeezing.

"A salad with grilled chicken or fish. Nothing fried. I can't keep eating crap while sitting on my butt all day. I'm starting to feel icky."

"Good call. I'll be back in a bit. You know the drill."

"Yes. Don't answer a knock at the door, even if it's you."

He closed the drapes before leaving the room and Layla crawled off the bed. She repeated her preparations from the night before, wondering as she pulled out another disposable razor if Brian was thinking at all about the box of condoms they'd left in the trash in the other motel.

Condoms were something they'd never used. She'd always been on the pill and they'd both been too addicted to the feeling of total connection to put a barrier between them, not to mention how spontaneous they were. He probably thought she was still on birth control.

She wasn't. What was the point when she wasn't having sex?

Remembering his assertion that he'd been celibate since they broke up, Layla felt a surge of guilt. She'd taken lovers after they'd broken up. Enough to prove what she had always suspected—no other man would ever make her feel like Brian did. She'd found men who were similarly attractive, men who had dark and ravenous appetites, men with experience and the patience to make sure she had a good time. But sex was just sex without love, no matter how good it was. She'd never gotten over the feeling that she was in bed with the wrong guy.

She took a long, leisurely shower. She shaved her legs smooth and rubbed the motel's complimentary lotion into her skin. Anticipation thrummed through her veins, along with the steady flow of adrenaline brought on by their circumstances and the desperation of knowing they were only two days away from losing each other again.

When she left the bathroom, she found Brian sprawled on the bed in just his jeans. He'd freed the buttons on his fly and sat with his back against the headboard and his bare feet crossed at the ankles. Holding the remote in one hand and a bottle of water in the other, he was watching the news until she came out. When he looked at her, his eyes became dark and hot with want.

"Feel better?" His voice was low. Rough.

Layla soaked up the sight of him. His chest was tanned from his daily shirtless runs, the broad expanse covered in a light dusting of hair that tapered into a thin line bisecting washboard abs. His arms were a work of art, the ripped biceps flexing when he lifted the water to his lips and drank deeply. His throat worked with each swallow, making her body tighten with need. She was starved for the feel of him.

He was so damn sexy. Deliciously powerful and virile.

She nodded.

"What are you thinking about, sweetheart?" He licked a drop of water off his lower lip.

"How bad I want your mouth on my pussy."

His low growl made her nipples hard. He came off the bed in an agile rush of movement. "Eat your dinner while I grab a shower. Then, I'll eat you."

The look he gave her made her nipples hard.

His gaze lowered to her chest as he approached and stopped in front of her. "I've been thinking about licking your mouthwatering cunt since you stopped me last night. I fantasized about pulling over at a rest stop, dragging you into the back of the Bronco, and tongue-fucking you until you screamed."

*"Brian."*

He pushed his hand into her panties and cupped her. "Umm . . . you're hot and juicy already."

Her legs parted at his urging, her heart racing. He was such a highly sexual man and unashamed of his needs. His lack of inhibition turned her on and drove her crazy.

She gripped his biceps as he parted her with his fingers and stroked over her clitoris. Her knees went weak. Her breathing was shallow and fast. His fingertips circled the clenching opening of her pussy, then two long fingers pushed inside her.

"Oh God," she whispered, welcoming his penetration with a hot rush of moisture. She returned the favor, reaching into his open fly and down the front of his boxer briefs. His cock fell heavily into her waiting palms, the plush head already slick with pre-cum.

He caught her leg with his free hand and urged it up to his waist, opening her to his touch. His fingers withdrew, then thrust deep, making her back arch on a gasp.

"How many times have we done this, baby?" he purred, pushing his cock into her grasping hands. "How many times did you need to come so badly I'd have to find the nearest corner and finger-fuck you to orgasm?"

"Not enough."

"It's never enough." He pumped his hand, working her with scissoring fingers and deft twists of his wrist. His thumb found her clit and massaged it, taking her to the edge of climax. "God, you're so beautiful. You make my chest ache."

Layla jacked his cock with both hands, using the fast, firm grip she knew he liked.

"You're so wet." He groaned. "I'm dying to taste you. And you're so close to making me come . . ."

"No." She stilled, giving him one last firm squeeze.

"Layla!" he protested, curling his fingers to rub her G-spot.

"When you come, you come inside me."

His green eyes narrowed dangerously a second before he bent his head and took her mouth. His kiss was softer and sweeter than she expected, lush and hot and leisurely. It was his kiss that kicked off her orgasm.

Her moan drifted into his mouth. Her pussy trembled around his fingers and her hands tightened convulsively on his cock.

He hissed, jerking in her grip. "You're killing me."

But he kept on thrusting gently, drawing out her climax until only sweet aftershocks remained. She leaned into him, breathing hard, relying on his support to keep her standing.

"I've got you," he murmured, nuzzling his cheek against the crown of her head. Releasing her leg, he caught her around the waist and drew her close.

"Shower later."

"I have stubble, sweetheart. I need to shave." Brian backed away. His face was flushed, his eyes feverish with lust. "I want you naked when I come out."

She was already stripping before he stepped into the bathroom. As she heard the shower come on, Layla grabbed her salad and crawled between the cool sheets. Needing to slow her raging heartbeat, she picked up the remote from the nightstand and turned on the television. A few channel switches later, she found a showing of *Navy SEALs*.

She started watching, her thoughts drifting to why a man would choose such a life. Jacob had chosen it because of their father, who had chosen it because of his father. But Brian never really had an answer to that question. He didn't have those family traditions. He'd been raised by a single mother, who never told him who his father was. When Layla had asked him why he'd joined the military, he'd shrugged and said, "What else was I going to do?"

But he was good at everything, from fixing transmissions to masonry to cooking. He could have done anything with his life that he wanted to.

"You'd better eat quick," he warned, when he turned the shower off. "I'm about to pounce."

Layla hit the mute button and feigned a loud snore.

"Ha! I know how to wake you up."

"Bring it on."

When he stepped out of the bathroom in all his naked glory, she felt her heart stop. Tears welled and blurred her vision. She dashed them away with impatient swipes, unwilling to lose even a second of the sight of him.

"God," she breathed, loving him so much her chest was tight with it.

He paused near the bed, letting her look her fill. He was leaner than she'd ever seen him, which told her he was working too hard, but his body was perfect in every way regardless. There was nothing she'd change about him, nothing more she could want. She closed her to-go box and set it on the nightstand without looking away.

Brian caught the edge of the sheet and tugged it down, revealing her body in slow increments. "I feel the same way when I look at you," he murmured. "Like I can't catch my breath. Like I can't blink, in case you disappear when I do."

He *saw* her. Truly saw her and who she was, knew her and cared about her with all her history and flaws. After feeling invisible for years, hidden behind a name and life that wasn't really hers, it meant so much to be with someone who *got* her. It meant the world to be with Brian now, during the most dangerous and stressful period of her life.

He set his palms down on the mattress, then his knees, crawling toward her in a luscious display of masculine strength and agility. His cock hung heavily between his legs, making her tummy flutter in anticipation. Her toes curled when he kissed the arch of her foot. His parted lips slid up to her ankle, his hand reaching for her other foot and squeezing.

"Brian?"

"Yeah, baby?"

"Come here."

His dark head lifted, his gaze snaring hers. "No."

"I'm not stopping you," she said huskily. "I just want to hold you a bit first."

He exhaled, then climbed over her, stretching out beside her.

She rolled into him, burying her face against his chest. His skin was still damp and cool, his heartbeat sure and strong. His arm draped over her and she tilted her head back, pressing tiny kisses to his clean-shaven jaw, so damn grateful for the opportunity to hold him in her arms again.

"Layla . . ." His voice was low and hoarse, with an aching note of yearning.

Even with a raging hard-on and her willingness, he'd taken the time to shave his evening stubble so as not to scratch her. He was always thinking of her, in both big and small ways. Always ready to give her whatever she needed.

Except when it came to his job.

"Make me understand," she whispered. "Why is it so important to you to risk your life?"

Brian stiffened, then rested his chin atop her head with a sigh. "It's not that."

"What is it, then?"

"I don't know. I've thought it over so many times. Lying in bed without you, wondering where you were, if you were okay, wondering why the hell I didn't just say to hell with the fucking job when you gave me the choice." His hands stroked down the curve of her spine.

She closed her eyes and nuzzled closer. "It gives you something I can't. Something you need."

"I don't need anything as much as I need you." He pushed her to her back and loomed over her. His thigh slid between hers, his weight settling atop her in the way that always made her feel safe and cherished. "That's what shreds me, that you'd ever believe I could love anything more than you . . . that I ever gave you a reason to think that."

Putting her fingers to his lips, Layla cut off anything else he might say. He nipped her fingertip with his teeth, the slight sting sending a quiver through her. His tongue flicked over the tiny hurt, his gaze unwavering on her face.

"Grab on to the pillow," he said gruffly. "Don't let go."

She reached up and did as he ordered, the position arching her back and lifting her breasts to his waiting mouth. He licked her nipple, and she made a soft noise of pleasure.

His breath blew softly over her skin. "I love the sounds you make."

"I love the way you touch me." As if she was the most precious thing in the world, as if her pleasure was the only thing that mattered.

"Then I won't stop."

Wet heat surrounded the sensitive point of her breast as he took her into his mouth. His cheeks hollowed on a soft, slow suck that radiated through her body. Her head fell back and she moaned. "Yes . . ."

Her pussy spasmed with jealousy. His hand cupped her other breast, kneading, his thumb and forefinger rolling and tugging her tight, sensitive nipple.

Her back arched, her lips parting on panting breaths. It felt as if she was being touched for the first time in years. The sensations were too fierce and hot, too vivid compared to the numbness she'd lived with since she left him. "God, Brian . . ."

His tongue lashed the tender tip of her breast, the drawing pulls of his mouth echoing in the throbbing between her legs. She pressed her pussy against him, slickening his skin with her desire, riding the hard muscle in an effort to ease her aching to be filled.

"You make me so hot," she breathed.

Sweat misted her skin. She felt almost sunburned, her flesh so sensitive it was nearly painful. When Brian's mouth moved to her other breast, she cried out, the surfeit of sensation intoxicating her. He sucked harder, his teeth grazing with just enough pressure to make her shudder.

Her fingers were cramping by the time he slid down between her thighs. She draped one leg over his shoulder; the other fell to the side.

"So pretty," he praised, parting her with his fingers. He flicked her clitoris with his stiffened tongue and she lifted to his mouth, seeking more. "And so sweet. I'm going to eat you for hours . . . make up for all the times I hungered for the taste of your pussy and you weren't there."

"Bri, please . . ."

"That's it, sweetheart." He licked through the saturated folds with a low groan of pleasure. "Beg me. Let me hear you."

Cupping her buttocks, Brian lowered his head and worked her clit with massaging rubs of the flat of his tongue. Her hips circled, grinding her trembling flesh against his firm lips. He traced her folds with slow, teasing glides, then rimmed the clenching opening to her pussy until she whimpered from the torture of it.

"Don't tease me," she whispered, so tense it hurt. "Make me come."

"Not yet."

"I've waited five years. Don't make me wait anymore."

"I won't be done," he warned.

Layla bit her lip, writhing beneath him. "Please."

Gripping her hips, he fucked her trembling pussy with rapid thrusts, his head tilting to deepen his reach. It was a fervent, wrenching kiss, his hungry growls making her hotter and wetter. The slick sounds of his avid mouth against her drenched sex were searingly erotic. Her hips churned, her pulse pounding in her neglected clit.

His plunging tongue felt so good she couldn't control the ferocity with which she bucked into the rhythmic penetration. The pleasure was too much, her love for him too powerful, his love for her too evident and fierce.

Brian moved with a groan, his lips surrounding her clit and suckling, licking, pushing her into an orgasm that shattered her.

# Chapter 7

No more." Layla pushed weakly at his head.

"One more time," Brian whispered, tonguing her swollen clitoris. "Just once more, baby."

He had lost count of how many times she'd come, but it could never be enough to satisfy him. His dick was pounding in demand for its turn at her slick, scorching cunt, but he held himself in check, needed her pleasure more than he needed his own.

With patient coaxing, he brought her to orgasm again, his groans muffled in the folds of her soft, sweet pussy as he fucked her rippling depths with his tongue. Her cries were low and hoarse, her perspiration-damp body trembling with exhaustion.

As he pulled away, her leg slid heavily off his shoulder, her body lax and replete. She was vulnerable now. Open. Almost where he needed her to be.

She curled on her side as he left the bed, her eyes on the thick stalk of his raging erection. She licked her lips. "I can suck you off."

He reached for the nightstand drawer.

A tiny whimper escaped her.

"You're soft and relaxed now," he soothed, gripping the lube in his fist. "You don't have to do anything. You don't even have to move. I'll take care of everything."

"Brian . . ."

"We need this, Layla. You know we do."

He watched the goose bumps sweep over her skin. She turned, lying prone, and he joined her on the bed, running his parted lips down her spine. "I can't tell you how often I dreamed of this . . . how many times I woke up hard and aching."

Grabbing a pillow, Brian slid one arm under her slim hips and lifted her, pushing the pillow beneath to cant her body to just the right angle.

Layla's hands fisted in the bottom sheet, her chest rose and fell with swift breaths. "You'll kill me . . . I can't take this. Not now."

He squeezed a line of lube in the seam between two of his fingers and a larger dollop on his fingertips. "You know it has to be now."

She shivered when he touched the pucker of her ass, the tight ring of muscle flexing. He rubbed in slow, gentle circles, willing to be patient. He knew what this act did to her, how much of herself she gave when he took her this way, how exposed and defenseless she felt. She'd shown him by example last night, made him experience in the flesh what he'd thought he understood in his mind.

"No one else has been here, have they, baby?" he asked softly.

Her lower lip quivered.

"You're still mine, aren't you, Layla? Just as I've always been yours."

"Brian, please . . . I can't bear it."

One fingertip pushed inside her, and she gasped. Her slender body shook.

He slid in and out, twisting his wrist. After a moment, another digit joined the first. She whispered a curse. Her hips began to move in tiny circles, seeking the pleasure of his touch.

She hissed when he pressed a third finger into the tightly stretched opening.

"You're so damn tight." He groaned when she clenched around his thrusting fingers. "And scorching hot."

"Oh God . . ."

He pulled free of her clinging depths and filled his palm with lubrication. He stroked his cock from root to tip, squeezing the thick pulsing length, imagining how damn good it was going to feel once he got inside her. More than the raw physicality of the act, it was her surrender that turned him inside out. He ceded to her in many ways, couldn't help himself from wanting to see to her happiness, found it almost impossible to say no to her, but in this one demand of his, she yielded completely.

If he'd needed proof that there was still an emotional wall between them, her token resistance was it. She'd never denied him anything, especially not in bed. But she was vulnerable now—weak from pleasure and falling for him all over again. After her expressionless face yesterday, he could finally read her tonight and he knew this was it—his chance to reach her, to make her feel his need and regret and pain. To feel the longing for her that was eating at him from the inside.

Brian gentled her quivering with a hand at her hip. Taking himself in hand, he ran the wide head of his cock up and down between her cheeks, teasing the flexing opening. With a sharp inhale, she pushed out, accepting him. He pressed forward, sliding into her, growling at the heat and damn near unbearable tightness.

Her exhale was shaky. *"Brian . . ."*

"I'm right here with you," he said hoarsely, sliding deeper. "It's tearing me up, too, baby. Killing me . . ."

Layla pushed back with her hips, taking him halfway. She was stretched tightly around him, clenching rhythmically. The pleasure was stealing his sanity. He could barely breathe through it. Sweat coursed down his chest and back, his hands trembled like a junky's, his mouth was so dry he could hardly swallow.

Reaching around and beneath her, Brian cupped her cunt, groaning at how wet and swollen she was. He pushed deeper into her rear, his fingers penetrating her pussy at the same time.

"Fuck," he bit out, feeling himself through the thin membrane between his fingers and cock. He struggled against the need to come before he was fully inside her.

She clawed at the sheets. Cries spilled from her throat, soft sounds of desperate hunger. Her legs slid farther apart; her ass lifted to take him deeper.

"That's it," he praised. She opened, and his cock slid in to the root. "There, baby. Right there."

"Bri . . ." Her voice broke.

Withdrawing his fingers, he yanked the pillow out from under her and tossed it aside. He caught her around the waist and rolled them as one, adjusting them so that he was spooned behind her, still deep inside her. His biceps cushioned her cheek, his other arm was slung over her waist. He linked his fingers with hers, holding their joined hands against her taut stomach, anchoring her in place as he began to thrust.

———

Layla felt herself unraveling . . . falling to pieces . . . and she couldn't stop it. She shook uncontrollably, as naked as she would ever be, her arousal so fierce and wild it frightened her with its power. It writhed beneath her skin, fighting to be freed.

Brian was everywhere—behind her, around her, inside her body and her mind. His chest heaved against her back. His skin was feverishly hot and wet with sweat, sealing them together.

She needed him so much. Too much. Needed his ferocity and hunger, which made her feel how deeply he needed her in return.

His hips pulled back, dragging the furled underside of his cockhead across hypersensitive tissues. The sensation was agonizingly exquisite, coaxing her to arch her buttocks against him to reclaim more of the stretching fullness.

"Easy, baby." His voice was made gruff by his raging lust. "Nice and easy."

He pushed back into her. The slow, sure glide ensured she absorbed every nuance of the penetration. The feelings of possession and dominance.

Her head fell back against his shoulder. The slight pain of his entry was its own pleasure. She clenched around the invading hardness, her body desperate to hold him as he began to withdraw again.

"Fuck, yeah," he growled, spurting a scorching wash of pre-cum inside her. "Keep squeezing me like that. You feel so good, Layla. So good . . ."

She moaned, her hand sliding downward to her pulsing swollen clit. He moved with her, their fingers still linked together.

"Let me." His index and middle fingers settled over her pussy, parting her, touching her so gently she felt like weeping.

His cock slid free until only the wide crest remained inside her, then he thrust home fast and deep. His serrated groan vibrated against her back. Two long, thick fingers pushed gently into her spasming pussy. His palm massaged her throbbing clitoris.

"I need . . ." Her words came slurred with pleasure. "Oh God . . . Fuck me. Please. Now."

Cupping her between the legs, Brian began to shaft her tender rear with smooth measured strokes. His hips worked like a well-oiled machine, pounding against the curve of her buttocks, his steel-hard cock caressing nerve endings only he'd ever touched.

Layla sobbed, her blood raging. The sounds he made spurred her dark hunger—the rough growls and muttered curses, the desperate groans of pleasure. The heel of his palm nudged her clit with every thrust, pushing her closer and closer to an orgasm she knew would destroy her. She'd have no defenses left against him by the time he was done with her, nothing to shield her from the pain of losing him all over again.

"I love you, Layla." His voice was a harsh rasp in her ear. "So damn much."

He pushed her forward slightly, gaining purchase with his knees. His strokes came faster, deeper . . . his fingers sliding in and out with the same perfect tempo.

"Love you." She gasped the agonizing truth, coming in a brutal rush. Her body seized, clamping down on his shuttling cock, tightening as he climaxed with heated spurts deep inside her.

Brian gripped her tightly. Holding her together. Holding her to him. For a moment the desperation melted away, leaving them alone with each other. The closest they'd ever been, while also the furthest away.

━━━━━━━

Layla awoke before Brian. She roused from sleep to the feel of his heavy arm draped over her and his leg tangled between hers. His face was buried against her nape, his rhythmic exhales soft against her skin.

Tomorrow she'd be in San Diego and Brian would go his own way. Again. It was a small comfort that he regretted allowing her to leave him that long-ago day. If they had a second chance, she knew they'd both do things differently.

She'd been so young when she left him. Barely nineteen. For all intents and purposes, Brian had been her first relationship. How childish she must have seemed to a mature twenty-five-year-old man, demanding he choose between her and the livelihood he'd worked so hard for. He'd chosen not to reenlist in the Navy because of her need to keep him close to home.

What had *she* sacrificed for *him*? Not enough. She'd been dizzy with adolescent yearning and seeking a Grand Gesture to prove his love for her. She had lacked confidence in her ability to keep Brian's interest and to satisfy his sometimes-dark, often-demanding appetites. And she'd mistaken his care and consideration as babying, feeling as if he was treating her like a child instead of the truth—he indulged her because he loved her and wanted her to be happy.

Now, it was too late.

She sighed. Brian tugged her closer.

"Don't think about it," he said gruffly, pressing his lips to her shoulder.

"I'm trying not to." She started thinking about running away instead, thinking about the viability of leaving the country and being on the lam together, and never letting him go. But neither of them could do that. Agent Sandoval had died saving her life; it was her responsibility to help bring to justice the men who'd killed him and Steph.

Lifting his hand to her lips, Layla kissed his knuckles, then rubbed her cheek against them. She felt his breath catch, then quicken. His embrace tightened.

"I'm sorry," she whispered. "So sorry."

"No, sweetheart. I fucked it up. I was the one who should have known better. You needed reassurance and I didn't give it to you."

She turned in his arms and snuggled into his hard chest. "I was worried that I was too inexperienced and undereducated to keep you from getting bored."

His smile made her chest tight. "You've always been a handful. Boredom has never been a concern."

"I was sick with jealousy whenever a woman nearer to your age flirted with you or gave you a please-fuck-me look. I felt inadequate every time I met one of your friends' wives or girlfriends and saw how mature and confident they were."

"While I was thinking I was the luckiest man in the room to have you."

Her tears wet his chest. "I kept thinking I'd blackmailed you into being with me. I knew you weren't ready, but I also knew you couldn't stand the thought of me with someone else. I put you in the position of being the lesser evil, but I never felt like you were really comfortable with it."

Brian's callused hands cradled her back. "I wasn't."

Layla looked up at him. His short hair was mussed and his eyes bloodshot. She thought he was the most gorgeous man she'd ever seen. "I knew it."

"I was worried I was too settled for you. I'd already had my fair share of late nights and too much to drink. When I was home, all I wanted was to be alone with you."

"I wanted that, too."

He exhaled harshly. "I felt old. I figured you'd get over your crush on me soon enough and it would gut me to lose you. The moment you broke it off was the last possible moment you could have done it and not killed me. I survived it only because I still hoped you'd come back. That when you were ready to settle down, I'd be the guy you would want to settle with."

"That's why you let me go? Because you still could?"

"Partly. And partly because I thought you needed to live a little. See what else was out there. You weren't the only one who was insecure. I wanted to be sure you didn't look back and wonder if there might have been someone better for you, if you'd just taken the time to look around."

Layla closed her eyes, sinking into an exhaustion that was more than physical. "I'm glad we had these few days together," she said softly. "Anytime I was set to meet a new deputy, I'd hold my breath and hope it would be you. I'd always feel this strange mix of relief and disappointment when it wasn't. It's good to have some closure. At least I know we saved some of the good—"

"Shh." He pressed his lips to hers. It was a reverent kiss. Full of tenderness and sorrow.

Layla pressed herself against him, wishing she could crawl inside him. Cherish him. Keep him.

God knew she loved him and had no idea how she was ever going to live without him. Knowing he was out there somewhere, still loving her . . .

"Don't think about it," he repeated.

Easier said than done when her heart was breaking all over again.

# Chapter 8

They drove straight through to Albuquerque with only a few quick stops for food and gas.

Pulling off I-40, Brian headed into the suburbs. Layla was quiet beside him, as she'd been most of the day. Her gaze was trained out the passenger window. He could feel the sadness radiating off her even though her face was hidden from him by the brim of a baseball cap. His own gut was tight with grief and frustration, his hands flexing restlessly on the wheel while he damned himself for not preventing this.

If he'd just talked to her when she needed reassurance, if he had given her a say in his plans, they would be in a totally different place in their lives now. She'd be safe, he would be with her, and they'd both be happy.

He pulled into a quiet residential neighborhood and she stirred, turning her head to look at him with her brows raised in inquiry.

"I've got a buddy out here," he explained, slowing down in front of a one-story ranch house with a Chevy Silverado in the driveway and a Sea-Doo trailer in the space beside it.

Parking, he left the keys in the ignition and said, "Let me see if he's home."

Before he could step out, the front door opened and Jack Killigrew appeared. Tall and dark in appearance and demeanor, the man was an SOG deputy like Brian, a Shadow Stalker Brian could trust with someone as precious as Layla.

"Sit tight," he murmured, getting out of the Bronco. Rounding the hood, he called out, "Hey, Killigrew. I'm in a bit of a bind."

"Understatement of the year." The other deputy held out his hand and they clasped forearms, pulling each other close for quick slaps to the back. "You're hotter than a bitch in heat. It's her, isn't it? Your Layla?"

"Of course."

A pretty blonde in a wisp of a summer dress stepped out of the house and offered him a tentative smile.

"Ah, shit," Brian muttered. "I didn't think about Rachel and Riley being here. We'll head out."

Jack had recently been in a similar position to Brian's—in love with a woman he couldn't have. But Jack had worked things out. He'd gotten the girl and the future he had once only dreamed of. Brian would be damned if he'd fuck that up.

"Riley's with his grandmother," Rachel interjected. "In California."

Brian extended his hand. "It's a pleasure to meet you, Rachel. Brian Simmons."

"Hi, Brian." She smiled. "We're getting ready to grill up some steaks. Jack bought enough for an army, as usual. I hope you're planning on staying for dinner."

He looked at Jack with a rueful smile. "I appreciate the offer, but I just stopped by for a moment."

"Bullshit," Jack said. "Your timing is perfect. I told everyone I was going to be at Rachel's in Monterey so they'd leave us alone. No one knows we're here."

"Jack—"

Jack ignored him and walked toward the Bronco. "I've got guest rooms. I'll move my car out of the drive and you can park in the garage."

Opening Layla's door, he introduced himself and gestured at the house. She looked to Brian and he shrugged.

Their eyes held for a moment, a surge of emotion passing between them.

So little time left. He hated to share even a moment of it, but he needed a fellow deputy's input and help, and Layla needed a place to decompress.

He held out his hand to her when she reached him. She linked her fingers with his and he led her into the house.

———

"How can I help?" Layla asked, watching as Rachel pulled the vegetables for a salad out of the fridge.

"Are you up for peeling a cucumber and chopping it up with some tomatoes?"

"Absolutely."

After rinsing and prepping, Layla joined Rachel at the granite-top kitchen island. She smiled at the friendly blonde, whose short golden curls perfectly framed a lovely face and kind blue eyes.

"You have a lovely home," Layla said, envying the other woman's happy family.

"It's not mine. Jack and I are still pretty new to each other. At least, in the romantic sense."

"I never would have guessed." Jack clearly doted on Rachel. In some ways, he reminded Layla of Brian. Both men were tough, no-nonsense guys . . . who just happened to have a soft underbelly they exposed only to the women they loved. When Jack looked at Rachel, the tender heat was obvious.

"We've known each other for years. He was my late husband's best friend and he's my son's godfather."

"You and I have a lot in common," Layla noted.

Rachel continued to shred a head of lettuce with her hands. "Jack gave me a brief rundown of why you're here. I can't imagine what you're going through right now, yet you're so pulled together and brave. You're amazing. Jack says you're from a military family?"

"Jack seems to know a lot about me."

"I said the same thing." Rachel laughed. "Apparently Brian talks about you a lot. It must be a relief to have him with you now."

"Huge." Layla began to dice the tomatoes. "It's ironic. We broke up, in large part, because of his job. And now I couldn't be more grateful that he does what he does and that he's helping me get through this."

"Jack's job got in the way for us, too. He felt like it was too dangerous for Riley and me, and that I'd eventually regret how often he's away."

"I never minded the separation so much," Layla said, thinking about it. "Maybe because I grew up living with it. My problem was—still is—his need to sign up for the most dangerous jobs, situations, whatever. I mean he couldn't just be a deputy U.S. marshal, right? He couldn't just be a sailor in the Navy. He had to go Special Forces all the way."

"It's scary when they're gone, I know."

"It's scarier when they don't come back."

Rachel paused, her gaze trained downward at the counter.

Exhaling in a rush, Layla stopped chopping. "I'm sorry. I shouldn't have said that."

"It's okay." Rachel left the counter and grabbed a beer out of the fridge. She held one up for Layla, but Layla shook her head. "I had to think long and hard about that very possibility before I pursued Jack. I had to be sure I was truly committed, because I was risking putting Riley through losing a stepfather as well as his own dad."

Layla set the knife down. "What made up your mind for you?"

"Jack. He deserves to be loved. He deserves to have someone to come home to. With all that he does for everyone else, he deserves something of his own." Rachel took a long pull on her beer, then set it down and got back to work. "Jack was raised in foster care. It took me a while to understand it, but the men he works with are his family, the only one he's ever had. I realized I have to look at his job the same way I would an unpleasant mother-in-law—it comes with the territory. I have to take him the way he is."

Gripping the counter, Layla forced herself to breathe in an even tempo while her heart lurched in her chest.

Dear God.

Families were supposed to be comprised of people who cared for you, people who would do anything for you . . . even die for you. She'd been blessed with that, but like Jack, Brian hadn't been. His mother was engrossed in the men in her life, losers who used her and eventually left her when the novelty wore off. Brian had no idea who his father was and no siblings he knew of.

So he'd chosen fields and jobs that would give him the support system of a family. Careers that provided him with people he trusted with his life. And hers.

She'd demanded he give that up for her. Coming from a young woman he feared might leave him at any moment, it must have seemed like an impossible request. He'd already lost Jacob.

Layla understood now why he hadn't been able to let the job go. It wasn't the job itself; it was the ties the job gave him. And she hadn't offered him a dependable alternative to that loss.

"Are you okay?" Rachel asked softly.

"Sorry. I'm just wiped out." Layla lifted her head. "I was already stressed about the trial. Then these last couple of days . . ."

"It'll be over soon, won't it?"

"It will never be over. Once I testify, I'll go back into WITSEC and wait for the possibility that they might need me again."

"Will Brian be with you?"

Layla shook her head. "He won't even know where I am or what my last name is. Today and tomorrow is all we've got."

"Then why the fuck are you in the kitchen with me?" Rachel asked without heat. "I've got dinner covered. Go spend some time with your man."

"I think he's talking with your man, actually." Layla felt herself smiling despite herself. She liked Rachel. She wished this sort of life was possible—spending time with people who were important to Brian, grilling a meal on a lovely day, commiserating with fellow significant others who knew what it was like to wait and worry and hope for the best. The worst part was that she'd once had the life she was now coveting and she had thrown it away.

"Then take a shower and a nap instead. It'll be a few hours yet before the food's ready."

"I'll feel like a mooch if I don't help."

"You can help me clean up later, how's that? I enjoy the prep part. It's the mess I don't much care for." Rachel rounded the island. "Let me show you to your room. The house has two masters, so you have your own bathroom."

"Thank you, Rachel." Layla met the blonde's blue-eyed gaze and tried to convey the depth of her gratitude. It meant so much to her that she and Brian had this brief respite with trusted friends in a home filled with love. It felt real and true, although she knew it was as much a moment out of time as the past two nights spent in rundown motels.

Rachel grabbed her hand and squeezed. "Anytime."

"You weren't fully briefed before you got there?" Jack asked.

"I was a last-minute replacement—" Brian's voice faded when Layla walked by the den's open double doors. The slump of her shoulders and low-hanging head told him so much about her mood.

Heaving out his breath, he leaned heavily into the front of Jack's desk. The other deputy stood with his back to the hallway, but he turned his head to follow Brian's gaze.

"What are you going to do about her?" Jack asked quietly.

"What wouldn't I do?" Brian shoved a hand through his hair. "She's blaming herself for us breaking up in the first place."

"Wasn't it her fault? She left you."

"We're both equally at fault," he said gruffly, feeling the need to protect Layla from censure. "We both needed something from each other that we couldn't vocalize at the time."

Jack grimaced in sympathy. "I've been there."

"None of which matters now. I can't even think about living without her again. It makes me insane." Brian forced his thoughts back to the most pressing issue at hand—keeping Layla safe. "I was brought in at the last minute because one of the deputies who was supposed to be on Layla's detail called in. I need you to find out who that person was."

"I'm sure they're working that angle, too, and if the deputy's involved, he or she has likely planned for that contingency, but I'll see what I can dig up." Jack crossed his arms. "The DEA has a big stake in this. This is personal for them."

Brian understood what Jack was saying. This was interagency business—reputations were on the line and the media attention was fierce. Every precaution would've been taken, most especially assigning only the most trustworthy, heavily vetted deputies. For one agency to have to admit to another that one of their own had gone rogue and betrayed the service was both embarrassing and the opening of a huge can of worms. "With any other situation I'd be betting on the witness fucking it up somehow. But not Layla. She knows better and she values the lives of others too much to jeopardize anyone needlessly. Someone had a price."

"What else can I do to help?"

Brian's mouth curved in a rueful half smile. "You're doing enough already. Layla's tired and scared and worried about things we can't change. She needed a safe haven that wasn't a dingy, by-the-hour dump."

"You'll stay the night." It wasn't a question.

"We'll be heading out before oh three hundred. I want to get her into San Diego prior to close of business so she can have at least a couple hours with the AUSA before she has to testify the next day."

Jack nodded.

"I could use new wheels," Brian said. "I was pushing my luck getting this far with Jim's Bronco. Could you help me get a rental with some teeth to it?"

"Take my truck."

"I can't do that. You're doing too much as it is."

"You and I both know a rental is unreliable and more likely to attract attention." Jack crossed his arms. "Take the truck."

Brian straightened. "I owe you."

"Big-time. Don't think I'm being completely selfless here. I'm coming out ahead by holding a favor from you in my pocket." Jack turned toward the door. "I'm going to spend some time with my woman. You do the same."

"Thanks, Jack."

His friend paused on the threshold. "Anytime."

━━━━━━━━━

Entering the bedroom, Brian heard the shower running and started to undress. Once he was stripped, he pushed the partly closed bathroom door open and stepped inside the steamy room. Layla stood with one hand on the tiles in front of her and her head bowed beneath the spray of the showerhead. Her long, dark hair hung heavily around her face.

Her pose was one of such pain and dejection Brian couldn't bear it. Opening the glass door, he stepped inside and turned her to face him, clasping her heaving body close. She was sobbing violently and his heart ached at her misery.

"Sweetheart," he murmured, running his hands up and down her back. "I can't stand it when you cry."

She wrapped her arms around him and buried her face in his chest.

He held her, whispering softly, offering what little comfort he could. Eventually, she quieted to hiccupping sobs and he took care of her as he should have been doing the last five years. He washed her hair and body, then bundled her up in a towel and carried her to the bed. They curled together beneath the blankets, falling wearily to sleep.

# Chapter 9

He walked in with my brother Jacob and I fell head over heels." Layla leaned back in her chair, enjoying the cool evening breeze that sifted through her hair. "I was sixteen. He was twenty-two and breathtaking. Gorgeous really, with a body built for sin. He had such intense sex appeal that it was like a match to my teenage hormones. He was the hottest man I'd ever seen."

Rachel laughed softly. "Sexual chemistry."

"To say the least. Totally ruined me for the guys in high school. They were fumbling little boys in comparison." Layla's fingertip circled the lip of her water glass. "But he only saw me as his best friend's annoying kid sister."

"If only," Brian interjected, coming up behind her and pressing a quick hard kiss to her temple. "She had me feeling like a lecher. Totally fucked me up. I wanted her more than I've ever wanted a woman before or since, and I couldn't have her until she grew up."

"Ha! Don't let him fool you, Rachel," Layla said, shooting him a glance. "He was no saint in the interim."

"Neither were you." He pulled out the Adirondack chair next to her and caught her hand in his. "You knew you were turning me inside out. You did it on purpose."

"You needed it. With the number of chicks falling all over you, you were getting full of yourself."

Jack returned from the kitchen with a fresh bottle of beer for Rachel. The look the other couple passed to each other was both loving and intimate.

Layla turned away, her gaze finding Brian with his head back and his eyes closed. He appeared relaxed, but she knew he was far from it. Neither of them had eaten much for dinner. They were both too worked up to fully enjoy Jack's skill at the grill.

"Want to crash?" she asked softly, knowing he was running on fumes despite their earlier nap.

He inhaled deeply and nodded. "We should. We'll be heading out in a few hours."

She looked at Rachel and Jack, who made such a striking couple. Rachel's short blond curls were a lovely contrast to Jack's dark good looks. "Thank you for dinner and for harboring fugitives in your home."

"Thank you for cleaning up after dinner." Rachel pushed gracefully to her feet. "I've really enjoyed having you, Layla. I hope this won't be the last time we see each other."

It would be. In a day or few, Layla Creed would cease to exist once again and she would become someone else. Layla pushed the thought away with a forced smile, choosing to take every moment as it came. Doing otherwise only drove her crazy. She hugged the other woman, then Jack.

The deputy looked down at her, his handsome face stark and austere. "I admire you, Layla. You've got balls taking on the Tijuana cartel *and* Simmons here. Stay tough and fierce."

Her eyes stung. Praise from a guy like Jack Killigrew was high and she appreciated it. "Take care of him for me, will you?" she asked softly.

He nodded.

She backed away. "Thank you."

"I'll be there in a minute," Brian told her, stroking his fingers through her hair.

She fled with relief, needing time to get her rioting emotions under control. When she got back to the room, she brushed her teeth and hair, then changed into the camisole she'd bought to sleep in. She climbed between the cool sheets and faced away from the middle, her gaze coming to rest on Brian's gun and badge on the nightstand.

He came in a few minutes later. He moved quietly through his evening routine without turning the lights on. When he got into the bed, he slid over to her side, fitting his hard body to her back.

She absorbed his warmth and breathed in the beloved scent of his skin. His cock was rigid against her buttocks and sexual tension tightened his frame. His firm lips whispered across her shoulder, while his hand at her waist slid beneath the hem of her top.

Layla responded to his proximity with familiar alacrity—her nipples beaded tight and hard, her breasts swelled, her pussy softened. She'd gone without his touch for too long. She hungered to hear his raw groans and feel his powerful muscles flexing against her flesh. Her arms ached from the need to hold him close.

"Layla," he murmured, nuzzling her nape. "Don't shut me out."

She looked at the clock, which counted down their remaining hours together. "I need you to promise me something."

His callused hand cupped the swell of her breast and squeezed gently. "Anything."

"Promise me you won't wait for me again. Promise me you'll find someone to love you and take care of you."

He stilled. "Correction: anything but that."

She turned to face him. His eyes glittered down at her in the semidarkness. The plantation shutters covering the windows weren't fully closed; they angled the moonlight upward to the ceiling, bathing the room in a soft silver glow. "I want you to have what Jack has with Rachel. A family, people who love you and are waiting at home for you. You deserve it. You need it. Don't let me fuck up your life any more than I already have."

"I can't have what Jack has without you."

Cupping his cheek, she said, "Because you're hanging on to a dream that's dead. I killed it, and now you have to let it go. You have to let me go."

Brian's fingers flexed restlessly into the muscles bracketing her spine. "Shut up, Layla."

"I wish I'd left you alone when Jacob started bringing you around." Her voice was hoarse with regret. "I wish I'd—"

He pressed his mouth to hers. Beneath the blankets, he caught the waistband of her panties in his fist and tore it. Then he kneed her legs open wider. He pushed the loosened crotch of her underwear aside and took himself in hand. The wide, silky crest of his cock parted the lips of her pussy and nudged her clitoris.

"Christ." He groaned. "I've been dying to push my cock into you since we woke up."

Perspiration misted her skin. He wanted what she did—the connection, the ephemeral feeling that they were one and could never be parted.

Layla averted her head, gasping. "Brian, damn it. You're deliberately distracting me."

"Stop talking and enjoy it." His lips slid across her jawline to her ear, where his tongue traced the shell. His breathing was harsh and loud, turning her on with the passion conveyed by the accelerated tempo. He stroked his cockhead down to the clenching opening of her pussy, notching himself briefly and growling at her trembling grip on that most sensitive part of him, before rubbing back up to nudge her swollen clit. "You're so wet, baby. So ready."

A soft sound escaped her as he continued to glide through the saturated folds of her sex with the heavy length of his beautiful cock.

"Promise me," she gasped, her hands gripping his hips.

"I've been riding you bareback, Layla," he murmured, his tongue worrying a hardened nipple through the thin cotton of her camisole. "And you specifically told me to come inside you. You're not protected, are you?"

She sucked in a shaky breath. "You don't know that."

He slid his cock downward to the entrance of her pussy and pushed the thick crown into her. "Your cunt is tight and greedy. You haven't taken a man inside you in a long time. Why take the pill if you're not having sex?"

She was briefly startled by how perfectly his words mimicked her thoughts from the day before. "That's not the only reason women take the pill, Bri."

"You're evading the question." His lips circled the tip of her breast.

He worked another few inches inside her. She trembled with desire, her body so sensitized by his confident, relentless seduction. His virility and potent sensuality were their own foreplay. Being the recipient of that intense focus and dominant need was impossible to resist.

"Brian . . ." Her hips arched in an effort to take more of him.

"Do you want my baby, Layla?" he purred darkly, rolling his hips to slide even deeper. "Are you hoping you'll walk away with a piece of me inside you?"

"You've always been inside me," she whispered.

Lowering his hips, he drove in to the hilt with a low hiss of pleasure. The headboard tapped against the wall. "You're asking me to let you go, while you're trying to hold on to something of me? Someone who's part of me?"

Her legs lifted and wrapped around his muscular thighs, holding him at that delicious point where he filled every centimeter of her. "Shut up, Brian. You're the one who wanted to fuck instead of talk."

Reaching behind him, he caught her wrist and pulled her hand up and away from his back. He pinned it to the mattress beside her head, then did the same with her other arm. His face was tight and hard with lust, his eyes dark, his sensual mouth drawn into a thin line. He withdrew slowly, stroking her inner walls with the wide head of his cock. Then he thrust home hard, ramming the headboard into the wall.

Layla bit her lip to stifle a moan. Heated pleasure raced through her veins.

"I'll have to take you slow and easy," he bit out, his jaw clenched tight. "Damn bed."

She tightened around him just to torment him.

"Witch." Circling his hips, he put pressure on her throbbing clit.

Her head pressed hard into the pillow as an orgasm hovered just out of reach.

Releasing her, he shoved another pillow under her shoulders. "Watch me fucking you, Layla. Watch what you do to me."

Brian pulled out, his cock thick and glistening. "See how hard you make me? I'm so hot for you. I'll never have enough of this, never have enough of you."

He eased the heavily veined length back inside her, his teeth grinding audibly.

"It's so good," she breathed, wanting it to last nearly as badly as she wanted to come. "You feel so good."

"As good as it gets," he said hoarsely, snaring her wrists again. "You know it, too. We're it for each other, baby. There's no one else out there for us. You can't tell me to settle. I won't."

He withdrew to the tip, then surged into her in a slow, deep glide. His harsh groan reverberated through the room. His head hung over her, his broad shoulders shivering as her pussy rippled helplessly around his hardness.

"I love you," Layla whispered, her entire being filled with a desperate longing. "I love you so much."

He caught her mouth with his own, his lips slanting across hers. His hips rose and fell, shafting her aching pussy with measured leisurely thrusts. Her pinioned hands clenched and released as she ate ravenously at his mouth, suckling his tongue as she longed to do to his cock. Sweat coated their skin, their bodies flexing and arching and straining together, their hips meeting each other with rhythmic erotic slaps. His heavy testicles swayed and smacked against her buttocks with every deep plunge, his chest heaving as the pleasure tore through them both.

The controlled pace was both maddening and delicious. They writhed against each other, driven by the need for a hard pounding tempo that would dull the reality of their inevitable parting.

Brian withdrew suddenly. She cried out in protest, her womb spasming with need.

"Fuck this noisy bed," he growled. He hauled her up and carried her to the wall by the bathroom, pinning her to the flat surface with a desperate thrust into her.

She gasped at the rough impalement, potently aroused by his ferocity, knowing it came from the need to ignore the swiftly passing time.

"*Yes,*" he hissed as her pussy spasmed in greedy delight. "Hold on, baby."

Clenching her hips in a fierce grip, he worked her up and down on his throbbing erection, his thrusts fast and furious.

She moaned, her nails digging into his back. "Harder. Deeper. *Yes.* Oh God . . . I'm coming."

He fucked through her climax, dragging it out, making it last, watching her quake with the force of the sensations tearing through her. "That's it. Give it to me, Layla."

Finally, the racking tension left her. Her body sagged in the aftermath of the violent orgasm. But Brian kept working her, slamming his hips against hers as he shoved his way through the tightened grip of her sated pussy.

As the pleasure built again, Layla moaned. "Brian."

"One more time," he rasped, the strain of holding out evident in his tightly clenched jaw.

Grinding his pelvis against her clit, he brought her off. He cursed as she cried out and rippled along his length, his cock jerking as he came in thick spurts of white-hot semen.

His knee hit the wall with a harsh thud; his big body crowded hers as he leaned into her for support. With his lips to her throat, he groaned through the wrenching orgasm, clutching her hard while she trembled in his arms.

"I love you." He nuzzled his perspiration-slick forehead against her cheek. "And your golden pussy, as you called it, is going to kill me. It's going to suck the life right out of me one day. But, man . . . what a way to go."

Layla laughed, his humor unexpected and welcome. She felt him smile against her skin, the moment as intimate as the climax they'd just shared. He stumbled back to the bed with her, staying inside her, even as they sank back into the mattress.

She pushed her hands into his sweat-soaked hair and held him close. "I want you to be happy. I want that more than anything in the world."

"I know." He pushed his arms beneath her shoulders and squeezed her.

"I don't want to make you miserable."

"Then stop talking about this, Layla."

"That is so like a man," she muttered. "Ignore a situation and hope it goes away."

He nipped the tender spot between her neck and shoulder with his teeth. "I'm not promising to forget you or move on without you. Give it up."

"Promise me you won't let my memory get in the way of having a good life." Her fingers massaged his scalp. "I can't bear the thought of you waiting around for another chance that we might see each other a decade or more down the road."

He lifted his head and looked down at her. "And if I did run across you, will you have moved on? Will you be married and happy?"

The mere thought caused physical pain in her chest. Perceptive as he was, Brian saw it. "Thought so. I rest my case."

"Brian—"

"Go to sleep."

She wondered how she was supposed to do that, with his heavy body atop hers and his cock still inside her. But she would never complain. She wanted the feeling imprinted on her skin, a vivid memory she would hold on to in the years to come.

# Chapter 10

Brian was staring out the kitchen window at the pre-dawn sky when Jack reentered the room. The other deputy had come in earlier to make coffee shortly after Brian first left his guest room. This time, Jack was dressed. Like Brian, he wore his shoulder holster, and his badge was clipped to his belt.

Brian tossed back the rest of his cooled coffee and went to the coffeemaker for another cup. Despite his lack of sleep, he was wired. It was a big day. The biggest of his life.

Leaning his back against the countertop, he crossed his feet at the ankles and looked Jack over. It wasn't yet three in the morning and the man had his boots on. "Why are you dressed?"

"I'm coming with you, of course."

"The hell you are."

Jack smiled. "You're a ray of sunshine in the morning, Simmons."

"Rachel needs you."

"She's got me."

"This is my gamble to make. Stay here."

"No can do." Jack's dark eyes were hard, his shoulders set. "That lady of yours has a very important appointment tomorrow and you need more eyes."

"Fuck." Brian couldn't argue against the need for help and more comprehensive protection for Layla. He wouldn't. The only argument he could make was a personal plea for Jack to put himself first, and Layla's testimony trumped that. "These guys aren't fucking around, Jack."

"Rachel accepts the risks. Did you call Jim?"

"I tried last night. Left a message. There was nothing in his recorded greeting that suggested trouble. He would have slipped in something I'd recognize if I needed to watch my back."

"Okay. So you and Layla will take my truck, and I'll follow in the Bronco."

Brian shoved a hand through his shower-damp hair. "For the record, I strongly object to your involvement, Killigrew."

"You'll get over it."

————

When they pulled over in Flagstaff for breakfast, Brian took a few minutes to leave a message on the AUSA's office voice mail. Then he switched to a new disposable cell phone and called Doug Preston, a supervisory deputy U.S. marshal in the Southern District of California. Relying on voice mail again, he explained the situation in a low, steady tone. He started with the explosion and ended with his anticipated arrival in San Diego. Aside from the last, he fully expected the information to be a rehash of what was already known, but Brian wanted his version of the events to be recorded in case something prevented him from giving a statement later. The closer they got to San Diego, the more dangerous the situation would become. He had to make sure he protected Layla with the truth as he knew it, even if he couldn't do so in the flesh.

Jack approached with a newly refilled soda in hand. "You sure you want to do that?"

Realizing the other deputy had eavesdropped, Brian shot him a wry glance as he pulled the battery from the phone. "You wouldn't if you were in my shoes?"

"I would, but I'm your friend. I have to ask."

Brian nodded, biting back further words when Layla stepped out of the restroom. He offered her a quick smile and she returned it, but they knew each other too well to hide anything from each other. She knew he was feeling raw. Twisted up over her, over her safety, over how much he loved her. Her eyes said it all in return.

"You ready?" he asked when she took his hand.

"No."

He tightened his grip on her and shielded her the distance to the trucks.

———

"Criminal justice, you said. Do you like it?"

Layla looked at Brian as they crossed the border from Arizona into California. He'd started trying to distract her about a half hour prior and she was going along with it as much as she was able, considering she had a knotted stomach and heavy heart. "I do."

"You sound surprised."

"It was a bit unexpected," she confessed. "I knew I wouldn't hate it, but I didn't realize I'd love it."

He glanced aside at her and smiled in the way she loved—half-wicked, half-tender.

She looked out the front window at the desert vista around them. "God, I've missed Cali."

"You're a native; you'll always miss it."

"How about you? Are you on the East Coast now?"

"For now. I've been moving around, taking transfers when I can."

"Do you like it?" she asked, tossing his question back at him. The thought of Brian living a nomadic existence filled her with sadness. "The hopping around?"

He lifted one shoulder in a shrug. "Moving keeps me busy."

"What did you do with your house?"

"I sold it."

"You loved that house." She had loved it, too. She'd been with him when he bought it and had seen the possibilities in the older Anaheim home. But what he'd done with it exceeded her imaginings. He had torn out the carpet and installed dark wood floors. Light rugs and walls paired with mostly black furniture had made the '50s-era home both modern and masculine. She'd given him a multicolored blown glass vase for a splash of color and he had placed it in a place of prominence, even installing track lighting to spotlight it.

"I loved the idea of the house," he corrected. "The idea of sharing it with you and watching you change it like you were changing me. Once you joined WITSEC I knew you'd never be coming back to SoCal, so the house lost its charm."

"Brian." Layla sucked in a shaky breath. "You're killing me."

He reached over and linked his fingers with hers. "No more than your change of major kills me."

"Have we both been living for a future we have no possibility of having? And making amends for mistakes, even though we couldn't know what the other was doing?"

He lifted her hand to his mouth and kissed her knuckles. "What else were we going to live for?"

It broke her heart to realize that he was right. Somewhere, in the back of her mind and deep in her heart, she'd been taking each day one at a time, waiting for the impossible moment when she'd see Brian again. She hadn't been able to picture a world in which they breathed the same air yet would be separated forever.

Her hand tightened on his. "I love you, Brian."

As often as she said it, she felt like she couldn't say it enough. The painful fact was that she'd given up on him when she walked out. If he took anything away from the last few days with her, she wanted it to be that he was loved.

"I know," he murmured, looking grim. "I love you, too, baby."

―――――

They pulled over for the final time at a gas station off I-8 to switch cars. Layla held Brian's flannel closed over her chest, concealing her body armor, and looked at Jack as he slid behind the wheel beside her. He'd swapped clothes with Brian while they'd been in the store; everything but their shoes.

He sighed as he settled into the seat. When he caught her gaze, he smiled sheepishly. "This seat is way more comfortable than the Bronco's."

He and Brian had been driving for nearly eleven hours. San Diego was only minutes away.

She was scared. Brian had left her with Jack and her heart was in her throat at the thought that she might not see him again. As soon as they checked in with the AUSA, he was going to face the consequences for going rogue with her. He could be tied up with interviews/interrogations for weeks. In the meantime, she'd be absorbed back into the system.

Jack started his truck. Brian was already merging the Bronco into the traffic on the street.

"What's going on?" she asked, knowing that something was up for them to switch places so thoroughly.

Jack looked over his shoulder for possible obstructions, then backed out of the parking space. "We can't get ahold of the owner of the Bronco. He's not answering his home phone and his cell goes straight to voice mail."

"What does that mean?"

"Could be nothing, but we can't take any chances. If the Bronco has been compromised, we don't want you in it."

Brian was in it. "Why don't we just leave it at the Park 'n' Ride?"

Jack looked at her. "If it's hot, keeping it on the road will deflect attention from this vehicle."

"Oh my God." She felt the blood drain from her face. Flashes of memory from the explosions in Maryland had her recoiling into the seat. "He's bait?"

"Hey," he said softly. "They're not going to launch grenades in the heart of San Diego, and at this late date, they need to make sure you're dead. They'll want to get up close and personal, which is where Brian is at his best."

"Is that supposed to make me feel better?" Her hand went to her throat, attempting to massage the tightness out of it.

"Brian has to do his job, Layla."

"By luring killers out after him?" Swallowing hard, she looked out the window. She felt like she was going to be sick. She wondered if Rachel had felt similarly when Jack left their bed that morning.

"For what it's worth," Jack murmured, "I believe everything happens for a reason. The chances of you and Brian crossing paths the way you did were pretty damn slim. Things stacked up for you two like a chain of dominoes: the prominence of the Sandoval trial warranted SOG deputies and Brian was in the right place at the right time. He saved your ass and his, and managed to get you across the country without incident. I can't believe you both would get this far for nothing. Have a little faith in fate or a higher power—whatever your poison is."

Layla shook her head. "You have no idea what it's like being the one who's always left behind. The one wringing their hands, pulling out their hair, and vomiting from the stress and god-awful terror."

"What do you think Brian went through when you joined WIT-SEC? You were the one with her ass on the line, the one in danger while he was stuck with the fear. He tried to keep it together around the rest of us, but sometimes his control slipped. I never called him on it, but I was really worried about him for a while."

Jesus. And she was about to do it to him again. Maybe that was what was making him so reckless now. Maybe he was throwing himself directly in the line of fire because he was in the same state she was— half out of his mind with grief and worry.

She sat up and straightened her shoulders. She needed to get someplace safe, so Brian could focus on all the shit that was about to blow up his career. It wasn't nearly enough, but it was all she could do. "Get me to the AUSA, Jack. Let's get this over with."

"That's the plan."

———

Brian was pulling into a motel on Pacific Coast Highway in San Diego when Jack's cell phone rang. He reached for it and answered, his greeting cut off by the impatience of Jack's regional supervisor on the other end of the line.

"Hey, Killigrew. I've got the information you asked for."

Brian parked and kept his gaze on the rearview mirror. "Who was it, sir?"

"James Reynolds was the deputy who called in that afternoon. He was questioned already and released, but his whereabouts are unknown now. Do you think he's colluding with Simmons?"

*Jim.* Fuck. "I'm absolutely certain he's not."

There was a moment of silence. "Who is this?"

"Killigrew should, at this very moment, be escorting Miss Creed into the AUSA's office." Brian exhaled, mentally kissing his career good-bye. "Thank you for your help, sir."

He hung up and slid out from behind the wheel. Standing in the apex between the open door and the body of the vehicle, he surveyed his surroundings. The end of the road was in front of him, but he was suddenly reluctant to get there. Jim had been his friend for a long time. Brian had trusted the deputy with his life more than once. Surely Jim was tracking them via the Bronco's theft recovery system. But he'd allowed them to get this far.

Why? Brian intended to ask the man that question directly.

———

Thank God he was wearing gloves. If not for them, Jim Reynolds doubted he could keep his grip on the Maglite in his hand. Breathing roughly, he wiped the blood off the end of the flashlight with a Kleenex, then dropped it on the corpse lying prone on the floor behind the front desk. He disabled the outdated and poorly placed security camera overlooking the closet-sized lobby area, then wiped the recording of the feed going back a solid twenty-four hours. It only took a moment to find a master keycard. Before Jim left, he placed the WILL RETURN SHORTLY sign on the counter.

"You're a lucky bastard, Reynolds," Jim muttered to himself, stepping out of the dimly-lit front office into the moonlit night beyond. He glanced down the road to where his Bronco was parked at a twenty-four-hour diner. He'd known Simmons long enough to be familiar with his routine. Out of the dozens of motels lining the street, he'd found the deputy and his witness girlfriend at the first one he tried. A quick flash of his badge and a picture of Simmons were all the desk clerk had needed to confirm his guess.

But then things had been going his way since Simmons first called him three days ago. It would have been simpler if the cartel had killed the girl in Maryland, but as far as fuckups went, the unexpected appearance of Simmons had worked in Jim's favor. The former SEAL was the only deputy who had a personal stake in Layla Creed. Anyone else would have seen her absorbed back into the system and Jim would have been scrambling to find her. Simmons was also the only one who would risk a last night in a motel instead of taking her directly in for witness prep, because his dick was driving

the bus. That gave Jim this opportunity to take out the girl and Simmons in a staged murder-suicide that would wrap everything up in a
nice, neat bow.

He pulled a roll of Rolaids out of his pocket and bit off three to
fight the burning ache of ulcers in his stomach. He didn't recognize
himself anymore. He'd become a man he hated. But as much as he
regretted what he was about to do, it would be a relief to end it.

Pausing outside Simmons's room, Jim noted the darkness within
and the silence. He gripped the master key in one hand and reached for
his Taser with the other. He'd have to be quick. Once the door opened,
Simmons would be a blur of movement if Jim missed his target.

He slid the keycard through the lock and threw the door wide,
aiming the Taser at the lumpy, disheveled bed and firing. An instant
of brightness lit the room as the electrical current sizzled. Then, he
heard the racking of a gun slide behind him.

He froze.

"Why, Jim?"

His eyes closed at the sound of Simmons's quiet voice behind
him. He'd lost his edge long ago and getting caught like this only
proved it. "When did you make me?"

"A couple hours ago, and I still can't believe it."

Jim turned around. A quick scope of the area revealed deputies
scurrying across the second floor breezeway and more encroaching
from the far left and right sides of the parking lot.

"Why?" Simmons asked again.

"Stella."

"What does your daughter have to do with this?"

"The cartel is far more determined than we give them credit for."
Jim's arms dropped listlessly to his sides. "Stella met a boy last year—
her first year in college. He's a handsome and cultured young man.
She brought him home for Christmas and I liked him. He spoils her
and makes her happy."

Simmons's expression was hard to read in the semidarkness. "He's with the cartel."

"Of course. He revealed himself to me a couple weeks ago. They've planned this for God knows how long. Think of the dedication involved . . . the patience and planning that went into finding me and my family, then finding the right guy to mesh with us, setting him up in school, giving him months to make sure Stella is so head-over-heels in love with him she won't believe he could do anything wrong. I've tried talking to her, but it's no use. She thinks she knows him, and now she's with him all the time. He can kill her at any moment—something he reminds me of every chance he gets. I can't imagine how many other deputies they've put the screws to, but I'm sure they've got their hooks into every deputy you call a friend. They've been drawing in their search net for years and it probably didn't take much digging to put you and Layla Creed together."

"You should have turned to the service for help."

"I couldn't take the risk." Jim's gut burned with a fresh wash of bile. "At least give me credit for the past three days. I could have taken you both out when you took my truck, but I felt I owed you some time with each other before all was said and done. Plus I really believe it would have been a mercy to finish you both together. Better than losing her to the system again, knowing those bastards are hunting her down."

"Christ, Jim."

"Will you look after Stella for me? Maybe now she'll believe that the man she's sleeping with is just waiting for the signal to kill her."

"You could have gone another way. You could have talked to me, let me help you." Simmons scrubbed the back of his neck wearily. "I'm really fucking sorry you didn't."

The deputy turned his back to Jim and the flanking deputies moved in.

# Chapter 11

The exhaustion Layla felt as she exited the courtroom was so profound, she felt almost as if she was drugged. Heaviness weighted her shoulders and eyelids, and her movements were sluggish enough to elicit concerned glances from the deputy beside her.

She hadn't seen Brian in over twenty-four hours.

Her grief over that was a mixed blessing. It dulled her anxiety, which allowed her to get through the AUSA's questioning. She faced more questions tomorrow, followed by cross-examination. She'd been dreading her court appearance for months, but now she was too consumed by fear and concern to devote any energy to nervousness.

"You did well today, Layla," AUSA Terri LeBow said with a reassuring smile.

For a moment, the cold dark eyes of the man who'd shot her and murdered Agent Sandoval invaded Layla's mind. As she'd relayed the events of that horrible night in Mexico to the jury, the reality of having her nightmare sitting just feet from her had brought a cold sweat to her skin. If not for the numbness brought on by Brian's disappearance, she might have broken down into a sobbing, quivering mess.

"I want that bastard to pay," she said with quiet grimness.

"We've got a strong case." Terri slowed, then stopped before a closed door. She gestured to it. "If you could step in here for a moment, I'll see about your escort."

With a sigh, Layla entered the room. She paused when she found two men bent over paperwork on the table and a third one standing behind them. For a moment, she stepped back, thinking she was intruding by accident. Then the man farthest away from her straightened and looked at her.

She sucked in a ragged breath. "Brian!"

He met her halfway, crushing her to his chest. "Sweetheart. I'm sorry I wasn't in the courtroom today; I had some things to take care of. I'll be there with you tomorrow."

"I don't care about that. I was worried sick about you." She pulled back to examine him. "Are you okay?"

"I will be." His smile had an edge. He looked tired, but there was an air of anticipation that lent him energy.

The other men in the room departed, the smiles on their faces defusing some of her worry. Still, she had to ask, "What's wrong?"

"Nothing." He looked down at her with heated eyes. "Depending on what you say next, things could be really damn right."

A flutter tickled her tummy. "Oh?"

Brian urged her toward a chair and she sat. He inhaled a deep breath, then sank to one knee.

"Oh my God," she breathed, feeling dizzy.

He reached into his back pocket and withdrew a ring box.

Her heart hammered in her chest. "What are you doing?"

"Getting ready to tell you I love you," he said softly. "And then asking you to marry me."

Her eyes fell to the ring he revealed, a large round diamond in an antique platinum setting. Her hands lifted to her mouth.

"Layla Creed. I love you and I really need you to marry me."

She looked at him over her fingers, her breathing rough and eyes wide. "What . . . ? How . . . ?"

Smiling, he explained, "I signed the contract to join you in WIT-SEC. The two gentlemen who left the room work for the county. One can get us squared away with a marriage license and the other can marry us in a civil ceremony. In about an hour, you can own me for life."

"I don't already?" she asked hoarsely, joking because her brain was unable to fully grasp the enormity of what he was offering to do for her.

"Let's make it official. We can make it pretty in a few months with a proper ceremony, once we settle wherever we're going to end up."

Layla exhaled in a rush, her hand lowering to touch the gorgeous ring. "Your job . . . ?"

He pulled the ring free of its velvet box and slid it onto her finger. "I've got money socked away from the sale of the house and the past five years of doing nothing but working. You'll get through school, then we'll start our own security firm. I can't imagine anything that would make me happier."

She cupped his cheek. Her lower lip quivered.

"Well?" he prompted. "I'm dying here."

"Shh."

His brows rose.

"If you wake me up," she warned, "I'm going to kick your ass."

His laughter broke through the chill she'd felt all day. "No more dreaming, baby. I want the real deal."

"What are the odds that we'd get this second chance?"

"Slim to none. Don't blow it."

Layla leaned forward and pressed her forehead to his. "I won't."

"Is that a yes?"

"That's a hell yes."

Brian stood and pulled her up with him, lifting her into the air.

"It won't be easy," she warned, remembering vividly how hard it was for her in the beginning of the program.

"I can take the heat."

Wrapping her arms around his shoulders, Layla seized what she wanted. "Take me instead," she purred.

"'Til death do us part," he vowed, carrying her to the door.

For more information about future Shadow Stalkers stories, visit www.sylviaday.com.

Coming Summer 2012

## Hot in Handcuffs

(with Shayla Black and Shiloh Walker)

## About the Author

**Sylvia Day** is the national bestselling author of more than a dozen novels. A wife and mother of two, she is a former Russian linguist for the U.S. Army Military Intelligence. Sylvia's work has been called an "exhilarating adventure" by *Publishers Weekly* and "wickedly entertaining" by *Booklist*. Her stories have been translated into Russian, Japanese, Portuguese, German, Czech, Italian, and Thai. She's been honored with the *Romantic Times* Reviewers' Choice Award, the EPPIE award, the National Readers' Choice Award, the Readers' Crown, and multiple finalist nominations for Romance Writers of America's prestigious RITA® Award of Excellence.